Songs My Mother Taught Me

Songs My Mother Taught Me

Stories, Plays, and Memoir

WAKAKO YAMAUCHI

Edited and with an Introduction by Garrett Hongo
Afterword by Valerie Miner

THE FEMINIST PRESS AT THE CITY UNIVERSITY OF NEW YORK
NEW YORK

Published 1994 by The Feminist Press at The City University of New York,
311 East 94 Street, New York, NY 10128

98 97 96 95 94 5 4 3 2 1

Library of Congress Cataloging-in-Publication Data
Yamauchi, Wakako.
  Songs my mother taught me : stories, plays, and memoir / Wakako Yamauchi ;
  edited and with an introduction by Garrett Hongo ; afterword by Valerie Miner.
    p. cm.
  ISBN 1-55861-086-3 (alk. paper) : $35.00. – ISBN 1-55861-086-3 (alk. paper :
  pbk.) : $14.95
  1. Japanese American women – Literary collections. 2. Japanese Americans –
  Literary collections. 3. Japanese American women – Biography. 4. Yamauchi,
  Wakako – Biography. I. Title.
PS3575.A447S66 1994
818'.5409 – dc20   93-45383
                                                                     CIP

This publication is made possible, in part, by public funds from the National Endow-
ment for the Arts and the New York State Council on the Arts. The Feminist Press is also
grateful to Sallie Bingham, Helene D. Goldfarb, Joanne Markell, Margaret Schink, and
Genevieve Vaughan for their generosity.

Text and cover design by Paula Martinac
Cover art: "Threads of Remembrance" quilt, from Strength & Diversity: Japanese
American Women's exhibit, National Japanese American Historical Society.

Typeset by AeroType, Inc., Amherst, New Hampshire
Printed in the United States of America on acid-free paper by McNaughton & Gunn, Inc.,
Saline, Michigan

Contents

Preface

M ost of the stories in this collection were written so long ago I sometimes can't feel their connection to me. But they are mine; I am responsible for all my children. And I know though they grow away from me, they carry with them all my misjudgments, misgivings, and the joys and pain of my past (even after I've taken the mystery and hurt out of them). Still, I can respect them for their endurance and the social history they recall.

My stories are about immigrants. There have always been immigrants. We were there in prehistory, travelers from another place, another continent, or just stragglers from a larger society. We are a tribe of wanderers remembering a garden we'd left or looking for an Eden that waits.

Immigrant stories have a certain commonality. Just as all dogs snarl, bite, hunger, and circle the nest before they rest, we as a species have common traits. We yearn for a more forgiving land, a truer love, and we huddle together for comfort and protection. We spring from this source and return to it for intimacy and warmth.

Why did I write these stories? I don't know. Why does anyone write? To record a time, maybe; to get things right. To build a personal monument? I don't think so. What for? We all get our fifteen minutes anyway. Without exception, they say.

Whatever the reason, my resources are only myself. My stories are as old as the skull of Peking Man and that soft stuff inside that triggered fear, anger, jealousy, and yes, love and loneliness; as ancient as the fossil footprints of two who walked on the damp clay of a prehistoric lake bed, met, walked together awhile (surely spoke some words or touched fingertips), separated, and continued their journeys alone. Just by chance two ordinary people transcended their brief lives and left evidence of a fleeting encounter on the lake bed.

I think that's why I write: for the hard skull that stubbornly remains, the soft stuff inside that disintegrates, for lost voices, a gossamer touch. I am asking, "Do you remember? Do you care?"

Well, I take some of it back. Immigrants, emigrants, natives, man, woman – we are all the same. We snarl, bite, hunger, and circle the nest before we rest. We love and we yearn. And we sing. It's in our genes.

Wakako Yamauchi

Acknowledgments

It's a long journey from there to here and almost no one makes it alone. I thank Garrett Hongo and The Feminist Press for the heart they put in this collection, and my friend Hisaye Yamamoto DeSoto for the writing that always inspires me and the support she has given so freely for so many years.

I thank *Rafu Shimpo, Aiiieeeee! An Anthology of Asian American Writers,* and *Amerasia Journal* for accepting my early stories, the UCLA Asian American Studies Center and Asian American educators for using them, and Mako and Nobu McCarthy of East-West Players for pushing and prodding me into playwriting.

And I give my profound thanks to Yasaku and Hamako Nakamura, Chester and Joy.

Wakako Yamauchi

My gratitude goes to many people who have been important to this project, especially to Hisaye Yamamoto and Henry Mori—a Nisei writer on the *Poston Chronicle* and a Nisei editor of the *Los Angeles Rafu Shimpo*. They were the first to acknowledge Wakako Yamauchi and to encourage her that what she had to say was important and artful. From the time I first proposed it, Florence Howe, Susannah Driver, and Neeti Madan at The Feminist Press have been enthusiastic and patient as we took the project through various stages. I received editorial advice from Amy Ling, director of Asian American Studies at the University of Wisconsin–Madison. With humor, grace, and much fire, Joy Yamauchi and Cynthia Thiessen have always given, through the years, two *Nikkei* writers their patient support and counsel. Three graduate students in creative writing at Oregon–David Shih, Ryan Iwanaga, and Sara Chan—took time away from working on their own stories and poems to help me make selections out of the entire body of Wakako Yamauchi's work. David Shih wrote useful summaries and evaluations, and they all helped my thinking about organizing the selections, orchestrating the rhythms of the tonal and narrative flow of the text. They helped me live in the work again, living in it with me. Writer Valerie Miner, who agreed early on to compose the afterword, wrote an admirable one. At Villa Montalvo, I enjoyed the genial support of Lori A. Wood and the staff. Finally, I am grateful to Wakako Yamauchi herself for all the passion given, all the restraint shown over a lifetime.

Garrett Hongo

Songs My Mother Taught Me

Introduction

I n 1975, when I was twenty-three and freshly sprung from graduate school
in Japanese literature, I found Wakako Yamauchi's poetic reminiscences
about Japanese American farm life in an anthology of Asian American
writers. She had been a teenager during the war, the endnotes said, and had
begun to write while an internee in the Poston Relocation Center in Arizona.
She was currently a "housewife." The story I read had the rhythm of song and
soliloquy; it was pitched to an emotional note I wanted myself. I was back
living with my parents, in the same town where Yamauchi lived. I found her
name in the phone book one morning and called her up. She answered, I
explained myself, and she invited me over immediately, asking me to breakfast.

Since then, she has fed me dinners, lunches, more breakfasts, and New Year's
feasts too, showing me her scripts-in-progress, talking to me about my wishes
for my own literary life. She introduced me into an understanding of the stoic
and shamed emotional world of mainland Japanese Americans. Through conversation and listening to stories, I learned from her that what mainstream
society perceived as "shame" and we younger Japanese Americans called "silence" or "passivity" was actually—in the way the Nisei themselves felt about it,
and in the way the first generation, the Issei who immigrated, felt about it—an
incredible burden of pain and disappointment. After the dispossession of the
war, after the loss of farms and possessions and half a lifetime of building a life,
the Issei who'd translated themselves over into becoming Americans were
simply heartbroken and exhausted. Many could not face starting over again,
and they certainly felt little inclination to *explain* themselves to their grand-

children. Perhaps detachment, a Buddhist recommendation, was the most they could muster in terms of an attitude toward their lives.

The Nisei, on the other hand, were kind of gung ho about things. They wanted to roll up their sleeves. They wanted their chance. Who had time to reflect on the past? On the camps? Who wanted to? It was too painful. An embarrassment. An anomalous experience that everyone wished to put behind them. Feelings about camp were things best left forgotten, and, anyway, what could anyone come up with that wouldn't be deliberately shallow or so painful that they would be completely withered by the recollection? The silence my generation had felt around the issue of the camp experience, the barrier to a link with a prewar history, was a necessary thing. It didn't arise to deny us, the younger generation, but to protect us and to protect the older generations from succumbing to the dire power of its tragedy. Wakako Yamauchi taught me, with regard for the Nisei and the untold stories of the prewar and relocation periods, a little about an emotional charity, an intellectual forgiveness for all the stoicism and denial I'd felt had gone on in our community.

This past winter, I was back in Seattle doing some poetry readings and meeting students, staying in a hotel in the university district up around 50th Street Northeast, where there is a long avenue of shops, coffeehouses, and restaurants. I once lived in the neighborhood during the seventies, when I was teaching Asian American literature at the university and was involved with a theater group we called "The Asian Exclusion Act." It was named after the various racist exclusionary laws forbidding Asian Americans from owning property, intermarrying with whites, or emigrating to the United States at all if they were single women. We staged about seven plays in the two years I was part of it, one of them a 1976 workshop production of Wakako Yamauchi's first play, *And the Soul Shall Dance*. In the cast were young people like me, all wanting something quite ephemeral and barely available in those days, I think–wishing for an emotional connection to our ethnic past and to lives our parents and grandparents might have lived. We were the descendants of Asian immigrants to this country whose stories were not much told to us in those days–not by our parents (particularly if they were Japanese Americans who suffered imprisonment in relocation centers during World War II); not by the educational system that promoted, more or less, an indomitably white American story that had neglected us or censored us out of it; and not much by our own literature either, as there was little or nothing in print written by Asian Americans except for the catalytic *Aiiieeeee! An Anthology of Asian American Writers*. We needed to *declare* ourselves. And we needed something of a narrative tie to a past we could then only barely imagine. Yamauchi's play was, for many of us, the strong beginning of belonging to that past in a way our souls could not have done without.

According to her birth certificate, Wakako Yamauchi was born Wakako Nakamura in Westmorland, California, on October 25, 1924, but she tells me her mother always said that was only the recorded date and that she was born a few days earlier, the third child of five. Her father, Yasaku Nakamura, was Issei, a first-generation immigrant, who came from Shimizu in Shizuoka Prefecture. Her mother, Hamako Machida, also Issei, also came from Shizuoka.

Yamauchi thus grew up in a household that constantly looked back to Japan for its traditions, values, and rewards. She lived, in fact, in the enclave community of Japanese American farmers in southern California's Imperial Valley, going to rural public schools, shunting back and forth within a divided, all but segregated, prewar world that was, outside of the enclave, completely American and yet struggling to be Japanese at home. This was the typical Nisei, second-generation, experience. Her family moved around according to fortune, first as tenant farmers (because of California's Alien Land Law, Japanese were forbidden to own real estate) and then running a hotel for itinerant Japanese farmworkers. She was a high-school senior in Oceanside, California, when Franklin D. Roosevelt's 1942 executive order evacuated her "to camp"– the Nisei euphemism for the ten wartime concentration camps–along with 120,000 other Japanese Americans living on the West Coast. She was sent with her family to the Poston Relocation Center in Arizona.

In Poston, Yamauchi found work as a layout artist with the *Poston Chronicle,* the camp newspaper. Its staff included the Nisei writer Hisaye Yamamoto, who was just slightly older than Yamauchi and had already written stories, columns, and articles that had appeared in the Japanese American vernacular press before the war. "It was *before camp* that I knew of her stuff," Yamauchi said in a private interview, "and it was the first time I'd read a writer who spoke about things I knew about–*chazuke* and *tsukemono* and *okazu*–poor people's meals–the kinds of lives we led before the war. She taught me not to be ashamed or afraid of being Japanese in my writing, in my heart." The young women became friends, fallen together as literary and artistic aspirants. "I used to follow Hisaye around her beat, you know," Yamauchi says, "while she walked around camp taking notes for her column on Nisei life."

Released from camp early for signing what was called a "loyalty oath," Yamauchi went to work for a candy factory in Chicago during the last war years, 1944 to 1945. She returned to camp in 1945 for the funeral of her father and then left again, among the last group of evacuees to be released, moving with her mother and siblings to San Diego. After a year working there as a photo-developer, she moved on by herself to Los Angeles, where she boarded in with her friend Hisaye Yamamoto. While Yamamoto worked as a columnist and copy editor with the *Los Angeles Tribune,* an African American weekly newspaper, Yamauchi attended night school at Otis Art Center. In the drawing, layout, and painting classes, Yamauchi was the only Japanese American among whites. She stayed there about a year, until she met Chester Yamauchi.

Chester Yamauchi's family–from Berkeley, California–had befriended Wakako's older brother during the war. Her brother refused to sign the "loyalty oath" and was separated from the family and sent to Tule Lake, California, a relocation center designated for the "hard cases" the U.S. government had attempted, in a largely failed plan, to "repatriate" to Japan. After the war, without ceremony or much further clearance, these internees also were released back into society. Her brother came with Chester Yamauchi to Los Angeles, where she and Chester met, and then were married in 1948. "Actually," Wakako Yamauchi says, "we were married *twice*—once in a private Las Vegas wedding, then again a few months later in a Los Angeles wedding for his parents." Chester studied political science at UCLA, while Wakako worked various day jobs, putting him through school, keeping house—her writing and finer artistic ambitions on hold. "I painted shower curtains," Yamauchi says, "daubing on pompon flowers with a sponge brush, shaping birds-of-paradise and chrysanthemums with a palette knife."

They lived in Los Angeles seventeen years, until 1965, when they moved just south of there to Gardena, an old satellite community then largely being settled by Nisei families empowered by a growing economic status enabled by things like the GI Bill and FHA loans, for which returning Nisei veterans were now eligible. Yamauchi still lives in the same house.

A daughter, Joy Yamauchi, had been born to them in 1955. By 1958, Wakako Yamauchi had begun to write again, quietly and on her own, laboring in obscurity even within the Japanese American community. Her life, up until that time, paralleled perfectly the group story of Japanese Americans—moving through the immigration period of rural farming and itinerancy, to the up-heaval of relocation, and then through the postwar return and the urbanization of the community. Yet, for all the economic improvements and the gains in security and the establishment of a family life, Yamauchi found herself still emotionally restless and questioning.

"I was reading these gay men—" Yamauchi said in a telephone interview, "Truman Capote's short stories, James Baldwin's essays, and Tennessee Williams's plays. I *loved* them—so much sensitivity and sorrow, and so eloquent. Capote wrote about things that others never wrote about. He implied *all* the unspoken—in the lives of common personalities, in outcasts. Baldwin had that passion and that beautiful anger. And I'd seen *The Glass Menagerie* in Chicago during the war, Laurette Taylor in the lead. So touching. So pure in emotion. They all inspired me."

In early fall of 1959, Henry Mori, editor of the *Los Angeles Rafu Shimpo,* a bilingual English-Japanese daily, knowing of Yamauchi's work as an artist on the *Poston Chronicle,* invited her to work as a graphic artist on *Rafu Shimpo.*

"He wanted me to draw pictures for their holiday supplement," Yamauchi said, "the Christmas and New Year's issue they produced every year. They needed drawings to dress it up and make it more lively than usual. Chester gave me the idea to make a deal. He'd become a businessman, a caterer, doing weddings and banquets for the Nisei community, and was used to negotiating and making bargains with people. So, coached by my husband, a go-getter, I told Mori that I would draw for him if he would publish my stories. Mori said okay, and believe it or not, that's how I got started publishing. I was a Nisei housewife who did a story a year for the *Rafu Shimpo* from 1960 until about 1974, when Frank Chin and the *Aiiieeeee!* boys found me and things changed."

In 1974, Frank Chin, a Chinese American fiction writer, had teamed with three other Asian American writers—Lawson Fusao Inada, Jeffrey Paul Chan, and Shawn Wong—to seek out and publish the works of pioneering Asian American authors in the anthology *Aiiieeeee!* (Howard University Press, 1974). Its title is an in-your-face reverse homage to the inarticulate suicide cries of dying Asians, friend and foe alike, in patriotic American propaganda movies about World War II. The anthology introduced two generations of Asian American writers and inspired another generation to write as well, creating a renaissance of interest in writers, either out of print or writing in obscurity, who had reached maturity during the forties and fifties. These writers included Filipino Americans Carlos Bulosan and Bienvenidos Santos, Chinese Americans Louis Chu and Diana Chang, and Nisei authors John Okada, Hisaye Yamamoto, Toshio Mori, and Wakako Yamauchi (a grouping that constituted, retrospectively, a kind of generational literary cohort). Even more than this renaissance of interest, the anthology, with its astute and provocative introduction, performed a powerful critique on the psychological and artistic damage that stereotypes promulgated by postmodern popular culture, censoring, and textual exclusion in public education have on Asian Americans attempting to work toward self-knowledge. It called for Asian Americans to produce our own literature, to reconstruct our images, our lives, and our world views in our own voices, in response to the history of voices raised before. Yamauchi's was, of course, one of those essential voices.

Divorced in 1975, Yamauchi began writing again almost full-time for a while, encouraged by younger writers and by Mako, artistic director of East-West Players, an Equity-waiver theater in Los Angeles made up almost entirely of Asian American actors. Mako had read Yamauchi's contribution to *Aiiieeeee!*, a short story entitled "And the Soul Shall Dance," and helped secure her a Rockefeller playwright-in-residence grant to adapt and expand on it for the stage. It worked. Yamauchi wrote a marvelous script which was enthusiastically reviewed by the drama critic of the *Los Angeles Times*. The house was packed for a run of two months, then for an extension, and then for a revival. So, in midlife, Yamauchi began a new career as a playwright, authoring, over the next fifteen years, a half-dozen full-length scripts that were produced on stages in Honolulu, Los Angeles, New Haven, New York, San Diego, San Francisco, and Seattle. *And the Soul Shall Dance* was produced by East-West Players in the winter of 1977 and re-produced by KCET in Los Angeles for PBS and aired nationally in 1977–78. *The Music Lessons,* her second play developed from the short story "In Heaven and Earth," was produced by Joseph Papp for the New York Public Theater in 1980. Several productions at East-West and elsewhere followed, culminating in two special events—the Yale Repertory Theater's staging of *The Memento* at Winterfest in 1987 and UCLA's production of *12-1-A* in 1992.

Throughout this period, Yamauchi continued to write short stories, memoir, and essays. Introduced to a wider audience by that first anthology appearance, she began to publish in academic ethnic studies journals, Third World women's anthologies, regional literary magazines, Asian American women's anthologies, and drama anthologies and annuals. An excerpt of *And the Soul Shall Dance* appeared in the *Burns Mantel Theatre Yearbook 1976–77*, accompanied by caricatures of the cast by entertainment cartoonist Hirschfield. Over the past fifteen years, her stories have appeared in *Amerasia Journal, Greenfield Review,* and *Southwest Review,* as well as regularly in *Rafu Shimpo,* her first home as a writer.

"Wakako Yamauchi is a superb master of the wistful and the poignant," writes literary critic Amy Ling, director of Asian American Studies at the University of Wisconsin–Madison. In preparing this volume, I wrote Ling for a characterization of the work, and she responded with a capsule analysis: "Yamauchi's themes – love unconsummated, opportunities missed, 'songs of longing' and resignation, of restraint and its psychic cost, of despair and renewal of hope – are handled with consummate skill, presented with beauty and grace. They are not depressing stories of 'victimization,' as women's and minority Americans' stories have been accused of being, but moving testaments to human endurance, survival, and strength. They are predominantly rooted in a particular people, a time and a place: the experience of Japanese American farmers in the 1930s in the Imperial Valley of California, but their resonance and significance extend – as with all lasting literature – to all people, everywhere."

Looking back over the publication history, one can track Yamauchi's literary emergence from first appearances in a literary tabloid supplement for an ethnic newspaper to inclusion in a polemical anthology, then to the stage of an Asian American theater and other anthologies and ethnic-studies journals, and finally on to stages at Yale and UCLA and publication in academic literary journals not exclusively dedicated to ethnic work. What this says about culture and society, however, what this says about the individual, is more than ambiguous. It can be interpreted in many ways, not only the readily available, politically coercive, and quite corny story of economic success, cultural assimilation, and social acceptance of Asian Americans by the mainstream culture of the United States. These interpretations invoke multiple concerns that have to do with history, politics, ethnicity, and the roles of women in our society. They also have to do with Yamauchi's development of a literary style and her choices of what were, up until her own writing, quite unconventional literary subjects – the common lives of Japanese Americans, and even more particularly, the highly circumscribed lives of two generations of Japanese American women.

"The repression, yearning, and inner life are the heart of my stories," writes Yamauchi in a recent letter. As one would suspect given her stated models in the heroic mix of Baldwin, Capote, Williams, and Yamamoto, Yamauchi's literary sensibilities call out for a style of emotional intensity and rhetorical control that would enable her to approach and capture that inner life. She develops a somewhat spare prose, therefore, nonetheless musical, graced with an affection for rendering physical details with precision, that carries the powerful freight of two generations of Japanese American emotional life. It is eloquent in understatement, rich in tone and drama, and sometimes operatic in the emotions it describes. From "And the Soul Shall Dance," the earliest story in this collection, here is a character sketch that turns on physical description and anecdote to portray the hidden inner life of the subject:

> Mrs. Oka was small and spare. Her clothes hung on her like loose skin, and when she walked, the skirt about her legs gave her a sort of webbed look. She was pretty in spite of the boniness and the dull calico and the barren look. I know now she couldn't have been over thirty. Her eyes were large and a little vacant, although once I saw them fill with tears—the time I insisted we take the old Victrola over and we played our Japanese records for her. Some of the songs were sad, and I imagined the nostalgia she felt, but my mother said the tears were probably from yawning or from the smoke of her cigarettes. (20)

I want to also cite a passage from a later piece entitled "So What; Who Cares?" In it, an aging Nisei mother who has had a stroke is being fed by her daughter. The story is a gathering of her reminiscences. It is the interior monologue of this silent invalid, her body incapacitated by illness and her emotions paralyzed by a fear of the invalidity of her life—perhaps at once a kind of metaphor for the social reticence of the Nisei and a lament for their sometimes emotionally paralytic state. She recollects a time during the war when, while she was a young widow with a baby, a mysterious suitor, full of need, once came calling:

> He came in while my father and sister were at a camp movie or someplace—I don't remember. He waited until he saw them leave. He lived in another block, a stranger. Well, not really. I'd seen him once or twice at the canteen. He had smiled at me. He was older, a Kibei, born in America, educated in Japan. He spoke mostly Japanese. He knocked and opened the door at the same time. I didn't know what to do—what to say. The baby cried and he picked her up. "*Yoshi-yoshi,*" he crooned. Then he put her in my arms and left.
>
> I lied. I had seen him often. I've told myself so many variations of the story, I can't separate fact from fiction anymore. At the camp talent shows he sang romantic Japanese songs of longing and loneliness. He was not good looking, not very tall, but his arms were strong and his eyes—they looked through you, past your fluttering heart, and all the way down to you-know-where. And when he finally came to see me, I didn't know what to do. Then the baby cried and he sang to her and he left. The only time a man came near me the whole four years. I've clung to this memory through four decades, embellishing it, stripping it to its bone, and putting on the flesh again. (233)

There is swift narrative painting here, a combination of summary and analysis, and also the powerful rendering of an emotional confession regarding the paucity of a *physical* life for this Nisei woman, a life *in the body*. It is an admission of her own barrenness, a commentary on the dysfunctional experience, sexually and socially, of an entire generation of Japanese Americans paralyzed by the fear of acquaintanceship, clumsy and uninitiated into styles of courtship and gender relations. They could not follow the sexual and stoical social codes of their immigrant parents who may have married in arrangements made by others and in Japan–a world away, who may have married through an exchange of pictures, who may not have been married, who may have fallen together in itinerancy. And the mores of white Americans were a mystery made even more mysterious by the movies–another world of liberty and self-possession, of physical sensuousness and emotional freedom. The Issei/Nisei world might have seemed dry by comparison, mis-partnered, strangely random, and roaming a desert of emotions.

We can see that, from early on in her work, Yamauchi took these themes of misspent sexuality and frustration over the ownership of the body and joined them to two others, closely related: personal freedom and the development of an aesthetic consciousness. In "And the Soul Shall Dance," Yamauchi contrasts two farm families–a seemingly childless couple and their neighbors who have a son and a daughter. The young girl, unnamed in the story, is mystified and admires the strangeness, the ethereality, and the sensuousness of Emiko, the woman who is her neighbor. Surrounded by boisterous men and stoical, dutiful women, Emiko smokes and drinks sake along with the men. As described in the passage quoted before, she weeps openly when she hears Japanese songs played on a Victrola, and she reminisces out loud about former times, lovers, a youth of studying dance. In contrast to Mrs. Murata, the Issei housewife who is the young girl's mother, Emiko is thus intensely subjectified, owning her own past, clinging to a prior life of consciousness and pleasure in Japan, and not only nostalgically, but actively, dancing crazily, alone inside her house and out in the desert, singing songs out loud, gathering flowers. The Nisei characters reject her as "strange" and "insane." Emiko, like other sexualized "outsiders" later in Yamauchi's oeuvre, is rejected by her husband (he abuses her physically) and stigmatized by the community, yet is empowered narratively, an active agent in Yamauchi's fiction, a heroine who insists on a measure of imaginative and emotional freedom in her life and initiates another into her way of being. The sensitivity for an aesthetic dimension and a powerful wish to live in a world not determined by necessity is stirred within the young girl, all of eleven or so, and the story portrays her spying on Emiko in her final dance, memorizing Japanese words to the sad sake-drinking song Emiko sings to accompany it.

There is a grand poignancy to all of this telling that Yamauchi, as a literary stylist, manages to fix in the mind with two literary techniques perhaps most familiar to poets: (1) She gathers up images from the landscape and from common life and weds them to narrative events; and (2) she ties new emotions, just emerging in the lives of her people and described in her fiction, to recognizable emotions already established in a tradition.

Again, from "And the Soul Shall Dance," Yamauchi describes Kiyoko, a schoolmate newly arrived from Japan and yet urgently Americanized, walking across farmlands:

> . . . with a permanent wave, her straight black hair became tangles of frantic curls, between her textbooks she carried copies of *Modern Screen* and *Photoplay,* her clothes were gay with print and piping, and she bought a pair of brown suede shoes with alligator trim. I can see her now, picking her way gingerly over the white peaks of alkaline crust. (23)

Drawn from life, these images articulate, with a physical precision, the contrasts in the Nisei world – their urge to acquire the material trappings of American life, objectifying an inner urge to *become American* that is painfully juxtaposed, in the image of the two-tone shoes skating over alkaline ground, with their condition as immigrants, tenant farmers, and itinerant workers laboring close to the earth and socially barely above it.

In the late story "Ōtōkō ," a retrospective piece in her grand style, Yamauchi reveals that part of her technique has sprung not only from stylistic roots in contemporary letters, but has had to do with her feeling for an extraordinary tradition – that of Japanese *song* – both the *shigin* tradition of narrative balladry and the one of folkloric and popular love songs. She has, as a background to her method and as a sort of emotional pitch-point, perhaps attached her new, American stories to the wealth of emotions invoked by Japanese lyricism. In "Ōtōkō ," as she has done previously in "And the Soul Shall Dance," Yamauchi quotes lyrics and invokes pentatonic, Oriental melodies from popular prewar Japanese culture and the older folk traditions of Japan, importing a wealth of memories and associated emotions, invoking the past and a separate inheritance of aestheticized melancholy unavailable in literature written exclusively in English. There are in these invocations a special, almost religious quality of emotion and an evocation to its lyric cadences quite unlike anything I know of in American letters. These are closer to the melancholy of Appalachian gospel tunes and have the resolute quality of black spirituals. When Yamauchi calls them forth, I feel, deep in my bones and in the strange, nearly imperceptible rushing of my blood, that huge inner evacuation of alienation and mystery that is a signal of the abolished emotional dissonance and historical distance between myself and those Issei immigrants who might have been my own ancestors.

In "Ōtōkō ," two aging Nisei siblings, a brother and a sister, chilled by contemporary suburban life, spend the occasion of the summer solstice together. The brother brings a recording of old Japanese songs that remind them of the distant life they began with, raised by Issei parents homesick for Japan. As Yamauchi dubs fragments of the Japanese lyrics into her story, as she invokes the melodies that accompany them, the brother and sister reminisce, fade back into similar memories, and draw together. My reader's heart lifts, even three generations removed, to the invocation of these songs and Yamauchi's juxtaposed stories of travail about those who spoke a language very different from the English I live in now. The Japanese term *sabi* is a word for the indescribable, plangent sadness for the poverty of being itself. It is a mode that invokes pity and a cast of mind in which compassion is born, and it is Yamauchi's grand mode as a writer. The storytelling and the narrator's voice themselves become pitched to the extraordinarily melancholy and balladic emotional tone of the Japanese tunes, and Yamauchi's writing seems to gain in susceptibility to the most delicate and ephemeral of recollections—whole swaths of generational experience. She describes Issei farmworkers inhabiting a transient hotel:

> Sometimes in the evening they would play wistful Japanese melodies on harmonicas or wooden flutes . . .
>
> The older men were scruffy and bowed from years of scraping along on their knees picking strawberries . . . and from bending over low grapevines. Their pants were caked with mud. They shook them out at night over the balcony. Conversations were colored with sexual references, and they laughed lewdly at the jokes. They spent their leisure playing *hana* (cards) or drinking sake which my mother kept warm for them at ten cents a cup.
>
> Once a man staggered off to the courtyard and passed out on the dirt, the ocean breeze cooling him, the sun warming him like the fruit he'd spent his youth harvesting. In the late afternoon he woke and walked away brushing himself off, without shame, as though it were his natural right as a man. Fruit of the land. (240)

The aesthetic enables her own nearly rapturous connection with the things of the earth and the small details of living, and, empowered by a rich tradition of stylized melancholy invoked by song, Yamauchi's stories, even as they describe an outer world, become symbolically invested with the amazing ability to reproduce the complicated and otherwise somewhat silenced *emotional* character, the Rilkean "inner life," of Nisei and Issei experiences.

I made the selection of these sixteen stories and memoir from approximately thirty narrative and essayistic pieces Wakako Yamauchi has written over the past thirty-five years or so. The two plays were chosen from among nine dramatic pieces, seven of them full-length two-act dramas. A complete works would run over five hundred printed pages and complete a chronicle of two generations of Japanese American lives, rendering into painful description, but for her grand and poignant storyteller's style, an almost subromantic seam running all the way through it. What follows, however, is a considered selection, chosen for literary qualities but also to represent the work as a whole—to demonstrate how Yamauchi's writing covers at least three periods of Japanese American history (early twentieth-century immigration and rural settlement, the wartime evacuation, and the postwar urbanization), two generations, and three literary genres. I divide the selection into four broad categories having to do with genre and/or locale: (1) Country Stories, (2) City Stories, (3) Plays, and (4) Recollections.

The five Country Stories include four among her earliest narrative pieces that establish her literary style and unique memoiristic and retrospective voice. "That Was All" is a late and decidedly memoiristic piece I grouped together with the rest for reasons of related locale, theme, and time frame. Like the rest of these country stories, it too is set in the tough, rural life of the Issei community before World War II and concerns the subjects of Issei/Nisei mis-partnering, thwarted sexuality, and the physical and spiritual loneliness of the immigrant generation witnessed by the first native one. Against a backdrop of the bleak California desert landscape, Yamauchi, in these five pieces, depicts the dreary lives of Japanese American tenant farmers and itinerant workers, teasing out of her own recollections stories of sexual and emotional thirst, commentaries on hidden and thwarted aspirations. They read as epic messages across a chasm of silence and shame that was the event of the Japanese American relocation—the government-ordered mass evacuation and stigmatizing of 120,000 citizens and resident aliens during World War II which resulted, arguably, in an obliteration of our history, the destruction of our communities, and the inheritance of an inner burden of self-hate for many of us. Another related, less markable but more terribly amorphous event these stories manage to overcome is the loss and abandonment of the Japanese language (its emotion and its memory) as the medium of our culture and society. Without Yamauchi's work here (and the work of the Nisei literary cohort which includes Yamamoto, Okada, and Mori), there would be a barrier of ignorance, a tremendous sacrifice of emotional legacy, and the sham of available history, far too intellectualized or merely factual, that somehow belies the full experience of the first Japanese Americans. As literature, her work has the advantage of symbol, summary, and subjectivity. She portrays an impoverished community that is also full of a highly emotional hunger—stoical men and women longing for tenderness, itinerant Issei bachelors and their roustabout societies thrown alongside lonely wives and young Nisei women, and families indentured to the land and its next crop of carrots and tomatoes. Yet, I believe that the stories also send out a strong note of independence from her own developing aesthetic consciousness that potentiates, in acts of contemplation, a certain freedom—from the beliefs of incompatible societies, Nisei or otherwise, and from the strangely limited and socialized body produced by those separate societies.

The first play in the collection, *The Music Lessons,* is set in the same rural surroundings and occurs during the same prewar, post-Depression period as Yamauchi's early stories. She depicts a family headed by a woman, an Issei widow who has lost her husband due to a farming accident. There are three children, a married male neighbor, and Kaoru, a robust, attractive, and violin-playing hired hand—the sexualized "intruder" of the play. The drama, much like the short story "In Heaven and Earth" from which it was developed, depicts the Issei generation dedicated to material survival – the men functioning as beasts of burden and the women as, normally, a helpmate to these beasts and mother of the family, a kind of servant and manager at the same time. When the mother discovers her teenage daughter's infatuation with the hired hand, exposed in a scene of mis-partnered seduction initiated by the young woman, she becomes enraged, confronted with her own sexual enfeeblement, and, as moral judge of the failed couple, banishes the man from her house. Metaphorically, she banishes her own sexualized body, along with its richer, more highly potentiated consciousness. She rules against subjectivity, the exploration of consciousness and ownership of the body. *The Music Lessons* thus exposes a sexual competition between Issei mother and Nisei teenage daughter and the conflict in values (and cultures?) regarding consciousness. The Issei woman is dedicated to *survival* – her goals are the laudatory but spiritually unfulfilling ones that commit to the avoidance of poverty, debt, and disgrace; to evacuating herself and her family of humiliation and stigma – while her Nisei daughter craves the romance of an imagined life, all potential, enspirited with poetry and music. The prize, of course, is Issei virility and cultural empowerment under the guise of city-educated, hired-hand Kaoru. Ambiguously masked and bound up in issues of cultural possession and individual power, the subtextual desire is for an intact society beyond the cares of necessity and caprices of vicissitude, released from the rural quotidian, perhaps not even *raced* (Kaoru is taught by a white woman teacher).

The section of City Stories, six narratives written in the decade between the mid-seventies and mid-eighties, represents the best of Yamauchi's fictional work that treats the period in the aftermath of the mass wartime evacuation – the Nisei postwar return from the relocation centers and the arc of their lives through adulthood and middle age. In each of them, Yamauchi sketches a narrative backdrop of industrious Nisei trying to accomplish the strange business of constructing mature *American* lives out of a people stigmatized by race and relocation.

In "The Sensei," for example, the first of these stories, a young Nisei couple just starting out in their marriage come upon an Issei man begging them for change while they are on a spree in Las Vegas. The sensei, a Buddhist priest, was once powerful and prominent as an uncompromising leader among dissident Japanese Americans in one of the camps, but in the aftermath of the war, after the release of the evacuees back into American life, he is beguiled by the glitter of the magical desert city – all potential and promise – and he gambles away his money, loses his self-possession, and cannot complete his trip from camp to Denver, where his family awaits him. He tries to keep gambling instead, borrowing money from other Japanese, humbling himself, slipping into a strange addiction. Throughout this story, and developed as well in "Shirley Temple, Hotcha-cha," there are undercurrents regarding the inadequacy of the Nisei husband – his blustery machismo, his naive and enthusiastic embrace of a mainstream male role as agent and adventurer in society, his potential for the betrayal of the narrator – his wife, a spousal helpmate – and a kind of choral commentator on the events of the story. I think the figure of the *sensei* himself, in this most abject of states, is a metonym of failure that represents the emasculation of Issei male culture (staunchly Japanese and unassimilated) by the war and also the Issei *fear* of coming back out of camp and having to start life over again. The entire tale can be read as an allegory for the older community's fear of again taking up an unreliable freedom and burdening the strange load of history sent by an inhospitable and racist country.

Yet, I think that Yamauchi's ultimate subject in these city stories is not acculturation but, as with the country stories, is again the thwarted sexual and emotional relations between people confused about their roles in society and with each other. Though each of the remaining five stories in this category, after their fashion, develop these themes further, I believe them most prominent in "Charted Lives" and "The Coward."

"Charted Lives," a somewhat sordid tale of masked origins, family secrets, and implied incest, is, I think, in fact an allegory regarding the third-generation's passion for knowing its origins, for knowing the father, for unmasking whatever it is that has been left untold by culture and society about who we are. A middle-aged Nisei woman is trying to recover from her divorce by taking on a clerical job in an office, where she is befriended by a young, Caucasian supervisor whose wife is Japanese American. The husband is fascinated that the Nisei and the Sansei women both paint, and the story turns on the developing mother-son relationship between the two co-workers and the deteriorating spousal relationship between the Caucasian man and his Sansei wife. Yet, the wife is not completely Japanese. It is revealed that her father was a Caucasian painter who had an affair with the woman's Nisei mother before she married her Nisei father! It is another mis-partnering. The Caucasian father enters their lives again, suggesting a reconciliation in Hawaii, and swiftly the marriage falls apart and the husband is left to confess a sordid story to his Nisei co-worker. As with Yamauchi's young-women characters in the country stories, this story's pivotal character, known to us exclusively by report, has a decidedly erotic fascination for what she has not known before, for what was hidden and perhaps proscribed by circumstance, by shame, and by loyalty to an enclave culture. The Sansei wife's passion for her estranged Caucasian father, styled as sexual in the story, seems a displacement for that deep spiritual thirst orphans have to know their origins. Sundered from the emotional character and from even the physical evidences of our ancestral past (where are our ethnic museums, our relics from relocation?), a third-generation Japanese American is a kind of orphan of history – in deep need to cross the cultural chasms that separate us from having an emotionally and intellectually accessible past and a public story regarding it that is available to others and kindly accepted by them as well. Her move to the father is the objectification of a fictive metaphor, the desperate enactment of a quest to be freed of ignorance, to be released from being bound within a social identity that represses a powerful hidden dimension of being.

"Charted Lives" reproduces Yamauchi's now recognizable and signature character configuration of a husband and wife threatened by a culturally empowered sexual intruder. In the country stories, the couple is Issei, the configuration includes their teenage or preteen Nisei daughter, and the intruder is a Japanese laborer with citified ways and a touch of glamour or culture. In "Charted Lives" and "The Coward," the intruder is a Caucasian painter.

In "The Coward," Yamauchi's Nisei narrator, another housewife in a dull and failing marriage, joins a group of amateur weekend painters, mostly other women, but including an attractive "pale European" man. As we read through her thoughts (the narrative is written as a kind of retrospective confession), we see her analyzing her marriage, examining how recent history may have determined her husband's ego-filled quest to demonstrate his power in the world, how heritage might have prescribed an unexamined and narrowly defined emotional and sexual identity for herself. In a passage that might serve as the summary statement regarding the de-sexualized identity of a kind of Nisei woman, the narrator makes these comments:

> My mother taught me a lot of things that were pertinent to then and me, a Japanese American country girl in an insecure economy, facing a bleak future. And however unrewarding the virtues she herself practiced, or inequitable the gods that judged her, she still pressed on me a sort of Japanese-Buddhist Victorianism. She spoke a lot about greed and need and hungers of the flesh, and all manner of nonessential material things as the devil's instruments. She taught me not to dream extravagantly, but with both feet on the ground and of attainable goals. She told me to be frugal with love and passion and she passed on an unspoken distrust of men. (137–38)

The marriage she finds herself in is utilitarian—her husband is an engineer who splurges on luxuries to demonstrate his lack of imagination, and she is a discontented economic and social helpmate with a thirst for something more. Like many unfortunates who have been thrown together, not knowing they are actually living out narratives that are at strong variance with one another's, these two seem locked in a marriage of incompatible karmas—the husband wanting a brand of American social and economic virility inaccessible to the generation of his father (wanting, in fact, a kind of social *revenge*), the wife wanting out of the role as helpmate to that power, wanting a relationship with *mercy* rather than with any worldly success. Through a group of artists, she begins to develop that relationship, evacuating herself of familial, ethnic, and historical identities, beginning to possess a nascent consciousness that is her unarticulated inner life. She lives, for a while, in a passionate titivation over paintings in galleries and museums, seeking mood and color and shape with which to release herself into the aesthetic dimension of an almost pure potential. She finds, within herself, a being without a past or a willed and determined future. She finds, suddenly, that she is curious about another man, an amateur painter like herself, a European with whom she takes up an unrequited love affair, arranging to meet in galleries until, finally, he invites her to his studio where the seduction is to take place. She is thrilled with his interest, his paintings, but rejects him, acknowledging her desire but prohibited from indulging in it because an inherited sexual morality has dispirited her into a kind of self-nausea for her own wretchedness, her own shame for the pathetic inner wish to be free and inspired to love.

Yamauchi's stories refuse to rewrite the past of consciousness and wishing. She will not have her character leap falsely into a freedom a woman of her time did not feel was available, nor will she glorify a consciousness that may have been only tentatively approached, incompletely achieved. However intense the desire might have been for political authority and moral freedom, the wishing to abide within imagined worlds unfettered by the truths of history, the message here is that these were not comfortably possessed by the Nisei generation. "The Coward," in this way, can be seen both as a tribute to the unacted-upon desires of a Nisei woman, and by extension, a troubled homage to an entire, outwardly quiescent generation. Formed by the circumstances of history, their heroicism was one of deep emotional caution and a problematized forbearance. If a passion has been expressed and released into the future that would be as powerful as a material force, then it would be the writer's own.

And the Soul Shall Dance, the two-act drama developed out of the original short story, follows the city stories in my sequencing. The script represents her most complex handling of the themes of sexuality and aesthetic consciousness, touches on the issue of women as property (the farmer Murata says, at one point, "Out here, a man's horse is as important as his wife"), and elevates Emiko, an eccentric Issei woman, who is a terrible misfit in her time and community, into a spellbinding martyr for art, culture, and independence of mind. Her martyrdom – going insane, intoning a sake-drinking song while dressed in fancy kimono and dancing among fields of carrots – is witnessed by Masako, the young teenage Nisei girl who is her neighbor, thus implying that a legacy of passion has been passed along and that a kind of permission has been given to succeeding generations to develop whatever consciousness might have been denied their ancestors. For the young Masako, madwoman Emiko functions as a troubled model of imaginative freedom in a time and culture in which the roles of women are highly bound by their circumstances, race, and gender status. The suggestion, at play's end, seems to be that Masako will own her own mind and body, that she will be empowered, invested with the ability to imagine and dictate an aspect of her own future. She will be free.

"Recollections," the final section of this collection, gathers short story and memoir together, the distinction between them sliding even a little more than it has over the rest of Yamauchi's mixed fictive and memoiristic oeuvre. Ostensibly, only "Old Times, Old Stories" – Yamauchi's personal essay looking back on her own life – can strictly be classed as pure memoir, yet each of the pieces has so powerful a retrospective cast, writing that seems to take final stock of things, that I've put them together as a group. They make a quintet of pieces treating the Nisei generation from middle age to retirement and some decrepitude. In the regretful "Makapuu Bay," the writer-narrator is a Nisei divorcee (like Yamauchi herself) who encounters an old flame she was infatuated with in camp, during the war, and is inspired to reminisce over her choices in life and lament a little over what did not transpire. "A Veteran of Foreign Wars" concerns the awkward, even unpleasant neighborhood encounters between a male amputee – a veteran of the famous Nisei combat team of World War II – and the divorcee who lives down his street. They cannot speak except to transform each other into tools, giving practical advice, preaching forbidding warnings, increasing the distance of emotional alienation between a man and a woman, both full of emotional need, who do not know what to do with one another. "So What; Who Cares?" and "Ōtōkō" reassert themes of mis-partnering, the ownership of the body, and the awkward sexual identities of the Nisei, even as the seemingly innocent, Adamic masculinity of Issei men is heroized. Of all the pieces in this collection, I think "Ōtōkō" puts forward Yamauchi's emotional and literary insights in a way that illuminates all the rest.

Overall, Wakako Yamauchi's work sets down the neglected social and emotional history of two entire generations of Japanese in this country. I believe that her writing is a cultural treasure, being testimonies in lyric prose that document our immigration and the painful process that attempts accultura-tion. Her words describe, without falling into bitterness or into obliged and sentimentalized angers, the privations of eking out a marginal existence farming desert scrublands in California, the mixed regard and resentment of women for their menfolk. Yet, though her stories do perform the necessary act of making a kind of chronicle and bear compelling witness to a difficult experience, they are written with such lyricism and depth of feeling that they all exceed mere function and take on the forms of small masterpieces. Hers is a sensuous and imaginative sensibility. She writes of the throng of World War II evacuees sent to camp and released to work in midwestern factories, describing their cultural exile with both acid and affection. She writes of regret and from an acute knowledge of the limits of passion and imagination to transform bleak and circumscribed lives. She writes of sexual desire coupled with social inadequacy. She has a Chekhovian insight into the small dramas huddled within larger social histories and the great narrative myths of culture. Wakako Yamauchi is our most mature literary artist, eloquent and completely informed of necessity and experienced in the wanton acts of history.

Garrett Hongo
Villa Montalvo

Country Stories

And the Soul Shall Dance

I t's all right to talk about it now. Most of the principals are dead, except, of course, me and my younger brother, and possibly Kiyoko Oka, who might be near forty-five now because, yes, I'm sure of it, she was fourteen then. I was nine, and my brother about four, so he hardly counts. Kiyoko's mother is dead, my father is dead, my mother is dead, and her father could not have lasted all these years with his tremendous appetite for alcohol and pickled chiles—those little yellow ones, so hot they could make your mouth hurt—he'd eat them like peanuts and tears would surge from his bulging thyroid eyes in great waves and stream down the coarse terrain of his face.

My father farmed then in the desert basin resolutely named Imperial Valley, in the township called Westmorland, twenty acres of tomatoes, ten of summer squash, or vice versa, and the Okas lived maybe a mile, mile and a half, across an alkaline road, a stretch of greasewood, tumbleweed, and white sand, to the south of us. We didn't hobnob much with them because, you see, they were a childless couple and we were a family: father, mother, daughter, and son, and we went to the Buddhist church on Sundays, where my mother taught Japanese, and the Okas kept pretty much to themselves. I don't mean they were unfriendly—Mr. Oka would sometimes walk over (he rarely drove) on rainy days, all dripping wet, short and squat under a soggy newspaper, pretending to need a plow blade or a file, and he would spend the afternoon in our kitchen drinking sake and eating chiles with my father. As he got drunk, his large mouth would draw down, and with the stream of tears, he looked like a kindly weeping bullfrog.

Not only were they childless, impractical in an area where large families were looked upon as labor potentials, but there was a certain strangeness about them. I became aware of it the summer our bathhouse burned down and my father didn't get right down to building another, and a Japanese without a bathhouse . . . well, Mr. Oka offered us the use of his. So every night that summer we drove to the Okas for our bath, and we came in frequent contact with Mrs. Oka, and this is where I found the strangeness.

Mrs. Oka was small and spare. Her clothes hung on her like loose skin, and when she walked, the skirt about her legs gave her a sort of webbed look. She was pretty in spite of the boniness and the dull calico and the barren look. I know now she couldn't have been over thirty. Her eyes were large and a little vacant, although once I saw them fill with tears – the time I insisted we take the old Victrola over and we played our Japanese records for her. Some of the songs were sad, and I imagined the nostalgia she felt, but my mother said the tears were probably from yawning or from the smoke of her cigarettes. I thought my mother resented her for not being more hospitable; indeed, never a cup of tea appeared before us, and between them the conversation of women was totally absent: the rise and fall of gentle voices, the arched eyebrows, the croon of polite surprise. But more than this, Mrs. Oka was different.

Obviously she was shy, but some nights she disappeared altogether. She would see us drive into her yard and then lurch from sight. She was gone all evening. Where could she have hidden in that two-room house – where in that silent desert? Some nights she would wait out our visit with enormous forbearance, quietly pushing wisps of stray hair behind her ears and waving gnats away from her great moist eyes, and some nights she moved about with nervous agitation, her khaki canvas shoes slapping loudly as she walked. And sometimes there appeared to be welts and bruises on her usually smooth brown face, and she would sit solemnly, hands on her lap, eyes large and intent on us. My mother hurried us home then: "Masako, no need to wash well. Hurry."

You see, being so poky, I was always last to bathe. I think the Okas bathed after we left because my mother often reminded me to keep the water clean. The routine was to lather outside the tub (there were buckets and pans and a small wooden stool), rinse off the soil and soap, and then soak in the tub of hot water and contemplate. Rivulets of perspiration would run down the scalp.

When my mother pushed me like this, I dispensed with ritual, rushed a bar of soap around me, and splashed about a pan of water. So hastily toweled, my wet skin trapped the clothes to me, impeding my already clumsy progress. Outside, my mother would be murmuring her many apologies and my father, I knew, would be carrying my brother whose feet were already sandy. We would hurry home.

I thought Mrs. Oka might be insane and I asked my mother about it, but she shook her head and smiled with her mouth drawn down and said that Mrs. Oka loved to drink. This was unusual, yes, but there were other unusual women we knew. Mrs. Naka was bought by her husband from a geisha house; Mrs. Tani was a militant Christian Scientist; Mrs. Abe, the midwife, was occult. My mother's statement explained much: sometimes Mrs. Oka was drunk and sometimes not. Her taste for liquor and cigarettes was a step into the realm of men; unusual for a Japanese wife, but at that time, in that place, and to me, Mrs. Oka loved her sake in the way my father and Mr. Oka loved theirs, the way I loved my candy. That her psychology may have demanded this anesthetic, that she lived with something unendurable, did not occur to me. Nor did I perceive the violence of the purple welts – or the masochism that permitted her to display these wounds to us.

In spite of her masculine habits, Mrs. Oka was never less than a woman. She was no lady in the area of social amenities, but the feminine in her was innate and never left her. Even in her disgrace she was a small broken sparrow, slightly floppy, too slowly enunciating her few words, too carefully rolling her Bull Durham, cocking her small head and moistening the ocher tissue. Her aberration was a protest of the life assigned her; it was obstinate but unobserved, alas, unattended. "Strange" was the only concession we granted her.

Toward the end of summer, my mother said we could not continue bathing at the Okas'; when winter set in we'd all catch our death from the commuting, and she'd always felt dreadful about our imposition on Mrs. Oka. So my father took the corrugated tin sheets he'd found on the highway and had been saving for some other use and built our bathhouse again. Mr. Oka came to help.

While they raised the quivering tin walls, Mr. Oka began to talk. His voice was sharp above the low thunder of the metal sheets.

He told my father he had been married previously in Japan to the present Mrs. Oka's older sister. He had a child by the marriage, Kiyoko, a girl. He had left the two to come to America, intending to send for them soon, but shortly after his departure, his wife passed away from an obscure stomach ailment. At the time, the present Mrs. Oka was young and had foolishly become involved with a man of poor reputation. The family was anxious to part the lovers and conveniently arranged a marriage by proxy and sent him his dead wife's sister. Well, that was all right, after all, they were kin and it would be good for the child when she came to join them. But things didn't work out that way – year after year he postponed calling for his daughter, couldn't get the price of the fare together, and the wife . . . ahhh, the wife . . . Mr. Oka's groan was lost in the rumble of his hammering.

He cleared his throat. The girl was now fourteen and begging to come to America to be with her own real family. The relatives had forgotten the favor he'd done in accepting a slightly used bride, and now they tormented his daughter for being forsaken. True, he'd not sent much money, but if they knew, if they only knew how it was here.

"Well," he sighed, "who could be blamed? It's only right she be with me anyway."

"That's right," my father said.

"Well, I sold the horse and some other things and managed to buy a third-class ticket on the Taiyo-Maru. Kiyoko will get here the first week of September." Mr. Oka glanced toward my father, but my father was peering into a bag of nails. "I'd be much obliged to you if your wife and little girl," he rolled his eyes toward me, "would take kindly to her. She'll be lonely."

Kiyoko-san came in September. I was surprised to see so very nearly a woman—short, robust, buxom—the female counterpart of her father: thyroid eyes and protruding teeth, straight black hair banded impudently into two bristly shucks, Cuban heels and white socks. Mr. Oka proudly brought her to us.

For the first time to my recollection, he touched me; he put his fat hand on the top of my head. "Little Masako here is very smart in school. She will help you with your schoolwork, Kiyoko," he said.

I had so looked forward to Kiyoko-san's arrival. She would be my soul mate; in my mind I had conjured a girl of my own proportions: thin and tall but with the refinement and beauty I didn't yet possess that would surely someday come to the fore. My disappointment was keen and apparent. Kiyoko-san stepped forward shyly, then retreated with a short bow and small giggle, her fingers pressed to her mouth.

My mother took her away. They talked for a long time—about Japan, about enrollment in American school, the clothes Kiyoko-san would need, and where to look for the best values. As I watched them, it occurred to me that I had been deceived. This was not a child, this was a woman. The smile pressed behind her fingers, the way of her nod, so brief, like my mother when father scolded her. The face was inscrutable, but something shrank visibly, like a piece of silk in water. I was disappointed. Kiyoko-san's soul was barricaded in her unenchanting appearance and the smile she fenced behind her fingers.

She started school from third grade, one below me, and as it turned out, she quickly passed me by. There wasn't much I could help her with except to drill her on pronunciation—the L and R sounds. Every morning walking to our rural school: land, leg, library, loan, lot. Every afternoon returning home: ran, rabbit, rim, rinse, roll. That was the extent of our communication—friendly but not close.

One particularly cold November night—the wind outside was icy—I was sitting on my bed, my brother's and mine, oiling the cracks on my chapped hands by lamplight—someone rapped urgently at our door. It was Kiyoko-san; she was hysterical, she wore no wrap, her teeth were chattering, and except for the thin straw zori, her feet were bare. My mother led her to the kitchen, started a pot of tea, and gestured to my brother and me to retire. I lay very still but, because of my brother's restless tossing and my father's snoring, was unable to hear much. I was aware, though, that drunken and savage brawling had brought Kiyoko-san to us. Presently they came to the bedroom. I feigned sleep. My mother gave Kiyoko-san a gown and pushed me over to make room for her. My mother spoke firmly: "Tomorrow you will return to them; you must not leave them again. They are your people." I could almost feel Kiyoko-san's short nod.

All night long I lay cramped and still, afraid to intrude into her hulking back. Two or three times her icy feet jabbed into mine and quickly retreated. In the morning I found my mother's gown neatly folded on the spare pillow. Kiyoko-san's place in bed was cold.

She never came to weep at our house again, but I know she cried. Her eyes were often swollen and red. She stopped much of her giggling and routinely pressed her fingers to her mouth. Our daily pronunciation drill petered off from lack of interest. She walked silently with her shoulders hunched, grasping her books with both arms, and when I spoke to her in my halting Japanese, she absently corrected my prepositions.

Spring comes early in the valley; in February the skies are clear though the air is still cold. By March, winds are vigorous and warm and wildflowers dot the desert floor, cockleburs are green and not yet tenacious, the sand is crusty underfoot, everywhere there is the smell of things growing, and the first tomatoes are showing green and bald.

As the weather changed, Kiyoko-san became noticeably more cheerful. Mr. Oka, who hated so to drive, could often be seen steering his dusty old Ford over the road that passes our house, and Kiyoko-san, sitting in front, would sometimes wave gaily to us. Mrs. Oka was never with them. I thought of these trips as the westernizing of Kiyoko-san: with a permanent wave, her straight black hair became tangles of frantic curls, between her textbooks she carried copies of *Modern Screen* and *Photoplay,* her clothes were gay with print and piping, and she bought a pair of brown suede shoes with alligator trim. I can see her now, picking her way gingerly over the white peaks of alkaline crust.

At first my mother watched their coming and going with vicarious pleasure. "Probably off to a picture show; the stores are all closed at this hour," she might say. Later her eyes would get distant and she would muse, "They've left her home again; Mrs. Oka is alone again."

Now when Kiyoko-san passed by or came in with me on her way home, my mother would ask about Mrs. Oka—how is she, how does she occupy herself these rainy days, or these windy or warm or cool days. Often the answers were polite: "Thank you, we are fine." But sometimes Kiyoko-san's upper lip would pull over her teeth, and her voice would become soft and she would say, "Always drinking and fighting." At those times my mother would invariably say, "Endure; soon you will be marrying and going away."

Once a young truck driver delivered crates at the Oka farm, and he dropped back to our place to tell my father that Mrs. Oka had lurched behind his truck while he was backing up and very nearly let him kill her. Only the daughter pulling her away saved her, he said. Thoroughly unnerved, he stopped by to rest himself and talk about it. Never, never, had he seen a drunken Japanese woman. My father nodded gravely. "Yes, it's unusual," he said and drummed his knee with his fingers.

Evenings were longer now, and when my mother's migraines drove me from the house in unbearable self-pity, I would take walks in the desert. One night with the warm wind against me, the primrose and yellow poppies closed and fluttering, the greasewood swaying in languid orbit, I lay on the white sand beneath a shrub and tried to disappear.

A voice clear and sweet cut through the half-dark of the evening:

Akai kuchibiru	Red lips
Kappu ni yosete	Press against a glass
Aoi sake nomya	Drink the green wine
Kokoro ga odoru	And the soul shall dance

Mrs. Oka appeared to be gathering flowers. Bending, plucking, standing, searching, she added to a small bouquet she clasped. She held them away, looked at them slyly, lids lowered, demure; then in a sudden and sinuous movement, she broke into a stately dance. She stopped, gathered more flowers, and breathed deeply into them. Tossing her head, she laughed softly from her dark throat. The picture of her imagined grandeur was lost to me, but the delusion that transformed a bouquet of tattered petals and sandy leaves, and the loneliness of a desert twilight into a fantasy that brought such joy and abandon made me stir with discomfort. The sound broke Mrs. Oka's dance. Her eyes grew large and her neck tense – like a cat on prowl. She spied me in the bushes. A peculiar chill ran through me. Then abruptly and with childlike delight, she scattered the flowers around her and walked away singing:

Falling, falling, petals on a wind . . .

That was the last time I saw Mrs. Oka. She died before the spring harvest. It was pneumonia. I didn't attend the funeral, but my mother said it was sad. Mrs. Oka looked peaceful, and the minister expressed the irony of the long separation of mother and child and the short-lived reunion. Hardly a year together, he said. We went to help Kiyoko-san address and stamp those black-bordered acknowledgments.

When harvest was over, Mr. Oka and Kiyoko-san moved out of the valley. We never heard from them or saw them again. I suppose in a large city, Mr. Oka found some sort of work, perhaps as a janitor or a dishwasher, and Kiyoko-san grew up and found someone to marry.

In Heaven and Earth

When Akiko Nagata was fifteen, her father had been dead for six years. He'd fallen one night from a catwalk bridging the All American Canal, and it was never established whether a seizure had sent him down, or whether the little bit of claret he'd had at the Kawaguchis' had been his undoing, or whether in a moment of abandon he'd made this final misstep. They'd found him in the morning caught in a large tumbleweed wedged in some rocks, the muddy Colorado water lapping gently around his face.

All those six years Akiko's mother and two older brothers—Taro, sixteen, and Tomu, seventeen—worked the farm: the mother, dark-skinned, hair bunned tightly back, driving the truck, grinding gears and roaring about the ranch; the boys loading, unloading, for all their tender years moving surely with the seasons, seeding, weeding, thinning, irrigating, harvesting. When one went to school, the other worked on the farm, alternating, both in the same class, one here, one there; one doggedly plugging away at some incomprehensible text, the other resolutely working furrow after furrow. The family kept up with their debts and maintained a frugal living, and Mrs. Nagata often reflected that this was no less than her husband had provided. The depression was not yet over for many.

Beginning the seventh year, in September, a stranger came looking for work—tall, handsome, with hands unlike any Akiko had seen on a working man. He'd been around the area inquiring and the Kawaguchis had sent him down. They'd said Mrs. Nagata could use help.

Mrs. Nagata looked him over skeptically—the sport coat, rayon shirt, a dusty violin case, canvas club bag, city shoes. She said no.

"Oh, there's plenty of work here," she said, "but I need a man who'd work like a horse and get paid in feed and maybe a little cigarette money. Can't do better. At least until after harvest."

He said, "I've lived in the city a long time and I'm pale and out of condition now. But I come from peasant stock and I know how to work. Just give me a chance. Let me work, put me up, and pay me what you can. When there's time," he said, "I can teach your children music, or Japanese. I can keep books for you too. That's what I did in the city – bookkeeping."

The muscles in Mrs. Nagata's jaw twitched. "Looks like you're a man of talent and culture. Why do you come to a dirt farm for work, and why at your age?" She cocked her head to glance at him. "In your thirties, aren't you?" she asked.

He drew an audible breath. "It's a long story and if I knew why, I wouldn't be here. I left Japan at eighteen and completed high school here." He sucked in his breath once more and wiped his violin case with the inner sleeve of his coat. "I have no reference or recommendation, Madam, but I'm honest and I'll work hard for you," he said.

Mrs. Nagata looked off to her newly seeded acreage. Soon there'd be thinning and weeding to do. The boys would be missing school again. She was tired – forty years, looking fifty, nineteen years riveted to this ranch, but after all, no more, no less than this stranger. Here and now, they stood in mutual need.

"I'll call the boys to move the tools out of the toolhouse. It's the newest outbuilding. You can move in there. Aki will call you when supper's ready," she said.

The boys cleaned out the cabin and set in a cot and some new crates, and the stranger, Kaoru Yanagita, moved in.

They called him Yanagita-san. He worked hard in the fields, and after supper with the family, he quietly retired. If there was a little daylight left, he sharpened or repaired tools. When nights grew longer, he stayed at the main house and sometimes helped the boys with their math. He talked as little as possible to Mrs. Nagata and Akiko, and always with a curious formality.

On his first day off, Mrs. Nagata gave him twenty dollars, an apology, and a lift to town. He would find his way back, he said, so after attending to some errands, Mrs. Nagata returned alone. Late that night Akiko heard him come in. He was singing softly as he walked into the yard, and in the still country night, the clumsy shuffling of his shoes could be heard.

The door was grabbed at, missed, and bounced. Drunk, Akiko thought. His first night off, drunk. She looked across the room to her mother. She was asleep.

In the silence, sounds began to stir. Light as leaves on a wind, Akiko heard the tentative plucking of a violin. Then the bow on the strings, at first almost inaudibly, then gaining assurance, now fast, now slow, with fire, with tenderness, now clear and cold. The sound of man's soul, Akiko thought, maybe this man's. She fell asleep to his music.

In the days that followed, Akiko tried to draw out the Yanagita of the music that moved her so. She stayed with him while he worked, often reading from a book of poems or humming mysterious melodies. The boys teased: "Hey, Aki, not the book, take a shovel instead." "Yeah, hit him with a shovel." Mrs. Nagata smiled, Yanagita smiled, but Akiko was not dismayed. She would get to him some day, and time would come when those beautiful hands, cracked and callused now, would stroke her hair, lift her face. At night she sat outside his cabin and listened to his music until her feet grew cold and stiff.

Mrs. Nagata spoke to Yanagita-san. "Akiko is lonely," she said. "She misses her father, though God knows he never paid mind to any of us. You've been so much help. We all have real respect for you, and I'd be much obliged if you'd be patient with Aki."

"It doesn't bother me," Yanagita-san shrugged. "She's young and romantic. With your permission I'd like to teach her to play the violin. I know she sits outside my cabin, and I can't help but wonder how cold and tired she must get."

Akiko was uneasy. She laughed nervously and chattered, "Of course, you know I'll never play well. My mother says I'm very clumsy with my hands."

Yanagita-san was serious. "There are more competent musicians than me," he said, "but music comes from here," he touched his heart, "and here," he pointed to his temple.

For weeks the sounds that came from the cabin reduced Mrs. Nagata and her boys to helpless laughter. Yanagita-san was heard above the miserable scraping, repeating phrases with frayed patience. Akiko grew impatient too. Many times she laid the instrument down, only to have it returned to her chin. Their relationship changed. Resentment grew for the foot that tapped out the time, the hand that touched hers for corrections, the voice that called: "Time for lessons, Aki-chan." Time for lessons, time for lessons, in silent mimicry she followed him to the cabin.

One evening Yanagita-san's voice rose, cracked under the strain of the day's heavy work and his student's paralytic fingering. On the varnished surface of the violin splashed a tear.

He took the instrument from her gently. "I've made you cry," he sighed. He wiped the violin. "I've made you cry."

Once a woman's tears had moved him and he had lingered too long. A woman's tears had enveloped him in a situation that haunted him still. How long ago had it been? Two years? Where was she now? Did she think of him? Why did the past plague him now in this ridiculous cabin with this hardly-more-than-a-child woman?

He tucked the violin under his chin and said brightly, "The master will play for you."

He played a cheerful exercise and then remarked, "You look so funny, your mouth all twisted like that. How will you grow to be a beautiful woman and marry?"

"Beauty isn't always seen with the eyes," Akiko said.

"You're right, you're right," Yanagita said and put his hand on the back of her neck. "Now back to the second measure, remember the sharp, and count 1–2–3, 1–2–3. . . ." What did it matter?

Yanagita grew less exacting after this. Often Akiko would carry a book to the cabin, and sometimes she could divert him and spend the music hour in discussion or demonstrations. Most of the time, on his insistence, she would dismally saw away.

Mrs. Nagata kept a careful ear toward the cabin, but they were, her integrity insisted, like father to daughter. She censored the conjugality such a relationship would require, repressed the picture of once more being a woman, remembered herself as a knotty pioneer carrying on the work bequeathed her—carrying on, carrying on. She was nevertheless relieved to note that Yanagita-san still spent his free days in town and returned late, usually in high spirits. Dark taverns, bought women. He invariably brought presents home: sweets and magazines for the family, always a bottle or two of wine for himself, once a flowering chiffon scarf for her (to flutter at her corded neck) and a small fly-specked volume of verse for Akiko.

"For the musician whose music is locked away," he said and tapped his heart.

By spring, Akiko learned a few scales and some simple melodies. However difficult it had been to make these small gains, neither pupil or master was highly gratified and the lessons degenerated to methodical corrections and short grunts and snorts of appraisal. Yanagita-san would often lie on his cot, a glass of wine on the crate beside him, and gaze beyond the tattered cobwebs on the rafters. "Again," he would say, moving only his lips. "The last three measures again."

One such evening, Akiko noticed the master had fallen asleep. She carefully put the violin on a crate, brought out her book, and sat on the floor, her back against the cot. She read in a whisper, rolling syllables, repeating lines, enjoying the hushed quality of her voice.

He touched her hair. He whispered, "How you dream, Akiko. You know so little about life. Flowers, stars, winds, eternity . . . words. What do you learn from them? Love is beautiful? Loneliness is sad?"

He sat up and sipped his wine. "Love," he started grandiosely and flung his arms out, then suddenly withering, he muttered, "It's ugly. It's full of pain. It's terrible and lonely. There's more to life than you can possibly imagine, Akiko," he said. In heaven and earth.

It seemed the right time. "Don't you feel it?" Akiko asked. "Don't you feel anything for me?"

Yanagita hung his head and stared at the floor. He was dizzy from the wine; he'd drunk more than he remembered.

"I loved a woman once," he said. "She didn't belong to me." He glanced at Akiko's thin brown legs and smiled. "Yoko was a woman—luminous skin, sensual—barred the door with her white arms. 'Don't leave me,' she begged. For years, 'Don't leave. . . .' "

Akiko was angry. "Why did you leave then?" she asked.

"You wouldn't understand. One meets someone he can love but the timing is wrong. For us it was too late. There were too many complications. I would have taken her away, but she couldn't come with me. There was her husband, their families . . . an insoluble situation.

"It grew ugly. I couldn't stay." The deceit, the pain of the days without her, the pain of the days with her. And finally the end; her voice pleading, Kaoru, come back to me. The baby is gone. I'm so sick, please come back.

Yanagita shook his head to deny the memory. He lifted his violin and plucked it lightly, a summer shower. He said, "It's past. Gone." No evidence of having been. Gone. Fetus washed away, down the drain.

"That's life," he said, "a little sorrow, a little joy." He sipped his wine. That's life.

He took Akiko's hand to help her to her feet and kept it a moment longer than he intended. She held on and moved toward him, but he wrenched free and rolled back on the cot.

Again, again, gravitating toward another impossible situation. Mother of God, where did it begin? The womb? Who was my mother and why did she abandon me? It's she that put this curse on me. Boy in a house of men: grandfather, senile and complaining, doing woman-chores, cooking, washing, scolding; silent embittered father planted calf-deep in the mud of a rice paddy. Where did she go? Did she desert us, did she die, was she sent away? Too frightened to ask. I looked for her in every face, every gesture of every woman, and dreamed of the day she would find me: the famous Yanagita, Kaoru. First step to fame: a cabin boy on a liner to America, wooed by a steward. Off the boat to work as a menial in a columned mansion, a schoolboy. The old Jap kid among freckled boys whose happiness hinged on the weekend football score. Wages hoarded and dropped into the moist palm of Miss White, the music teacher. "I don't want your money, Karl [she couldn't say Kaoru], but everything good is earned." "You have such talent, Karl, I wish you had come to me ten years ago." Ten years ago I was a small boy in Japan dreaming of abundance and fame, and you were already a full-bloomed woman, American. "Perhaps it's not too late, Karl; it will be hard work, but there's a chance we can make something of you. I know how difficult it is for you financially, dear Karl; I'd like you to come live with me – a business arrangement, of course. You can help around the house." "Call me Alma, Karl. *Alma* means soul." Ensconced in the bosom of tenacious possessive Soul: "Where are you going tonight, Karl? Are you sure you're not seeing a girl?" Eyes glittering, smile pressed against laboratory teeth. "Books on accounting, Karl? Really now, you know you're a musician." Running, running, and trapped again. This time in the dismal loneliness of a room above Arnie's American Restaurant. One flight down and all of man's outer life is attended to: food, work, camaraderie. One flight up and all of man's inner life awaits. Empty. Then Yoko, married to an anonymous man, warm like the nest of a cozy bed on a cold morning, and like the cold morning, relentless, chilling. And the final break, an exercise in pain, pizzicato. How many towns, jobs, mornings after have passed, and now this child, breasts hardly swelling, tiny nipples embossed on faded calico, destined to be yoked to some hayseed forever. Shall I give her something to remember? A small lesson on the treachery of loneliness, perhaps. And lechery.

He reached for her arm and drew her to the narrow cot. "Akiko," his voice was hoarse, "you do love me, don't you?"

In this barren environment, love was an excessive word. The feeling was there. Yes.

He kissed her and stroked her small breasts. The powerful erotic response this evoked confused itself with more familiar emotions and released a surge of tears. How could he seduce a weeping child? He wanted to cry too.

They lay there quietly clinging to each other, consoling their separate griefs. A draft of cool air blew into the room.

Mrs. Nagata stood against the evening light. Her fists were clenched, her eyes triangles of fury.

"Obscene! Disgusting!" she screamed. She snatched the violin and flung it against the wall. She split the bow and threw it across the room in splinters and tangled hair.

"Lessons indeed! My God, Akiko!"

Yanagita held up his hand. "Madam, calm down, calm down. We . . . I did nothing. Believe me, nothing."

"I trusted you! Take your things and get out. Get out, get out!"

"I have no money, Madam."

"I'll give you money. Get out! Tonight! Now!"

Akiko began to cry, "Please, Mama, don't do this to us. Please, it was my fault. I love him. . . ."

"Love? What do you know about love?" Mrs. Nagata sneered. "Do you suppose this man—this man old enough to be your father—loves you? Don't you suppose he's been tramping through one town after another, getting in and out of situations like this? Where do you think he goes on his days off? Have you stopped to think of a future with him? No permanence. No roots. Going from town to town. Maybe one day being abandoned. Think, Akiko. One day all by yourself. Maybe then you'll realize. This has nothing to do with love, Akiko. You don't know what love is." Nor do I.

Akiko opened her mouth and the words came out: "If you send him away, I shall go with him."

"Go, then, go!"

It can't happen like this. They were like actors in a burned-out play, mouthing words out of obligation to finish the drama. It shouldn't happen this way. Yet she walked away, closing the door behind her.

Yanagita put his arm around Akiko. "I can't take you with me; you know that, don't you?" he said.

"But I can't stay here; I'll die without you."

"You won't die. People don't die so easily. I know."

"But I'll be all alone. What will I do?"

"You'll go to her and apologize. And you'll go on living."

"And you too?"

"Like she said: another town, another job." Another story, another death.

In the house, Mrs. Nagata sat at the kitchen table grasping a roll of bills. When Akiko came in, she stood up and gave her the money, saying, "This is all we have. Take it. And take care of yourself." Her eyes welled with tears as though she believed it would really happen.

"I'm not going," Akiko said.

Mrs. Nagata stifled a sigh. "It's better you don't. I'm glad. Your brothers need not know anything. It never happened."

But it did happen. And I'll be knowing it a long time.

"Give him the money and say good-bye." Tomorrow is another day. Mr. Kodama at the general store will carry us until the harvest. Tomorrow everything will be the same again. Almost. "That's the only way."

In the spring twilight Yanagita came to Akiko smelling strongly of the last of the wine. He carried his small club bag.

"Where's the violin?" Akiko asked.

"She broke it."

"Where will you go?"

"I'll decide at the bus depot." This is a good time of the year. There'll be harvesting all along the California coast—droves of men like myself, working, laughing, singing, complaining, bragging about their sexual exploits, keeping alive worn-out dreams. Like myself.

"Will you write to me?"

"You know I can't do that."

Akiko passed him the roll of bills, and her hand lingered over his. He patted her arm, counted the money, and said, "Don't worry, Aki-chan."

She watched him cross the yard and move on to the road. In the half-light, she saw the dust rise from his feet in a small gray cloud. Then the night absorbed him.

Songs My Mother
Taught Me

I was eleven in the summer of 1935. My father was farming then in the valley of the Santa Rosa, San Jacinto, and Chocolate Mountain ranges called Imperial Valley near the Mexican border of California. The land was fertilized with tons of chicken manure and irrigated by the All American Canal that flowed out of the Colorado River. Planting started in late September: tomatoes, squash, cantaloupe. All during the winter months, it was thinning the seedlings, weeding, building brush covers for them, repairing the covers after a storm, and starting the smudge pots to ward off the frost. In early spring, it was harvesting the crops. By May, after the broiling sun had reduced the plants to dry twigs, the plowing began. Then the land was flooded to start the weeds and fallen seeds growing, after which there was another plowing to destroy these sprouts, and once again fertilizing, furrowing, and preparing the land for late-September planting.

At best, the entire process kept us alive and clothed. There were five of us: my father, Junsaburo Kato; mother, Hatsue; sister Nami, fourteen; brother Tetsuo, thirteen; and myself, Sachiko. Why my father kept at this unrewarding work, I never knew or questioned or thought about. Maybe there was nothing else he could do. Maybe he worked in hope that one day that merciful God (to whom we prayed, before whose lacquered shrine we burned our incense) would provide the miracle crop that would lift us to Japan, rich and triumphant.

My father was a quiet man. If he suspected this was the whole cloth of his life, that he would live and die this way, he never showed it. He never revealed his dream for us, his children, in America, or articulated his own dreams. But sometimes when he was in his cups, when the winter rain drowned his hopes for a good harvest, he would sing the saddest and loneliest Japanese songs. My mother spoke often of returning to Japan, of smelling again the piney woods, tasting the exquisite fruits, of seeing her beloved sisters. The stories of her Japan came on like a flashback in the movies—misty, wavering, ethereal, and her beautiful eyes would grow soft.

Summer is unbearable in the valley. The sun beats on miles of scrub prairie, and the air is deathly still. One listless day succeeds another, without incident, without change. The farmers who had had some luck with their harvest usually spent their summer north along the coast in San Pedro, where a colony of Japanese resided permanently, occupied with fishing and canning. On a small island off the mainland called Terminal Island, most of the valley people rented cheap houses and spent the summer fishing off the scummy San Pedro wharf, clamming, crabbing, and swimming in the Pacific. My mother said it was hard to believe these same waters broke on the shores of Japan.

The harvest of 1935 was a good one. That summer we started north in early July, after we popped off the firecrackers my father had bought for Tets. They loved firecrackers; I can't remember a year that we didn't have some, no matter how poor we were. Usually, though, they couldn't wait until the fourth, and they'd fire off a few each night, until there was nothing left for the fourth. So, on Independence Day we often sat outside and watched the neighbors' fireworks a quarter mile away. Sometimes my mother made iced tea with sugar and lemons while we waited for the dark. That year we had enough to string out until the actual celebration.

After the fourth, we packed our old gray Chevrolet and drove three hundred miles north to Terminal Island. It was always a hot tiresome trip, and when we finally drove up to the drawbridge that spans the narrow channel and recognized the Ford plant to the left, we let out whoops of delight. My father quieted us with a grunt. He hated noise.

There was already a group of people from the valley, townspeople we knew from the Buddhist church. We rented a small four-room house for the summer.

The days were filled with vacation fun. We trapped crab at the piling of a demolished pier. When the sun went down, we boiled the catch in large galvanized tubs and ate the sweet meat, our skin chilled on one side by the night air and seared on the other by the campfire. There were roasts; I can still taste the succulent meat and the bitter ash. There were hot days in the sun, blistered backs, and the good pain. In the evening, the older folks sat on front stoops or wandered from house to house looking to start a card game or a session of go, and we were allowed to play outside until darkness blurred our faces and hide-and-seek became too hazardous. We went everywhere with friends, huge contingents of raucous children and adults. Every day was a holiday, far removed from the isolated farm and its chores and the terror of another blighted year.

But there was a subtle change in the family. I don't know if Nami or Tets felt it. If they did, they said nothing. Maybe I too would not have noticed if Sayo, my summer friend, had not called attention to it. Sayo was two years older, and wiser, more perceptive, and knowledgeable than I. She wrote poetry and read masses of books and knew all the latest Japanese songs and the meaning of the lyrics. She said, "Your mother plays the same record again and again. Why is she so sad?"

I said, "Maybe she likes the song. Maybe she wants to learn it."

It was true. My mother joined our excursions less and less. Often I found her sitting at the kitchen table writing, nibbling at the stub of a pencil, and looking past the window. It was also true that she played the Victrola, usually the same record over and over: "*Mujo No Tsuki*," which Sayo said meant transient moon. She translated the lyrics for me:

Samishiku kyo mo	Today too
Kurete uki	Passes in solitude
Yuhi wa toku	The evening sun is distant
Umi no hate	Beyond the rim of the sea
Dare ga yobuno ka	Who is it that calls
Sagasu no ka yo?	Who, that seeks me?
Namima ni sakebu	The seabirds that
Hama chidori	Cry from the shore

It was all true. But I couldn't always remember to think about it while everyone else appeared so happy. I laughed with them and fought with them and pretended, like Nami and Tets, that nothing was wrong.

After one of those quarrels at the beach, I returned home alone. Nami and Tets always sided against me, and though I had a well-honed tongue for my age, I couldn't match the two together. I begged my father to come home with me, but he was playing cards with some cronies and waved me off like an annoying fly. I walked home alone sulky and morose and went to the rear of the house to brush the sand off my feet. Mrs. Griffin, the landlady, lived within eyeshot, and she was very particular about sand in her threadbare rug. We called her *Okorimbo*, which is a diminutive for Angry One. Okorimbo's face was permanently creased in a pattern of rage. She spent the daylight hours at her window, and when she caught us heading toward the front door, she rushed from her house, her ragged slippers flapping, screaming, "Go to the back, to the back!"

I was rubbing sand from my legs when I heard soft voices. My mother had company. Not wanting to be seen, I crouched behind a privet hedge. There's a humiliating routine a Japanese child must endure from adults: the pat on the head, the examination, the appraisal, "How tall she's growing! She will be beautiful some day. She looks very bright!" Then: "Not at all, very small for her age, homely like her mother, not very smart, no help at all around the house, lazy . . ."

Within fifteen minutes, the visitor left through the rear door and passed very close to the hedge where I was hiding. I could smell the polish on his shoes. I recognized him as Yamada-san, the young man from northern California who earlier that spring had come to the valley with a group of laborers. He was a *Kibei*, a Japanese born in America and reared in Japan. My father had hired him to help us with our good harvest. Yamada-san was different from my father—handsome and younger. He came to the dinner table in a fresh shirt, his hair combed back with good-smelling oil. My father, like most farmers, wore his hair so short that neither comb nor rain (nor sun) changed its shape. Yamada-san had eyes that looked at you. When you talked, he committed himself to you. My father's eyes were squinty from the sun, and he hardly saw or heard you.

My father had been dissatisfied with Yamada-san. For a man of few words, I was surprised how strongly he spoke.

"Someone like that I wouldn't want around here long. He's a bad example for our Tetsuo," he said.

"How can we finish harvesting without him?" my mother had asked. "He works hard, Kato, you know that."

"You see how he is—plucking at that frivolous mandolin all the time—like he was practicing for the pictures or something. The clothes he wears—those two-tone shoes, that downtown haircut, the fancy cigarettes. Like a woman! Do you want Tetsuo to get like that? So he works hard. So? He stays only until harvest is over. I won't tolerate him after May! I don't want him in the house except at mealtime. Tell him."

"Kato, I can't tell him this."

Some of what my father said was true. But I watched Yamada-san's sure body move effortlessly, and I knew he worked hard. He was not like a woman. He had a quality of the Orient my father did not have. He was the affirmation of my mother's Japan—the haunting flutes, the cherry blossoms, the poetry, the fatalism. My mother changed when he was around. Her smile was softer, her voice more gentle. I suspect this was what my father disliked more than the man himself—the change he brought over the rest of us.

Though we loved to listen to Yamada-san's mandolin, loved to touch the pearl frets and pluck the strings, we began to avoid him. He sensed the change in us and thereafter confined his visits to mealtimes. He lived in the cabin my father had built for Tets, but Tets didn't like sleeping away from the rest of us, so it had stayed unused until now. I pictured Yamada-san sitting on his cot reading by lamplight, or mending his clothes, or singing his songs alone. We pretended not to hear the lonely music that came from his quarters; we pretended not to notice how each of us missed him.

Immediately after the harvest, Yamada-san packed his things and shook hands with us. My father drove him to the bus station. I went to the vacant cabin. The cot was in the corner with a naked mattress on top and the bedclothes neatly folded at one end. He'd left an empty jar of pomade on the table.

I saw Yamada-san one more time before summer was over. One evening Sayo and I crept away from the other children and walked to the dunes, where the sea figs sprawled to the edge of the surf. The sky was still pinkish from the dying sun and a warm wind blew in from the west. I saw only his back. He was standing against the wind, facing the sea. When he heard us, he walked away without turning, flicking the stub of his fancy cigarette to the wind.

As summer drew to a close, my mother's malaise would not be ignored. She spent a lot of time in bed. Nami and my father did the cooking because the smell of food sent her retching to the bathroom. My father finally called Dr. Matsuno. It was a frightening time for me because I remembered years before when my mother was very sick and had to stay with friends in town. They had recommended the blood of carp, so live carp was kept in a tub on the back porch for her. My mother told me she put her mouth directly to the living fish. When she didn't improve, a white doctor was called. He diagnosed the illness as typhoid, and we all went to his office to get shots. I was very frightened. I thought often of her dying, and my heart would contract.

We waited disconsolately on Okorimbo's ratty couch not saying a word to one another. The doctor had closed the door behind him. When he finally emerged, he told us there was nothing to worry about. "She will give birth in late March," he said.

The next day we strapped the luggage to the top of our car and started the dismal trip back to the valley.

The baby grew steadily in my mother's belly, distending and misshaping her body. The black hair she wore in a smooth coil at her neck grew crisp and faded. Broken strands hung from her temples like dry summer grass, and brown splotches appeared on her skin.

She withdrew from us. I couldn't coax a smile from her. My father was kinder than he'd ever been, but everyone seemed to retreat to a separate place. I wanted someone to make room for me, someone to tell me what was going on, to assure me everything was all right. But no one would let me in. I was too afraid to ask. It was as though each prepared to fight this monstrous condition alone, with silence, and will it back to its dark origin.

I looked for someone to turn to. I chose the highest source.

In December, the Jodo Shinshu sect of the Buddhist church headquartered in Los Angeles sent down a new minister to stimulate religious life in the valley. The previous man was a bachelor, too handsome and too popular for his own good. Many members of the Ladies' Auxiliary desired him for their daughters. He may have asked for his own transfer.

There was something disconcerting about the new minister, Reverend Umino, his eczema, his full lips, his obesity (in contrast to ideals of austerity and self-denial), but he appealed to me just because of these very human traits. I thought if God could accept so ordinary a man for His emissary, there was a good chance He would listen to *me*. I thought if prayer and faith could heal the sickness in our house, I would build a faith matched by no one, and I would pray with every breath I drew. So with limited knowledge of ritual, I prayed to my eastern deity in western methods. The request was always the same: Sweet Buddha, let us be happy again. Let there be six living people in our family. I was afraid something terrible and unmentionable would happen to my mother or the baby. After a while the prayers became so abbreviated, only Buddha could have understood them. I slipped them into all the activities of school and home—while turning pages in my reader, while cleaning lamp chimneys, "Six, six, six . . ."

On the morning of the birth, Nami shook me awake: "Sachiko, wake up! Something's happening!" We ran to my mother's room. She lay twisting, clutching the metal bars of the bed, and breathing in short gasps. Tets stood beside her, his head low, his tears dropping to the floor.

"Papa has gone to get Mrs. Nakagawa," she said. Mrs. Nakagawa was the midwife who delivered most of the Japanese babies. She lived in town, her husband was an accountant, and they were both religious Buddhists. "Go quickly to school, be good children, and take care of the little one," she said. She touched my face.

It was the first time in a long time she had touched me. I screamed, "Mama, don't die!"

"Don't worry," she said.

At school I was unable to concentrate. I loitered behind everyone so I could whisper privately into my joined palms, "Six, six, six . . ." I spoke to no one. Two or three times the teacher peered into my face and shook her head.

Once home, I went directly to my mother's room and watched until I caught the movement of my mother's breathing. The baby was lying next to her.

Buddha had saved this infant for me; Kenji was very special. I loved him, cared for him, changed his diapers, pretended he was my own. I spoiled him. But he took only my mother's milk, and when it was gone, he would refuse a bottle. Then he'd fret and cry, and Nami and I took turns carrying him, rocking and teasing him until her milk returned. Times when we were already in bed, my mother would get up and carry him off to the desert. I listened to her footsteps on the soft sand, terrified they would not return. The more he cried, the less she liked him; the less she liked him, the more he cried.

She grew despondent from this perpetual drain on her body and her emotions, and slipped farther and farther from us, often staring vacantly into space. Every day I rushed home from school to take care of the baby so he wouldn't start my mother's terrible strangled sighs.

One evening after supper, Kenji began his crying again. My mother snatched him from his bed and walked rigidly away, bouncing him erratically. I followed her, begging her to let me carry him, assuring her that I could quiet him.

"Go back!" she snarled. I was frightened, but I would not turn back, and half running, I followed her to the packing shed. By this time Kenji, shocked by the unnatural motion, had stopped his crying. My mother, too, had calmed down, but she saw a hatchet my father had left outside his toolbox, and she lifted it.

While I stood there watching, my blood chilling, she lay the blade on the baby's forehead. I began to cry, and she pulled me to her and cried too. She said, "My children are all grown. I didn't want this baby—I didn't want this baby. . . ."

I know now what she meant: that time was passing her by, that with the new baby she was irrevocably bound to this futile life, that dreams of returning to Japan were shattered, that through the eyes of a younger man she had glimpsed what might have been, could never and would never be.

I turned to prayer again.

Sunday service was largely a congregation of children and adolescents. Adults were at the fields preparing for Monday's market. Whereas the previous minister geared his sermons to the young, using simple parables and theatrical gestures, Reverend Umino never talked down to us. He spoke on abstract philosophies in rhetoric too difficult to follow. Peculiarly responsive to shifting feet and rustling hymn books, he often stopped abruptly, leaving the lectern massaging the festering eczema on his wrists. The church people who lived in the city and had the most influence didn't like him, but I didn't care. I only hoped he'd sense my need and put in a special word for me.

The spring harvest was meager and market prices low. My father couldn't afford the hired help of the year before. Tets and Nami helped wherever and whenever they could. My father would rise before daylight and work until dark. He grew morose and short with us.

That summer there wasn't enough money for a vacation. Sometimes my father would drive us to town and give each of us fifteen cents for the movies: ten cents for admission and a nickel for popcorn. I loved the movies, but I couldn't enjoy them, I was so worried about my mother and Kenji. Most of the summer we played cards. The baby grew rapidly in spite of the lack of breast milk and mother love. He responded to his name, slouching like a giant doll in an attempt to sit up. My father went to the burning fields to parcel out the land for flooding.

Then one day toward the end of August, it happened. As it had its beginning in August, so it found its end then.

A hot wind blew in from the desert, drying the summer grass and parching throat and skin. Tets had gone out to help my father with flooding, controlling the flow of water at the water gate. My father was at the far end of the field repairing the leaks.

I was playing with Kenji, who was sitting in a shallow tub of water. He loved water. It was one of the few ways to keep him happy. With one hand he grasped the rim of the tub and with the other he pawed at a little red boat I pushed around for him. My father bought the boat for Kenji shortly after he was born. Nami was reading an old Big-Little book, carefully turning the brittle pages. My mother had prepared some rice balls and a Mason jar of green tea for my father's lunch, and since Tets was also in the fields, she divided the lunch in two separate cloths and sent Nami and me to take them to the men. We went together, first to Tets, then to my father.

My father had seen us coming and waited for us by the scant noonday shade of a cottonwood tree. We sat together quietly while he ate his riceballs. A riceball is to a Japanese what a sandwich is to an American – a portable meal. It's a molded ball of rice sprinkled with sesame seeds and salt, and inside there's usually a red pickled plum. My mother once told me it was the mainstay of Japan's Imperial Army, the symbol of her flag: the red plum with the white rice around it. Nami poured tea for my father into a small white cup decorated with a few gold and black strokes – a tiny boat, a lone fisherman, a mountain, and a full moon.

The sound of my hungry father devouring his lunch, gulping his pale yellow tea, the rustle of wind in the cottonwood leaves, the put-put of a car far away – these lonely sounds depressed me so, I wanted to cry. Across the acres of flat land, the view to the house was unbroken. It stood bleached in the sun in awful isolation. A car turned up the road that led to our house.

I shaded my eyes. Far in the distance I saw the small form of my mother waving frantically and running toward us. I pulled my father's sleeve and the three of us ran to her. I could see she clutched our baby. His arms dangled limply. My heart fell.

The front of my mother's dress was stained with water. "I left him only a minute, and I found him face down in the water! I've killed him, forgive me, I've killed him!" she wept.

My father tore the baby from her, turned him upside down, and thumped his back. He put him on the ground and blew into his mouth. The car that had entered our yard lurched over the fields. Reverend Umino, perspiring in his black suit and tie, jumped out. "Come, we will take him to a doctor," he said. My father looked dazed. He carried the naked baby into the car. He brushed away the dirt and grass from our baby's face. The reverend drove off, steering the car like a madman, reeling and bouncing through the fields toward the road to town.

When Tets came home, we all cried together. Waiting for my father that afternoon, my mother roamed from room to room, holding Kenji's kimono to her cheek. We followed her everywhere. Outside, the tub sat with its four inches of water and the toy boat listing, impervious to our tears. From habit, I said my prayers, "Six, six, six."

The reverend brought my father home in the evening. With his hand-kerchief he wiped the dust from our family shrine and lit the incense. He chanted his sutras while we sat behind him, our heads bowed. He stayed a while longer murmuring to my mother, assuring my father that everything would be attended to. My mother gave him clothes for the baby: diapers, pins, a small white gown he had never worn, a slip. The reverend received them with both hands. He put a palm to my mother's shoulder and left.

There was only a small group in the chapel, those few who were unable to go away for the summer. The flowers that surrounded Kenji's white coffin were the last of summer, and their scent along with the smoking incense filled the room.

Candles flickered in tall brass stands, and the light glittered on the gold of the shrine. In the first pew reserved for the family, we five sat huddled, at last together in our grief. Reverend Umino's sutras hung in the air with the oppressive smoke. He began the requiem: "An infant, child without sin, pure as the day he was born, is swept from the loving arms of parents and siblings. Who can say why? Trust. Believe. There is an Ultimate Plan. Amida Buddha is Infinite Mercy. The child is now in His sleeve, now one with Him. . . ." In his elegant vestments, the tunic of gold brocade, the scarlet tassels, with his broad chest heaving, Reverend Umino swabbed at his swarthy neck. "Providence sent me to this family at this extreme hour. I was there to witness the hand of Amida. . . ." And the reverend went on to tell the story of that dreadful day in flawless detail. The assembly wept.

Pictures of that day, the days of the gestation, the summer before, the terrible days following the birth, reeled before me. Someone in the congregation sobbed. Scratching at his eczema, the reverend motioned the group to rise. My father helped my mother to her feet. She gripped my hand. It seemed to me that if my tears would stop, I would never cry again. And it was a long time before I could believe in God again.

The Boatmen on
Toneh River

Kimi Sumida knew the end was near. The bed she'd lived in for many months now ceased to resist the jutting bones of her body, and prolonged attitudes of discomfort reached a stage of stonelike numbness. The cancer that ate at her lungs had no more to feed on.

Where once the long day steadily, slowly moved into night, now darkness descended without warning—dark and light, dark and light, and dreams, always dreams. Sometimes daylight and reality seemed just beyond a door of pain—now near, now distant—on the other side of pain. "Mari, do I have to remind a seven-year-old every day to brush her teeth? What will your teacher say?" "Give me time, Daddy, you never give me enough time." "Ssshhsh. Not so loud." "Mommy still sleeping?" "Ssshhsh . . ." Like a stone at the bottom of the sea, Kimi lay on the ocean floor and the tide flowed over her. "Ryo! Mari! Me: wife and mother! Do you not need me?" Did she cry out?

The door opened and a thin light poured into the room with Ryo. A sandwich on the nightstand indicated it was still day—late afternoon.

"How do you feel now, dear?"

Did I feel worse before? How long before? His mien is one of enormous cheer: he has on his cheer face. What happened to your other face, Ryo, the one that mirrors your heart? Did you discard it along with hope for my recovery? Honor me with a little honesty, the reality of my disease. Despair a little, feel free to despair a little with me. This is the time to be yourself. I hear the things you tell Mari: that I am going away, that we will all meet again some day, that this is not the time of sorrow, that flowers are sometimes broken in bud or plucked in bloom, or sometimes mature to seed and fruition and seed again. Are these words to take the edge off the rawness of death, or do you really believe, or do you only wish to believe? But you haven't known this desperate reluctance to leave life—you don't know the terror of the things I face. You don't even see me anymore; you turn your back while the doctor presses, turns, and probes me like a vegetable, and mutters, "Comatose; can't see what keeps her here."

Once you looked at me with eyes soft and tender; eyes dull with desire. Now only this cheer. You won't acknowledge me. I'm the woman who moved you through those many dark streets, hurrying, rushing to meet me; the woman who brought the fire to your loins. I'm the one! Wasted now; my hair is too black against the fearful pallor of my skin. Do I frighten you? Do you drop your cheerful mask in alarm when you close my door? Do you keep my Mari from me to protect her from the horror of seeing me? Are you afraid I will sear the color from her warm lips, sow seeds of my disease in her tender body? But she's mine. Mine. And I have the right to insist she share my experience, just as, yes, just as my mother had shared hers with me. And she will no doubt travel the lonely channels I've charted, paths like the narrow canals on my cracked ceiling that angle off here, stop abruptly there, byways I've come to know as well as I know the palm of my hand. I'm at one of those dead ends now.

The door closed but the light remained and turned blood-red with pain. Slowly the red tide subsided, and throbbing with the beat of her pulse, Kimi heard her own mother's voice call: "Kimi . . . Kimi . . ." Warm, a mother's voice. She opened her eyes.

This is the country kitchen of my childhood: furniture of raw unfinished wood, bare floors, sweaters on pegs, gray dishcloths drying on the sink rim, cosmic dust slowly sifting. And beyond the windows, the stretch of desert, broken nearby with rows of furrowed earth. All there. Am I the mother or am I the child; am I the caller or the called?

"Kimi, go fix the bath for Father. He'll be back from the fields and will want his bath."

"Not now, Mother. I'll be back soon, and I will do it then."

"Now. Now. Every evening you go off when I need you. What's in this compulsion to commune with this nothing land. I need your help here; do you think this wild desert changes a whit for your walking through a piece of it? Stay here and use the strength God gave you where it'd do some good. Make the bath."

My Kimi, where do you go; what do you dream? Fancy clothes? Glittering lights? Love? There're none of these here. I was seventeen, the caress of my mother's fingers still warm in my hair, when they married me to a stranger from the next province. He must have a young healthy woman to help him in America, they said, and soon I would return, a rich, proud, honored lady. I looked forward to the promise in dewy-eyed innocence—unaware, unaware of even the conjugal night that lay before me. The years have devoured me with work and poverty and anxieties: early frost, fluctuating market, price of rice—what chance had love? They told me that with this black mole on my earlobe, I couldn't fail; a black mole on the earlobe is a sure sign of fame and fortune, they said. I waited for this fortune, worked and waited, and when finally my time was up, I counted my fortune. Fifty years of living and what was there to show? Ten thousand nights I lay there remembering my Japan: clear lakes, lonely shrines, the lyric of flowering cherry trees, street vendors' calls, plaintive and sweet as a mother's lullabies, the sound of a flute on a summer evening. I spent a lifetime waiting to return to these. I thought my happiness was bound to these. I reached too far for what was always here, in the dust, in the sunrise, in the sunset, in you.

"Kimi, make the bath."

"Yes, I'll do it now."

I'm going now to heat the bath with sage that you and I gathered and spread out to dry in early summer. It will shoot up in crackling flames and tiny sparks, and I'll think of your fireflies in Japan. Though you may not believe it, I've found something here in this arid desert that is gentle and sweet too. I want to ask you about it, but to put it to words or to your critical eye may be to profane it. And now the tall summer reeds bend in the wind, cicadas hum, shadows lengthen, cottonwood leaves catch the last flutter of sunlight, and the lad who pedals down the warm dusty road each evening at this time is passing by, and I am not there. I shall not see the wind move through his black hair and touch his smooth brown cheeks and fill his blouse with air. I want to be as close to him as that wind. Where he comes from, where he pedals to, I don't know, but when I watch him, I see west winds in the sage, I see tumbleweeds lope across the prairie, and primrose petals fall, and I am moved. From my hiding place in the reeds, I watch him scan the horizon, and I wonder if he looks for me. Does he watch for me? Does he yearn for me?

Kimi, how extravagantly you dream; what disenchantment you court. What loneliness you will know.

The room was dark and cold. Night had come; the sandwich on the nightstand had been removed and a covered tray replaced it. This is Ryo's acknowledgement of me, Kimi thought; ashes of dreams he prepares for me. I am still here.

"Still here! Kimi, drat it! I tell you, put the dog out. He's still here!"

Three days of steady rain now; one more day and the tiny seedlings that last week pushed their tender shoots from the overworked earth will rot. The kitchen is dank and murky with smoke from Bull Durhams and the smell of sake warming on the coal-oil stove. The patriarch sits at the table with Mr. Nagata, one of a legion of shifting rootless men who follow crops along the length of California. They sip the warm rice wine and talk, tugging exaggeratedly at one another's sleeves. They laugh; they sing half-remembered songs.

"Kimi, I tell you, put the dog out! If there's anything that annoys me, it's the smell of a wet dog. I've got troubles enough without that. The stench comes from the floor like something stepped on in the dark. Eh, Nagata-*kun?* Heh-heh. . . . What a life, eh? Heh-heh."

Yah, those seedlings. A month's work destroyed. You sow one more row before sundown, pull one more weed before nightfall, for what? Rain, more seeding, more weeding. Don't look at me like that, Kimi; I didn't order this rain. I didn't ask for this kind of life. What would you have me do? Run out and stop the rain with my bare hands? I can't change the shape of fate. I know. I tried. I left my native shore to tread these "gold-paved" streets, heh-heh, to live and die, unseen, among aliens. And I've found that when it rains there's nothing to do but jump into bed and pull the covers over your head, or find a friend and drink a little wine, sing a few songs, and explore those feelings you've forgotten you'd had, so remote, so beautiful, so fragile they are. And then you can pull out your koto *(chin-chiri-rin)* and close your eyes and leave this soggy lifestyle. Heh-heh. What would you have me do?

The smell of a wet dog isn't bad. There's hardly any smell sadder than the smell of sake and rain together. I read in schoolbooks where fathers return from work and kiss their wives and toss their children in the air, their pockets bulging with candies and balloons, and the smell of supper cooking on the range permeates the air. I'd like that. Warm smells and good sounds. Here rain drums on the tar-paper roof, and you and your crony sit and drink, and you close your eyes and with this expression of tender sorrow, you pluck your imaginary koto, brown hands moving on the air, thick fingers touching phantom strings *(chin-chiri-rin)*.

I am a dying reed by the river bed
As thou, a drying dying reed
Alas, our lives together lie
Blossomless, on the river bed.

Whether we live or whether die
Tides will ebb and flow
Come then, thou with me, to dwell
As boatmen on Toneh River.

Now you come to me. You come to haunt me as I had never permitted you to do when I was stronger. Sly old man. You waited until there was only a membrane between you and me. Is there still unfinished business? What do you want to tell me? That you are me and I am you, and today is the same as yesterday, and tomorrow will be the same as today? I thought I could change the pattern of my life; I thought I could deny your existence, deny our lonely past together, but alas, I had preserved it carefully, and when all the frills and furbelows are stripped away, you are here, the backbone of my life, the bleached hull of my shipwreck. And here between yesterday and today, I sing the same lonely song as you. I should not have denied you; I should have woven my life within the framework of our past. I should have loved you. Now my guilt comes home to me.

It's all right, Kimi. The pattern doesn't change and the guilt doesn't change. It's too late now; too late for might-have-been and would-have-liked. Give yourself to the tide, give yourself to the river; the sun is setting, the desert is cooling. . . .

Kimi.

A nebulous anticipation filled Kimi's bowels as she drifted to a cold dimension. She surrendered to the chill that enveloped her, her lips twisted in a pain akin to joy as she moved with a wind that carried her out, back to the country road, and against the smooth brown cheeks of a lad on a bicycle, and into the blouse that billowed behind him.

That Was All

L ast night I dreamed about a man I hadn't thought about in many years. He was my father's friend, a holdover from his bachelor days. As far back as I can remember, starting somewhere in the late twenties, Suzuki-san visited us – though not frequently – and my earliest memory of him begins with these visits when, at four or five, I used to run from him. I hated the feel of his hands; they were rough and callused from farm work. My father's bachelor friends were constantly reaching for me – perhaps they were amazed that he, bachelor of bachelors, had settled down to domesticity with this beautiful woman, himself not so handsome, not so cunning (still not losing his bachelor ways – the drinking, the gambling), and had this scrawny kid, or perhaps they were recalling other children spawned in other wombs and brought to life only by seeing and feeling me and remembering. At that early age I suspected something sinister about their caresses because I did not find this touch-touch attitude in men with families. Japanese people rarely touch, and my father . . . I cannot recall the warmth of my father's hand, except the sharp snap of it against my thigh when I misbehaved. My father acted as though I should accept these attentions from his friends as accommodations to him. I thought they were more for my mother's sake.

Raised on that desert farm under the patronage of two adults wrapped in their own set of problems and isolated from peer values, my imagination was left to run rampant. Although I cannot now believe it was entirely a misconception, I had the suspicion that all men were secretly and madly in love with my mother, who was the most beautiful and charming of all women. Magically emerging from that desert floor, she endured the harsh daylight realities and blossomed in the cool of the evening. After the bath. And I was sure no man in his proper mind could resist her. My father, I thought, was not in his proper mind.

My mother was a perfect Japanese wife except with my father in the bright light of day, when she did the bulk of her nagging. My father's strength was his silence which he applied in varying pressures from Arctic chill to rock-mountain imperturbability to wide open, no horizon, uninhabitable desert silence. My mother's emotional variances were my barometer: today she sings—fair and mild; today she remembers Japan—scattered showers; today he has made her unhappy again.

Suzuki-san lived in Niland thirty or forty miles from us in a treeless landscape of sand and tumbleweed. I don't know why this area, not so distant, seemed more desolate than where we lived, maybe because where we lived there was a mother and father and a child, and where Suzuki-san lived, there was only him and two bleak structures, a kitchen and a bedroom, and the land beyond this complex and ranch was untouched from year to year, century to century—only the desert animals pocking its surface and the rain streaking the sand in a flash flood now and then. That seemed awesome to me.

I remember a visit to his homestead. I was six or seven. It was winter, and my mother bundled me in a heavy coat and packed the car with pillows and blankets, and we drove for what seemed hours. I was disappointed when we got there because there was no one and nothing to play with; and in this incredibly boring place, the sun was blinding, the wind biting, and my mother was again in the kitchen cooking and mending Suzuki-san's clothes, and my father was walking up and down the furrows with Suzuki-san. I tried staying with my mother, but the kitchen depressed me; without a woman's touch, it looked like the inside of a garage—no embroidered dish towels, crocheted potholders, nor a window with a swatch of dotted swiss fluttering.

I walked along with my father and Suzuki-san, but their frequent stopping to examine plants, scratch the earth, turn over equipment, bored me and I wandered off to the desert. My father was not alarmed; on that windswept land a few loud bellows carried for miles and would quickly draw me back to him. Besides, there was no shrub taller than myself I could hide behind, no ditch I could drown in, and snakes and vipers were not considered a threat.

I wandered around looking for—I don't know what—maybe some indication that someone had been here before me and left something for me, and finding nothing, I stood by the fine pure sand the winds had pushed against a shrub and mused that it was possible I was the first person who had ever been on this particular mound of sand and put my shoe to that dust that began with creation and then my hand and then my cheek and then my hair and finally rolled myself on it and fell asleep.

My mother said later, brushing the sand from my coat with hard quick hands, "I think she rolled in the dirt," and my father said contemptuously, "Like a dog," and Suzuki-san looked at my mother with those bemused eyes that pretended to know something he didn't, and I grew very angry and denied it all.

It was his mocking eyes that I disliked.

Intuitively I knew that my father, close to forty, and my mother, perhaps not yet thirty, had abiding ties with Suzuki-san that started earlier than my arrival, perhaps somewhere back in Japan in Shizuoka, and perhaps on something less mysterious than appeared on the surface. I thought later maybe Suzuki-san had loaned my father a vast sum of money.

Suzuki-san was unlike my father's other bachelor friends who still followed the crops along the length of California, cutting lettuce in Dinuba, harvesting grapes in Fresno, plums, peaches, and finally strawberries in Oceanside and those little-known places—Vista, Escondido, Encinitas. They spent their money as soon as they got it—drinking, gambling, carousing—until at the southernmost end of the state, they looked for us and stayed two or three months eating my mother's cooking, and drinking my father's wine, oblivious to my mother's sighs which grew deeper as the visits wore on. Although Suzuki-san drank with my father too, he never permitted himself the coarse laughing and out-of-control drunkenness characteristic of the other roustabouts. Also, Suzuki-san leased a parcel of land and farmed it like a family man—although he had no family that anyone spoke of either here in America or in Japan—nor did he show any apparent need for family, nor did my father or mother show interest in seeing him married. The need only surfaced now and then when he would catch me unaware and hold me squirming in his sandpaper grasp. Or sometimes it showed in the way he looked at my mother with his amused eyes. Perhaps when these needs were strongest, Suzuki-san came to us and ate with us, often bringing something special for my mother to cook, examining each morsel on his *hashi* before bringing it to his lips and chewing slowly—movements as sensual and private as making love. Once when he caught me watching him, he laughed and slipped some food into my mouth in a gesture so intimate I flushed warm and my father coughed suddenly. Those days he would stay overnight, sleeping on a cot in the kitchen and leaving in the morning after my mother's good breakfast.

Then about the time I turned fifteen, something very strange happened to me.

Suzuki-san was visiting us on this summer evening. We had finished supper; the day's warmth was still with us as we sat on the porch fanning away gnats and insects that flew past us toward the light of the small kerosene lantern. The air was still and the cicadas hummed without beginning or end. Suzuki-san returned from his bath stripped to his waist and sat next to me.

In the half dark I saw his brown body and smelled his warm scent, and in the summer night with the cicadas' pervasive drone and the scent and sight of Suzuki-san's body assailing my better judgment, I fell in love.

I sat in the protective shadows of the night and watched the face I'd never before regarded as handsome and scrutinized the eyes that always seemed to mock me. I wondered about the wasted years this man had kept his perfect body to himself, never giving or receiving the love that was most certainly available to him. I wondered why he continued to work in his self-imposed exile and what future he hoped for himself . . . and whom he would share it with. An indescribable loneliness and sorrow came over me. I wished he would touch me again. He'd long ago stopped that.

Then he looked at me. My stomach turned and roiled with things terrible and sublime and sensual and sexual and rotten that I was unable to contain. They passed through me and fouled the still night. My father grunted and walked away. My mother glared at me and fanned the air away from herself and Suzuki-san.

I was mortified. My mother should have found a way out for me. Instead she separated herself, denied me, and remained aloof, the lady of evening dew, and I . . . I was humiliated. Suzuki-san's eyes did not change. I went into the house.

That was all; that was all.

A few years later my father, unable to stave off the economic disaster that was our inexorable fate, moved us to Oceanside. And a few years after that, war with Japan broke out, changed the course of our lives, and we along with thousands of Japanese and Japanese Americans were incarcerated in Arizona. Maybe Suzuki-san was also in the same camp. I don't remember seeing him.

And I fell in love at least three times thereafter – each time with the same brown body, the same mocking eyes; and the last time, I was drawn into a tumultuous love affair that spanned twenty-five years and ended on a rainy January morning. And perhaps I should add, I have not loved since.

And last night I had this dream:

I was living in a lean-to which I instinctively knew was part of Suzuki-san's house. The house itself was in terrible disrepair. It looked like a wrecking ball had been put to it. The floors buckled and the walls caved inward.

I felt I should offer to do something for the man who kindly shared his house with me, battered though it was. I was thinking of my mother who had so long ago done his cooking and mending. I went about gathering clothes I might wash for him. While going from room to room, I passed a cracked and dusty mirror, and in the fragmented reflection I saw myself – older than my mother had ever been, older than I remembered myself to be.

I found two items to wash: an ancient pair of twills, moldy and stiff but unworn, and a sock, which I recognized as my own, half filled with sand.

Then I saw him in one of the rooms.

As it is with dreams, I was not surprised when I saw he was the same man I remember on the summer night when I so suddenly fell in love. He was naked to the waist, his body was tight and brown, he wore the same pants. In my head I thought, "He hasn't changed at all – still thirty-five. . . . What would he want with this fifty-year-old woman I've grown to be?" But my mouth said, "I hope you're not paying a lot of rent for this place."

He said, "The rent is cheap."

It was my fault. I should not have started a conversation sounding so shrewish. I looked in his face to see if I could find some recognition of me . . . the me that he once wanted to hold . . . the me that was part of my mother's evening dew . . . the me that was gone forever.

I watched him until he could avoid me no longer, and in my dream his eyes mocked me again . . . as they have always done.

The Music Lessons

The first production of *The Music Lessons* was March 18–April 3, 1980, at the New York Public Theater. It was produced by Joseph Papp and directed by Mako.

Cast

Sab Shimono	KAORU KAWAGUCHI
Haunani Minn	CHIZUKO SAKATA
Lauren Tom	AKI
Keenan Shimizu	ICHIRO
Gedde Watanabe	TOMU
Dana Lee	NAKAMURA
Kestutis Nakas	BILLY
Jane Mandy	WAITRESS

Characters

KAORU KAWAGUCHI, 33, Japanese male, itinerant
CHIZUKO SAKATA, 38, Issei widow farmer, mother
AKI SAKATA, 15, daughter of Chizuko
ICHIRO SAKATA, 17, son of Chizuko
TOMU SAKATA, 16, son of Chizuko
NAKAMURA, 45, male, Issei farmer
BILLY KANE, 15, white, friend of the children
WAITRESS, middle-aged, non-Asian

ACT I

Scene i September afternoon, 1935. Sakata kitchen
Scene ii October afternoon. Kaoru's shed
Scene iii Shortly after. Pool hall
Scene iv That evening. Sakata yard

ACT II

Scene i The following day. Sakata yard
Scene ii November, early evening. Sakata yard
Scene iii A few months later, winter night. Sakata kitchen
Scene iv Shortly after. Sakata kitchen
Scene v A spring evening. Kaoru's shed
Scene vi Immediately after. Sakata kitchen

ACT I
Scene i

September afternoon, 1935

ON RISE: *Center stage left is the interior of the Sakata kitchen. It is spare, almost stark. There is a table with at least three chairs, some crockery (water pitcher, glasses) on a cupboard. An upstage door leads to the bedrooms. Upstage left is a screen door leading outside.*

Stage right is a toolshed. A cot lies on its side, crates and tools lie scattered. The interior of the shed is dark until it is in use.

NAKAMURA, Issei farmer, in farm clothes of the era, and KAORU KAWAGUCHI, Japanese itinerant, in a sport coat and hat and carrying a violin case and an old-fashioned suitcase, enter from stage left.

NAKAMURA: I don't see the truck. Maybe she's not home.

KAORU: You're sure she'll hire me?

NAKAMURA: Well, I'm not *sure*. You said you're looking for work and I thought, well, maybe Chizuko. She runs this farm all by herself and . . . *[calling]* Chizuko-san! One thing you ought to know about farming; there's always work to be done; the problem is money. There's not a lot of it around these days. *[He opens the door and peers in.]* I guess she went out. Depression's still here for us farmers, you know.

KAORU: Yes, I know.

NAKAMURA *[looking at his pocket watch]*: Well, I gotta be going.

[KAORU picks up his violin case.]

NAKAMURA *[continuing, stopping him from following]*: You ought to wait for her. She'll be back (soon) . . .

KAORU *[quickly]*: You do all your own work? I'd like to . . . you know, you don't have to pay me right (away) . . .

NAKAMURA: *[ha-ha]* I got two grown sons to help me. Now Chizuko, her boys are still young, and well, it's hard for her. It's hard for *me;* it's gotta be rough for her. You wait here. She'll be back soon.

[KAORU puts down his violin and wipes his brow.]

NAKAMURA *[continuing]*: Not used to the heat, eh? 'Nother thing: I'd hide the violin if I was you. *[He almost takes the case from KAORU.]* No good to look too . . . You gotta look like you can *work*. You know what I mean?

KAORU: I see.

NAKAMURA: Why don't you mosey around while you're waiting? See what people do on a farm. *[ha-ha]* Maybe you won't *want* to work here.

KAORU: Yes, I'll do that.

NAKAMURA: I live about a mile down this road. If Chizuko don't want you, come on down and I'll give you a lift back to town.

KAORU: Thank you. Thank you for being so kind to a stranger.

NAKAMURA: Japanese stick together, eh? *[He stops on his way out.]* Oh, you tell her you picked grapes in Fresno and cut lettuce in Salinas. Tell her I sent you.

KAORU: Yes, I will. Thank you.

NAKAMURA: Well, good luck.

> *[NAKAMURA exits left. KAORU puts his suitcase in an inconspicuous place, and still carrying his violin, he walks upstage center and exits behind the toolshed.]*
>
> *[The Sakata children, ICHIRO, son, in cotton twills and plaid shirt, hair cut short; TOMU, son, similarly dressed; and AKI, daughter, hair clasped with one metal barrette at her neck, in a cotton dress of the period, return from shopping for staples. They enter carrying the groceries.]*

AKI: It's no fun shopping: shoyu, rice, miso . . . always the same old stuff.

ICHIRO: Stop complaining. Next time, don't go.

AKI: Boy, Ichiro, you're getting just like Mama. Wouldn't even give me a quarter. You could have loaned it to me. I would have paid you back.

ICHIRO: With what? Tomatoes?

AKI: I could do extra work for Mama.

ICHIRO: Who gets paid for extra work?

TOMU: Ma doesn't pay for work. Period.

ICHIRO: You get food in your belly, consider yourself paid.

> *[CHIZUKO SAKATA, Issei, gaunt and capable looking, hair bunned back, wearing her dead husband's shirt, pants, heavy shoes, and hat, enters from stage right. She does not see the suitcase. She carries a basket of peas.]*

AKI: He wouldn't even give me a quarter, Mama.

CHIZUKO: What do you want a quarter for?

[They enter the kitchen.]

AKI: I just wanted to get a small book, Mama.

ICHIRO *[giving CHIZUKO the bill and change]*: It's all there.

CHIZUKO *[counting the change and putting it away in a jar]*: Money has to last until spring.

AKI: But Mama, a quarter . . .

CHIZUKO: A quarter buys two pounds of meat.

TOMU: We ought to be able to spend for something else besides just keeping alive.

ICHIRO: Quit complaining, will you?

CHIZUKO: After harvest you can have treats.

AKI: I won't want it then.

TOMU: She only wanted a quarter, Ma.

ICHIRO *[silencing the two]*: Hey!

CHIZUKO: I told you we don't spend right now.

TOMU: Yeah, Ma.

AKI: It was different when Papa was here.

ICHIRO: Well, Pop's *not* here.

AKI: He always brought stuff for us. Remember that dog, Tomu?

TOMU: Oh, yeah. Maru.

ICHIRO: Well, it's different now. You might as well get used to it.

> *[KAORU enters from upstage center. He picks up his suitcase. ICHIRO notices him in the yard and goes out.]*

KAORU: Oh. Hello.

ICHIRO: Hello.

CHIZUKO: Who is it, Ichiro? *[She comes to the yard.]*

KAORU: Oh. You are . . . Sakata-san?

CHIZUKO: Yes.

KAORU: Ah! I am Kawaguchi.

> *[KAORU extends a hand and CHIZUKO reluctantly takes it. It's not a Japanese custom to shake hands.]*

CHIZUKO: Kawaguchi-san?

KAORU: Kaoru, I was . . . a . . . with Nakamura-san a little while ago. He brought me here. He said you might be needing help and I . . .

[*Aki and Tomu come out. Visitors are few and they are very interested.*]

CHIZUKO: Nakamura-san brought you? [*She feels obligated to invite KAORU in.*] *Sah, dozo.*

[*CHIZUKO opens the door and everyone enters the house. ICHIRO pulls out a chair for KAORU.*]

KAORU: Yes, yes. I was looking for work, and he thought you might be able to use me.

CHIZUKO: I don't know why he'd do that. He knows I don't have the money to hire. There's plenty of work here, but I just don't have the money right now.

KAORU: We can talk about that later . . . when the crop is (harvested) . . .

CHIZUKO: Well, we never know how it turns out. Sometimes it's good; sometimes, bad. A lot depends on weather, prices . . . things like that. Besides . . . [*She looks him over shamelessly.*] I need a man who can work like a horse.

KAORU: Ma'am, I know how to work. I come from peasant stock.

CHIZUKO: Then sometimes, when it rains, there's nothing to do.

KAORU: Pay me what you can.

CHIZUKO[*dubiously*]: You look like a city man.

KAORU [*pressing*]: If you put me up, I'll only need a little now and then – not right away – for cigarettes and things, you know.

CHIZUKO: Well . . .

KAORU: If you do well with the harvest, we can settle then. I promise you I won't be idle. When there's time, I can . . . [*He brushes the dust from his violin case and changes his mind.*] Can I help your boys with their math work?

TOMU: Boy, I can sure use some help there.

AKI: Maybe you'll make a *C* this year.

KAORU: I can keep books for you. That's what I did in the city – bookkeeping.

CHIZUKO [*shelling peas*]: Looks like you're a man of talent – culture.

KAORU:[*ha-ha*] Well, I came to America as a boy. I finished high school here. You know, schoolboy. Live-in. I lived with rich white folks and did the gardening and cleaning while I went to school. The lady I worked for was a musician. She taught me to play this. *[He laughs wryly.]* She wanted me to be a musician.

CHIZUKO: Oh? What happened?

> *[AKI gives KAORU a glass of water. KAORU gratefully drinks it.]*

KAORU: Thank you. Well, I don't know. As soon as I was able, I left them. I wanted to be on my own. But there's no chance for a Japanese violinist in America.

CHIZUKO: You worked in the city all the time?

KAORU: Most of the time, yes. Or maybe I wasn't good enough.

CHIZUKO: What did you do?

KAORU: This and that. Waited tables, cooked—worked as a fry cook. And bookkeeping. I did that the last few years.

CHIZUKO: Maybe better you stay at a nice clean job like that than work on a dirt farm like this. Why did you want to come out here?

KAORU: Oh, I didn't get fired. To be honest, I wanted to . . . to start something new. I was tired of city life. I wanted a change.

CHIZUKO: I want a change too. But some of us . . . *[She glances at her children.]* we're not free to do that. Change.

> *[KAORU sees the futility of going on. He almost gives up but tries one last time.]*

KAORU: I understand your doubts about me. I have no references or recommendations, but I'm an honest man and I'll work hard for you. I give you my word.

> *[CHIZUKO looks quickly at ICHIRO. The children are excited.]*

CHIZUKO: All right. But no pay until after the harvest.

KAORU: You won't regret this, Ma'am.

> *[From stage left, BILLY KANE, white neighbor, pedals his bicycle into the yard. It's equipped with a raccoon tail, reflectors, stickers, etc.]*

BILLY: Tomu! Hey, Tomu!

TOMU: That'll be Billy.

KAORU *[to CHIZUKO]*: You have another son?

ICHIRO: It's Billy Kane. He lives down the road.

AKI: He comes over a lot. They're rich.

[TOMU goes downstage to meet BILLY.]

TOMU *[to BILLY]*: Hi.

ICHIRO: They're not *that* rich. His father works for the American Fruit Growers. On salary.

BILLY *[astride his bicycle]*: Guess what? We went to Yosemite last week.

[The conversation is heard in the kitchen.]

TOMU: Oh, yeah?

CHIZUKO *[to KAORU]*: My boys spent summer here – flooding, plowing, getting ready for planting. It was hot. Hundred ten degrees.

ICHIRO: We bought the seed today. Cash.

BILLY *[to TOMU]*: There was a stream just outside the tent. It was cold!

TOMU: That right? *[He gets on Billy's bicycle.]*

BILLY *[showing Tomu a postcard]*: See this?

CHIZUKO *[to ICHIRO]*: You and Tomu clean the toolshed. Aki, get the blankets and sheets for Kawaguchi-san.

[AKI exits through the upstage door; ICHIRO goes outside to join TOMU and BILLY.]

BILLY: We cooked over a fire. You know, the fish Dad caught.

ICHIRO: Come on, let's get this done. *[to BILLY]* You too.

CHIZUKO *[to KAORU]*: Looks like an act of Providence. We start planting tomorrow. If we get through in a week, the boys can start school together this year. I don't want them to get behind.

[AKI appears with the bedding.]

AKI: They're both in the same class.

CHIZUKO *[impatiently]*: They *have* to be so they can teach each other.

KAORU: How's that?

AKI: They take turns going to school, and the one that goes teaches the other what he missed.

CHIZUKO: Not all the time. Only when work piles up. Some things just *have* to be done on time.

AKI: That's why they take the same subjects.

> *[CHIZUKO waves AKI away. AKI joins the boys in the shed.]*

CHIZUKO: When did you say you came to America?

KAORU: Nineteen nineteen. I was sixteen.

> *[The children are in the shed making the place livable.]*

CHIZUKO: I'll call you when supper's ready.

KAORU *[taking the cue to leave]*: Yes, thank you.

> *[He follows the voices to the shed. CHIZUKO begins chopping vegetables. AKI enters the kitchen.]*

AKI *[watching the chopping]*: Oh, Mama, don't make *that* again.

> *[Fade out]*

> *[The stage is dark. KAORU is in the shed changing. Country-western music of the thirties plays over the radio ("Now and Then"). The announcer makes a weather report.]*

ANNOUNCER: This is Bucky Burns with the extended forecast for Saturday through Monday. Fair weather except for night and morning clouds. A slight warming trend with highs ranging from seventy-five to eighty degrees. Lows in the upper sixties. Northwesterly winds at five to ten miles. Generally fair for the next three days. Now back to your old favorites.

> *[Country music continues until costume changes are made.]*

ACT I
Scene ii

October afternoon

ON RISE: *In Kaoru's shed. KAORU has just returned from town. He's dressed in his good clothes. It's his day off, and on the bed is a paper bag containing a small book of poems, magazines, some candy, and a pretty chiffon scarf. Kaoru's door is closed.*

NAKAMURA enters from stage left. He carries a small bottle of wine in his back pocket.

NAKAMURA: Chizuko-san . . . *[He opens the kitchen door and peers in.]* Chizuko-san!

KAORU *[opening his shed door]*: Hello!

NAKAMURA: Oh! Chizuko told me she hired you.

KAORU: Come in. Come in.

[NAKAMURA enters the shed.]

KAORU *[continuing]*: Been almost a month now. Been meaning to thank you. Today's my day off.

[NAKAMURA looks for a place to sit and picks up the paper bag.]

NAKAMURA: Been to town already, eh? Been shopping.

KAORU: Just some things for the kids. They don't get much of anything.

NAKAMURA: You're a good man, Kawa. *[He looks in the bag.]*

KAORU: No-no. Nothing much.

NAKAMURA *[bringing out the book]*: What's this?

KAORU: For the girl. She likes to read.

[NAKAMURA pulls out the scarf (which should show the kind of woman KAORU loves) and looks at KAORU questioningly.]

KAORU *[continuing]*: Oh, that. Reminded me of someone I once knew. I'm thinking of sending it to her.

NAKAMURA: Oh, yeah? *[He drinks from his bottle.]*

KAORU: Maybe it's foolish.

NAKAMURA: No-no. *[He offers KAORU a sip.]* Where's Chizuko-san?

KAORU *[refusing the drink]*: I don't know. I just got back from town.

[NAKAMURA looks around and lowers his voice.]

NAKAMURA: That woman never lets up. Works like a man. Maybe better, eh?

KAORU: Maybe.

NAKAMURA: Says she found a good man, Kawa. Thanked me for sending you down. *[He laughs raucously.]* Yeah. Thinks we're old friends.

KAORU: I'm working hard. I'm going to try to get her a good harvest so I can make some money too.

NAKAMURA *[laughing hard]*: You think all you got to do to make money is to work hard? If that's the way, I'd be a millionaire now.

KAORU: You don't have to be a millionaire to have a farm. I want to save some money and start my own place.

[*NAKAMURA scoffs.*]

KAORU [*continuing*]: Sure. I'll work here a while and get the feel of it; save my money and . . .

NAKAMURA: "Save!" Horseshit! Only way to do is borrow money.

KAORU: Who's going to lend me money? I got nothing. No collateral.

NAKAMURA: Well, first you get some names together. Good names. You can use mine. Sponsors, you know? Then you go to a produce company—in Los Angeles. That's where they all are. Put on a good suit, talk big . . . how you going to make big money for them. Get in debt. Then you pay back after the harvest. [*The futility of it occurs to him.*] Then you borrow again next year. Then you pay back. If you can. Same thing again next year. You never get the farm. The farm gets you. [*He drinks.*]

KAORU: You never get the farm?

NAKAMURA: 'S true. Orientals can't own land here. It's the law.

KAORU: The law? Then how is it that (you) . . .

NAKAMURA: Well, I lease. If you have a son old enough, you can buy land under his name. He's 'Merican citizen, you see? That's if you have enough money.

KAORU: I'll apply for citizenship then.

NAKAMURA: There's a law against that too. Orientals can't be citizens.

KAORU: We can't?

NAKAMURA: That's the law. Didn't you know?

> [*NAKAMURA again offers KAORU a drink. This time he accepts and drains the bottle. NAKAMURA looks at the empty bottle.*]

NAKAMURA [*continuing*]: Hey, let's go to town.

KAORU: I just came from there.

NAKAMURA: Yeah, me too. Come on, we'll get some more wine. [*He lowers his voice.*] You know, Chizuko don't like drinking. Her old man used to [*ha-ha*] drink a little. Like me. He drowned in a canal, you know. Fell off a catwalk.

KAORU [*putting on his coat*]: Is that right?

NAKAMURA: Yeah, six . . . almost seven years ago.

KAORU: That long?

NAKAMURA: Yeah. She got lucky with tomatoes a couple of years ago and paid back all her old man's debts. People never expected to see their money again, but she did it. She paid them back. Now she never borrows—lives close to the belly—stingy, tight. That's the way she stays ahead. Not much ahead, but . . .

[They exit talking.]

KAORU: That so?

NAKAMURA: What's she planting this year?

KAORU: Squash, tomatoes . . .

NAKAMURA: Tomatoes again?

ACT I
Scene iii

Shortly after

ON RISE: *On stage right there is a setup for a poolhall. There are a table, two chairs, and a thirties beer sign on the wall.*

WAITRESS, heavily made up, non-Asian, sits on one of the chairs, her feet propped on the other. She files her nails. Country music plays softly.

NAKAMURA and KAORU enter talking.

NAKAMURA: And the day after he was buried, she's out there plowing the field. *[to the WAITRESS]* Oi!

WAITRESS: Oi???

NAKAMURA: I couldn't believe it. The day after the funeral. *[to the WAITRESS]* Wine!

WAITRESS *[shining up to KAORU]*: What kind of wine? Red? White?

NAKAMURA: Red! *[to KAORU]* Can you believe it? A woman behind the ass of a horse the day after her man's funeral. It ain't right.

[The WAITRESS brings the wine to the table and KAORU pays her in small change while NAKAMURA fumbles with his pinch purse.]

WAITRESS: *Arigato!*

[KAORU looks the WAITRESS over. NAKAMURA is irritated and waves the woman away. Since they are speaking

in Japanese, the WAITRESS doesn't understand them except when they talk directly to her.]

NAKAMURA: She'll give you a disease, Kawa. You don't want to fool around with that kind.

[KAORU laughs.]

NAKAMURA *[continuing]*: I mean it. They can get you in a lot of trouble.

KAORU *[laughing]*: I know, I know.

NAKAMURA: Japanese stick to Japanese. Better that way.

KAORU: Yeah.

NAKAMURA: So I tell her, "Chizuko-san, you got a right to cry. Take time out to cry." She says no. So I say, "I'll do your plowing. Stay home for a while." And you know what she said?

KAORU: What'd she say?

NAKAMURA: She said that's the way she cries. By working. *[to WAITRESS]* Oi!

KAORU: I guess there're all kinds of ways.

NAKAMURA: She must be crying all the time, the way she works.

[They have a good laugh on CHIZUKO.]

NAKAMURA: Too bad. She's getting all stringy and dried up. Heh. I remember when she was young—kinda pretty—but she's getting all . . . oh-oh.

[The WAITRESS pours again and NAKAMURA makes a feeble attempt to reach for his purse. KAORU pays again.]

WAITRESS *[to KAORU]*: You're a real gentleman. Thank you. *[She winks at him and leaves.]*

NAKAMURA: Bet you had plenty of them, eh? All kinds?

KAORU *[laughing]*: All kinds.

[They're feeling loose.]

NAKAMURA: Yeah? Bet you been in heaps of trouble, eh?

KAORU: Oh-yeah. *[He pushes up his sleeve.]* See this? Bullet went clean through this arm.

NAKAMURA: Ever get one in trouble?

KAORU: Hunh?

NAKAMURA: Ever get one pregnant?

KAORU: Well . . .

NAKAMURA: Liked her a lot, eh? Woman of the scarf?

KAORU: Yeah.

NAKAMURA: Never been that way myself. A woman's a woman to me. Never been that way. *[He feels sad.]* What's it like, Kawa? Never been that way. Must be a good feeling.

KAORU: Sometimes.

NAKAMURA: Old bastard like me, been married, the same woman – picture bride – twenty years. Still don't know that feeling. *[He drinks.]* Is it good? Kawa, what's it like?

KAORU: Sometimes it hurts like hell. Rather be shot, sometimes.

NAKAMURA: Why's it gotta hurt like that?

KAORU: Don't know. Sometimes they're married. Then everybody gets hurt.

NAKAMURA: Married! What kind of woman's that?

KAORU: That's the way it happened.

NAKAMURA: What's the matter you do like that?

KAORU: Don' know.

NAKAMURA: You had a baby, no? What happened to the baby?

KAORU: No baby. Aborted.

NAKAMURA: Waah! You lucky to get away from that kind.

KAORU: I know. *[He's still morose.]*

NAKAMURA: No good, Kawa! You got twenty, thirty more years. Let a woman grab your balls and you good for nothing. 'Specially that kind.

KAORU: You're right.

NAKAMURA: Sure, I'm right. I'm right. *[to WAITRESS]* Oi!

KAORU: No-no. No more for me. Well, maybe I'll take one for later.

NAKAMURA: Get my friend a bottle.

WAITRESS: To go?

NAKAMURA: Sure, I'm right. Laugh about it. You gotta move on.

KAORU: 'S what I'm tryna do.

NAKAMURA *[reluctantly standing]*: You think 'bout what I said.

WAITRESS *[to KAORU]*: You going already?

KAORU: Yeah.

WAITRESS *[whispering]*: I'll be off in a couple of minutes.

NAKAMURA: Kawa, you coming?

KAORU *[his attention to the WAITRESS]*: Yeah, yeah.

NAKAMURA: Come on, come on!

KAORU: All right. *[But he doesn't move.]*

NAKAMURA *[understanding]*: Well, I'll pick you up later.

KAORU: That's fine.

> *[Light fades on KAORU and the WAITRESS sitting together and whispering.]*
>
> *[Fade out]*

ACT I
Scene iv

That evening

ON RISE: *Interior of the Sakata kitchen.*

Dinner is just over. ICHIRO and TOMU are seated at the table. AKI clears the dishes and CHIZUKO puts out textbooks. A place is still set for KAORU.

TOMU *[picking his teeth]*: The food is getting better around here.

ICHIRO: What you call company dinner.

AKI: It was good, wasn't it?

TOMU: Too bad Kaoru-san couldn't eat with us.

CHIZUKO *[worried]*: Maybe something happened.

TOMU: Maybe he couldn't get a ride back.

ICHIRO: Maybe he's looking around town.

AKI: Not much to look at. Five blocks and you're out of it.

TOMU: Why don't we go pick him up?

ICHIRO: Aw, he'll find his way back.

TOMU: But it's getting late. Eight miles is a long . . .

ICHIRO: No one ever worried about me walking eight miles. He'll catch a ride.

CHIZUKO: Ichiro's right. He'll get a ride.

AKI: There're hardly any cars on the road at night, Mama.

CHIZUKO: He'll find his way back.

ICHIRO: Or maybe he won't come back.

TOMU: He'll come back. He left his violin.

CHIZUKO: He'll come back.

TOMU: Besides, where would he go? Ma didn't give him much money.

CHIZUKO: I gave him as much as I could. After the har(vest) . . .

AKI: Yeah, we know. After the harvest.

CHIZUKO: Well, we'll make it up to him later.

> *[BILLY drives into the yard on his bicycle. He bleeps his new horn. The boys look up from their books.]*

BILLY: Tomu . . .

ICHIRO: Your friend, Tomu.

AKI *[to ICHIRO]*: I suppose he has something else to show us.

> *[TOMU goes out.]*

TOMU *[to BILLY]*: Hi!

ICHIRO: The horn. Didn't you hear it?

> *[BILLY and TOMU can be heard in the kitchen. The yard remains dark.]*

BILLY *[honking the horn]*: Look at this.

TOMU: Swell! Did you buy it?

BILLY: Sold twenty-four Wolverine salves for it.

TOMU: Salves? What's that?

BILLY: You know, like Vaseline. You can get one too. Just sell the salves. My dad bought all mine.

TOMU: No thanks. I might get stuck with them. What'd I do with twenty-four salves?

ICHIRO *[leaning toward the window]*: What'd you do with a bicycle horn? You ain't even got a bicycle.

BILLY *[to TOMU]*: You can give them away. My mom's going to give them to friends for Christmas.

[TOMU honks the horn several times.]

CHIZUKO *[leaning out the door]*: Shhh!

TOMU: My mom'd hit the ceiling.

AKI *[to ICHIRO]*: Maybe he'll get one one day. How do you know?

ICHIRO: Yeah, when he's fifty.

> *[BILLY and TOMU walk into the kitchen. BILLY gives CHIZUKO a quick nod.]*

BILLY: Hi. Ich, want to see what I got?

ICHIRO: Don't have time.

BILLY: Aki?

AKI: I'm busy.

BILLY: Busy, busy, busy. You guys are always busy. What do you do for fun?

ICHIRO: Oh, we have fun. We . . . we seed, we weed, we irrigate, and in winter we light smudge pots.

BILLY: That's fun?

ICHIRO: Lots of fun. Two o'clock in the morning . . . cold as hell. And pretty soon we'll be doing brush covers.

> *[AKI snickers. CHIZUKO shrinks in pain.]*

TOMU: Yeah, and all the other times we study, study, study. That's the kind of fun we have.

CHIZUKO: It'll be better this year.

BILLY *[to AKI]*: Aren't you going to ask me to sit down?

AKI: Sit down.

TOMU: Come on, Billy, let's go to my room.

> *[But BILLY sits down. Offstage we hear the sound of a car driving into the yard. NAKAMURA and KAORU enter with a bottle. They sing and laugh. The family sits frozen.]*

KAORU AND NAKAMURA: *Oyu no naka ni wa / Korya hana ga saku yo / Choyna, choyna* . . . (an old Japanese drinking song)

KAORU *[half stumbling]*: Oh-oh.

NAKAMURA: You all right?

KAORU: Sure. Thanks alot. 'Preciate it.

NAKAMURA: 'S all right. We do it again sometime, eh?

AKI: He drinks, Mama.

CHIZUKO: That's not your business.

> [NAKAMURA exits left and KAORU goes into his shed, sees the paper bag with the presents, picks it up, and with his bottle, crosses the yard and enters the kitchen, his laugh still on his face.]

KAORU: Hello-hello. What a nice family picture.

CHIZUKO [dispassionately]: Did you eat?

KAORU: Oh-yeah. Ate, drank, and [ha-ha] . . . Got a ride back with Nakamura-san. Very friendly, nice man. Spent most of the day with him.

CHIZUKO: With a family waiting supper for him.

KAORU: [ha-ha] Got some things here.

> [He spills the presents, candy, magazines, and book on the table—all but the scarf. The scarf may fall partially out. He distributes the magazines.]

ICHIRO: What for? What's this for?

KAORU: They're presents.

> [The children come alive. BILLY is happy for them. The bag with the scarf falls to the floor. The children's talk overlaps.]

BILLY: How about that?

TOMU: Gee, thanks. Thank you.

ICHIRO: Thanks alot.

> [KAORU presents the book to AKI with exaggerated gallantry.]

KAORU: And . . . for . . . Aki-chan!

AKI: Thank you.

KAORU: Now would you get me a small glass, Aki-chan?

AKI: Oh, sure.

> [CHIZUKO gets the glass for KAORU and plants it firmly in front of him.]

KAORU [*still in good spirits*]: Thank you, Chizuko-san.

CHIZUKO [*clearing away KAORU's dishes*]: You sure you don't want something to eat?

KAORU: No-no. Nothing.

> [*KAORU pours the wine and lifts the glass in a toast. The family stares, CHIZUKO with disapproval. There is an uncomfortable silence.*]

KAORU [*continuing*]: Well, I'd better go.

AKI [*holding her book*]: Thank you, Kaoru-san.

KAORU: Good night.

ICHIRO AND TOMU: Yeah, thanks.

BILLY [*chewing the candy*]: Good night. Good candy!

> [*KAORU leaves. The children look at their magazines.*]

TOMU: Look, Billy.

BILLY: Oh! Hey, can I borrow that?

TOMU [*kidding*]: No. I ain't even *looked* through it yet.

BILLY: Man-o-man. [*to AKI*] Let's see the book.

> [*AKI flicks it briefly in BILLY's face. TOMU catches a look.*]

TOMU: So-nets from the . . . What are so-nets?

AKI: Sonnets, dopey. Poems.

ICHIRO: Poems?

BILLY: Oh-boy.

AKI [*reading from the book*]: "What can I give thee back, O liberal / And princely giver, who hast brought the gold / And purple of thine heart . . ."

TOMU: What's she talking about?

BILLY: Beats me.

AKI: ". . . unstained, untold, / And laid them on the outside of the wall / For such as I to take or leave withal / In unexpected largesse? am I cold . . ."

ICHIRO: Largesse?

TOMU: Woo-woo!

> [*AKI continues to read as much of the poem* (Sonnets from the Portuguese — *Elizabeth Barrett Browning*) *as*

it takes for KAORU to get to the shed and start playing the violin.]

AKI: "Ungrateful, that for these most manifold / High gifts, I render nothing back at all? / Not so; not cold, – but very poor instead / Ask God who knows. For frequent tears have run / The colors from my life, and left so dead / And pale a stuff, it were not fitly done / To give the same as pillow to thy head / Go farther! let it serve to trample on."

[From the shed comes beautiful music that breaks the silence of the desert (Bach?). Everyone is still for a while. Then AKI closes her book and starts out the door.]

BILLY: Hey, where you going?

ICHIRO: I think they're playing our song.

TOMU: *That's* our song?

BILLY: Aki, is that *our* song?

ICHIRO: "When I'm calling you ooooooo . . ."

AKI: I'm going to the toilet!

BILLY: Don't forget to request some potty music.

[AKI is already out the door.]

BILLY *[continuing]*: Just kidding, Aki. Aki . . . ?

[AKI stands at Kaoru's door and listens to the music.]

BILLY *[continuing]*: I think I'll go home now.

TOMU *[his nose in the magazine]*: Yeah? Already? Well, okay.

[Downstage is dark. In the kitchen, the boys are reading; CHIZUKO stands by the window. KAORU plays the violin in a dim light, a half-filled glass of wine beside him. The room is neat.]

[BILLY joins AKI.]

BILLY: What're you doing out here?

AKI: Shh!

BILLY: I'm going home now.

AKI *[listening to the music]*: Go home.

[BILLY gets on his bicycle, bleeps his horn, and exits. KAORU hears the horn and comes out.]

KAORU: Oh. Aren't you cold out here, Aki-chan?

AKI: The music is beautiful.

KAORU: Come inside. I'll teach you to play this. *[He holds the door open for her.]*

AKI: Oh, I don't know if I can . . .

KAORU: Sure, you can.

> *[KAORU tucks the violin under AKI's chin and shows her how to hold the bow and lets her draw her own sounds. The noise is terrible.]*

KAORU *[continuing]*: Put your chin . . . that's right. Elbow in . . . unhunh . . . Hold your fingers like so. Now draw down. Up . . . down . . .

> *[In the kitchen CHIZUKO and the boys hear the sounds and are shocked. Then they start to laugh.]*

ICHIRO: Sounds like a cat with a bellyache.

TOMU *[holding his stomach]*: Oooooo-eeee . . .

ICHIRO: That's what you call the horse's tail hitting the cat gut.

TOMU: Maybe something under the horse's tail, hunh?

CHIZUKO *[stifling a laugh]*: Well, she's got to start somewhere.

ICHIRO: Yeah, but why here?

TOMU: Yeah. Why not in Siberia?

CHIZUKO: She's pretty bold, walking right in and asking to learn.

TOMU: You think she walked in his room and asked him to teach her?

ICHIRO: What else?

TOMU: I don't think Aki'd do that.

> *[The music stops.]*

ICHIRO: That girl'll do anything.

> *[In the shed AKI hands KAORU the violin.]*

AKI: It sounds awful. Play something for me.

KAORU: What would you like to hear?

AKI: Oh, something . . . something romantic. Something that will remind you of me . . . no matter where you are.

> *[KAORU ignores the implication. He plays "Two Guitars." The boys return to their books. CHIZUKO finds the paper*

bag, looks inside and finds the scarf. Light fades as she slowly returns the scarf to the bag.]

[Fade out]

ACT II
Scene i

The following day

ON RISE: *The Sakata yard. KAORU and CHIZUKO enter from upstage right (behind Kaoru's shed), carrying hoes.]*

CHIZUKO: We got lots of work done. Almost half the field.

KAORU: I could have moved faster, but . . .

CHIZUKO: You did good. There's a big difference between the work of a man and the work of boys.

KAORU *[has a hangover]*: I'm not so good today. Don't feel so good.

CHIZUKO: Maybe too much wine last night.

> *[KAORU laughs weakly. CHIZUKO grows self-conscious and smooths her hair. She looks better these days.]*

CHIZUKO *[continuing]*: Well, we'll stop for today. You want something to eat?

KAORU: No-no. Not hungry.

> *[KAORU starts toward his shed. CHIZUKO follows him.]*

CHIZUKO: How about coffee?

KAORU: Sounds good. I could use that.

> *[KAORU lies on his cot as CHIZUKO goes to heat the coffee. She lights the stove and looks into the paper bag that KAORU left the night before. She takes out the scarf, returns it to the bag, and carries it to KAORU.]*

CHIZUKO: Kaoru-san. Thank you for all the gifts last night. You did too much.

KAORU: No-no. It's nothing. Unless you don't want me to.

CHIZUKO: It's not that. I didn't give you much money, and it's not right for you to spend it all on the children.

KAORU: Just cheap presents.

> *[CHIZUKO takes a tentative step into Kaoru's room.]*

CHIZUKO: You left this bag last night.

> *[Puzzled, KAORU looks into the bag. He sees the scarf he bought for someone else. He pushes the bag back to CHIZUKO.]*

KAORU: Oh. You can have it.

CHIZUKO *[not accepting the bag]*: Didn't you buy it for someone?

KAORU: Oh. No. No one. It's for you. *[He takes the scarf and hands it to her.]*

CHIZUKO: But it's too . . .

KAORU: It's yours.

CHIZUKO: . . . too nice for me.

KAORU: Not at all. Please keep it. Wear it. *[He hangs it on CHIZUKO's neck.]*

CHIZUKO *[embarrassed]*: I'll have to find someplace to wear it to. Oh! Coffee! *[She rushes to the kitchen.]*

KAORU: Don't hurry.

> *[KAORU slowly walks to the bench outside as CHIZUKO enters the kitchen, hums a small tune, feels the soft fabric of the scarf around her neck, picks up the coffeepot (with a cloth) and a cup and returns to KAORU. She pours the coffee.]*

KAORU *[continuing]*: This will make me like new. I can still get in a few hours of work.

CHIZUKO: We'll stop for today.

KAORU: There're three good hours of daylight left.

CHIZUKO: Please. Kaoru-san, I . . . Thank you for the scarf.

KAORU: Nnn.

CHIZUKO: You're so kind. My children, my boys . . . they do good in school now.

KAORU: That's good.

CHIZUKO: And Aki . . . you teaching Aki to play music. Thank you, Kaoru-san.

KAORU: You don't have to say anything. It's my pleasure.

CHIZUKO: She seemed so happy last night.

KAORU: Aki is, you know . . . a very lonely little girl.

CHIZUKO: They miss their father.

KAORU: Yes, of course.

CHIZUKO: They miss him. *[Her voice goes dead.]* Funny. He never paid attention to them – to any of us. Well, I guess this work wasn't suited for him. He was always too late or too early for everything: planting, harvesting . . . and dying like that – so soon – so suddenly. Leaving us with . . . But the children miss him.

KAORU *[reluctantly]*: It must be lonely for you too.

CHIZUKO: When I left Japan I never knew it would be like this. The babies came so fast . . . and me, by myself, no mother, no sister – no one – to talk to. I was so young . . . never dreamed it would be like this. Never thought my life would be so hard. I don't know what it is to be a . . . a woman anymore . . . to laugh . . . to be soft . . . to talk nice . . . *[She can't look at KAORU.]*

KAORU: Well . . . *[ha-ha]*

CHIZUKO: I hear myself: "Don't do this; don't do that. Wear your sweater; study hard. . . ." I try to say other things: "How smart you are; how pretty you look . . ." but my mouth won't let me. I keep thinking, life is hard. I shouldn't let them think it would be easy.

KAORU: That's true.

CHIZUKO: Well, they're used to me like I am. If I change now, they'd think I went crazy.

KAORU: The important thing is, you're here. It's no good without a mother, Chizuko-san. I know.

CHIZUKO: You . . .

KAORU: My grandfather brought me up. My father was always in the rice paddy. He was a bitter old man. Old and bitter on a rice paddy. Growing old in the mud. I didn't want to die like that too. That's why I came to America.

CHIZUKO: And you never married?

> *[KAORU reaches for another cup of coffee. CHIZUKO rushes to pour it.]*

KAORU: When you're young you think youth will last forever. You throw it away foolishly. When you finally decide you want more – a family, maybe, it's too late. Family means roots, money, and you're like one of those tumbleweeds out there. Seed's all run out of your pockets and you have no roots. No one wants a tumbleweed.

CHIZUKO: But you're not a (tumbleweed) . . .

KAORU: There're lots of tumbleweeds out there. Some have wives in Japan; some even children. Some . . . well, like me . . . never got started, or started on the wrong foot, and before they know it, time passed them by and it's too late . . . too late. [He moves away from CHIZUKO.] The stories are always the same. You hear them all over: in bars, gambling dens . . . forgotten men laughing at lost dreams.

CHIZUKO: I'm forgotten too. My dreams are lost too. And my stories are all the same: one year following another, all the same.

KAORU: You have lots to look forward to: fine sons, a nice daughter.

CHIZUKO: I wonder sometimes, if it will not be the same for them too.

KAORU [trying to change the mood]: Cheer up, Chizuko-san. One of these days it will be time to harvest. Say! Nakamura-san told me yesterday he thinks you . . . you're getting quite pretty.

CHIZUKO [embarrassed]: Nakamura's an old goat.

KAORU: He's all right. I like him.

CHIZUKO: I don't know how I managed all these years by myself. I don't know how I did it. It's been a hard seven years. I don't think I can do it again.

KAORU [laughing]: Sure, you can.

CHIZUKO: I've been thinking . . . a . . . wondering how you'd feel about . . . what you think about staying on . . . on this farm, I mean. With us. [She waits; KAORU is silent.] I mean, share the profits . . . a partnership.

KAORU: I have no money, Chizuko-san.

CHIZUKO [quickly]: Oh, you pay nothing. I mean a joint venture. More or less. This farm is too much for a woman alone and I . . .

KAORO: Well, to be honest, I planned to work a piece of land for myself one day.

CHIZUKO: You don't have to. You can stay right here.

KAORU [drawing away]: Well . . .

CHIZUKO: You don't like it here? You mean you . . .

KAORU [quickly]: No-no. Don't think me ungrateful. I mean, right now, I don't have anything to offer.

CHIZUKO: You give only what you can.

[KAORU is silent.]

CHIZUKO [continuing]: We like you. All of us. As a family, well, the children are quarrelsome sometimes but . . .

KAORU: They're good kids. You should be proud.

CHIZUKO: They're good kids. They're not mean . . . no trouble.

KAORU: You should be proud.

CHIZUKO: I . . . I promise to do my best to make it . . . nice for you. *[with some discomfort]* I know I'm not an easy woman to get along with – being so set in my ways.

KAORU: You're a fine person.

CHIZUKO *[desperately]*: I'm so tired. Sometimes I wish . . .

KAORU: Chizuko-san, this is not a day to be so solemn. Look, the sun is shining, birds are singing. . . .

CHIZUKO *[depressed at not getting through]*: Yes.

KAORU: Don't worry. Everything's going to be all right. Another couple of days and the weeding will be done. I think you'll have a great harvest.

CHIZUKO: If the weather holds.

KAORU: It will. Nakamura-san said it'll be a mild winter. His son heard it over the radio.

CHIZUKO: They have a radio?

KAORU: A crystal set. Maybe I can get one for Ichiro to assemble. Then you . . . we can get the weather reports.

CHIZUKO: Ichiro can do that?

KAORU: Sure, he can. He's smart.

CHIZUKO *[brightening]*: After harvest, we can buy a small radio for everyone to enjoy. We can listen to it in the evenings.

KAORU: That will be nice.

CHIZUKO: Maybe we can get a bicycle for Tomu. A used one.

> *[AKI enters from stage left. She wears schoolclothes and carries books. She comes bounding in.]*

AKI: A used what? Are we buying something? Hi!

> *[CHIZUKO pulls the scarf from her neck and stuffs it into her pocket.]*

KAORU: Hello there, Aki-chan.

CHIZUKO: Where are your brothers, Aki?

AKI: They're coming.

CHIZUKO: You got home early today.

AKI: I took a shortcut.

KAORU [laughing]: Your face is flushed.

AKI: I ran all the way.

CHIZUKO: Go change your clothes.

> [KAORU heads toward the shed, unbuttoning his shirt,
> preparing to start back into town.]

AKI: Where are you going?

KAORU: Well, we quit for the day and I thought I'd go to (town) . . .

CHIZUKO: Maybe this is a good time to repair the barn. There's a big hole in the north wall.

AKI: That's been there since before Papa died.

CHIZUKO: Change your clothes, Aki.

KAORU: Yes, I noticed it. I'll fix it. Winter's coming and the wind will blow right through.

> [CHIZUKO pushes AKI toward the house. AKI goes. ICHIRO
> and TOMU enter from the left. KAORU, toolbox in hand,
> sees them.]

KAORU [continuing]: Hello, boys, how's school? Math any easier?

TOMU: Lots easier.

ICHIRO [overlapping]: Not bad, not bad.

TOMU [to CHIZUKO]: Did Aki get home?

CHIZUKO: She's here. What's the matter with you, Ichiro? I told you always to walk together. You're the oldest and . . .

TOMU: She ran away from us, Ma.

> [KAORU exits to the right. The boys and CHIZUKO enter
> the house.]

ICHIRO: God, she's a big girl now. I can't watch her all the time.

CHIZUKO: I want you to walk together. I told you that. Anything can happen.

ICHIRO: Like what?

CHIZUKO: Anything. Snakes, scorpions . . .

ICHIRO: Snakes? Scorpions?

TOMU: How about spiders and lizards?

ICHIRO *[overlapping]*: And man-eating ants.

AKI *[offstage, reading]*: "A heavy heart, Beloved, have I borne / From year to year until I saw thy face . . ."

> *[TOMU and ICHIRO groan and exit through the upstage door. AKI continues reading as the light slowly fades on CHIZUKO taking the scarf from her pocket and looking at it.]*

AKI *[continuing]*: "And sorrow after sorrow took the place / Of all those natural joys as lightly worn."

> *[Fade out]*

ACT II
Scene ii

November, early evening

ON RISE: *KAORU, ICHIRO, and TOMU sharpen tools downstage. The sun is setting, there is an orange glow that slowly turns dark as the scene progresses.*

TOMU *[to KAORU]*: Is this sharp enough?

KAORU *[feeling the edge]*: Just a little more. On the angle.

ICHIRO *[teasing]*: That'll cut butter real good. In summer. *[He takes the hoe from TOMU.]* Here, I'll do it.

> *[NAKAMURA enters from stage left.]*

TOMU *[imitating NAKAMURA]*: Haro-haro, Nakamura-san.

NAKAMURA: Haro-haro. You can stop now. Sun's gone down, you know.

KAORU: *[ha-ha]* How you been?

NAKAMURA: Caught it from Chizuko-san, eh? I didn't know work was catching.

KAORU: Just honing tools for tomorrow.

NAKAMURA: Go easy. You'll be all worn out by harvest time.

> *[AKI enters.]*

NAKAMURA: Oh, Aki-chan.

AKI: Hello, *Oji*-san.

KAORU *[to AKI]*: Go in and start. I'll be there soon.

AKI: Okay. *[She enters the shed and prepares to practice.]*

NAKAMURA *[watching her pass him]*: They grow up before you know it, eh?

KAORU: Before you know it.

NAKAMURA: Yeah. Before you know it. Next year my son—the oldest—be twenty. If it was the old country, I'd think about . . . about giving him a parcel of land. . . . *[He laughs dourly.]*

NAKAMURA *[continuing]*: Well, maybe in a couple of years I can get together a down payment for . . . maybe ten acres. Put it in his name . . .

[AKI starts practicing. NAKAMURA is surprised.]

NAKAMURA *[continuing]*: Ah! She can play the violin!

ICHIRO: No, she can't.

KAORU: Well, I've been trying to teach her.

NAKAMURA: Oh, yeah?

KAORU: She's not a good player, but she's smart. She . . .

ICHIRO *[to TOMU]*: Let's get out of here.

TOMU *[his finger in his ear]*: Yeah, let's go to Billy's.

[They exit left.]

NAKAMURA: Chizuko's kids are all smart. Nice boys. Nice family.

[CHIZUKO appears in the yard with a basket of laundry. NAKAMURA sees her first.]

NAKAMURA *[continuing]*: Ah! Chizuko-san! Nice, eh? Nice evening. I'm enjoying the nice music.

CHIZUKO: She's just a beginner. Sometimes I wish I were deaf.

[AKI hits some sour notes.]

NAKAMURA: You know, Chizuko-san, when I first saw him in town—no job, nothing—just a suitcase and a violin—I felt sorry for him, then I thought of (you) . . .

CHIZUKO: Nakamura-san, did you . . . How is your family?

NAKAMURA: Fine. Fine.

[AKI's playing grows worse. She tries to get KAORU's attention. NAKAMURA winces and prepares to leave.]

NAKAMURA [*continuing*]: Well, I better . . . Eh! I almost forgot what I came for. Chizuko-san, I'm irrigating tomorrow. You want water too? Might as well order same time, eh?

CHIZUKO: Well . . .

NAKAMURA: No trouble for me.

CHIZUKO: Kaoru-san, what do you think?

KAORU: Maybe we should finish thinning first.

CHIZUKO: Yes. We'll wait a few days. Thank you anyway.

KAORU [*hearing the bad music*]: I'd better get in there.

[*AKI stops playing.*]

NAKAMURA: Ah . . . that's better.

KAORU [*in the shed, softly*]: You'll drive our visitors away with your playing.

AKI: Why, thank you sir.

CHIZUKO [*to NAKAMURA*]: It was nice of you to ask.

NAKAMURA: Oh. Yeah. It's all right.

CHIZUKO: Would you like a cup of tea?

NAKAMURA: Tea? No-no. No tea [*heh-heh*].

[*There's an awkward silence.*]

NAKAMURA [*continuing*]: Aki-chan's growing up fast, eh?

CHIZUKO: No, not so.

NAKAMURA: They're like weeds. You don't give them water, but they grow anyway.

CHIZUKO: That's true.

NAKAMURA: Pretty soon the yard be full of young men. Maybe my sons come too, eh? Chizuko-san, you chase them out with your broom, eh? [*He laughs heartily, but CHIZUKO doesn't find it funny.*] I better be going. Well . . . good night. You're sure about the water, eh?

CHIZUKO: I'm sure. Good night.

NAKAMURA: Good night. Good night. [*He exits.*]

CHIZUKO [*calling to KAORU*]: Kaoru-san, you want . . . would you like tea?

KAORU [*calling out*]: No tea, thank you.

[Soft laughter from the shed as light fades.]

[Fade out]

ACT II
Scene iii

A few months later, winter night

ON RISE: The lantern shines dimly in the Sakata kitchen. ICHIRO reads at the table. TOMU has already retired.

AKI practices in Kaoru's shed. There is a bottle of wine and a glass on an upturned crate. KAORU sits on the cot listening.

CHIZUKO sweeps the floor, opening the door to sweep out the dust. The music stops. CHIZUKO steps to the window. She returns to the table to work out some figures.

The music starts again.

ICHIRO *[looking at CHIZUKO]*: So long as she keeps playing, eh Ma?

CHIZUKO: What do you mean?

ICHIRO: Want me to talk to her?

CHIZUKO: About what?

ICHIRO: Okay.

[ICHIRO shakes his head and retires. Light fades in the kitchen and turns up in the shed.]

[KAORU watches AKI. It's been a bad day for both. AKI hits a wrong note.]

KAORU *[pointing to the music sheet]*: See this symbol? That's a sharp. All the Fs are sharped. I told you that.

AKI: I know. I forgot.

KAORU: That's the third time.

AKI *[sarcastically]*: Sorry!

KAORU: Now. The last three measures again.

AKI: The last three?

KAORU: You have a hearing problem? That's what I said.

AKI [muttering]: The last three . . .

> [She plays and makes another error. KAORU jumps to his feet.]

KAORU: Those are eighth notes. One-half of a quarter. Quarters go: [He taps.] one, two, three, four. Eighths: one and two and . . . You should know this.

> [AKI starts over, making another error.]

KAORU [continuing]: Sharp! Sharp! [He tears the violin from her.] Here!

> [AKI cries softly. KAORU reconsiders.]

KAORU [continuing]: I'm sorry, Aki-chan. I guess I'm tired. Here. Lie down.

> [AKI is sullen and hesitant.]

KAORU [continuing]: Go on. Lie down. Close your eyes. Now this is how it should sound.

> [He plays the exercise. He taps her knee with the bow. He plays a beautiful gypsy song.]

KAORU [continuing]: Think of yourself as the violin. Feel the music coming from inside. Deep inside. Listen to it. Does it tell you what you want to hear?

AKI: Not my music.

KAORU [laughing]: No, not yet. You see, this instrument is not so different from people. The songs that come from us depend on how we are touched. If you want sweet music, you must coax and stroke . . . coax and stroke.

AKI: I can't do it.

KAORU: Yes, you can. If you hear it and feel it, then it's only a matter of time. I know you can do it. Tell me why you want to play this, Aki-chan.

AKI: I don't *want* to play it.

KAORU [He stops playing.]: Oh. [pause] All right.

AKI: Learning and practicing destroys all the . . . I just want to hear it and feel the romance and mystery of that other world out there. I want to be a part of it.

KAORU: When you learn to play this, you'll always be a part of it.

AKI: How long will it take?

KAORU: Depends on *you*.

AKI: Five years?

KAORU: More than that.

AKI: Ten? Twenty?

KAORU: Maybe. Maybe more. Depends on how hard you want to work.

AKI: I don't want to work twenty years and just be a second-rate fiddler.

KAORU [*suddenly depressed*]: I see.

AKI: It's only for fun anyway, isn't it?

KAORU: That's right.

AKI: Then why do we have to be so . . . so serious? Why do we have to be so strict?

KAORU: That's right. What does it matter?

AKI: I love the book you gave me.

KAORU [*putting the violin away*]: That's good.

[*AKI takes the book from her pocket.*]

AKI: Listen, Kaoru-san: "The face of all the world is changed, I think / Since first I heard the footsteps of thy soul / Move still, oh, still, beside me, as they (stole) . . ." Do you like it?

KAORU: We'll stop now.

AKI: Will we practice again?

KAORU: If you like. Next week.

[*KAORU does not turn. AKI waits. She finally leaves.*]

[*Fade out*]

ACT II
Scene iv

Shortly after

ON RISE: *Sakata kitchen. CHIZUKO sits at the table deep in thought.*

AKI, after waiting in the dark thinking, finally enters the kitchen. She carefully closes the door.

AKI: Oh. You're still up.

CHIZUKO [*casually*]: That was a long lesson.

AKI [*trying to get away*]: Un-hunh.

CHIZUKO: I didn't hear you play much tonight.

AKI: We talked. I guess he knows I'll never be a good player, so we just talked. About music. That's just as important.

CHIZUKO: For playing the violin?

AKI: We do have to talk, you know.

CHIZUKO: About what?

AKI: Things. *[She starts for the bedroom.]*

CHIZUKO: What kind of things?

AKI *[impatiently]*: Music. Composers. What kind of music they write. Why. Where they come from. We talk about other things too. Books, writers. He's been to high school, you know. Why do you ask?

CHIZUKO: I . . . I don't like you staying up so late. *[She folds clothes.]* You have a hard time in the morning . . . getting up. You have a hard . . . You know that!

AKI: Tomorrow's Saturday!

CHIZUKO: Shhh!

AKI: Then why do I have to go to bed so early?

CHIZUKO: The boys have to get up and work tomorrow. It's not fair to them.

AKI: *They* don't care!

CHIZUKO: Kaoru-san works tomorrow too.

AKI: I know that.

CHIZUKO: Then you shouldn't keep him up so late.

AKI: I'm not keeping him up!

CHIZUKO: Shhh!

AKI: Well, if he wanted me to leave, he'd tell me.

CHIZUKO: He's too polite to tell you.

AKI: It's not that late anyway. God, he's a grown man. He can stay up as long as he wants and still do your old work. Work-work-work. That's all you think about.

CHIZUKO *[warning]*: Aki . . .

AKI: Well, it's true. You're always telling me what to do and how to do it. You're always trying to tell everybody what to do around here.

CHIZUKO: I'm not trying to tell every(one) . . .

AKI: You're going to drive Kaoru-san away from here – bossing him around like that.

CHIZUKO: Watch how you talk to me.

AKI: Nobody likes that. Especially a man like him.

CHIZUKO: Enough. I'm not trying to tell every(one) . . .

AKI: Yes, you are! You're trying to control everything. It's a free country. If we want to talk, what's wrong with that?

CHIZUKO: You can talk in the kitchen.

AKI: We *can't* talk in the kitchen.

CHIZUKO *[looking innocent]*: Oh? Why?

AKI: Ma, you *know* why. Ichiro and Tomu sitting around all the time making all those cracks. And you sitting there listening and making those faces. I *know* those faces. Telling me what to say and when to say it . . . when I should shut up and . . .

CHIZUKO: You don't want me to listen? You saying things you don't want me to hear?

AKI: No! But I try to talk about . . . about . . . *things,* and there's Ichiro and you . . . I know what you're thinking. "How stupid; how dumb." Yes! I don't want you to hear what I say!

CHIZUKO: You think you're the only one with feelings? You think no one else has feelings they want to talk about?

AKI: Well, let them talk about them. I don't care. *[She starts for the bedroom.]*

CHIZUKO: You don't care!

AKI: I don't care who talks to who!

CHIZUKO: That's what I mean. You don't care about anyone but yourself. You don't care how anyone feels.

AKI *[turning back]*: You mean *you?*

CHIZUKO: I mean other people! How do you think it looks: you all the time in a man's room?

AKI: I don't care how it looks.

CHIZUKO *[lowering her voice]*: I'm not saying you're doing anything wrong. I'm saying . . .

AKI: You're saying *you* don't like it. No one else cares. You're saying . . .

CHIZUKO: Aki-chan. It's not like that. You don't understand. Kaoru-san is a grown man.

AKI: I just told you that.

CHIZUKO: He's twice your age.

AKI: He is not.

CHIZUKO: If you want a friend to talk to, find someone your age who can understand you.

AKI: Who? Name me one.

CHIZUKO: There's lots of boys *and* girls. Friend doesn't have to be a grown man. Nakamura-san has two sons.

AKI: Hunh!

CHIZUKO: There's Billy.

AKI: He's a baby.

CHIZUKO: He's your age.

AKI: You think he understands me? You don't even know what I'm talking about, do you.

CHIZUKO: Kaoru-san is old (enough) . . .

AKI: He's not twice my age. He's not old enough to be my father, and if he were, I don't care!

CHIZUKO: I know you don't care . . . right now. I'm just saying you shouldn't let your emotions run away with you.

AKI: Emotions? What do you know about emotions? You don't have any.

CHIZUKO *[overlapping]*: How can you say that?

AKI: I'm not going to live like you. I'm not going to live all tied up in knots like you: afraid of what people say, afraid of spending money, afraid of laughing, afraid (of) . . .

CHIZUKO: Do you understand my problems? Do you think just once about *my* prob(lems) . . .

AKI: Afraid you're going to love someone. Afraid (you) . . .

CHIZUKO: I have lots to worry about. I got to see you have enough to eat, give you an education, see you're dressed right . . . decent, so people won't say, "Those kids don't have a father." See you're not left with debts, like what happened to me. See you don't make a mess (of your life). . . .

AKI: I know you work hard. I'm grateful. But I can't . . . you can't tell me how to feel or how to live or . . .

CHIZUKO: I don't want you to get hurt, Aki.

AKI: It's *my* life!

CHIZUKO: Your life is my life. We're one.

AKI: No! We're not! We're not the same!

CHIZUKO: I mean when you hurt, I hurt.

AKI: That's not true. I hurt when I see how you live: dead! Nothing to look forward to. You think that's good. You want me to live like that. Well, I won't. I want more.

CHIZUKO: You will have more. Things are not like they were for me. You're young. You have lots to look forward to. I just don't (want) . . .

AKI: God, you never give up.

CHIZUKO: Someone more your age . . .

AKI [*It dawns on her.*]: You're jealous!

CHIZUKO: Jealous?

AKI: Yes, because he . . .

CHIZUKO: What're you talking about?

AKI: Yes, because he pays attention to (me) . . .

CHIZUKO: That's ridiculous! He likes all of us! He told me!

AKI: It's more!

CHIZUKO [*screaming*]: No! No more!

> [*ICHIRO enters from the bedroom. Both women stop immediately.*]

ICHIRO: Go to bed, Aki!

> [*AKI exits. ICHIRO stands looking at CHIZUKO, who avoids his eyes.*]
>
> [*We hear Kaoru's violin ("Two Guitars"), and we know he also does not sleep.*]
>
> [*Fade out*]

ACT II
Scene v

A spring evening

ON RISE: *Interior of KAORU's quarters. A bottle of wine and a small glass sit on an upturned crate. The rest of the stage is dark.*

AKI is practicing. KAORU lies on the cot after a hard day's work. He appears to be listening, keeping time with his foot.

AKI's playing is improved but not much. She stops momentarily.

KAORU: Go on. Continue.

[AKI resumes. KAORU looks at the ceiling and tries to keep awake.]

KAORU *[continuing]*: Getting old. Tired . . . *[He falls asleep.]*

AKI watches KAORU and her playing slows and finally stops. She sits on the floor, opens the violin case, and puts the violin away, holding it a moment first.]

AKI: "My cricket chirps against thy mandolin. / Hush, call no echo up in further proof / Of desolation! there's a voice within / That weeps . . . as thou must sing . . . alone, aloof." (E. B. Browning, *Sonnets from the Portuguese*)

KAORU: You know so little about life. What do you learn from those words?

[KAORU sits up and pours a drink.]

KAORU *[continuing]*: Love is beautiful?

AKI: Of course.

KAORU *[teasing]*: Tell me about it. What do you know about it?

AKI: Oh . . . love is . . . Oh, you wake up in the morning knowing good things are going to happen. It's making . . . making people like me—nobodies—feel special. You *know* there's a heart beating inside, pumping, singing, and you *know* this is what people are born to feel. Everyone. It's eternal and forever (and) . . .

KAORU: *[ho-ho]* So that's what it is: beating and singing and eternal and forever.

AKI: Don't laugh at me.

KAORU: Let me tell you something, Aki. Loves doesn't always sing. Sometimes it pulls you to the bottom. It drags everything along with it. Then all sense of right or wrong goes too.

AKI: I don't believe you.

KAORU: It turns sour and pretty soon you start enjoying the sick smell of it.

AKI: That's not love. Love isn't like that.

KAORU: I loved someone once. *[He drinks.]* Her name was Yoko. She didn't want me to leave. She begged me to stay.

AKI *[angry and jealous]*: Well, why'd you leave? Why didn't you stay with her?

KAORU: She wouldn't marry me.

AKI: Well, why not? If she loved you, why wouldn't she marry you?

KAORU: It's a long story. She had a husband. She had a family.

AKI: That's awful!

KAORU: Things like that happen sometimes.

AKI: That's no excuse!

KAORU: Sometimes you meet someone you can love at the wrong time. Too late. She was already married.

AKI: You shouldn't have let that happen!

KAORU: I didn't try to make it happen. It just did, that's all. It's something *[heh]* you wouldn't understand. Maybe one day it will happen to you. Maybe you'll understand then.

AKI: Never! I wouldn't let it!

KAORU: What does it matter? It's past. Gone. *[He drinks.]* I've never been long with a woman. Even my mother left me. Everytime I saw a pretty lady, I thought maybe she was my mother. I thought she was waiting for me somewhere. Somehow I wouldn't believe she was dead.

AKI: Was she?

KAORU: Who knows? Maybe she did die. Maybe she ran away with someone. No one talked about it.

AKI *[sympathetically]*: Oh . . . Kaoru-san.

KAORU: I never stayed long in one place.

AKI: But you will here, won't you?

KAORU: Always wandering away; always running. With Yoko was the longest.

AKI: But she was no good (for you). . . .

KAORU: She was warm . . . sweet . . . she was—you're right—no good. *[He buries his head in his hands.]* Too much wine. I'm a little drunk. *[He sits on the cot.]*

[*Aki watches him for a moment, then sits on the cot and slowly, tentatively puts her arm around him. Kaoru shrugs her off.*]

Kaoru [*continuing*]: Don't.

[*Aki persists.*]

Kaoru [*continuing*]: Don't do that.

[*Aki will not let him go. His vision blurs; he sees Aki's innocent longing and responds to her embrace. They kiss and hold for a long moment before Kaoru puts her down on the cot. The embrace grows sensual.*]

[*Chizuko, who has been sitting in the kitchen, gets up and walks to the shed. She listens for sounds of music and talking, and not hearing any, she flings open the door.*]

Chizuko: What's this! What are you doing?

[*Kaoru and Aki jump apart.*]

Kaoru: Chizuko-san . . .

Chizuko [*overlapping, to Aki*]: Get in the house. [*She pushes Aki out.*]

Aki: Mama . . .

Kaoru: Chizuko-san, please let me explain. Please . . .

Chizuko: "Please-please-please." Don't beg now! Pack your things and get out now! [*She pulls shirts and things off pegs and throws them on the bed.*]

Kaoru: Chizuko-san!

Aki [*overlapping*]: Mama! Don't!

[*Chizuko picks up the violin case, but Kaoru prevents her from throwing it. There is pandemonium.*]

Kaoru [*trying to hold her*]: Chizu(ko-san) . . .

Chizuko: Don't touch me! Don't call my name!

Kaoru: Calm down. Please calm down.

Chizuko: You thought you could fool me. You . . . violated my trust. You violated my daugh(ter) . . .

Kaoru: Vio . . . ? I did nothing. Believe me, I did nothing.

Aki: Nothing, Ma. Nothing!

Chizuko: Get in the house!

AKI: It's not his fault!

CHIZUKO: I'll fix you. I'll get the police! You'll never work here (anymore). . . .

KAORU: Be reasonable. Let's talk this over.

CHIZUKO: I said out! Tonight! Now! *[She pulls AKI downstage.]*

AKI *[balking]*: Mama! Don't do this to us!

CHIZUKO: "Us?" What is "us"?

KAORU: Believe me. I meant no harm. . . .

CHIZUKO: What did you do to *me?*

AKI: I'm sorry, Mama. It was my fault. All of it. I did it. I started it. It was me, Mama. Blame me.

CHIZUKO: I know his kind, Aki. He preys on women with his talk . . . his sweet talk and gifts. *[She tries to touch AKI but AKI draws away.]* That's what I tried to tell you. How many women do you think he's lured with his . . . his sweet . . . Little country girls like you.

KAORU: I've made no pretenses. From the beginning I told you . . .

> *[CHIZUKO stops him before he says the terrible words that prove how foolish she was to dream.]*

CHIZUKO: I trusted you. I trusted you.

KAORU: I didn't betray that trust. Tonight I . . . I had too much to drink. I know that's no ex(cuse) . . .

CHIZUKO: Get out.

KAORU: I have no money.

CHIZUKO: I'll give you money!

> *[She starts toward the house, dragging AKI with her.]*

AKI: Don't! Don't, Mama, I love him!

> *[CHIZUKO stops at the word love.]*

CHIZUKO: Don't say that. Don't say that word!

AKI: I do. I love him.

CHIZUKO: And do you think this . . . this old man loves you?

> *[AKI looks at KAORU. He avoids her eyes.]*

CHIZUKO *[continuing]*: He doesn't know the meaning of the word. I know his kind. Where do you think he goes on his days off? To women! he goes to women, Aki!

AKI: If you send him away, I'll go with him.

CHIZUKO: You don't know what you're saying.

AKI: I will. I'll go with him.

> *[She runs to KAORU and holds his arm. KAORU reacts, drawing away.]*

CHIZUKO *[pulling AKI away]*: You know what you're asking for? From town to town . . . no roots . . . no home . . . nothing. Maybe one day, he'll get tired of you . . . throw you out . . . leave you in some dirty hotel for another fool woman. Think, Aki. And you'll come crawling ho(me) . . .

AKI: I'll never come home! I'll never come back to you! You're not a mother. You're a witch!

> *[KAORU goes back to his quarters and starts packing.]*

CHIZUKO: Witch? Who you calling witch? Me who sacrificed everything for you?

AKI: You didn't sacrifice for me.

CHIZUKO: No? No? You think I like this life? You think I *like* grubbing in dirt and manure (and) . . .

AKI: That's the only way you know to live. You don't want to change your life.

CHIZUKO: You believe that? You believe this is all I want? That I lived with a man I hardly knew, didn't understand, didn't respect because (I) . . .

AKI: You didn't love him! You didn't love him, did you?

CHIZUKO: How could I? How could I love, when all the time I was keeping our heads above water. Single-handed! Yes! While he was still alive, until the merciful day he drowned! Growing old before I was ready . . . dying before I ever lived. . . .

AKI: Then you've never loved. Then you don't know anything about love.

CHIZUKO: I do! *You* don't know! What do you know about my feelings?

AKI: I know, and I don't want to stick around to be the kind of woman you are.

CHIZUKO *[in a towering rage]*: *[Anngh!]* Go then. Go! Go! You'll find out. And when things get rough, remember tonight!

AKI: I'll never forget tonight.

CHIZUKO: You think you know all the answers. You think everything's so simple. You haven't tasted pain yet. You'll find out.

AKI: So I'll find out! *[She runs to the house.]*

CHIZUKO: Aki . . .

AKI: Leave me alone!

> [*AKI slams the door behind her. CHIZUKO is stunned. She sits on a bench until ICHIRO comes out (in the next scene).*]

> [*Fade out*]

ACT II
Scene vi

Immediately after

ON RISE: *Awakened by the sound of angry voices, ICHIRO, in pajamas, enters from the bedroom. He peers through the screen door.*

ICHIRO: You all right, Ma?

> [*CHIZUKO enters the kitchen.*]

CHIZUKO: Everything went wrong. Get the money jar.

ICHIRO: What?

CHIZUKO: Kaoru-san's leaving.

ICHIRO: What happened?

CHIZUKO: I don't know. I don't know what happened. Suddenly . . . everything happened and . . . and he's leaving us.

ICHIRO [*with regret*]: Ahh!

CHIZUKO: Aki too.

ICHIRO: Aki? Goddam kid.

> [*TOMU enters. He wears pajamas. He rubs his sleepy eyes.*]

CHIZUKO: I don't what happened. Suddenly . . . Ichiro, what went wrong? She's going with him. How can things turn so bad?

TOMU: What turned bad? What happened to Aki? Where's she going?

ICHIRO: She's going with him. That stupid brat!

TOMU: Why?

ICHIRO: Never mind why.

TOMU: What's going on?

CHIZUKO: Get the money. I have to give them money.

TOMU: Don't let her go, Ma.

CHIZUKO: She wants to. We have to let her go.

TOMU: You can stop her, Ma. Stop her!

CHIZUKO: I can't. I can't anymore.

ICHIRO: Never mind. Give them money and let them go.

[ICHIRO gets the money jar.]

TOMU: Ma, stop her. Stop her! *[He starts to the door.]* Aki!

ICHIRO *[grabbing him]*: Get back here, dammit!

CHIZUKO: Don't get mad. Let's not fight anymore.

ICHIRO *[counting the money]*: I knew what was going on; I should have knocked some sense . . .

CHIZUKO: No. If . . . no. I was thinking of myself all the time. I was thinking of the farm. It was easier with a man helping. I was thinking, I'm getting old . . . tired.

TOMU: Why can't they both stay then?

CHIZUKO: That's not possible.

ICHIRO *[overlapping]*: Shut up, Tomu.

CHIZUKO: We can't stay here anymore. It'll be too hard for us.

ICHIRO: Don't worry, Ma. We can make it. I'll quit school (and) . . .

CHIZUKO: No. It's no good. We have to move.

TOMU: Ma . . .

CHIZUKO: You can't quit school.

ICHIRO: Where will we go? The crop . . .

CHIZUKO: After the harvest. I was thinking . . . maybe San Pedro.

ICHIRO: Where?

CHIZUKO: Terminal Island. I hear there's lots of Japanese there. And the canneries. You boys can get part-time work. After school. That way you don't miss school so much . . . like you been doing.

TOMU: We didn't miss any this year.

CHIZUKO: We sell everything. Maybe just keep the truck and the beds . . . and some furniture. Rent an apartment. How much should we give them?

ICHIRO: Just enough to get out of town.

CHIZUKO: Aki will need some too. Poor Aki.

ICHIRO: Don't waste sympathy, Ma. She asked for it. She's no good.

CHIZUKO: She's a good girl. She's not to blame.

TOMU: She's a good girl.

ICHIRO: She's a selfish brat. *[He finishes counting the money.]* This should be enough.

> *[CHIZUKO adds the rest of the bills.]*

ICHIRO *[continuing]*: That doesn't leave us much.

CHIZUKO: That's all right. We can get credit at the store. Ishi-san will give us credit.

> *[AKI comes out of the bedroom with her clothes in a pillowcase.]*

ICHIRO: You spoiled everything for everybody.

> *[ICHIRO follows AKI downstage hoping to say a few more things, but he sees KAORU waiting with his violin case and bag, and he stops. He slams the money on the bench.]*

ICHIRO *[continuing]*: Here. Give him that.

> *[AKI gives KAORU the money. KAORU looks at it and slips it in his pocket. AKI takes his arm preparing to leave with him.]*

KAORU *[gently detaining her]*: I can't take you with me; you can't come with me. You know that, don't you?

AKI: But I have to! I can't stay here.

KAORU: You understand why, don't you?

AKI: But what will I do here all by myself? You got to take me. Please take me with you.

KAORU: I can't. You know why.

AKI: Because you don't love me?

> *[KAORU smiles gently.]*

AKI *[continuing]*: Please take me . . . take me. *[She tries to embrace him, but he will not permit it.]* I'm going to die, Kaoru-san.

KAORU *[firmly]*: No, you won't.

AKI: Take me . . .

KAORU: Now go inside and apologize to your mother. Try to explain. . . .

AKI: She won't understand. She won't take me back. Please . . .

KAORU: She will take you back. In time you'll both forget.

AKI: I'll remember all my life. *[She tries to embrace him.]*

KAORU *[stopping her]*: You must stop this.

AKI: Please . . .

KAORU: Stop it!

AKI *[after a moment]*: What will you do? Where will you go?

KAORU: I don't know. First to the bus depot. This time of year there'll be harvesting all along California. Grapes . . . peaches . . . Like she said: another town, another job.

AKI: Another woman?

KAORU: Another? *[He laughs.]* You're not a woman yet. When you grow up to be a real woman, I'll be an old man. You'll be all right. Now be a good girl and say good-bye.

> *[AKI embraces him, and he permits it without responding. She releases him.]*

AKI: Will you write me?

KAORU *[without turning]*: You know I can't do that.

> *[KAORU exits. AKI watches him go.]*

> *[TOMU comes from the house. He reaches in his pajama pocket and gives AKI some coins.]*

TOMU: Take this with you, Aki.

AKI: I'm not going.

TOMU: You're not going?

> *[We hear a truck approaching from a distance.]*

TOMU *[continuing]*: Ma! Did you hear that? She's not going!

> *[He runs in the house taking AKI with him.]*

ICHIRO: He won't take you, eh? You should have figured that out yourself.

> *[CHIZUKO hushes him.]*

> *[KAORU hails the truck.]*

KAORU [offstage]: Hey . . . hey. Stop.

[The truck stops.]

KAORU [continuing]: Can (you give me) a lift to town?

TRUCK DRIVER [offstage]: Hop in.

[AKI stands by the screen door until the truck starts again
and stays there until she can no longer hear it. Then she
slowly moves to the bedroom and light fades out.]

City Stories

The Sensei

There's a story I'd like to tell. It's been a long time on my mind, changing form, eras, situations, characters, but I think there's only one way to tell this story: the way it happened.

It starts back at the beginning of World War II, maybe earlier, but for my purpose this is where it begins. Some people may say everything begins much earlier; with each situation and relationship we bring along data from birth, and some say the data is accumulated through previous lives. My husband Jim would say, "Leave the thinking to the thinkers, Utako." So I'll get on with it.

When the United States and Japan entered into war, the Japanese and Japanese Americans living on the West Coast were shunted off to various internment centers in the more isolated areas of the United States. For security reasons, they said. I went to Poston, Arizona, with my family; I was seventeen then and very resentful of my loyalty being questioned and my rights being violated, but at seventeen, what could I do? A protest needs strong organization and that's one thing we Nisei (Japanese Americans) lacked.

Inside this particular camp, as in others (there were ten of them), there were many political factions: pro-America, pro-Japan, pro-rights, fence sitters, indifferents, and at least one pacifist. There was quite a bit of internal tension, rumors, blacklists, beatings, and a pro-Japan strike. Actually it wasn't pro-Japan. It was anti-informant. I attended this. We stayed up all night in block groups, block standards waving in the icy wind, Japanese military music blaring over the loudspeaker, campfires blazing. My friend (she was the pacifist) and I huddled together and sang ballads. Very conspiratorial.

About this time, the government decided to separate the pros from the cons. Questionnaires were passed to all American citizens, and somewhere in the middle of the list (numbers twenty-seven and twenty-eight), there were two important questions: Would you renounce all ties with Japan, and would you volunteer your services to the United States (in legalese)? The people were sorted on the basis of their answers. I said yes-yes; after all, what did I know about Japan, and what branch of service would take me? But my brother Toshio was a no-no.

It was hard on the old folks. They were brought up in the spirit of Yamato: patriotism and filial piety. Though the old folks weren't required to answer the questions, the government offered to repatriate those who wanted to return to Japan. These people, repatriates, and no-noes and yes-noes and no-yeses were sent to Tule Lake, California, to await transfer to Japan. Some went in family clans, some left their young folk, and some left their old folk. My brother Toshio went alone. It was hard on everybody.

There's where Toshio met Jim Morita, the man I was to marry later. Toshio used to write to me about life in Tule, the 6:00 A.M. calisthenics, Japanese language studies, the friends he'd made, the Morita clan in particular who were so kind to him, the extremists who shaved their heads, *banzai* meetings (*Banzai* is a battle cry; it means Hurray! or Long Live the Emperor!), beatings, and knifings. They stayed in Tule quite a while; there was a long waiting list and only one boat, the *Swedish Gripsholm*. Toshio wrote about contingents who left for Japan, how they wept. I sent candy bars, cookies, and once I saved up my clothing allowance and sent him a sweater. You know, my brother's keeper.

By the time war ended, we in other camps had gradually been processed (investigated and cleared) into the mainstream of outside life. We scattered all over: Chicago, New York, Cincinnati, Boston, but most of us returned to the West Coast. My family moved back to Los Angeles. There was a huge group left stranded in Tule. They too were processed and allowed to sift back. Toshio returned to us.

The Morita family went back to Walnut Creek in northern California where they'd farmed before. Only Jim came to Los Angeles to attend the university here. That's when I met him.

I wish I could tell you about our courtship—the joy, the pain. But that's not pertinent to my story. I'm glad we married before we had sense enough not to. We're both from Buddhist families, so we had a Buddhist wedding, and the reverend said he was so happy to unite two Buddhist families. Suddenly the awesome responsibility of family—generations from my womb—scared me and I wanted to cry. That's what I mean about getting married before I had sense enough. I wondered what Jim was thinking, but we were like in separate rooms.

The first years were rough. We got a small basement apartment for keeping the yard mowed. I worked at a shower-curtain factory hand-painting shower curtains—you've seen them: flamingos, palm fronds, sailboats. I've always loved to paint, and this was as close to it as I could get. Every four and a half months we scraped the barrel to meet nonresident fees at school. Jim's citizenship was revoked when he answered no-no to the questionnaire, and he did not qualify as a resident. His major was international relations, and his dream was to work in the reconstruction of Japan. Phoenix from the ashes.

We spent most of our weekends in our basement apartment playing penny-ante poker with Jim's colleagues who were also needy. Sometimes he'd go to the House, one of the dorms, for a big game. "I've got to make tuition," he'd say, and most of the time he'd get it. He's what they call a tight player. But Jim's very superstitious, and he could never go to these games without a smile and kiss from me. Sometimes I simply couldn't smile and kiss, and he'd say, "Well, I just won't go if you don't want me to. I'll just go on to bed." And he'd lie in the bed next to me (I'd have retired by then, sulky) with his coat and shoes on. That would make me laugh, and I'd smile and kiss him and watch him go off like a kid running to catch the ice-cream man. I said to myself, when we have money he will stop this. He needs the money.

Jim heard about Las Vegas from these boys at the House. They planned systems and worked out mathematical theories, and Jim would come home all excited and tell me about them. There was gambling around the clock, night lit like day, money flowing like water, free drinks, free breakfasts; we had to go.

It was winter. I cashed my fifty-dollar bonus check, and we agreed not to write checks or use the tuition money. I tucked an extra ten dollars in the secret compartment of my wallet. I'd also heard about Las Vegas, of people coming home broke and hungry and running out of gas the last mile and pushing the car home. This was before credit cards.

We lost most of our money at the gaudiest, plushest casino downtown, the Golden Nugget. There were only a few dollars left, so we went across the street to the Boulder Club, where dime and quarter bets were allowed. The clientele differed there—some of them looked like grizzled prospectors, refugees from a TV western. I sat at the Keno seats and bought a quarter card and pretended to mark numbers. They won't let you sit down unless you're playing the game. In a little while Jim came along and jerked his head, let's go home.

While we were walking to the door, Jim pulled my arm and said, "Look at the man at the water fountain." I looked. He was small and thin, Japanese, about forty or more. His face kind of hung on his neck like a rag on a peg. He was deeply tanned, with creases like gullies on his face, his hair was thinning, and his eyes were terribly tired. His two-color loafer jacket was faded and dirty; he looked like a strip of bent clay. "He asked me for money," Jim said.

"Did you give it to him?" I asked.

"Hell no. I didn't have any to give."

The man leaned over the fountain and took a long drink, and from where I stood I could hear the water rushing into his empty gullet.

We were maybe five miles out of town, driving in the cold glare of the desert sun when Jim spoke, "I can't get over it. A Japanese begging."

"Oh, please," I said irritably. This whole trip had been a pain—a pain in the pocketbook and a big pain in the ass. "Who can be responsible for all the Japanese the world over? Why, there must be thousands begging on the streets of Tokyo, or Hong Kong, or wherever. Besides, what could you do? You didn't have the money."

"I can't help thinking of him," Jim said and pulled the car over to the side. "I know him," he said.

I was shook up. "Why didn't you say so?" I asked.

"Well, I don't exactly know him, but I've seen him around Tule Lake. He was known as Kondo Sensei (*sensei* means master or teacher). At that time he was a Buddhist priest. He was a powerful man in camp—feared and respected. He had a big following. Fanatics. Some people called them his goon squad. They shaved their heads like the monks in Japan, and they moved in bands and terrorized people. Now look. I can't believe it. Begging . . ."

We turned back.

Jim found him at the Boulder Club still standing where we last saw him, leaning against the water fountain. We drove to a restaurant. I can't remember what we ate, but they were two-fifty dinners, all three of them. While we waited for our order, the sensei told how he hadn't eaten for three days nor had he slept for as long except to doze on his feet. He said he hadn't bathed for two weeks, and I believed him. He explained how he was on his way to Denver and stopped off to change trains and had become so fascinated by this town and the abundance and glitter of its money that he was compelled to stop for a day to study the situation. That was a month ago, and all his possessions were now pawned and he had nothing, not even self-respect, and ah, how low must a man sink before his senses return. If God would permit him one last chance to continue to Denver, he would never again falter in the face of temptation. All the while, he talked slowly with his eyes closed and seemed to catch mininaps between phrases. During one of these lulls, Jim mentioned how he remembered him as Kondo Sensei of Tule Lake. He didn't even open his eyes. "Yes, yes," he said, "and they are waiting for me in Denver." I wondered if it was the parish that waited, but it didn't seem proper to ask.

"Sensei," Jim said, "your family, your wife and children must be worried about you."

"Yes, yes, I must hurry on to Denver," he said, and, "So you were in Tule. Ah, yes, I remember the Moritas, fine people. Your father, yes, he was very active, was he not? He worked with the block council?"

"Well," Jim said, "you're probably thinking of some other Morita. My father worked in the kitchen." He gave a small laugh.

"Yes, that's right. A fine man." The sensei dozed off again.

Jim left us to see about cashing a check, and when he returned, he passed the sensei some money and offered to drive him to the Greyhound depot and buy his ticket for him. "I know your family is waiting for you," Jim said.

The sensei's hands fluttered like they'd drop off. "No-no-no," he said, "I wouldn't think of putting you to such trouble. You've done enough for me. When I get back to Denver I shall repay this money. You've rescued me as sure as if you'd plucked me from deep water. I shall never forget you, Mr. Morita. The depot is not far from here, and walking will keep me awake." There was a crystal tear in the mucus around his eyes.

Jim slipped him more money. He bowed deeply, and as we turned the corner, I saw him raise his arm in a forlorn salute. Jim asked me not to tell anyone about this encounter with the sensei. I guess he didn't want people laughing over it. I kept it to myself even though he got a lot of laughs talking about *my* friends.

We went to Vegas quite often after the first taste of being so close to so much money. During one of these junkets, Jim came rushing over to me. I was pumping the arm of one of those slot machines. If you stay at one machine long enough, it seems to get into a sort of frenzy and sometimes you can hit a jackpot. So, seven dollars on a nickel machine. It gave me something to do. "Let's get out of here," Jim whispered. "The sensei's here."

I didn't want to leave. I'd already dribbled two Dixie cups of nickels into this particular machine. They give you paper cups to use, and two dollars' worth of nickels doesn't quite fill one of them, and I didn't want to leave. "Oh, Jim," I was irritated, "he won't see us." And still pumping, I asked, "Where is he?" Jim jerked his head toward a blackjack table.

The sensei stood behind the seated players and watched the game. He kept his hands in his pockets, and they moved as though impatiently fingering coins. He looked better than when we first saw him – tidier, but his eyes still had that weary look. They say if you stare long enough, a person will eventually feel it; the sensei turned, then walked quickly away.

That was a number of years ago. We don't go to Vegas much now. If we were married in '48, and Jim went to school for four years, this sensei thing happened along '49 and '52. All that time I was painting shower curtains. Oh, it wasn't that bad. I did other things. Once I took a course in ceramics – Jim even bought me a potter's wheel and would have bought a kiln, but we couldn't cart it home. I studied anthropology too. You pay two-fifty for registration and you can take as many courses as you can bear. But it wasn't that good either; there were some bitter quarrels. And once Jim said that when he got through school he would no longer need me and he would shuck me like an old shoe. Machiavellian.

Jim got his B.A. and went to work for an importing firm as a stockboy. After a while he was made foreman and he had me quit my job. He said now I could paint anything I wanted, but you paint flamingos and palm fronds and sailboats for four years and you hardly want to hold a brush or remember the things you wanted to paint before. Something like spirit leaves, and you don't even remember that you once lay awake nights thinking about color and form and space. Maybe that's part of growing up. Maybe that's what people mean when they say you've matured – you've lost your dreams.

Jim got restless working in that stockroom, and after a couple of years, he opened a small record shop. He stayed with that three years and then sold out. It never seemed to work with his taking all his buddies out to lunch so often. He said that wasn't true; he would have left the business sooner or later because he couldn't stand the noise. All those teenagers, you know, and never buying.

Right now he's selling cars. It's been all right; he wears a suit and tie every day, and he usually has a pocketful of money. And he's among men. That seems to be important. They go off for a drink now and then, and they play liar's poker. That's a game that must have been invented by two people on a desert island with a hat full of money. It has something to do with bluffing about the serial numbers on currency, and the good thing is that you don't need a lot of equipment. Just money. But it's got to be genuine government issue.

He seems to be happy at this job, and we always have a good model car to use. Evenings he's often busy with clients, or poker, or a staff meeting. And he loves cars. This business is seasonal, of course. Sometimes the money is plentiful, but there's a long dry spell that's pretty rough just before the new models come out. I try to look out for these bad days, but there never seems to be enough surplus to tide us over in any but the most frugal style. When things get too rough, we pack a bag and take a trip for a few days to Ventura, where my brother Toshio now lives. He married a girl from there who didn't like Los Angeles.

I had just finished packing the old Gladstone for this trip to Ventura, and Jim was on the front-room floor fastening the straps on our bag, and we were laughing about the many times we'd packed it for Vegas and never opened it. We'd lose the money before we could register at a hotel. The front door was ajar because we'd been to and from the car. It was a soft September evening and a pale gray light came through the door. I heard a shuffle of feet on the rubber link mat we have outside. I saw only a silhouette, but believe it or not, I mean it had been seven or eight years, I knew who it was.

"Oh, Sensei," Jim said, bowing before he quite got to his feet. "My, my . . ."

The sensei bowed. "I have never forgotten you, Mr. Morita. I see you're planning a trip. I don't want to detain you."

Jim glanced at his watch. "We have a few minutes, Sir, please sit down," he said. I turned on the lights.

The sensei looked as if he had walked all the way from Vegas. His shoes were cracked and dusty, and his hat and coat were stained with sweat. It was the same or similar two-color coat he wore when we first saw him. He looked as though he'd lived on those paper bags tossed out by motorists.

"Make a sandwich for Sensei, Utako," Jim ordered, "and a cup of tea."

The sensei fluttered his hand as he did eight years ago. "No-no-no," he said, "you were just leaving for someplace. I won't detain you."

"We have a few minutes," Jim said. "My wife will make a sandwich for you."

I could hear them from the kitchen. The sensei asked Jim how things were with him. "Not bad," Jim said. "I'm in the car business now, and I have to see a client in half an hour. Then we plan to drive to Ventura." The sensei almost purred. He said that fate had been kind to a most deserving individual – the beautiful car, the lovely home, and weekend motor trips. Jim didn't explain the car was on loan, the house mortgage and furniture payments were in arrears. There was a painful pause before Jim reluctantly asked, "And how does it go with you, Sensei-san?"

It came pouring out – the troubles he'd had, the heartaches. Five, six years of bad luck. He'd gone into business with a partner, produce, in Anaheim. Yes, partnerships are bad. Two bosses, different goals, no good at all. The debt, the incredible debt this unscrupulous man incurred. The lying, the cheating . . . yes, bankrupt . . . had to dissolve the business. The anxieties, the terrible stress! Yes, even considered suicide; very seriously considered it. Oh, yes, a cardinal sin.

They both stopped talking when I walked in with the sandwich. I was glad, because I could see that Jim was looking a little uncomfortable. I pushed the sandwich under the sensei's long face.

"You should not have made it, Madam. You are too kind, far too kind for such a worthless fool," he swallowed the juices in his mouth. "I haven't eaten in over three days, and sleep . . . ," he passed a yearning look to our couch, "I haven't slept for as many nights. I have considered suicide."

I remembered the first time we'd met he'd also said he'd not eaten nor slept for three days and nights, and I wondered how many other people had heard this story unchanged and unchanging throughout those miserable years of the sensei's misfortune. I had the sympathy, but it was way deep inside of me, not ready to come out yet. "Perish forbid," I said.

Jim glanced at his watch. "Sensei," he said, "I don't want to rush you, but I have an appointment in a few minutes. May I drive you somewhere?"

"No-no," the sensei protested, "you have done too much already. I can catch a trolley. I came to Los Angeles to call on a friend, but he wasn't home. I'll try him again later. He isn't home now. I'll be all right. Excuse me for imposing my foolish self on you."

"Still," Jim persisted, "we must leave in a few minutes. I have this appointment, you see. It won't take long; you can wait in the car with my wife until I'm through. Then I'll drive you over to Japanese town, Little Tokyo. I'm sure you'll see someone you know there. Everyone turns out on Saturday nights."

The sensei sat quite still chewing his sandwich. He nodded slowly, and his eyes moved once more to our couch before he surrendered to Jim.

While we sat in the dark car waiting for Jim, I asked the sensei how he came to find us in this big city. We had moved several times since we gave our address to him years ago.

"Telephone book," he answered sullenly. I thought he might be mad at me for being so unfeeling earlier, and I felt real bad.

I tried again. "I hear Las Vegas has really grown since we used to go there. I understand they've extended the strip with lots of luxury hotels, and the shows they put on are fabulous. It must be quite a town."

He turned to life. "Ah, yes, yes," he said. "It's quite a town." He was still for a while, and as though he'd shuffled through his files and had come to a final analysis, he said again, "Yes, it's quite a town."

Sometimes I could kick myself for talking when silence is better observed, but it's like when you're with a fat person and you want to avoid the word *fat,* so everything comes out like elephant or gargantuan or monumental or something. So I kept right on. "You know, if all the hopes and dreams of those many people who go to Las Vegas were converted to units of energy, imagine what could be accomplished." I don't know why I was talking that way; I really didn't want to moralize. But I could see the sensei sweating all week at some miserable job, maybe washing dishes, only to lose his pay at the tables, and I knew the hopelessness he felt as the last of his money slipped away. All that energy.

"And all the tears that have stained the sleeves of men," the sensei said. "Still I love Las Vegas." That made me feel good.

Jim came back and asked, "I wasn't gone long, was I?" We both answered no together.

It was a short ride to Japanese town from there. I pointed out the landmarks: the Statler Hotel, the water and power building, city hall, the new police station. The sensei was polite. When we got to the fringe of Little Tokyo, he pressed Jim's shoulder and said, "Here, let me off here."

He got out of the car and bowed. "Thank you for your kindness," he said. He nearly stumbled on a piece of sidewalk litter, then walked on toward the lights of Little Tokyo. The Ginza Club, Miyako Hotel, Mikawaya—green, red, yellow, green, red, yellow—alternating, the colors blinked on the sensei's shapeless hat. He stopped, waited for a light to change, then disappeared in the pedestrian traffic.

Shirley Temple, Hotcha-cha

I met Jobo Endo at Kazawa, a winter resort near Karuizawa, the vacation spa of Japan. I had already been in Japan two years. I'd left Heber, California, at fourteen to further my education in my parents' homeland. It was the winter of 1939. Jobo had also come from America, from an obscure place called Inglewood on the outskirts of Los Angeles. His family were farmers like mine, and they had struck a good year and sent their only son to Japan. It was common practice with the Japanese living in America, to send their more promising children to Japan for an education. Because of the prevailing racial discrimination, the future of Japanese in America was pretty bleak.

I am one of two girls. My sister Momo is three years younger.

I was then boarding at Keisen, an all-girl high school in Tokyo, and spending summer and winter holidays in Shizuoka with the Kodamas. They were *tokoro-no-mono*, people from the same prefecture, and although we had been family friends for a long time, the Kodamas were city people in America and Mr. Kodama, an insurance man, had made a killing in something or other and had retired in Japan with a substantial income. They were childless, and I suspect I had become a surrogate daughter because they bought all my clothes and books, and they had selected the school I attended, and bought me gifts my father could not afford. They'd always prefaced these gifts with oblique references to my father, but I knew he was not as clever as Mr. Kodama; our life in America was always one of poverty. At first I tried to believe that my father finally drew money from that desert farm, but letters from home made it clear that nothing had changed.

It was hard for me in Japan. I'd been thrown into a class of my peers, first year in high school, and I had a lot of catching up to do. I had to wrestle with the language, the written and spoken word, plus the courses themselves, and all those ideograms that a stroke displaced meant a whole different thing. I spent all my time studying; I read everything: newspapers, novels, want ads, labels . . . everything.

That winter I had come back to Shizuoka wan and worn, and Mrs. Kodama suggested the trip to the snow country to take my mind off of studies. The Kodamas were somewhat different from the average Japanese couple; maybe because they'd spent so much time in America, maybe because they had no children of their own, they were closer than most. If, as I'd heard later, Mr. Kodama had kept a mistress in Tokyo, I would not have guessed it. I loved them in a way not unlike the way I loved my parents, but of course, my mother was special and not replaced for all her manipulations and obsessive frugality. I was always made to feel guilty about the Kodama gifts. Poor Momo did not enjoy such luxuries, my mother said, and she herself had not bought a pair of shoes in six years.

The Kodamas had taken me to the snows. I remember clearly how it happened. As it is everywhere in Japan, there was a crowd of people milling around in bright snow clothes. Looking at them—rich daughters in Paris outfits, handsome young men in turtlenecks—one wouldn't guess there was a poor working class in Japan or that there was a war going on with China. It could have been a resort in America except for the language. But I was bored. I'd come with two elderly people who spent most of their time in the inn. Also I did not ski.

Jobo was standing outside the lodge attending to his gear when I brushed by and nearly tripped over his skis. His friend—he'd come with three or four colleagues—gave me a cross look, and Jobo said, "Hey, watch it!"

I was startled because he'd spoken to me in English, and I thought I passed for a native Japanese.

"How did you know I spoke English?" I asked.

"You can't walk like *that* and expect to pass for a Japanese girl," he said. He smiled and winked. "These skis are my magic carpet. They take me away from . . . ," he waved his hand, "everything." I knew then that he too studied hard to keep up. But I could tell he was more a survivor than I. His friends looked annoyed by my intrusion, and as he slowly and meticulously waxed his skis, they grumbled and went up the slope without him.

We spent the afternoon together. I watched as his red snow cap, among hundreds like it, skimmed in and out against the green pines and white snow. He was magnificent.

It was the best winter I'd had. I hadn't used my English for two years, but as we talked, I could feel the language return to me, rolling on my tongue and moving through my throat. It was like renewing ties with a long-lost friend. The carefree language released feelings from deeper still and bound me to Jobo with delight and intimacy. It was like sharing a secret from all of Japan.

The Kodamas liked him too. In those days, boy and girl relationships were discouraged, but they indulged us. I was seventeen and Jobo, twenty-one.

We exchanged addresses. He was attending Waseda University, also in Tokyo, and he suggested we meet again, away from school, away from the Kodamas.

Although I didn't know it then, Japan, already into the Sino-Japanese war, was preparing for the bigger one. I was so involved in studying and becoming a native, I was unaware of what was happening in the country. Jobo was the light of that winter; he gave purpose to everything.

It was the Christmas my mother sent the Shirley Temple doll. All my childhood on that barren farm, I wanted a Shirley Temple doll. I wished for her on every Christmas, every birthday, but she never showed up. For that long time, Shirley Temple was a symbol of the American world: ruffles, bows, straight legs, large eyes, curly hair, Jell-O for dessert, the pursuit of happiness, all those things that separated me from white America. Now at seventeen, when I was too old for her, after I left the American me behind, she came to me.

My mother wrote: "Mie-chan, you've always wanted a Shirley Temple doll and though you're a little old for it now, I've prevailed upon your father to buy one for you." Implicit, another year without new shoes; something else put off.

I cried when I opened the package. Mrs. Kodama said I was too old for dolls. Mr. Kodama said, "If I had known, I'd have bought one long ago."

Shirley became my dearest friend. She sat at my desk, her knowing eyes reminded me of a secret love that sent my heart leaping. Sometimes when frustration and fatigue gnawed at my brain, her smile turned warm and, in a voice remarkably like my mother's, she called my name: "Mieko, Mieko . . ." Her unflagging smile assured me of a serene and confident future.

Jobo graduated the following spring. In his last year at Waseda his parents cut back his allowance. I knew this when our Saturday meetings changed from teahouses and noodle shops to a lamppost on the street, a stone bench in a park. Most of the time I took along my homework which Jobo helped me finish, and we would spend endless hours walking through gravel parkways, crowded department stores, never daring to touch except when jostled against each other by the crowd. His arm reached out to steady me then, and I felt the keen pleasure and security of his strong body.

On his graduation Jobo's parents sent a token gift, a small check, and a letter of congratulations and apology saying they knew he worked hard and they were very proud but could not afford more. He showed me a tiny gold tie clasp. "I guess I'm on my own now," he said and returned the clasp to his pocket.

Shortly after, he found a cheap apartment on the second floor, one room where he could sleep and cook his meals, and he got a job with the Japanese government translating letters and documents. After considerable hesitation ("I won't hurt you, Mie," he'd said), I consented to meet him at his apartment, and we left the inconvenience of park benches behind. I studied there, ate the meals he cooked, talked with him, and (it was the night he told me of his grave fear for the future) made love with him.

"Mie," he said, "if we're to see America again, we must go now."

That was in October. I still had another year in school, and neither of us had the fare. I started to cry. Jobo then said I should talk to the Kodamas and arrange for a loan, and we should take the necessary steps to leave Japan.

"Together?" I asked.

"We'll marry first, of course," he said.

"You'd marry me just to get back to America?"

"I'd marry you for any reason. You know I love you, don't you?" he said.

When I returned to Shizuoka that winter, I spoke to the Kodamas about Jobo's plan. They were shocked, but in their restrained way, they said they'd thought Jobo was a bit of an opportunist and that I should not make too much over this man. After all, what did we know of his background? And besides, Mrs. Kodama said, they already had a young man, a relative, a grandnephew, in mind for me, and they had planned to work out arrangements for a family meeting after I graduated. Mr. Kodama hastily pointed out that because they had no children of their own, they hoped this nephew and I would marry, come to live with them, and take over the family interests.

"I've already committed myself to Jobo," I said.

Mrs. Kodama grew quite agitated. "Mieko," she said, "these things are not determined on personal whim. We already have an understanding with your parents. Why do you think you came to live with us?"

"I see," I said, "I've been sold."

"Not true," Mr. Kodama said and went on to recommend we talk about it later when we were all more calm. Whatever, there was no hurry since spring was still a winter away, and as for returning to America, well, that would certainly have to wait until then.

Later I heard them whispering, Mr. Kodama saying, "*Shikata ga nai*. Love is love." Then, "Maybe it'll wear off by spring."

My mother wrote saying she could hardly believe that just last winter she had sent a doll to the same girl who spoke of marriage today and that I should remember I was still on the edge of childhood, emotions rampant, not ready to make such a serious decision, and that I should also not forget that the good Kodamas had my best interest in mind. "They've always loved you, Mieko," she wrote. No mention of contract; implicit, my obligations. In any case I should wait until after graduating before thinking of returning to America.

When I told Jobo all this, he grew very quiet. "It will be too late then," he said.

In spring the Kodamas gave me a small wedding reception in Shizuoka, replete with two sham *baishakunin*, matchmakers. At the time I wasn't sure I was pregnant, but I told them anyway, and they hastened to arrange this small wedding. It so happened I wasn't; I later explained this as a miscarriage because already I felt a coolness from them. Well, I can't complain. They gave me a wedding and let me go. True, under pressure, but they did let me go and with a certain grace.

Jobo and I started housekeeping in his second-floor apartment. And he was right, it was too late. With his salary, saving for fare back to America was impossible, and because of what I did to the Kodamas, I couldn't ask for money again. That didn't matter to me; I was happy with Jobo, playing his young wife (I was nineteen), still with my Shirley doll, who watched from the dresser as we made love on the tatami.

Jobo continued skiing when he could, but because of the increasing strain of war, traveling was curtailed and finally prohibited. Food was rationed from the beginning, and the rations grew smaller; there was hardly any place to go for recreation, and our first winter together, on the first snowfall of the season, Jobo simply sat at home and waxed his skis.

"We won't be going to the snows for a while, Jobo," I said.

"Someday, when this is over, we'll go back to Kazawa," he said.

That December Japan sent her planes to bomb the U.S. fleet in Pearl Harbor. All Jobo's fears had come to pass. We wept together the night we heard the news. We talked about our families in America; I held my Shirley, and the three of us went to bed. We clung together and Jobo said, "At least we have each other."

"And Shirley," I was thinking of my mother.

"Hotcha-cha," he said.

When I look back on those days, my mind blocks out the physical deprivation. And too, that was nothing compared to what was yet to come, and later when things got really bad, we spoke of those earlier days as "the good old days." In spite of short rations, the lack of everything imaginable, we were together and that was good. We'd heard of the awful things that were happening to our families in America, that all Japanese had been imprisoned behind barbed wire, and we began to speak of them as though they were already dead. "My mother was . . . ," I said. Jobo talked about his sisters Kiku and the younger Mary in the past tense too. We made a pact to survive. "We will live through this," we vowed, "and we will return to America and walk that good earth again."

Jobo, whose father's farm had apricot and fig trees, and five acres of berries, told me endless stories of how he would one day pick strawberries for me and drown them in fresh cream from the dairy not a quarter mile away. I saw the red berries bleeding into the white cream and tasted its fragrance. He spoke of the two eggs he'd always had for breakfast like two old friends he'd lost in the war. He said that when he returned, he would have those two eggs again, with bacon that crumbled to the touch, or a piece of pink ham maybe left over from dinner the night before. We spoke of food constantly—while rereading old letters from America we found casual references to food; while recycling a moth-eaten sweater, Jobo remarked it was the color of a ripe pear. I was knitting the yarn for a baby shawl. I was pregnant. I wondered how we would keep this baby alive, but Jobo said we must take only one day at a time.

That was in 1944. Japan was losing badly and soon the bombers came from America. Already we were required to limit the use of gas and electricity during certain hours of the day, but when the bombs fell, both services were shut off immediately. Coal and firewood were unavailable except through black market. The streets were picked clean of everything, every shred of burnable material for these emergency cookouts for our meager rations. Day after day we ate rice gruel with bits of potato or carrot, sometimes without the vegetables, sometimes without the rice. But we were still luckier than some.

One night incendiary bombs were dropped in a circle around Asakusa, fencing in the industrial center with a ring of fire. I was in my fourth month. When the alert sounded, I ran to the window. Explosions tore the sky and lit it an angry red. Heat from the fires struck my face. Sirens shrieked. In spite of the warning to keep inside, residents poured into the streets, crying for their trapped families. I thought of Jobo and panicked. Was he there on an official mission? My back gave out and I fell to the floor. My body turned numb. I remembered that Jobo had said if the bombs should strike our house while he was away, I should walk north and he would find me. My mind went cold and blank. I remained on the floor until Jobo came home.

I lost my baby that night. Jobo paid the doctor with his ration of rice.

While convalescing, an old neighbor who had clucked her tongue when she first heard of my pregnancy, and continued to cluck as I grew larger, came to help. Mrs. Domoto didn't look as underfed as the rest of us; her clothes were not as mean. All the neighbors remarked about this – these things came to our attention at the time. When Jobo brought her to see me she said, clucking again, "Better this way, Mie-san. Better. Too hard for children in this world."

In spite of her kindness, there was a cunning about Mrs. Domoto that made me uneasy, but I was unable to get on my feet, and she brought her own rice, and sometimes a little extra for us. Twice she brought some tiny pieces of salt fish. "You must get well," she said.

When I remember Mrs. Domoto, I get a weird feeling because there was something uncanny about her coming to us at a time when we needed help so desperately, and then moving on to Hiroshima almost immediately after.

She came for eight days. For three days she admired my Shirley. She stroked her fine legs and ran a dry wrinkled finger over her blue eyes. She touched the organdy tissue of her dress and felt the velvet polka dots. Her eyes turned upward as though she were recalling a dream. The fourth day, Mrs. Domoto offered a pound of rice for Shirley. I smiled weakly. On the fifth day she brought the first salt fish and made another offer. I shook my head. "Shirley is my contact with my mother," I explained.

"Mie-san," Mrs. Domoto said, "you must learn to survive. After all, this is only a doll. There's no more rice in the bin."

"Jobo will bring some home tonight."

"Your husband is growing very thin," she said. "I will bring you five pounds."

On the eighth day she came with the rice and the second fish, and when Jobo returned from work, she took my Shirley, wrapped her carefully in a *furoshiki*, bowed, and left. Neighbors told me later she went to join her daughter in Hiroshima. Jobo said he would make it up to me someday.

The city was bombed again the following day. The gas and electricity were shut off, and because I was too weak to go scavenging for firewood, we had nothing to cook with. And our apartment was bare. Piece by piece with each bombing we had burned everything we could spare. We were very hungry.

Jobo pretended to look for something to burn.

"There's nothing left," I said, and tried not to look at the skis that were leaning against a doorless cupboard. Jobo walked around the room once more and stopped in front of them. He ran his hand along the waxed surfaces. He started to laugh. We both laughed. We laughed so hard we cried. With all the waxing, the skis burned beautifully, and for the first time in years, we went to bed with our stomachs full.

About two weeks later, Mr. Kodama came to take me away from the city. He said he'd heard I was ill with a pregnancy, and it would be safer for me in Shizuoka. For the baby's sake, he said. I had to tell him once more that I'd lost the child. Tears came to his eyes then. He cried where I could not. "Ah, Mie-chan, *unn ga nai* . . ." He meant I had no luck.

He took me back with him, and there I never lacked for food even though the national condition worsened. Mr. Kodama had *unn*. And except for brief meetings, Jobo and I were separated until the end of the war.

Once near the end of the war, Mrs. Kodama packed a lunch and some supplies for Jobo, and I took a train to Tokyo. The Kodamas provided these treats for us maybe twice a year; they took care of everything: fare, a few tins of food, and some small items—a bar of soap, a used shirt, a *tenugui*, a washcloth.

It was a particularly muggy day and Jobo looked tired. The apartment was depressing; I had forgotten how small and dark and hot it was. I asked Jobo if we couldn't take our lunch to the park where we used to meet. He said it wasn't the same anymore; everything had changed.

"We'll pretend it's the same," I said. "We'll pretend there is no war and we're young and in love."

I hadn't realized what had happened while I'd been away. The plants and trees—stems burned by heat from the bombs, foliage picked clean by residents—struggled for life like the rest of us. Ragged children with bloated bellies lay listlessly on the dry grass. The scrappier ones lurked in the leafless shrubs and eyed us carefully.

"Who are they? Don't they belong to someone?" I asked.

Jobo shrugged. "They're all over the place. Orphans, I guess. People get killed in wars and a lot of them are parents," he said. He unwrapped our lunch and began to eat.

"Jobo, how can you?" I asked.

"What? How can I what?"

"Eat . . . with those hungry kids looking at you."

"Everyone in the country's hungry," he said and continued eating. "I can, same as you can behind the Kodama walls," he said.

While we talked, one little fellow sprinted forward and snatched a rice ball. "Now, you see?" Jobo said sullenly. "We should have stayed home."

The other children salivated and groaned as the bold one gulped down the stolen rice ball. I divided the lunch in half; rewrapped Jobo's portion and set my half on the bench.

Jobo said, "It's no use, Mie. It's too big. You can't fix it with a couple of rice balls."

I knew that, but at that moment I remembered my own lost baby and some other feelings rushed at me. The Jobo I didn't know frightened me, and I started to cry.

Jobo stalked away. We walked home in silence.

That night when I went to lay out the bed, I found a hairpin in the futon. My body went cold like the time of the Asakusa bombing. When you reach a certain level of despair, feelings become more or less the same. Later I was to find still another level, but at that time the same cold blankness squeezed my brain. I couldn't function; I couldn't talk. Jobo thought the children in the park had upset me, and he tried hard to make me forget, but toward the end of the evening he grew quite peeved. He said, "You come for one visit in six months, and you turn it into a wake."

The Kodamas were concerned because I spent a lot of time crying. Finally I had to confess what had happened, and Mr. Kodama said I should be realistic – after all, except for a few visits, Jobo had been without me for almost two years. I should understand that. Tokyo is full of beautiful hungry women, he said. With all that hunger and loneliness and the political chaos, who could be blamed? War was the culprit. Mrs. Kodama thought we should stop giving things to Jobo, but Mr. Kodama quickly said no, we couldn't do that. He advised me not to think of it as a betrayal – men were that way . . . different from women – and I shouldn't blame the other woman because while I had enough to eat here, there were many who didn't, and when there's nothing left to barter and perhaps children to feed, well, I should try to understand that too.

The war ended in August with Hiroshima, Nagasaki, and the atom bomb. I can't talk about that bomb because everytime I think about it, something happens to me, and if it's true that nothing goes to waste, I must wonder what this experience was for, what my own life is for, and confront all those thoughts that make the silent hours of our lives so unbearable. I want to cry then, the same tears I shed for Shirley, the same I shed over the hairpin in the futon, and it doesn't make sense.

After the war, the food situation got worse – if you can imagine that. Tokyo was closed to the refugees because of this and the housing shortage. I stayed for a while longer in Shizuoka, maybe not quite a year, then Jobo found an apartment, again on the second floor, in Hayama, a fishing village not far from Tokyo.

By that time we got word from our families in America. My father had died in an internment camp; my mother and Momo had relocated to Chicago, where my sister attended the university. My mother worked in a candy factory. She sent us candy bars and small items that were good for bartering.

In the evenings I stood by our window facing the sea and waited for the fishing boats to come in. Those of us whose men worked in the city rushed out to meet the boats and tried to buy fish. The fishermen were prohibited from selling outside the markets so that the full catch could reach the starving urban residents. I would take my candy bar, or a cup of sugar, or a small tin of meat, and the men pushed to wait on me.

Jobo's parents had relocated to Cleveland. His father worked in maintenance, janitorial work, and his two sisters, Kiku and Mary, had cushy office jobs. They sent us things my mother could not afford–clothes, towels, bedding, food. I was pregnant again, and Jobo's dad wrote concerned letters on what I should eat. He prescribed a diet for me: proteins, beef, chicken, fish – pork is not important, he said–vegetables, yellow and green, milk, cheese– leave out the sweets. Jobo is his line to immortality, he said. I took the Endo gifts to the city for trading.

At the railroad station, signs of the occupation were everywhere. Apple-cheeked soldiers with neat haircuts and snappy uniforms (it was incredible that these laughing men had won that terrible war) were always present, often carrying with them family treasures, a sword, an ancient urn, a daughter. *Pan-pan* girls with brightly painted lips in dance-hall dresses lay in wait for them there, their conversation dripping sweet in broken English, like shards of a wind chime trying to make sounds in stagnant air. When I first saw them, the hairpin in the futon came to mind. And Mr. Kodama's advice. Would love ever be the same for them? After a while I stopped thinking about it.

This pregnancy also miscarried, and I had to believe something in me was to blame. Jobo and I didn't talk about it, but I knew he knew too. The economic situation improved, and we moved back to Tokyo. I never got pregnant again.

During the five years there, I often thought of the Kodamas. I wanted to ask Mrs. Kodama how she managed to survive those childless years and the possible infidelity. I supposed there were moments of unspeakable distress for her. I supposed that if I could hang in there, our marriage would reach a more gratifying state, and maybe we too would find someone to carry on Jobo's name. They had found a wife for the grandnephew.

Once I suggested we adopt a war orphan.

"I don't want nobody else's kid," Jobo said.

My mother had a coronary in the candy factory. She'd worked there through the thick and thin of getting Momo through school. She was proud; I can see her discreetly mentioning her psychologist daughter to her candy buddies. A claim to fame. Momo married a white fellow psychologist.

After her stroke, my mother told Momo she must see that I returned to America. She said they owed me that. So Momo sent us money, and Jobo and I applied for permanent residency—I'd always kept my American citizenship—and we left Japan.

It didn't go well in Chicago. My mother and I had traveled too far, too long on different roads to meet again on the same ground. For days on end, my mother, confined to a wheelchair, spoke of the indignities of the camp experience, the inadequate medical facilities, my father's dying there, the awful food, the gossiping, and when she went full circle, she started from the top again, as though her life would end if she stopped. Once she paused long enough to ask if we suffered much in Japan. I said yes. But it was past. I did not care to bring back the pain—or inflict it.

It didn't go well. Jobo with his Waseda diploma would not work in a factory. He said we simply had to move on.

We went to Cleveland. Jobo's father still worked in maintenance, but Kiku had a great job as a legal secretary. Mary had married and left the family. Mother Endo stayed home.

Jobo hired in at a realtor's on commission, so we lived on the Endo charity, and it didn't work. There was too much tension with three women in the house—Kiku, sophisticated and patronizing; Mother, sly and insinuating; and myself, slow, unable to cope with mechanized housekeeping, unable to speak up for my feelings, always on the edge of hysteria. Dad was all right, but his constant talk of babies and pregnancies was perhaps the most devastating of all.

It was my turn. I asked to move on, but Jobo was unwilling.

"Give me a chance to get started. I'm tired of moving," he said.

"I want to go back to California. I want to feel that sun again; I want to be free. I want my own house."

"That's nonsense," he said. "We have no money. Besides, Dad wants us all to be together."

"Together? They hate me!" I screamed.

But it was nothing I could prove. There was always this cloying politeness covering the barbs, and Jobo only saw the candy coating. He said I was paranoid. He said it was my own insecurity. It was the old Chinese water torture.

I took too long to think about it, and by the time I'd borrowed money from Momo, the whole of Cleveland wasn't big enough for us Endo women. Jobo, caught in the middle, defended Kiku, defended his mother, and sometimes even defended me. It was a miserable place to be, yet he would have stayed but for my determination to leave Cleveland, taking Jobo with me—my final revenge on the Endos.

I told him that in California, near a Japanese community, there would be plenty of opportunities for a smart bilingual man, especially in real estate. It would be a chance to help our Japanese-speaking people, I said. I could go to work, wait tables, anything, and maybe together we could buy a piece of property with fruit trees. I reminded him of our dream back in Japan during the terrible war years. I said we could have children.

Jobo told an elaborate lie about a fantastic job offer in Los Angeles, and the Endos, pretending to believe, let us go.

The lie became a reality. Jobo happened in on a real-estate boom; he sold from the start. Before the first year was up, we bought a modest frame house. I couldn't believe it. But I was hardly through furnishing it – sewing curtains, hunting bargains – when Jobo bought a larger house, and I no more got used to living in those surroundings when he bought a still larger and more beautiful house.

Now there was no longer need for me to select furnishings. There were people for that – decorators and landscapers – people for everything but my loneliness. I asked Jobo why we didn't ever buy that place in Inglewood, his old hometown, and he said, "No resale value. A noisy airport there . . . the place is changed. Everything changes. Keep up with the times, girl."

And we changed. Jobo was a super salesman. He became more and more occupied with work and related activities, the lunches, dinners, the clubs, the drinking; he often stayed out late, sometimes returning in the morning.

"Had too much to drink and slept it off in the car," he said then.

We quarreled a lot – bitterly. We bickered over every detail of our lives, what to buy, where to go, what to eat. After a while it got so ridiculous, I stopped snapping at every lead.

Momo came to visit us two springs after we moved into the fancy house. In spite of Jobo's noisy welcome, she immediately sniffed out trouble, and with quiet restraint she asked if I planned to spend the rest of my life knitting afghans and waiting for Jobo.

"What else is there for me?" I asked.

"You'll have to find your own alternatives," she said.

"Forty-five is too old to start a new life," I said.

"That's your choice," she said.

That summer I enrolled in a typing class, and before the season was over, I found work in an insurance office. It seemed unfair to take this job with so many women really needing the work, but it was a matter of survival for me too. I had decided to let go; to leave Jobo alone until, on his own, he returned to our marriage, and I couldn't stay idle all that painful time.

There were almost five more years of clothes, cars, parties, late hours, and further estrangement.

Well, I guess I gave him too much rope. All that affluence finally attracted a smart woman who outwitted Jobo. She got herself pregnant. She was from Japan, divorced from a white sailor, a hostess in one of the restaurants in town. Jobo said he hadn't meant the affair to go so far, but now he wanted a divorce. He wanted a new life. He wanted this child.

He came home one morning while I was having my coffee and preparing for work. He said he wanted to talk to me and casually tossed a paper bag on the table. "Brought you something," he said.

I looked in the bag and found a battered Shirley Temple doll. I held back my tears. Somewhere in his new lifestyle he had kept the memory of that time when we were so young, so poor, so close.

I said, "I owe you one, Jobo. A pair of skis . . . I owe you a pair of skis. . . ."

"You owe me nothing," he said. "I want to talk to you. I want a divorce."

The treachery, the betrayal! My anger came spewing out. "Is that why you brought me the doll? You set me up for this! You brought the doll and meant to bomb me with her!" I screamed.

"No," he said. "I found the doll months ago . . . three or four months ago in a junk shop. I saw it and I thought of you. I left it in the trunk of my car and forgot about it. Mie, I want a divorce. I got a girl pregnant and I have to marry her."

"Three or four months? In the trunk of your car? Oh, Jobo, why didn't you bring her to me then?"

"I forgot, I told you. Mie, don't you hear me? I said I want a divorce."

We didn't quarrel then. I cried a little; I asked him if he loved her. He thought so. I asked if she loved him. He thought so. It was hard for me to believe that this woman – young and beautiful, I supposed – could love an old rich man who'd grown pompous, obese, and unyielding. It was not so easy for me to love him, even remembering the hard-muscled skier he once was, the sweet vulnerable man who wept with me long ago.

"I'm sorry, Mie," he said. And an era passed.

It's been three years since that day. In the first year following, I found that deeper level of pain I spoke about earlier. Sometimes at night, memories of the old days came at me: the terror, the hunger, the sweet intimacy of early love, *pan-pan* girls walking through my room, their voices tinkling, a cup of sugar dropped from my trembling hand, dissolving into the beach sand, swarms of fish in the cool gray of a Hayama twilight, dying at my feet, and Jobo coming to me, once again young, once again loving, warming my blood once again. Those kind of dreams.

Awake, there were other confrontations: What was the reason for surviving the war, to come to this? What is the purpose of heartbreak? And if it all dies with me, what indeed was the use of it? Am I only a segment of a larger drama? Is there still another act?

I wonder sometimes if Jobo thinks of these things too. But I suppose with the new family, more immediate problems occupy him, putting off the day of reckoning. Maybe there is no such day. Maybe he will die happy, the answer in his grasp. Maybe love is the answer. Maybe neither of us loved enough.

Well, you can go on like this until the sun sets, but some truths simply will not be hurried to reveal themselves. And after a while, even pain gets boring, and one has to get on with it. Get on with life. And that—life—does not stop just because you'd like to jump off here and hop on somewhere else later. You go on, and somehow some of the old vitality returns.

My Shirley doll sits on my dresser now. I bought her a new wig and made a fancy nylon dress for her. She smiles at me. Her lips are cracked, she's a bit sallow, the luster is gone from her blue eyes. She's not what she used to be. But she's been around a long time now.

The Handkerchief

I t was Benjamin Tanaka's ninth birthday. After the evening meal of rice and *okazu,* Mama brought out a cake that Mary had baked and frosted a vivid blue, the last of the artificial colors. There were eight shopworn candles on it; not the right number but, as Mary said, better than nothing. The candles had lain in the drawer with stray buttons, old rubber bands, and other small things for a whole year, and this was the last of them. Maybe next year there would be a new package of candles, but the next birthday was Mary's and she would be fourteen, and George's seventh one followed, and unless someone bought another package, there would be only two on his next cake.

Afterward, Mary presented him with a green yo-yo meticulously wrapped in Christmas paper, and Mama brought out the catcher's mitt, not regulation size but real leather nevertheless, and Benji's heart grew large with that good feeling. George screamed with delight, but Papa continued to eat his cake with the jabbing way he had with forks.

That night as Benji lay in bed, his presents by his pillow, the yo-yo giving off the scent of wood and paint, the pungent smell of the leather mitt intermittently bringing back that good feeling, he heard Mama and Papa talking in the next room.

It was summer and the doors and windows were open to catch the breeze, and voices, even Mama's whispers, carried to his room—and the ominous silences and stabbing staccato of Papa's anger. Benji didn't understand all of the language, but he knew Papa's "*Katte ni se!*" was suppressed rage.

Mama said, "Don't you understand? It isn't my choice. My sister is ill. Be reasonable; it's only for a month."

"Who will do the cooking? We have to eat too."

"Mary can do it. School's out and the boys will help her. She's almost fourteen; it's time she learned to keep house."

Benji put the cool surface of his yo-yo to his cheek and buried his face in the mitt. The soft fingers caressed his ear. The voices went on. He pulled the sheet over his face and dozed off until Mama's fierce whispers woke him.

"It's always like this. I've devoted eighteen years to you—without complaint, without demands. I'm not made of stone. I have feelings too."

"So now it comes out! *Katte ni se!* If you want to go, go. The door is open!"

The yo-yo rolled off Benji's pillow and clattered to the floor. The voices stopped.

In the morning Mama explained to the children that she would be away for a month to help care for her ailing sister in San Francisco, and while she was gone, Mary was to take charge and Benji and George were to help her. So it was settled.

Five hundred miles for thirty days may well have been across the Pacific and forever to Benji. But Mary was quick to rise to the challenge and with notebook in hand, she began taking notes on chores and shopping tips. George screamed and kicked the wall and went out to play.

At the depot they stood around Mama and listened to last-minute instructions until the train left. Benji's throat tightened with pain. He envied Mary's offhand chattery manner in talking to Mama, wishing Auntie a speedy recovery. He couldn't trust his voice, so he stared at his scuffed shoes until the tears slid into the soft curve of his nostrils. Mama pressed her handkerchief into Benji's hand. Though he did not use it, he could smell the bleach and soap so characteristic of her. Only after the train began to move did he look up. Mama peered from the window with her fingers to her mouth.

Papa walked rigidly ahead of the children, back to the car. He drove home in silence, and Benji, remembering Mama's hand on her mouth, clutched the handkerchief she gave him.

That month was endless. Mary took her job seriously and the house was never cleaner, never neater; the meals, such as they were, were served at 5:30, never a minute later. She pushed the boys mercilessly. It was as though she were preparing for one of her school exams, meaning to make it to the top of the class. She had no patience with the small aches and pains growing boys are heir to, especially during dishwashing time.

George was more adaptable than Benji. He dropped a few dishes early in the tyranny and was relegated to such chores as drying flatware and emptying wastebaskets. He watched the climate of Mary's eyes, and whenever he saw a storm brewing, he sped from room to room gathering wastebaskets. Although his sympathies were largely with Benji, he capitalized on Mary's susceptibility to flattery and could often be found outside while the silver dried itself in white rings and baskets accumulated their waste.

Benji knew the phrases that could release him from the meaner jobs (you're the best cook; you're the prettiest), but the words stuck on his tongue and his eyes betrayed him and Mary was not deceived. So while Benji committed himself to an uneasy integrity, outside the butterflies fluttered freely and inside the birthday mitt caught only the dust that Mary permitted to enter. One day, one day, he thought.

Benji schemed to get even. He wanted to hurt Mary; he wanted to hear her cry for mercy, yes, to feel a pain deep enough to instill a little humility in her. But he couldn't do it alone; she was bigger than him. He would need help.

The time was chosen and George was enlisted to attack Mary's legs, bite one of her calves, while Benji went for her neck. But George couldn't get himself to bite, and Mary quickly reached down and pinched his nose to submission. All Benji could do was watch.

It had occurred to him to talk to Papa about Mary–about the work load, about his unhappiness, his loneliness–no, not that. Loneliness was a weakness; a man didn't expose that soft underside. Papa was airtight, strong–a man of few words, fewer emotions. You asked him only for things: a nickel, a dime, a ride to the library. The exchange was simple: yes, no, later–not of multiple words or explanations. Tidy. The untidiness was underneath, just below the surface of the skin, under the twitch of an eyelid, under a clammy palm. And if you said, "I hurt," you better have something Papa could see.

Because Papa himself didn't hurt. Even with Mama gone, his routine did not change: In the morning, after breakfast, on the back porch lacing his boots to his knees, driving off in his pickup loaded with hoses, mower, edger, scythes, clippers; in the evening returning drenched in sweat and unlacing his boots on the back porch. Then the bath, supper, and later the bedroom with the door closing behind him.

No one seemed to hurt. Not George or Mary. Only he, Benji with too much of that underside. But no one else had been awake the night of his birthday.

One particularly trying day, after the house had been vacuumed, the peas shelled, the greens washed, Mary announced, "From tomorrow, we will use day-old bread. It's half price and we can save the money and buy a new tablecloth. Benji, you'll go to the store for it." Just like that. Incredible. What other tortures did she plan?

"Mama never said anything about day-old bread. Why do we need a new tablecloth? Why do I have to go? You thought of it, you want the tablecloth, you go." "Yeah, yeah," George supported. But Mary turned her back.

Benji stormed out of the kitchen and locked himself in his room. The words he knew were inadequate. Troublemaker! Witch! Ass! He threw himself on his bed and cried without control. He pictured himself walking furtively to the store, plucking the clerk's sleeve, and whispering, "Day-old bread, please. For my ducks." The guys from Oak Street would be lurking behind the stalls, "You startin' to quack now, Benj?" And the obscene quacking.

The sounds from his mental images, sounds from the street, and his own sobbing conjured Mama's voice. "Benji, a man doesn't cry."

A sweet loneliness dissolved the anger. Benji walked to the closet to touch the coat he wore to the depot. It still hung on the peg where he'd left it when they returned. Without Mama. The handkerchief was in his pocket. Benji put it to his nose—bleach and soap. The smell evoked a memory of a scant few weeks ago when order and mercy prevailed—the smell of an orderly house, the father, mother, members of the family in their proper places, chain of command undisturbed. Damn! Damn that aunt that took Mama away. Die; get well; do something. Disorder was everywhere in this neat house. Mama, come home. Benji cried into the handkerchief.

In the middle of the fourth week, Papa read a letter from Mama. Not the first one that came, Mary confided. Papa's eyes skimmed through half of the first page until they came upon the passages he read aloud. "I'm glad that Mary is keeping the house in order and the boys are helping her. As you say, she is getting good training and her cooking will improve as the days pass. I'm glad the children are getting along together. Please tell them for me, I am unable to come back as scheduled; my sister is not yet well enough for me to leave her. Perhaps next month . . ."

Papa didn't finish the letter. Mary wandered off to dust a table with the corner of her apron. George, bewildered, followed close behind her. Benji went to his room.

He closed the door carefully and got out the handkerchief. He put it to his nose. The smell was not quite the same. "How come? How come?" he asked. He did not cry.

The second month passed, and Mama wrote to say she would probably return before school resumed in fall. She was now helping a friend in his restaurant, she said. Just helping out—sometimes in the kitchen, sometimes at the counter—helping and earning a little money besides. This man had been widowed recently, and without his wife he was unable to carry on the business—just until he got competent help, she said. Papa read it from the first page of her letter. No word was said about Auntie's condition.

Benji was furious. He stamped to his room and slammed the door. He rushed to the closet and tore the handkerchief from his coat pocket and screamed into it: "How come!" He put it to his mouth, ready to bite the deceitful cloth, but the smell stopped him. It was sour. Was it from his sweating palms or his tears or did the handkerchief change? He threw it on the floor and stamped on it. "Damn you," he said.

Mary knocked on the door. Her voice was gentle. "Benji," she said, "let's have some ice cream."

"You too; goddam you," he muttered and ran from the room, past Mary and into the backyard. Papa was pulling out of the driveway, going somewhere.

For a few days Papa appeared grim and talked even less, but that passed, and maybe because the nights were so warm, his bedroom door now remained open. He seemed more friendly. He made half-jokes now and then, and the children responded quickly to show their appreciation. Mary changed too. The house was less tidy, the food more varied, the bread fresher. She was kinder.

One day shortly before school opened, Mary spoke to Benji about back-to-school clothes. They had just finished supper; George had already gone outside. The sun had not yet set, and Papa was in the backyard.

Benji was startled. "How come?" he asked.

"We have to get ready for school," Mary said.

"She's not coming back?"

"I don't know." With her chin, Mary indicated Papa in the yard. "He said we have to go shopping." She cleared her throat. "He got a letter today. He didn't read it to us. Why don't you ask him about it?"

Benji was reluctant, but Mary pushed him past the door.

Papa was squatting on the ground. He seemed to be burning something. When Benji approached him, he looked up quickly and showed his teeth in a semblance of a smile. Benji smiled back, but Papa was already walking to his truck. He said, "I'm going to see Yamaguchi-san about some tools." He didn't look back.

Benji examined the flakes of ashes Papa left behind. It had been a letter. He saw the Japanese words on the unburned fragments. He poked at it with his shoe.

Benji looked around. Everything was the same – the grass, the shrubs, the fence, the lilies of the Nile, the clothesline with the morning's wash. How could everything be the same when nothing was really the same? He walked to the clothesline. Mary would want the clothes down before night fell. He saw the handkerchief between Papa's good shirt and Mary's scarf. It was pink and stiff, as though it had taken the colors of Mary's scarf and fallen into the starch with Papa's shirt.

Benji removed the handkerchief from the line and looked at it. He walked to the fence and dropped it on the other side. A freak wind blew in from nowhere and carried the handkerchief off, past the next lot and into the distance, and the same wind scattered the ashes of the letter.

Charted Lives

S ome people's lives are so convoluted, you wonder how so much can happen to any one individual. I have watched such a one unfold as logically as the scenes of a play with the characters pulled along the compelling force of its theme. I wonder sometimes if all our lives are not already charted and we simply live them out.

It was a time when twenty-five-year-old marriages were going to pot six months before or after anniversaries, and I was one of the casualties of this social epidemic. Most of my married life I'd been a dutiful Japanese American (Nisei) wife and mother, and suffice it to say, I reared two children who left home at a reasonable age–reasonable enough to suspend critical judgment of me as a mother. As a wife now, that's a different story.

I was too muddled then to think clearly, and one of my daughters, who'd married and relocated to Hawaii, invited me to stay with her until I got my act together. So in this land of tropical rain and turquoise sea, she encouraged me to take a refresher course in clerical work to brush up on my "marketable skills" in order to find "gainful employment" in the "mainstream." It's true, my ten-year hobby of painting sixty-dollar pictures was not marketable. I sold as many as four of these a year. Tops.

And since divine intervention was not immediately forthcoming, I put on a brave smile and sallied forth to the "marketplace." Like those who grin: "My mother died yesterday; my car was totaled; my house burned to the ground; . . . my husband left me."

Back in California, I got a bottom-rung job in an insurance firm. "It's okay for starts," my other daughter said. I think my qualifications had less to do with my placement than being Japanese and/or a painter. Stephen Turner, the man who interviewed me, looked over my application and said, "Oh, you paint. My wife paints. She's Japanese too." But I was ready to accept any advantage. Years ago during World War II, being Japanese was a total nil, and I figured I'd paid my dues.

I would guess that Steve, he insisted I call him that, was in his late twenties. I am purposely vague about his position in the firm for reasons of my own. I will say, however, that in this vast complex, he had an office of his own and a secretary he shared with another man. The secretary, Elaine, was on leave, and on this first week, the pileup of work was so enormous that it was agreed Elaine was doing far more than anyone guessed, and the hunt was on to find someone not ambitious enough to replace her, but competent enough to do the drudge work. I was hired.

In a few days, through office gossip and observations of my own, I found that Steve's job, despite his preoccupied frown, his dashing in and out, his hurried phone calls, was not as important as it seemed. But I should complain; he always found time to be friendly. He asked often if things were all right. "Feel free to ask any questions, any at all. Be sure to speak up. We want to keep an open line here," he said. A couple of times I noticed that he hovered over me as I worked. I finally asked him, "Am I doing something wrong?"

"No, no," he said and moved away self-consciously. The talk was that Steve was a serious and somewhat humorless man, and his attention to anyone, much less a middle-aged Japanese American divorcee was unusual. But I let it go. There was just too much work to do.

One day he called me to his office to pick up some material he wanted copied. Before I got out the door, he asked, "Have you been painting lately?"

"No," I smiled. Every day I came home exhausted and only had the energy to bolt down my supper, shower, and stagger off to bed. Weekends I cleaned house, did the laundry and small repairs. I hadn't painted since the days before the divorce. I started toward the door.

"You're very quiet," Steve said. "You remind me of my wife."

"I do?" I waited for the other shoe.

"She's quiet too. She's Japanese, did I tell you?"

"Japanese Japanese or Japanese American?" I asked.

"Japanese American. Third generation." He drew out a picture from his wallet. I looked.

"She's very pretty," I said. "She's not pure Japanese, is she?"

The smile hung on his face. Obviously I said the wrong thing. But it wasn't my idea to start the conversation.

"Misa and I were high-school sweethearts," he said. He put the wallet back in his pocket. "She's always been quiet. Like you."

"That's nice," I said, my hand on the doorknob.

"Her parents are from Hawaii."

"Yes, lots of Japanese in this area come from Hawaii."

"Are you from Hawaii too?"

"No."

"Have you ever been there?"

"I spent two months with my daughter in Manoa." Actually I spent a semester there. "Hawaii is so beautiful, I don't know why anyone would want to leave it." I thought I should make another statement and that sounded safe enough.

Steve came to life. "Is it really so great? I heard it's getting pretty commercial. . . ."

"I suppose that's true, but it's still very beautiful. Your wife must miss it very much."

"Oh, Misa's never been in Hawaii. Her parents moved here right after they were married. Or maybe before. I'm not sure."

"Is that so?"

"You think I might enjoy it there?"

"Of course. You really should go."

"I've been trying to talk Misa into going but she . . ." He stopped. "Well, we were wondering where to go this year. I'd really like to see Hawaii."

"Why don't you ask your in-laws about it. They could probably map out a nice itinerary for you," I said.

"Oh, yeah. I suppose they could."

"Misa probably has a lot of relatives there. You'll have a good time."

"Well, they haven't really kept in touch."

"Are her folks from Oahu?"

"Maybe we won't go."

Here it was again. Again drawn in and pushed away. Well, I turned the knob and got out of there pronto. Seconds later, Steve came to me as though to talk, then moved on into the hall. If you can believe it.

A couple of days later Steve brought a cup of coffee to my desk and said, "Congratulations. You won."

I won?

"You talked Misa into a Hawaiian vacation. I'm really happy for you."

Now, that's got to be a joke, right? So I went along with it. "That means you got a ticket for me too?"

"Ha-ha . . ."

"I better talk to my supervisor about it. She'll have to get a replacement for me. Next week, you say?"

"Ha-ha. Yeah, next week." And he ha-haad himself backward into his office.

The day before Steve left, he dropped by to let me wish him bon voyage. How I got to be such a friend, I don't know; our relationship was certainly no more than I've stated here. But he was happy and excited, and I couldn't let on that I sensed a need that counted heavily on a small commonality: that I, like his wife, painted; that I was Japanese, like his wife. Still Misa was not all Japanese; I could see it from a snapshot. Wasn't it clear to him?

He was gone a couple of weeks. In the meantime I was too busy to think about either Steve or his mysterious Misa, particularly after it was announced that Elaine was not returning to the company. There was a flurry of activity as I was pushed half a step upward in the arena. I wondered if Elaine was Japanese too.

Steve returned brown and rested. He was not upset to learn Elaine had left us for good. "No problem," he said. "You can do it." And smiling, he said, "You were right. Hawaii is magnificent."

"You had a good time then?"

"You bet. When I catch up with my work, we'll look at the pictures I took. I got some nice shots."

He soon made good his threat. Laden with envelopes from the photo-finisher, and unmindful of my work, he called me in. He was so proud of his snaps. Tediously he explained the light, lens, and angle. I politely went through scores of scenes and pictures they had taken, first of one and then the other, like honeymooners. There was Misa in Hanauma, Steve posing stiffly at the Pali, Misa in a bikini at Waikiki, Steve in Kaneohe raising a rigid arm. Then the pictures changed. There were shots of Misa and Steve together with Steve's head cut off at the crown; Misa looking radiant on the rocks in Hana but only half of Steve.

"Who took these?" I asked. Steve seemed not to have heard so I dropped it. Then a third person appeared. "Who's this?" I asked.

"He's a painter."

"You met a painter there?"

"Yeah."

No more. After a few more snaps I suggested we finish them another day.

It was summer. The office manager frantically juggled schedules to accommodate vacations and fought to equalize the workload for those of us that remained. It was awhile before I realized I hadn't finished admiring Steve's Hawaii pictures. But Steve was busy too and didn't seem to remember, so that was all right. Then summer was over.

At the close of a work day near the end of September, I rode the elevator down with Steve. He seemed kind of low.

"Everything all right?" I asked.

"Well, I have to go home and cook something. Misa's not home," he said.

Misa not home? Shame on me if I hadn't learned by now not to ask questions. I didn't bite.

"I'm tired," he said. "How about let's go out to eat?"

Well, it was one of those Indian summer days, far too warm to go home and start the stove going and too lonely to eat alone. Steve suggested a quiet restaurant with something cool to drink. I had my doubts, but after all, what could happen? So we'll turn a few heads – an odd couple, a young white man and a middle-aged "Oriental." So what else could happen? No more than an occasional silence we'd have to struggle through while finding something to say. I could deal with that.

Steve brightened as we sat in the restaurant. "This reminds me of summers in New York," he said. "Muggy, hot . . . On days like this, we used to have supper on the porch. My mother usually made potato salad and gallons of iced tea."

"You're from New York?"

"Upstate."

"Are your folks still there?" I asked and nearly clapped my hand over my mouth. Too nosy again.

"Well, no one's there now. My mother died when I was a kid, and my father remarried. Edith is from Oregon. She's twice divorced. It was too lonely for Dad, I guess, ha-ha."

I know, I almost said.

"Edith didn't like New York, so she decided we'd move to California. I sure kicked up a ruckus then, but they said they couldn't leave me there alone . . . a kid of thirteen. So they sold the property and we came to California." He smiled. "I hated to leave that old house. Memories, you know. Well, maybe that's why she wanted my father out of there, and I had to come with them. That's all there was to it."

"Your folks are here, then?"

"No. They moved on to Seattle. Edith has this wanderlust and keeps on a-moving. They waited till I graduated and went on. I stayed here by myself."

"It must have been lonely for you." There are times when you have to say something.

"Yeah, well. I didn't have a friend in the world when I started Belmont High. Until I met Misa. She's pretty much a loner too, so we naturally . . . we naturally got to be buddies." He ordered iced tea. "I didn't want to leave her, ha-ha."

Steve paid for my dinner over my protests. "You get the next one," he said. The next one? We left, awash with iced tea.

Should I have guessed what was happening with Steve? He was late for work; he had dark circles under his eyes; he was absentminded. Even his posture changed. My supervisor asked if I knew anything. "He's obviously troubled," she said.

One evening he threw a casual "Let's go out to eat tonight" at me. Misa wasn't home again?

"I can't," I said. He looked like I'd slapped him. "I didn't bring any money." That was all I could think of at the moment.

"No problem," he said. "I'll pay."

"But it's my turn." No-no-no, but-but-but; Steve looked so wretched, I let him help clear my desk and we left for dinner.

When we settled in at the cafe, I bore the silence for a while and then said, "What's on your mind, Steve?" and bit my tongue.

"Do you remember when you said Misa was part white?" he asked. That's not exactly the way I remembered it, but I nodded anyway. "Well, her maiden name is Yoshida, and both her parents are full-blood Japanese Americans."

So all right. I don't care. I didn't answer. "She doesn't look all-Japanese, does she?" he said. I shrugged. "She has two younger sisters who look very Oriental." Okay. "When she was little she asked her mother why she didn't look like the rest of the family, and her mother said, 'Because your nose is too big; your eyes are too large.' All her life she's been teased about it."

"I'm sorry," I said.

"She told me she always thought it was her fault." My God, what we do to our kids. "I think that's why she's so quiet."

"You said Misa was a painter. What kind of work does she do?" I asked.

"I don't know," he said. "She's been painting since those high-school art classes. I can't understand her stuff."

"She must be pretty good, then," I laughed.

"I have to tell you something," he said seriously.

Oh-boy. "Steve," I said, "you don't have to tell me anything. In fact, I'd rather you don't."

"I just want to say that you were right. Misa *is* part white."

"So?"

"I know. I don't care either. But Misa . . . well, she always knew something was wrong, but no one in the family would talk about it. It was a no-no, if you get what I mean. So when we married . . ." He stopped.

"Did you have a big wedding?"

"Just Misa's parents and her sisters. And my dad flew in from Seattle. It was at the courthouse. I didn't even have a best man. Or Misa, a what-you-call-it?—maid of honor." I got the picture.

"We got all of four presents. My dad gave us money, and Misa's father too, and a bottle of champagne, and her mom gave us a small package. It was wrapped in, you know, in wedding paper."

"It was weird," he said. "That night, our wedding night, you know, after the Chinese dinner with the folks? We came home and opened the champagne. Misa was so happy. We got on the bed, and she made this big show of opening our gift."

I saw it: alone at last, champagne in tumblers, giddy from the wine, Misa giggling, climbing unsteadily onto the bed, her little finger lifted, carefully untying the ribbon, saving the silver wrapper.

Steve reached into the inner pocket of his coat and brought out a packet. "This is the present," he said.

"Letters?"

"Yeah, I want to know what you think."

Why, he meant to talk about it all along. He left the house this morning, carefully tucking these frayed envelopes in his pocket, patting down the bulge it made.

"I don't want to read them," I said. "Misa wouldn't want you to show them to me."

"She won't know." He pushed the packet toward me. I turned away, but he thrust them in my hand and excused himself.

There were four letters. The one on top was a wedding card. Inside were the usual sentiments and, handwritten: "To Misa and Steve – Love, Mom and Dad, Karen and Judy." Over in the lower corner in very small script: "Forgive me – Mom." The other three envelopes were yellowed and brittle. All of them bore Hawaii postmarks; the first, over twenty-five years old, was addressed to Miss Fumi Motoyoshi in Honolulu. It read:

Dear Fumi,

You have forgotten the agreement we made at the very beginning that we would not hurt each other or hurt ourselves. And remember too, what I told you: that you are a sensitive and talented artist, and you must let nothing stand in the way of your work. It will give you more than any mere man, especially one like me. I don't deny the feeling I have for you, but I've devoted more years to painting than you have lived on this earth, and I intend to stick with it. If I have to die in obscurity, so be it. I thought that was amply clear. It's the first thing you should have understood about me.

W. B.

The second letter was postmarked later that same year and was addressed to Mrs. Fumi Motoyoshi Yoshida, Los Angeles:

My dearest,

I heard rumors that you had eloped, but I did not want to believe it. I thought maybe you were sulking and, in your own way, trying to make me come to terms with our relationship. It was a month before I worked up the courage to see your parents, pretending to inquire why you had stopped attending classes and to ask if I should hold your paintings or send them to you, wherever you are. Your father was abrupt. He said, "She's dead." But your mother followed me out and slipped me your address. She said you'd left for California with young Yoshida. She said you were pregnant.

My darling, why couldn't you have told me? Or why hadn't I understood it the night you came to the studio to cry. I wrote that callous note, and I never saw you again. I think of you two children in the wilderness bravely fighting dragons, and I am heartsick to know that I am the dragon. Forgive me. You are so brave; you have such spunk. Would it hurt too much to say that I love you? I can hear you spit back to me, "Too late!" If I had known, maybe things would be different. Maybe it would be the same. I admire Yoshida for taking the burden of another man's child – for loving you to that extent. For all my bravado, I am unable to do what this young son of a Maui farmer has found heart to do. For you.

I'm sending the proceeds from a painting I recently sold. I would like to keep in touch if it's possible. If not, I will understand.

Love,

W. B.

The third letter was postmarked a year later:

My dear Fumi,

I've asked all around, but no one will give me *any* information. It's as though you'd never existed. If that's true, how is it that I have these paintings? How is it that you appear so regularly in my dreams? Sometimes you seethe in with a wind and tear at my clothes. Sometimes you simply stand in the shadows. Have mercy, Fumi. Write me. Tell me you are happy and well. Tell me it's only my conscience that plagues me with these sad tricks. Tell me about the baby. Is it a boy? Is it a girl? Does it laugh? Write me a line, I beg you. I am unable to paint.

Love,

W. B.

Steve came back, drying his hands on his handkerchief. He'd apparently washed his face too.

"That was some wedding gift," I said. "That lady's sense of timing is something else."

"I don't think she meant to hurt Misa," Steve said. "She probably just wanted to get it off her chest."

"Misa must have felt terrible," I said.

"She didn't even cry. Didn't shed a tear."

"What stamina," I said.

"Well, she's lived with it all these years. I'm the one who cried." Steve's eyes swelled. Mine too, I think.

"What did she say?" I asked.

"Nothing. Well, she said, 'I didn't know my mother painted.' That's all. We didn't talk about it. Isn't that something? I guess she's used to putting things away. I thought she might want to talk, but she didn't."

Maybe it's easier to cry for someone else.

"You remember when you told us to go to Hawaii?" Steve asked.

Yes, I did do that. I encouraged them to go.

"Well, at first she didn't think much of the idea, but she changed her mind later. I told her how nice you said it was. And I guess . . . I guess we knew we'd have to go someday."

"But you said you had a good time."

"We had a great time. I showed you those pictures, didn't I?"

"Sure."

"Well, just a few days before we left, we decided to look for Blake—that's his name—and we found him in the telephone book."

"Just like that? I bet he was shocked."

"Shocked, shaking, the works. Misa too . . . crying like a dam burst, both of them. I couldn't take it. I left her there—figured they'd want to talk—so I left them alone for a while. I went to a movie. Then he spent the rest of the time with us. Went everywhere with us. All the time."

"She must have been happy."

"I never saw her like that before. Laughing all the time. Made me feel good." Steve looked pretty miserable for a man trying to recall how good he felt.

I finally said, "That's a nice story, Steve. Thanks for telling me." He smiled like it hurt.

"Is your daughter still in Hawaii?" he asked.

"I doubt if she'll ever leave. She loves it there," I said.

"Could I ask a favor?" This was the hook.

"I don't know. Let's see what it is, first."

"I was thinking . . . you know, Misa came home with me but . . . well, she went back."

"She went back? You let her go?"

"I couldn't help it. She was depressed . . . crying all the time. She said she didn't get a chance to talk to him. She said . . . Well, you know, they're both artists."

"You shouldn't have let her go, Steve."

"I couldn't help it. Besides, I wanted her to go. She was miserable; I had to let her go. She said she'd be back in a few days. That was three weeks ago. She wrote once, but . . . I tried calling, but they don't answer. I don't know why. Her parents don't know anything about this, and, well, I'm running out of excuses."

"You ought to tell them, Steve."

"I can't. They'd worry. I want to find out what's going on, first. And that's what I wanted to ask you . . . to ask your daughter if . . . well, I know she can take care of herself, but I'm kind of worried, and I thought maybe your daughter could check it out for me."

"I don't know if she will. She's not that kind of . . ."

"I don't mean to spy on them. Maybe she could give them a message for me."

"I don't know if she will."

"I wish we'd never gone to Hawaii," he said. "I'm worried sick." It's true; he looked bad. I promised to write.

I didn't sleep most of the night. Steve's predicament brought back old pain, and I grew angry with myself, angry again with my ex-husband, angry with Steve and Misa. And Blake? Everyone should have learned about him from the experience of Fumi Motoyoshi Yoshida. And Mr. Yoshida. The blameless Mr. Yoshida, the brave Mr. Yoshida, who every day for twenty and more years faced the evidence of his wife's first love but could not state honestly, "This is the situation." Yes, that's what this thing needed. Some good old-fashioned honesty. Straight talk. And me. How did I get caught in this mess? Just because I said, "Yes, you should visit Hawaii"? Did I say, "I'll break your arm if you don't go"? Why, I didn't even know Misa. I was so cautious, so cautious, and still I'm in this mess. Maybe I should have told him outright, at the very beginning: "Leave me out of this. I have problems of my own. I resent you for taking me back to places I don't want to be."

I took two fingers of bourbon at four o'clock and woke up late.

In the morning Steve, all clean and shining, came directly to my desk and said, "It's all right! She was home when I got back last night!" He was wearing a tasteful aloha shirt; I guess someone could search three weeks for one so tasteful. He gave me a tin of macadamia nuts. "Try to forget what I told you last night. If you can, ha-ha."

Well, two days after the aloha-shirt–macadamia-nut homecoming, Steve told me that Misa was leaving for good. She had only come home to get her things and say good-bye.

"Don't let her go, Steve," I said. "That will be the end. Stand up for yourself. Make her stay!"

"I can't," he said. "She says she doesn't love me. She wants to be with Blake."

"But that's her father!"

"I know."

"I don't believe what I'm hearing," I said. "I don't believe it."

"That's what she said."

"She doesn't know what she's talking about. She's mixed up, Steve. You have to straighten her out."

"That's what she said." He moved away from me.

Later that day we filled out a transfer form, and before the term was over, he moved to Chicago–for a fresh start. Without memories, without friends.

The Coward

I have always had this spot in the back of my head that I keep clear, and I have often stood like a third party on the periphery of activity and watched the physical part of me perform. From there, I have observed myself reacting to fear, or grief, reacting to sensuality – all the time acutely aware of the situation and its sometimes irrelevant externals. I suppose some of this is due to the era in which I was born, early depression years, and some to the origin of my birth: Japanese immigrants settled in a desert valley near the Mexican border of California, scratching out a meager living in the barren soil. Those words: immigrants, desert valley, Mexican border, conjures up the whole ashes-in-the-mouth picture. I mean, in the interests of survival, it was wise to stand somewhat removed from a situation, not become too involved, and still remain part of its reality.

The living was basic: the house, the food, the work that supported the life, and sometimes a laugh or so. It was that way with us then: things were either not so good or very bad; we didn't dwell too much on it, and we started from that point and worked up. I suppose it gave me a lot of endurance for hardship, but it didn't prepare me for some of the joys of life.

My mother taught me a lot of things that were pertinent to then and me, a Japanese American country girl in an insecure economy, facing a bleak future. And however unrewarding the virtues she herself practiced, or inequitable the gods that judged her, she still pressed on me a sort of Japanese-Buddhist Victorianism. She spoke a lot about greed and need and hungers of the flesh, and all manner of nonessential material things as the devil's instruments. She taught me not to dream extravagantly, but with both feet on the ground and of attainable goals. She told me to be frugal with love and passion, and she passed on an unspoken distrust of men.

Some of the stuff has been useful; in a land where living is hard won, the philosophies she offered were often practical if not necessary; but some were burdensome and unrealistic, and I discarded them about the time I first discovered that my mother's wisdom was not that of Solomon (may she rest in peace). And some that she imposed on me, like the habit of dreaming in tiny proportions, were downright hard to shake and kept my heart too small to know the joy of abandon, too small to taste the quality of despair. The year I went to art school and met a young man who did maintenance work at the school grounds to finance his education in civil engineering, I ignored her most repeated advice. I told this man I loved him.

It was after the end of the Second World War, and there wasn't too much going for the Japanese in America then. We had spent some years in a detention camp for the Japanese in America; my father died there, and my mother followed shortly after we were permitted to return to the West Coast. We had settled in Los Angeles.

I started classes in basic art, working my way through as a part-time domestic. I had always wanted to paint, but my small dream was to find a job in the art field, perhaps drawing lines or making erasures, or even washing brushes – anything – but to be there where my heart was. This young man was undaunted by the prevailing racial antipathy. He wasn't too proud to haul rubbish and wash toilets for the sake of a greater goal. He planned to build and create, and no job was too menial to help prepare for this purpose.

Besides his extraordinary drive, he had other extraordinary traits. His medium was steel, concrete, and resilient timbers – permanence; his nature was strong but tensile. His dreams were built on solid foundation: his determination and ambition. He was kind and thoughtful to me and would not let me toy with his emotions. He was handsome, heavy-browed, and sullen-eyed; I was totally attracted to him. He added a new dimension to my life: among all the lovely young women he could have loved, he chose me.

I was in the bloom of youth then, I mean to the extent a desert flower could blossom. Still far from beautiful, some distance from delectable, this young man loved me, and I began to love myself. I was adored; my entire life changed; I found that all the world did indeed love a lover. I gave him the whole of myself.

I became pregnant and we married. Yes, in that order. He found a better-paying job and attended classes at night, and after our son arrived and I was well enough, I did clerical work at the Department of Motor Vehicles, typing, filing, and he returned to school full time. I dropped the art course.

It wasn't easy. There were days when, after the books and paper were bought, only the baby could eat. There were days of incredible weariness and bickering and tears. But there were good days too, and the years passed quickly. Before long, our boy was five, my husband got his papers, and I quit my job.

After the money began to flow in, there wasn't anything my husband wouldn't buy for our son and me: toys, appliances, expensive clothes, gimmicks, and a beautiful house. I suppose it has something to do with man's image of himself, the kindly god of abundance and power, the proof of manhood. He often said, "Stick with me, kid, and you'll never go hungry," his chest expanding with pride. Sometimes he would add "again."

But I had long ago cut away the wheat from the chaff; maybe much earlier than I knew. There weren't a whole lot of things I couldn't do without. To me these acquisitions were all those things my mother never had, and they burdened me with guilt. It was the seduction of material goods that she had warned me against. I looked for something else. This was my fixation, and I couldn't enjoy, enjoy. I was afraid we would grow old like this, and in the end all that remained of us would be a heap of used appliances and broken toys; the worthwhile things having withered from inattention. I have accused him of abandoning ideals, he accused me of standing on a pedestal with blinders yet, and while I tried to bring up our boy with a feeling for himself and his individuality, my husband impressed on him the value of self-restraint and negotiation. I guess the restrictions of his work, his respect for rules, and his cunning in the field had a lot to do with his attitude.

He asked, "What would happen to us if I did as I pleased? If I were as unyielding as you? How could we live? How would we pay for all this?" His arms swept the rooms, the cars, the food we ate, the company we kept.

Our boy, however, had a strong sense of survival, and as he developed, I noticed he proceeded with extreme caution. That's what he had found most digestible, I suppose.

In the years that followed, I spent a great deal of time in that zone I spoke of earlier – the periphery of myself – observing, processing, validating; and while time mellowed the two of us, we learned to tolerate each other's eccentricities, walk softly around them, and between us there developed a real feeling for each other. A feeling without understanding, a concern . . . perhaps something closer to love than the earlier passion.

It showed itself one day in January; he brought me a box of paints and brushes. He'd bought them from a young man who had given up painting. "I thought you might like these," he said modestly. "Now with the boy gone" (our son had left us to attend a northern university earlier that fall), "you can think a little of yourself," he said. "Paint!" he shouted with rare abandon. "Paint, without compromise!" He spread both arms. "I'll face the world and do the compromising." I fell on him laughing.

I had forgotten what it once meant to me. The smell of paint and turpentine awakened old dreams . . . that I, like God, could create man, woman, forms, light, shadow, joy, sorrow, and could move into another man's sphere of experience, touch him, move him, change him. Like one possessed, I painted, studied painters, and frequented galleries. I was there for most of the new shows and often two or three times thereafter. There was much to learn, and time was pressing on me.

There is a camaraderie among people with common interests who meet in the heat of day or drizzle of rain while all normal folk work. And in art galleries there are those who form a silent club. They are hot-eyed and intense, independent of the trivialities of amenities. They come to *feel* pictures, to seek mood, color, or a shape that evokes in them an inner passion, a completion of self. They respect silence and privacy, and their alliance is acknowledged with only the slightest nod or glint of eye contact. They snort or groan – few words are spoken. They usually travel alone.

I met one such person. I had seen him two or three times before; a pale European, tall, with great piercing eyes, probably over fifty. He had wild curly hair thinning on the top back, these eyes that stabbed, and a thin sharp nose. He was usually clean-shaven. He dressed neither poorly nor well, rather darkly, conservatively. Sometimes a wine-red scarf flowed from his breast pocket.

I had stepped back to study a painting, and I backed into him, my high heel, spiked like a nail, impaled his instep. He groaned. I whipped around babbling many apologies and found his great eyes glaring at me in contempt: clumsy dilettante, disturber of peace. When there was nothing more to say, I stopped my gibbering, and the silence that followed was awesome. Finally he said, "You did not hurt me, Madam."

After that, when he saw me and felt like speaking, he would bow and say, "You did not hurt me." I never spoke first.

At the beginning he really scared me. The memory of his wrath was vivid. My conversation was monosyllabic; I guarded my ignorance with noncommittal replies and what I hoped were knowing nods and smiles.

One hot July day, he came upon me by the fountain at the County Art Museum. He was delighted. "Come," he said, "I will show you a painting." He took my arm and stood me before a Soutine. "See this man? See the passion of his strokes? The colors?" He traced his fingers lightly over the trees.

The poplars were wild, writhing like the hair of Medusa. The skies were defiant.

"Feel his love for children?" he asked. Under the treacherous trees, two misty children walked a perilous red road, defenseless and vulnerable.

He said, "To paint, you must feel. You have no right to paint without this," he indicated his heart. He gripped my arm: "Feel that?" he asked. He stroked the back of my hand, "Feel that?"

"Feel the texture of this man's tragedy, his compassion, his love. A painting becomes immortal when one can feel its pain, hear its laughter, smell its soil." He put his fingers to his nose.

I stood humble beside him. How does one paint love, a swelling of the heart, the flowing of glands? How does one paint an unshed tear, a joy? Can a color, a shape bring to mind all the recollections of childhood, or terrors or tendernesses yet to know? Man reaches out to clasp another through this abstract means. How does he know when he's found home? Why is this particular man so kind, so interested that I should catch his message? Does he reach past the graying hair, the neck turning crepey, the propriety by habit? Does he find some warmth worth sharing, worth uttering, worth painting? Or is he only mystified by the Oriental me, inscrutable and restrained. I am a woman, no less than any other, no more.

"Why are you so kind to me?" I asked.

"Because you are a beautiful woman," he said. "That's the important thing."

Aha. Old man, I'm on to you, I thought. I saw myself—the true me, picky, petty, and often irritable. What did he know about me? A woman is a woman; sometimes good, sometimes unbearable; sometimes everything; sometimes nothing. The rest was fantasy.

I protested, "I never expected to hear that from you. What do you know about me? Nothing." My voice returned to me whining.

"You've never even seen my work," I added lamely . . . as though that was the crucial point.

"Please don't misunderstand me," he said. "I see with an inner eye." He studied the ceiling. "I know how you paint," he said. "I see it now. It is soft, but it says nothing because you don't know what you want to say. Am I right? You must make a statement in your work. You must dig into your canvas and look for yourself."

"Maybe that's the real me—indecisive and soft . . ."

He saw the disturbance in my face and smiled. "It's like anything else," he said. "You plant a seed and tend it; care for it. It will grow and flower. I know."

"Yeah," I said. I was thinking perhaps this man knows there are already too many bad pictures. Maybe he's saying if I can't make paintings with my heart, I should give up. But I couldn't give up. It was all I had of myself. I was thinking how long it would take from now until I could really paint. I was thinking of how old I already was, and the years I had not tended that seed. How long would the hand hold up, the eyes, the heart, the hope? A wave of sadness passed over me. I asked, "How long will it take? Ten years? Twenty years?" Forty-four and twenty make sixty-four.

"Forever," he laughed. He took my hand. "And after you die you paint some more. Then you have a head start next time."

He told me he would see the Matisse show at Barnsdall Park on opening day. Then he left.

That's the way we would meet. He'd indicate where he'd be one week, two weeks later. And we'd walk through the galleries hand in hand. We never asked questions of our other lives. I know he wore a wedding band, and I'm sure he noticed mine. I knew he was a painter, but I wasn't perceptive enough to see his pictures as he did mine. I knew his wife would be kind and tender; he could love no other kind. Perhaps he had children—he seemed especially fond of them.

Sometimes when I returned home, I would want to tell my husband about this man who inspired in me such admiration and affection and this feeling of communion, but I was afraid that to speak of the relationship might destroy everything. Perhaps it would be an accusation of the void in our marriage. And that wasn't fair. This marriage was more than my mother had ever dreamed for me. It was more than I could ask for in a union of two people like ourselves: he'd given me all he had been able to give. It was I who withheld. But perhaps his eyes would inquire, "Is that the whole cloth? Platonic love? Is that all?" and I couldn't endure that. They were questions I couldn't ask myself. But I knew one day I would have to.

It crept upon me with stealth, and I became aware that his touch, his smile, could spring me to life. I would come home shaken. Alone at home I would sit before my canvas thinking: paint a love, paint a desire.

I tried to reason with myself: love is caring, comforting, wanting the best for someone. I love my husband; he's given me all he can. If it isn't enough for me, the fault lies in myself. It took years to build our marriage to this point; to threaten it with such a tenuous dream would be to destroy twenty years of living. What do I know of this other man who reveals only the best in himself? But who of us wants to reveal less, and what really counts but the best in us? Why should we not love the best in one another? All right, but we commit ourselves to only one. Desire is not the same as love. Yes, I love him, I yearn for him, yes. But there's no danger in that as long as I can hold these to myself until they can be stilled, until they turn to ashes. Besides, he wouldn't permit himself to hurt his family. After all, it's only a middle-age fantasy – not uncommon. A cinder in the eye, a heel in the instep, a sharing of interests – only variations of the old theme. What would he see in me anyway? An aging woman making a final thrust to transcend herself. Pathetic. A graying Japanese woman, a once-young Japanese woman who never visualized in her parsimonious dreams a fulfillment so near perfection. So near. It doesn't matter. It's only a dream. I can't harbor these thoughts any longer. It would hurt my husband too much. It would destroy his faith in himself – the bountiful provider. I couldn't stand between another man and his wife anyway. If I were his wife, I would die from the theft.

Still, I couldn't prevent myself from going to meet him.

One day we didn't look at pictures. It was toward the end of September. We had met at the Otis Gallery, and instead we walked across the street to Westlake Park. We strolled on the asphalt walk among the iridescent pigeons and happy children and scolding parents and old folks sunning. We stopped now and then to watch some little play or speak a few words. I was completely happy.

He held my hand and spoke softly: "Observe the light, how it passes through those leaves and down around the soft felt brim of the man's hat, and over his porous nose, and soft again on his grizzled chin. Look under the brim; his eyelids catch a reflected light, almost transparent. What does he dream?"

A fat young woman waddled by, licking a huge cone of ice cream. As she walked away from us, he said, "That woman is fat, and she's acting, 'I don't care. I eat and I don't care. I don't care if no one admires me,' but inside she's crying,'Look at me closely; I'm beautiful. I need you to love me,' and she's crying this loudly–louder than any thin woman." He stepped back and looked at me over his nose. "Louder than you," he said.

I was stunned; I couldn't speak. After a while he said, "I will kiss you."

"Now?" I asked.

He smiled. "Not now. I will tell you when."

"You ought not to–I don't think so," I said. I was having a time pulling myself together, and my voice was getting shrill.

"I think so," he said softly.

"No . . ."

"At any rate, come to my studio," he said. "I must talk to you."

"No. I can't . . . I can't . . ."

He was incredulous. "Why?" he asked.

"I've got to get home," I said.

"I won't keep you long. Come." He took my arm.

"I can't. I've got to go home." I stood rooted. A pigeon cocked its head at me. The muscles of my right cheek fluttered in distress.

"Well then, tomorrow at three," he said. He looked at me sternly, gave me his studio address and left.

I walked through the park alone, trying to get hold of myself. Under the trees, over the knoll, around the benches, and along the paved shores of the artificial lake. I was trying to find the third-person me who's always been able to help. But nowhere . . . nowhere. The phrase "I can't, I can't" repeated itself insanely as though it were the problem and the solution. Finally, when my knees felt stronger and my shoes began to pinch, I started home.

At night I lay in my husband's arms and wanted to cry. I wanted to tell what had transpired; he could comfort me, tell me what to do. With precision he could cut to the bone of a structure and find the weakness in it. He knew what to do for anything and how to mend it, strengthen it. But we didn't deal with stone and steel here. It wasn't a wedge here, a support there, and everything will be all right. From where he stood, this affair would lay like a rotten clot, dark in the shadows, the stench pervading his beautiful house. No. It wasn't right. I couldn't do it . . . couldn't go.

But I did. I pulled myself together and went. I knew I would only be playing games with myself and with him, but I couldn't endure the thought of him waiting for me, believing in me, until the daylight left his window.

I knew what I had to say. I rehearsed it: I've given you the only good thing that's me, and you have shown me more than I've ever expected to know or feel. Nothing is more precious than these, and I am not willing to tarnish them with furtive trysts. I've made a commitment years ago that I cannot ignore. You've often spoken of love and compassion; I ask you to extend them to me now. Perhaps I should not have loved so much–perhaps I don't love enough. Still, love cannot flourish in the anguish of others.

That was the essence of it.

I arrived there before three, because in the back of my mind I was still looking for a way to slip out of this situation without hurting him or damaging his feeling for me. The studio was up a flight of weather-worn stairs. I stopped at the landing and breathed the fresh wind before knocking on the door. I was relieved to find he was not yet there. I rummaged through my purse for paper and found a coupon that I could write on. I began:

"I came as you asked but am unable to stay. I can't ever stay. Ever."

I was looking for a phrase that might convey finality and still show how much I felt for him. I didn't hear him come up the stairs. His breath was warm on my neck.

"What are you doing?" he asked.

"I planned to leave a note for you," I said.

"You're being foolish," he said. He smiled tolerantly, took the note, and opened his door.

Up to then I was so filled with anxieties about conducting myself, I wasn't prepared for his paintings—didn't even think of them. He took my hand and led me as he always did.

It was like what the first bite of food is to a stomach in pain from hunger. All the senses stir and rush out to meet this food in great urgency, and the digestive juices flow over and claim it. And the outer body trembles, not aware of what is occurring, only that this particular condition and that particular substance is causing this reaction.

I was overwhelmed. The canvases were enormous and hung on every wall. He painted in abstraction, passionately, angrily, happily, contemptuously, tenderly, hopelessly; each unmistakable in its statement: fruit unreal yet juicier, sweeter than life; shafts of sunlight warm as a spring morning; skies bluer than any I'd known, with nostalgia of another place, another homeland.

I stood moved, inadequate. It seemed like I could find something profound to say, but all I could muster up was "They're beautiful." My words were like an obscenity.

He pulled me toward him, took me in his arms. I put my head against the coarse cloth of his coat, and it was as though I had finally come home. I felt a peace; I could have stayed like this forever. But I knew I was at a very precarious place. He lifted my face and kissed me; it was like a promise—everything in me yearned to return it. I knew if I didn't hang in there, I would be lost.

I pulled away muttering, "I can't . . . I've got to leave . . ."

"My dear," he said, "would you leave me like this?"

All those beautiful words I had rehearsed were nowhere to be found. I was ready to cry; I couldn't look at him with my wretched emotions spread baldly over my face. I kept my eyes on the floor. Finally I managed, "We would hurt too many people."

"We're hurting no one," he said. "My life is to feel."

Hurting no one. Hurting no one! I'd heard of people who lived like that. But not this man—not those who loved him. It wasn't true we were hurting no one. I alone would leave a devastating swath of hurt. Amazing how that one phrase brought me plummeting to the ground.

"But I live a more prosaic life," I said. "I couldn't do this to people I love."

Yes, prosaic. That was my heritage and my mother's before me and countless daughters of mothers before her. Yes, commonplace. Ordinary. Was his perhaps the real way to live: love and give totally, without regret or obligation, to extend one's self to the limit of his capacity of love, of pain, of feeling, of giving and taking, and still be true (darling in my fashion) to the commitments one's made?

Commitments . . . tattered remnants of my speech fluttered back to me. Well, too late now. Commitments, compassion, love, anguish—we spoke a different language. There was no use saying anything now.

"I have to go," I said in my mother's daughter's voice, and from somewhere back there I could see myself pulling away, regretfully, of course.

"My dear," he bowed. There was pity for me.

He walked me to his door and outside to the landing. The sun was out, and there was a strong cool breeze that blew away the warmth of his room, his embrace, the confusion of the moment before.

I scampered down the stairs and walked briskly across the parking lot. I looked back and saw that he still stood leaning on the railing. He had worn his wine-red scarf—it fluttered at his breast pocket like a wound. I smiled and waved and mouthed, "Good-bye." It seemed to me he called out something, but with the wind and traffic sounds, I was unable to hear. I cupped my ear to him. He smiled broadly, raised his hand, and called out again. It was unmistakable:

"Coward!"

I nodded and bowed in the manner he often did for me and said more to myself than to him, "You did not hurt me, Sir."

Maybe

W hen I am out of sorts, I often drive to the outer edge of the city to
calm myself. I love the outskirts. It reminds me of the land as it must
have looked before we covered the earth with cement. I find there a
feeling of the prairie where I was born. Sometimes when I see an old house with
peeling paint squatting on a mound of dry weeds, the setting sun bleaching its
west wall, I think I hear the children that have played there, perhaps now as old
as myself—if they have survived the depression, three wars, sickness, and
heartbreak. At this point I remember where I am in the scheme of things,
smaller than a grain of sand and as dispensable. It comforts me.

One day on such a drive, I found the factory just outside of town. Here
narrow roads burrow through low hills; and frame houses, shutters askew like
unfocused eyes, along with rusting cars and oil drums, are enclosed by the
chain-link fence that banks the city drain. The lots are oddly shaped; city
planners had exercised eminent domain and sliced the properties at their
convenience, creating instant prosperity to the owners (providing rabbit-skin
coats and hand-tooled boots), maiming the lots for that brief prosperity (a tuft
of fur caught in the chain links, a weathered boot lying with the flotsam in the
weeds). A sign on the outer wall of the factory: HELP, succinct, desperate, still
with a touch of humor, gave me courage to walk in. After all, I was no less in
need, my alimony had dwindled to a trickle; after eight years, that's about par
for course, my attorney said. Even after twenty-five years of marriage, he said.
That's life. The owner himself, Chuck White, took me in like a lost member of a
tribe. We're of the same generation.

I am embarrassed to tell you the name of the company; it's too presumptuous for the two stories of rotting wood and broken windows and air conditioners hanging off the walls. Those that still function spin out tails of spidery dust in the tepid air. But that's only in the offices, not for the majority of us.

I will call it Zodiac Prints. When I joined them, they were printing signs of the zodiac on T-shirts and cloth posters. I was hired as a quality-control person. They put me at the end of a long conveyor belt that slowly passes through several silk screens, each a different color, and a drying process. I check the colors, the print, and the material for flaws, and I stack and bundle the finished product. They don't say Zodiac till *I* say they say Zodiac.

Although I was the last hired, I was sent to the end of the belt largely because of Chuck White. White people (no pun intended) do not observe the difference between native Japanese and Japanese Americans. As I said, I was born in the southern California desert, but people are often amazed that I can speak English, and I guess Chuck White associates me with Japanese industry (Sony, Toyota, et cetera), and just for walking in and asking for a job, I went to the back of the line which in this case is the top of the bottom. This inability of white America to differentiate worked against thousands of us Japanese Americans in 1942 when we were all put in concentration camps, blamed for Japan's attack on Pearl Harbor. Since then there have been other harrowing moments—the save-the-whale issue, the slaughter of dolphins, and always during trade treaties over Japanese exports—each sending waves of guilt by association. On the extreme, some of us have been clubbed to death by our superpatriots, and we have always been admonished to go back where we came from.

Anyway, back at Zodiac, the story I hear is that Chuck White was having financial trouble and had taken steps toward declaring bankruptcy. He planned to drop out, wipe off the slate of debts, and start clean at another place under his wife's name—Zenobia. They say it isn't the first time Chuck did this, but the first with the new wife.

Preparations for the change had been made; a new site was selected, new business cards with Zenobia's name were printed, and Zenobia was coming in daily to get a working knowledge of the business. Then, suddenly the orders came pouring in and with it thousands of dollars. New people had to be hired. The factory started to hum again, and the move was postponed. This is where I came in.

They say that Zenobia—Colombian by birth, a ravishing overweight beauty at least twenty years Chuck White's junior (like my husband's new wife)—changed from a quiet housewife to a formidable boss as easily as she would put on a coat, wearing all the executive qualities, the harassed eyes, the no-nonsense walk, the imperial forefinger, and also a touch of paternal benevolence—the sodas and tacos on the days that we worked overtime. Most of the workers are from Mexico, Nicaragua, and Costa Rica. The sales staff is white, but they are often not at the factory.

Zenobia watches me when she thinks I'm not looking. I catch her reflection on the dirty glass panes, and when I turn to face her, she flashes her perfect teeth. She doesn't like me. Maybe I remind her of someone. Maybe she's amazed that I can speak English. China, she calls me. Maybe she thinks I'm a communist.

Most of the time, she's busy on the phone or is rushing off somewhere in her silver Mercedes. Probably to the bank. She wears Gloria Vanderbilt jeans and carries a Gucci bag and smells of expensive perfume. When Chuck White is out of town, she moves me from one floor to the other for unimportant reasons. Just to let me know how superfluous I am.

So it goes. I've had worse things happen to me, and nothing about this job causes me to lose sleep. Almost nothing. There's a certain confidence in knowing you're overqualified, and Zenobia does not diminish me. Besides, I like the second floor; the project is more interesting. They tie-dye there. Twenty people bend over paint troughs, dipping and squeezing shirts, skirts, and other things, and the items hang to dry on rows and rows of lines, dripping and making puddles of color on the worn floor.

There are three big German shepherd dogs in the factory. During the worst of his days (I'm told), Chuck White had to sell his Bel Air house, but Zenobia would not let him sell the dogs. So the dogs live in the ramshackle factory, and they follow Umberto, who feeds and cleans up after them, everywhere he goes— roaming the floors (they're not permitted outside), in and out of rooms, up and down the stairs, stumbled on and cursed at by the workers. When Umberto is not here, these monstrous animals lie disconsolately on the floor wherever their depression happens to drop them. Umberto calls them by name and rubs their monster heads, and they thump their powerful tails and slosh him with saliva. He's patient and gentle. He's twenty-four and quite handsome.

Everyone here who is from the other Americas is between seventeen and twenty-five. They all speak Spanish, some a little English, and they generally work quietly, obeying Zenobia or Rachel (the floorlady) without question or comment. In the late afternoons and on paydays, Jesus (El Savior) begins to sing and an excitement prevails, even though we groan and laugh at his comic straining for high notes. I am reminded of my own youth, after being released from camp, the period that I spent working in factories, looking over the boys, waiting for the end of the day, looking forward to my paycheck, mentally parceling out the money—to the layaway at Lerner's, for rent, food, for bus tokens. Fridays were just like these, with another Jesus singing and cutting up, with everyone waiting for the factory whistle so we could go on with our real lives. I've come full circle, back to a place that has remained unchanged in the changing times, in the age of Pac-Man and the computer. Maybe all displaced people go through a period of innocence before the desire to own, the ambition to be, propel us away from simple pleasures. The return is sweet with re-membrance, along with a little sorrow—for the loss of innocence. But I'm older now, and none of the senses are so acute and no pain so unbearable. And yet . . .

On a coffee break, I walk to the low hills for a breath of fresh air. Reynaldo and Anabella sit on top of the knoll on a scrap of plastic. Reynaldo is in charge of the keys to the factory and is married to Anabella. She doesn't speak much English, so she always stays close to him, letting him transact the business of their lives. Faded pop cans lie in the dry grass.

"How romantic," I say to them.

"It is hot in the factory," Reynaldo says. Anabella whispers something.

"We are talking about our son," Reynaldo says.

Why, Anabella looks no more than seventeen. I tell him this.

"She is twenty-one, same as me," Reynaldo says. "We are married already five years. Our son is in Mexico still. Today is his birthday."

Walking down the hill, I am filled with their longing. I stop to look back at them. Anabella waves.

Umberto is not conscientious about cleaning the factory. The women's bathroom is dotted with dog droppings. I complain, and Umberto tells me not to use it.

"I cannot clean everything all the time and do the work also," he says. "The dogs, you know, they do it all the time. I cannot keep up. Go to the office toilet."

He tells me they pay him three dollars and thirty-five cents an hour – the minimum. He gets up at four to come to work; his bus fare is three dollars, and lunch from the catering truck almost always costs six dollars a day. He is so tired at the end of day, he cannot stay awake. He shakes his head. "I am still a young man," he says.

The reedy whistle of the catering truck rises above factory noises and a surge of people run to meet it. The chatter grows bright with food words: *tortillas, pollo, naranja*. My high-school Spanish is inadequate; I wish I knew what else is said. Umberto sits on the ground to eat, carefully placing the paper plate in the circle of his legs. I feel the sublime intimacy of the man and his food.

To get to the office bathroom, I must pass through Chuck White's office. He sits at a big desk looking over invoices in a pool of sunlight. The floor is carpeted, the walls are papered; the room is an oasis in the factory. He looks up briefly and smiles – almost an apology. "The other bathroom is filthy," I say. He nods and returns to his papers. No doubt he's heard of the fastidious Japanese.

Someone tried to bring some class to the bathroom and had painted the walls a dark green and installed a pair of fancy faucets in the sink. An electric hotplate on a crate destroys the ambiance, and there is a bottle of shampoo on the floor. The toilet here doesn't flush right either.

Umberto tells me that Reynaldo and Anabella live in the factory at night. I see no bed, no blankets, no clothes – only the hotplate and shampoo in the office bathroom. I think about the eerie loneliness of this huge factory at night, the three dogs groaning and snuffling and shuffling, the doors that hardly close, and Reynaldo and Anabella copulating on the production table with the smell of the dogs and the spoiling vegetable dyes and the summer moon shining on their skin. And in the morning I see them putting away the evidence of their living: the underwear, the socks, the toothbrushes, combs, and towels.

But Umberto says Zenobia knows about this. She lets them stay because they have nowhere else to go. Umberto himself shares rent with six other people. "I have no room for them," he says.

In winter, icy winds will blow through those broken windows and ill-fitting doors, and the production table will be cold and hard, I tell Umberto.

"That's winter," he shrugs.

Reynaldo makes a sandwich from a loaf of Weber's bread and pressed meat. He spreads the bread with a thin swipe of mayonnaise and eats this with a gusto that can come only from hunger or habit. Anabella buys fried chicken, frijoles, and tortillas from the truck and shares these with Reynaldo. She eats slowly and sensually, careful not to lose a morsel from the chicken bones. She eats a sandwich too. I make fun; I point to her stomach and ask, "How many months?" She holds up four fingers.

I have a feeling Zenobia likes the sales staff as little as she does me. They bring her extravagant gifts and she puts on a dazzling smile and turns away, quickly dropping the smile as though she hopes her hypocrisy would be discovered. But on her birthday she invites them all to a party—everyone except me. I'd already contributed five dollars toward her gift, and I had signed the birthday card.

She's happy all day, smiling and humming, but I pretend not to know what's up and try to look happy too. What do I care? If she has a conscience at all, she'll feel rotten when she sees my name on the card. I wish Rachel had let me do the shopping; I'd have fixed her good (I thought I'd given up feelings like that).

At the party they say Zenobia drinks too much and kisses all the young men. That's because she married an old man, Umberto says. Late in the evening she sniffs cocaine and turns up the music and wants to dance with all the guys. Chuck White serves the cake and goes to bed. Neighbors call to complain about the noise, and everyone gets nervous thinking about police and raids and such things. These are always on the top of an undocumented alien's mind, Umberto says. Zenobia doesn't care; she married a white man and holds a green card. Umberto says everyone in the factory except the sales staff is undocumented. Reynaldo comes to sit with us.

"Are you illegal too?" I ask.

Reynaldo nods. "Everybody is. In this factory, in all the restaurants around here, all these places," he waves his hands. "These places, they would not stand without us." He pokes my arm and laughs. "Hey, you want to marry me? I'll give you one thousand dollars," he says.

"What will we do with Anabella?" I say.

"After our divorce, I will marry her," he says.

"But I have children older than you," I say.

He moves away and calls back, "One thousand dollars, Florence." Anabella smiles at me.

Andrea stands at the bus stop with a plastic purse clasped to her breast. She is seventeen and the prettiest girl in the factory, but today she looks awful. It's before the lunch hour. "Is she sick?" I ask Umberto.

"Well, Chuck told her to go home," he says.

The story is, Zenobia was so anxious to get an order off, she told Andrea to remove the bands before time and dry the shirts. Andrea did this, but she put the shirts in the tumble dryer, and the wet dyes ran together and the whole order was ruined. Chuck White found the mess and fired Andrea. Even after he was told about Zenobia's instructions, he would not relent. "She should know better," he said and went to his office and closed the door.

Umberto taps his head. "She should know better," he says.

"Look how she holds her purse," I say.

"Well, she's sad," he says.

"Her mother will ask what happened, and she'll have to say she lost her job."

"Rachel will find another for her," Umberto says.

"What will happen if she doesn't?" I ask.

"Then I will find for her," he says.

Reynaldo punches my arm every time he passes by, mocking me softly, "One thousand dollars, Florence." Sometimes he catches my eye from across the room and mouths, "One thousand dollars."

I call a young single friend to ask if she would marry Reynaldo. She is divorced and always in need of money, but she tells me that immigration laws require a full three years of marriage before they will issue green cards. "That's longer than some real marriages last," my friend says. "One thousand dollars for three years is three hundred and thirty-three dollars a year," she says.

"And thirty-three cents," I add.

"I turned down ten thousand for the same service," she says. "And I could very well meet someone myself in three years. A real marriage, you know what I mean?"

I give Reynaldo the bad news. He looks hurt even though we only joke about it. I tell him my friend says three years is too long to be tied to a stranger.

"I just want a green card so I can bring my son here," he says. "My son was two years when we left him. He already forgot me, I think." Anabella turns her face away.

"I can't marry you, Reynaldo," I say.

"I know," he says. After a while he walks away.

I'm afraid I shall leave Zodiac soon. In the deceptive simplicity of the lives here, there is a quality I am unable to face. It's the underbelly of a smile. I know it well.

I remember our life in the Arizona camp—the first day our family entered that empty barracks room (our home for the next four years), my father squatted on the dusty floor, his head deep in his shoulders, and my mother unwrapped a roll of salami and sliced it for us. I wanted so much to cry, but my mother gripped my arm and gave me the meat. I turned to my father; he looked

Maybe – 151

up and smiled. Two years later, the day I was to leave them and relocate to Chicago, my mother stood by the army truck that was to take us to the train in Parker. She had not wanted me to leave because my father was in the hospital with stomach ulcers. She did not touch me. The corners of her mouth wavered once, then turned up in a smile. And in the same tradition, I smiled when my husband told me he was marrying a young woman from Japan. "That's good," I said.

It did not seem so brave or so sad then. Maybe living it is easier than remembering or watching someone else living it. My son is in Mexico still, ha-ha; he will soon forget me.

Late in the afternoon Reynaldo comes back to me and pokes my arm. "Thank you for telling your friend to marry me," he says.

"I'm sorry it didn't work out," I say. I ask him if he crossed the border at Tijuana. My sister lives in National City, just north of the border. I remember those immigration roundups that show periodically on television nightly news: soft gray blurs running in the California twilight, crouching, routed out of bushes, herded into covered pickup trucks, their faces impassive.

"We crossed the river in Texas," he says.

"You swam the Rio Grande at night?" I ask.

Reynaldo nods. "Anabella, you know, she does not swim so I . . ." He crooks his left arm to make a circle for Anabella's head and with his right arm he makes swimming strokes and looks at me and smiles.

Maybe it does not seem so brave or so sad to him. Maybe I should spare myself the pain.

And the Soul
Shall Dance

The first production of *And the Soul Shall Dance* was February 23–April 16, 1977 (extended run), at East-West Players. It was produced by Rae Creavy and Clyde Kusatsu and directed by Mako and Alberto Issac.

Double Cast

Shizuko Hoshi, Haunani Minn	EMIKO
J. Maseras Pepito, Pat Li	HANA
Jim Ishida, Sab Shimono	MURATA
Keone Young, Yuki Shimoda	OKA
Mimosa Iwamatsu, Denice Kumagai	MASAKO
Susan Inouye, Diane Takei	KIYOKO

Characters

MURATA, 40, Issei farmer
HANA, 35, Issei wife of Murata
MASAKO, 11, Nisei daughter of the Muratas
OKA, 45, Issei farmer
EMIKO, 30, wife of Oka
KIYOKO, 14, Oka's daughter

ACT I	Scene i Summer afternoon, 1935. Muratas' kitchen
	Scene ii That evening. Okas' yard and beyond
	Scene iii The same evening. Okas' yard
ACT II	Scene i Mid-September afternoon. Muratas' kitchen and yard
	Scene ii November night. Muratas' kitchen
	Scene iii The next morning. Muratas' yard
	Scene iv The following spring afternoon. Okas' yard
	Scene v Same day, late afternoon. Muratas' yard
	Scene vi Same evening. Desert

Kokoro Ga Odoru

Akai kuchibiru
Kappu ni yosete
Aoi sake nomya
Kokoro ga odoru

Kurai yoru no yume
Setsu nasa yo
Aoi sake nomya
Yume ga odoru

Asa no munashisa
Yume wo chirasu
Sora to kokoro wa
Sake shidai

Futari wakare no
Samishisa yo
Hitori sake nomya
Kokoro ga odoru

And the Soul Shall Dance

Red lips
Press against a glass
Drink the green wine
And the soul shall dance

In the dark night
Dreams are unbearable
Drink the green wine
And the dreams will dance

The morning's truth
Scatter the dreams
Sky and soul
Are suspended by wine

In the separation
The desolation
Drink the wine
And the soul shall dance

ACT I
Scene i

Summer afternoon, 1935

ON RISE: *Interior of the Murata house. The set is spare. There are a kitchen table, four chairs, a bed, and on the wall, a calendar indicating the year and month: June 1935. A doorway leads to the other room. Props are: a bottle of sake, two cups, a dish of chiles, a phonograph, and two towels hanging on pegs on the wall. A wide wooden bench is outside.*

The bathhouse has just burned to the ground due to MASAKO's carelessness. Offstage there are sounds of MURATA putting out the fire.

Inside, HANA MURATA, in a drab housedress, confronts MASAKO (in summer dress). MASAKO is sullen and defiant.

HANA: How could you be so careless, Masako? You know you should be extra careful with fire. How often have I told you? Now the whole bathhouse is gone. I told you time and again—when you stoke a fire, you must see that everything is swept into the fireplace.

[MURATA enters. He is in old work clothes. He suffers from heat and exhaustion.]

MURATA *[coughing]*: Shack went up like a matchbox. This kind of weather dries everything . . . just takes a spark to make a bonfire out of that dry timber.

HANA: Did you save any of it?

MURATA: No. Couldn't.

HANA *[to MASAKO]*: How many times have I told you . . .

[MASAKO moves nervously.]

MURATA: No use crying about it now. *Shikata ga nai*. It's gone now. No more bathhouse. That's all.

HANA: But you've got to tell her. Otherwise she'll make the same mistake. You'll be building a bathhouse every year.

[MURATA removes his shirt and wipes off his face. He throws his shirt on a chair and sits at the table.]

MURATA: *Baka!* Ridiculous!

MASAKO: I didn't do it on purpose.

156 – And the Soul Shall Dance

[MASAKO goes to the bed. She opens a book. HANA follows her.]

HANA: I know that, but you know what this means? It means we bathe in a bucket . . . inside the house. Carry water in from the pond, heat it on the stove . . . we'll use more kerosene.

MURATA: Tub's still there. And the fireplace. We can still build a fire under the tub.

HANA *[shocked]*: But no walls! Everyone in the country can see us!

MURATA: Wait till dark then. Wait till dark.

HANA: We'll be using a lantern. They'll still see us.

MURATA: Angh! Who? Who'll see us? You think everyone in the country waits to watch us take a bath? Hunh! You know how stupid you sound? Who cares about a couple of farmers taking a bath at night?

HANA *[defensively]*: It'll be inconvenient.

[HANA is saved by a rap on the door. OKA enters. He is short and stout. He wears faded work clothes.]

OKA: Hello! Hello! *Oi!* What's going on here? Hey! Was there some kind of fire?

[HANA rushes to the door to let OKA in. He stamps the dust from his shoes and enters.]

HANA: Oka-san! You just wouldn't believe . . . We had a terrible thing happen.

OKA: Yeah. Saw the smoke from down the road. Thought it was your house. Came rushing over. Is the fire out?

[MURATA half rises and sits back again. He's exhausted.]

MURATA *[gesturing]*: *Oi, oi.* Come in. Sit down. No big problem. It was just our bathhouse.

OKA: Just the *furoba*, eh?

MURATA: Just the bath.

HANA: Our Musako was careless, and the *furoba* caught fire. There's nothing left but the tub.

[MASAKO looks up from her book, pained. She makes a small sound.]

OKA: Long as the tub's there, no problem. I'll help you with it.

[He starts to roll up his sleeves.]

MURATA: What . . . now? Now?

OKA: *[heh-heh]* Long as I'm here.

HANA: Oh, Papa. Aren't we lucky to have such friends?

MURATA *[to HANA]*: We can't work on it now. The ashes are still hot. I just now put the damned fire out. Let me rest a while. *[to OKA]* Oi, how about a little sake? *[gesturing to HANA]* Make sake for Oka-san.

> *[OKA sits at the table. HANA goes to prepare the sake. She heats it, gets out the cups, and pours it for the men.]*

MURATA *[continuing]*: I'm tired . . . I am *tired.*

HANA: Oka-san has so generously offered his help. . . .

> *[OKA is uncomfortable. He looks around and sees MASAKO sitting on the bed.]*

OKA: Hello, there, Masako-chan. You studying?

MASAKO: No, it's summer vacation.

MURATA *[sucking in his breath]*: Kids nowadays . . . no manners.

HANA: She's sulking because I had to scold her.

> *[MASAKO makes a small moan.]*

MURATA: Drink, Oka-san.

OKA *[sipping]*: Ahhhh . . . That's good.

MURATA: Eh, you not working today?

OKA: No-no. I took the afternoon off today. I was driving over to Nagata-san's when I saw this big black cloud of smoke coming from your yard.

HANA: It went up so fast.

MURATA: What's up at Nagata-kun's? *[to HANA]* Get out the chiles. Oka-san loves chiles.

> *[HANA opens a jar of chiles and puts them on a plate. She serves them and gets out her mending basket and walks to MASAKO. MASAKO makes room for her.]*

OKA *[helping himself]*: Ah, chiles.

> *[MURATA waits for an answer.]*

OKA *[continuing]*: Well, I want to see him about my horse. I'm thinking of selling my horse.

MURATA: Sell your horse?

OKA *[scratching his head]*: The fact is, I need some money. Nagata-san's the only one around made money this year, and I'm thinking he might want another horse.

MURATA: Yeah, he made a little this year. And he's talking big . . . big! Says he's leasing twenty more acres this fall.

OKA: Twenty acres?

MURATA: Yeah. He might want another horse.

OKA: Twenty acres, eh?

MURATA: That's what he says. But you know his old woman makes all the decisions at that house.

[OKA scratches his head.]

HANA: They're doing all right.

MURATA: Heh. Nagata-kun's so henpecked, it's pathetic. Peko-peko. *[He makes henpecking motions.]*

OKA *[feeling the strain]*: I better get over there.

MURATA: Why the hell you selling your horse?

OKA: Well . . . a . . . I need cash.

MURATA: Oh yeah. I could use some too. Seems like everyone's getting out of the depression but the poor farmers. Nothing changes for us. We go on and on planting our tomatoes and summer squash and eating them. Well, at least it's healthy.

HANA: Papa, do you have lumber?

MURATA: Lumber? For what?

HANA: The bath . . .

MURATA *[impatiently]*: Don't worry about that. We need more sake now.

[HANA rises wearily.]

OKA: You sure Nagata-kun's working twenty more?

MURATA: Last I heard. What the hell, if you need a few bucks, I can loan (you) . . .

OKA: A few hundred. I need a few hundred dollars.

MURATA: Oh, a few hundred. But what the hell you going to do without a horse? Out here a man's horse is as important as his wife.

OKA *[seriously]*: I don't think Nagata will buy my wife.

> *[The men laugh, but HANA doesn't find it so funny. MURATA glances at her. She fills the cups again. OKA makes a half-hearted gesture to stop her. MASAKO watches the pantomime carefully. OKA finishes his drink.]*

OKA *[continuing]*: I better get moving.

MURATA: What's the big hurry?

OKA: Like to get the horse business done.

MURATA: Eh . . . relax. Do it tomorrow. He's not going to die, is he?

OKA *[laughing]*: Hey, he's a good horse. I want to get it settled today. If Nagata-kun won't buy, I got to find someone else.

OKA *[continuing]*: You think maybe Kawaguchi-kun . . . ?

MURATA: No-no. Not Kawaguchi. Maybe Yamamoto.

HANA: What is all the money for, Oka-san? Does Emiko-san need an operation?

OKA: No-no. Nothing like that.

HANA: Sounds very mysterious.

OKA: No mystery, Missus. No mystery. No sale, no money, no story.

MURATA *[laughing]*: That's a good one. "No sale, no money, no . . ." Eh, Mama . . . *[He points to the empty cups.]*

HANA *[filling the cups, muttering]*: I see we won't be getting any work done today. *[to MASAKO]* Are you reading again? Maybe we'd still have a bath if you . . .

MASAKO: I didn't do it on purpose.

MURATA *[loudly]*: I sure hope you know what you're doing, Oka-kun. What'd you do without a horse?

OKA: I was hoping you'd lend me yours now and then. *[He looks at HANA.]* I'll pay for some of the feed.

MURATA: Sure! Sure!

OKA: The fact is, I need that money. I got a daughter in Japan, and I just got to send for her this year.

[HANA leaves her mending and sits at the table.]

HANA: A daughter? You have a daughter in Japan? Why, I didn't know you had children. Emiko-san and you . . . I thought you were childless.

OKA *[scratching his head]*: We are. I was married before.

MURATA: You son-of-a-gun!

HANA *[overlapping]*: Is that so? How old is your daughter?

OKA: Kiyoko must be . . . fifteen now. Yeah, fifteen.

HANA: Fifteen! Oh, that *would* be too old for Emiko-san, child. Is Kiyoko-san living with relatives in Japan?

OKA *[reluctantly]*: With grandparents. Shizue's parents. *[pause]* Well, the fact is, Shizue – that's my first wife – Shizue and Emiko were sisters. They come from a family with no sons. I was a boy when I went to work for them . . . as an apprentice. They're blacksmiths. Later I married Shizue and took on the family name – you know, *yoshi* – because they had no sons. My real name is Sakakihara.

MURATA: Sakakihara! That's a great name!

HANA: A magnificent name!

OKA: No one knows me by that here.

MURATA: Should have kept that – Sakakihara.

OKA *[muttering]*: I don't even know myself by that name.

HANA: And Shizue-san passed away and you married Emiko-san?

OKA: Oh. Well, Shizue and I lived with the family for a while, and we had the baby – you know, Kiyoko. *[He gets looser with the liquor.]* Well, while I was serving apprentice with the family, they always looked down their noses at me. After I married, it got worse.

HANA *[distressed]*: Worse!

OKA: That old man . . . *[unnnnh!]* Always pushing me around, making me look bad in front of my wife and kid. That old man was the meanest . . . ugliest . . .

MURATA: Yeah, I heard about that apprentice work – *detchi-boko*. Heard it was damned humiliating.

OKA: That's the God's truth!

MURATA: Never had to do it myself. I came to America instead. They say *detchi-boko* is blood work.

OKA: The work's all right. I'm not afraid of work. It's the humiliation! I hated them! Pushing me around like I was still a boy. Me, a grown man! And married to their daughter!

[MURATA and HANA groan in sympathy.]

OKA *[continuing]*: Well, Shizue and I talked it over, and we decided the best thing was to get away. We thought if I came to America and made some money . . . you know, send her money until we had enough, and I'd go back and we'd leave the family . . . you know, move to another province . . . start a small business, maybe in the city . . . a noodle shop or something.

MURATA: That's everyone's dream. Make money, go home, and live like a king.

And the Soul Shall Dance – 161

OKA: I worked like a dog. Sent every penny to Shizue. And then she dies. She died on me!

> [HANA *and* MURATA *observe a moment of silence in respect for* OKA'*s anguish.*]

HANA: And you married Emiko-san.

OKA: I didn't marry her. They married her to me! Right after Shizue died.

HANA: But Oka-san, you were lu(cky) . . .

OKA: Before the body was cold! No respect. By proxy. The old man wrote me that they were arranging a marriage by proxy for me and Emiko. They said she'd grown to be a beautiful woman and would serve me well.

HANA: Emiko-san *is* a beautiful woman.

OKA: And they sent her to me. Took care of everything! Immigration, fare, everything.

HANA: But she's your sister-in-law. Kiyoko's aunt. It's good to keep the family together.

OKA: That's what I thought. But hear this: Emiko was the favored one. Shizue was not so pretty, not so smart. They were grooming Emiko for a rich man – his name was Yamato – lived in a grand house in the village. They sent her to schools; you know, the culture thing: the dance, tea ceremony, you know, all that. They didn't even like me, and suddenly they married her to me.

MURATA: Yeah. You don't need all that formal training to make it over here. Just a strong back.

HANA: And a strong will.

OKA: It was all arranged. I couldn't do anything about it.

HANA: It'll be all right. With Kiyoko-san coming . . .

OKA [*dubiously*]: I hope so. [*pause*] I never knew human beings could be so cruel. You know how they mistreated my daughter? After Emiko came here, things got from bad to worse, and I *never* had enough money to send to Kiyoko and . . .

MURATA: They don't know what it's like here. They think money's picked off the ground here.

OKA: And they treated Kiyoko so bad. They told her I forgot about her. They told her I didn't care . . . said I abandoned her. Well, she knew better. She wrote to me all the time, and I always told her I'd send for her . . . as soon as I got the money. [*He shakes his head.*] I just got to do something this year.

HANA: She'll be happier here. She'll know her father cares.

OKA: Kids tormented her for being an orphan.

MURATA: Kids are cruel.

HANA: Masako will help her. She'll help her get started at school. She'll make friends. She'll be all right.

OKA: I hope so. She'll need friends. *[He tries to convince himself he's making the right decision.]* What could I say to her? Stay there? It's not what you think over here? I can't help her? I just have to do this thing. I just have to do this one thing for her.

MURATA: Sure.

HANA: Don't worry. It'll work out fine.

[MURATA gestures to HANA. She gets the sake.]

MURATA: You talk about selling your horse, I thought you were pulling out.

OKA: I wish I could. But there's nothing else I can do.

MURATA: Without money, yeah.

OKA: You can go into some kind of business with money, but a man like me . . . no education . . . there's no kind of job I can do. I'd starve in the city.

MURATA: Dishwashing, maybe. Janitor.

OKA: At least here we can eat. Carrots, maybe, but we can eat.

[They laugh. HANA starts to pour more wine.]

OKA: I better not drink anymore. Got to drive to Nagata-san's yet. *[He walks over to MASAKO.]* You study hard, don't you? You'll teach Kiyoko English, eh? When she gets here . . . ?

HANA: Oh, yes, she will.

MURATA: Kiyoko-san could probably teach her a thing or two.

OKA: She won't know about American ways.

MASAKO: I'll help her.

HANA: Don't worry, Oka-san. She'll have a good friend in our Masako.

[They move to the door.]

OKA: Well, thanks for the sake. I guess I talk too much when I drink. *[He scratches his head and laughs.]* Oh. I'm sorry about the fire. By the way, come to my house for your bath . . . until you build yours again.

HANA: Oh, a . . . thank you. I don't know if . . .

MURATA: Good, good! I need a good hot bath tonight.

OKA: Tonight, then.

MURATA: We'll be there.

HANA [*bowing*]: Thank you very much. *Sayonara*.

OKA [*nodding*]: See you tonight.

> [*OKA leaves. HANA faces MURATA as soon as the door closes.*]

HANA: Papa, I don't know about going over there.

MURATA [*surprised*]: Why?

HANA: Well, Emiko-san . . .

MURATA [*irritated*]: What's the matter with you? We need a bath and Oka's invited us over.

HANA [*to MASAKO*]: Help me clear the table.

> [*MASAKO reluctantly leaves her book.*]

HANA [*continuing*]: Papa, you know we've been neighbors already three, four years, and Emiko-san's never been very hospitable.

MURATA: She's shy, that's all.

HANA: Not just shy. She's strange. I feel like she's pushing me off. She makes me feel like—I don't know—like I'm prying or something.

MURATA: Maybe you are.

HANA: And never puts out a cup of tea . . . If she had all that training in the graces . . . why, a cup of tea . . .

MURATA: So if you want tea, ask for it.

HANA: I can't do that, Papa. [*pause*] She's strange. . . . I don't know . . . [*to MASAKO*] When we go there, be very careful not to say anything wrong.

MASAKO: I never say anything anyway.

HANA [*thoughtfully*]: Would you believe the story Oka-san just told? Why, I never knew . . .

MURATA: There're lots of things you don't know. Just because a man don't . . . don't talk about them, don't mean he don't feel . . . don't think about . . .

HANA [*looking around*]: We'll have to take something. There's nothing to take. Papa, maybe you can dig up some carrots.

MURATA: God, Mama, be sensible. They got carrots. Everybody's got carrots.

HANA: Something . . . Maybe I should make something.

MURATA: Hell, they're not expecting anything.

HANA: It's not good manners to go empty-handed.

MURATA: We'll take the sake.

[HANA grimaces. MASAKO sees the phonograph.]

MASAKO: I know, Mama. We can take the Victrola! We can play records for Mrs. Oka. Then nobody has to talk.

[MURATA laughs.]

[Fade out]

ACT I
Scene ii

That evening

ON RISE: | *The exterior wall of the Okas' weathered house. There is a workable screen door and a large screened window. Outside there is a wide wooden bench that can accommodate three or four people. There is one separate chair, and a lantern stands against the house.*

The last rays of the sun light the area in a soft golden glow. This light grows gray as the scene progresses, and it is quite dark by the end of the scene.

Through the screened window, EMIKO can be seen walking erratically back and forth. She wears drab cotton but her grace and femininity come through. Her hair is bunned back in the style of the Issei women of the era.

OKA sits cross-legged on the bench. He wears a Japanese summer robe (yukata) and fans himself with a round Japanese fan.

The MURATAS enter. MURATA carries towels and a bottle of sake. HANA carries the Victrola, and MASAKO, a package containing their yukata.

OKA *[standing to greet the MURATAS]*: Oh, you've come. Welcome!

MURATA: *Yah* . . . Good of you to ask us.

HANA *[bowing]*: Yes, thank you very much. *[to MASAKO]* Say hello, Masako.

MASAKO: Hello.

And the Soul Shall Dance – 165

HANA: And thank you.

MASAKO: Thank you.

> *[OKA makes motions of protest. EMIKO stops her pacing and watches from the window.]*

HANA *[glancing briefly at the window]*: And how is Emiko-san this evening?

OKA *[turning to the house]*: Emi! Emiko!

HANA: That's all right. Don't call her out. She must be busy.

OKA: Emiko!

> *[EMIKO comes to the door. HANA starts a bow toward the house.]*

MURATA: *Konbanwa!* (Good evening)

HANA: *Konbanwa,* Emiko-san. I feel so badly about this intrusion. *[pause]* Your husband has told you our bathhouse was destroyed by fire, and he graciously invited us to come use yours.

> *[EMIKO shakes her head.]*

OKA: I didn't have a chance to . . .

> *[HANA recovers and nudges MASAKO.]*

HANA: Say hello to Mrs. Oka.

MASAKO: Hello, Mrs. Oka.

> *[HANA lowers the Victrola to the bench.]*

OKA: What's this? You brought a phonograph?

MASAKO: It's a Victrola.

HANA *[laughing indulgently]*: Yes. Masako wanted to bring this over and play some records.

MURATA *[extending the wine]*: Brought a little sake too.

OKA *[taking the bottle]*: Ah, now that I like. Emiko, bring out the cups.

> *[OKA waves at his wife, but she doesn't move. He starts to ask again but decides to get them himself. He enters the house and returns with two cups.]*

> *[EMIKO seats herself on the single chair. The MURATAS unload their paraphernalia; OKA pours the wine, the men drink, HANA chatters and sorts the records. MASAKO stands by helping her.]*

HANA: Yes, our Masako loves to play records. I like records too, and Papa, he . . .

MURATA [*watching EMIKO*]: They take me back home. The only way I can get there. In my mind.

HANA: Do you like music, Emiko-san?

[*EMIKO looks vague, but smiles.*]

HANA [*continuing*]: Oka-san, you like them, don't you?

OKA: Yeah. But I don't have a player. No chance to hear them.

MURATA: I had to get this for them. They wouldn't leave me alone until I got it. Well . . . a phonograph . . . what the hell; they got to have *some* fun.

HANA: We don't have to play them, if you'd rather not.

OKA: Play. Play them.

HANA: I thought we could listen to them and relax. [*She extends some records to EMIKO.*] Would you like to look through these, Emiko-san?

[*EMIKO doesn't respond. She pulls out a sack of Bull Durham and begins to roll a cigarette. HANA pushes MASAKO to her.*]

HANA [*continuing*]: Take these to her.

[*MASAKO goes to EMIKO with the records. She stands watching her as EMIKO lights a cigarette.*]

HANA [*continuing*]: Some of these are very old. You might know them, Emiko-san. [*She sees MASAKO watching EMIKO.*] Masako, bring those over here. [*She laughs uncomfortably.*] You might like this one, Emiko-san. [*She starts the player.*] Do you know it?

[*The record whines out "Kago No Tori." EMIKO listens with her head cocked.*]

[*She smokes her cigarette. She is wrapped in nostalgia and memories of the past. MASAKO watches her carefully.*]

MASAKO [*whispering*]: Mama, she's crying.

[*Startled, HANA and MURATA look toward EMIKO.*]

HANA [*pinching MASAKO*]: Shhh. The smoke is in her eyes.

MURATA: Did you bring the record I like, Mama?

[*EMIKO rises abruptly and enters the house.*]

MASAKO: They're tears, Mama.

And the Soul Shall Dance — 167

HANA: From yawning, Masako. *[regretfully to OKA]* I'm afraid we offended her.

OKA *[unaware]*: Hunh? Aw . . . no . . . pay no attention. No offense.

> *[MASAKO looks toward the window. EMIKO stands forlornly and slowly drifts into a dance.]*

HANA: I'm very sorry. Children, you know . . . they'll say anything. Anything that's on their minds.

> *[MURATA notices MASAKO looking through the window and tries to divert her attention.]*

MURATA: The needles. Masako, where're the needles?

MASAKO *[still watching]*: I forgot them.

> *[HANA sees what's going on. OKA is unaware.]*

HANA: Masako, go take your bath now. Masako . . .

> *[MASAKO reluctantly takes her towel and leaves.]*

OKA: Yeah, yeah. Take your bath, Masako-chan.

MURATA *[sees EMIKO still dancing]*: Change the record, Mama.

OKA *[still unaware]*: That's kind of sad.

MURATA: No use to get sick over a record. We're supposed to enjoy.

> *[HANA stops the record. EMIKO disappears from the window. HANA selects a lively ondo ("Tokyo Ondo").]*

HANA: We'll find something more fun.

> *[The three tap to the music.]*

HANA *[continuing]*: Can't you just see the festival? The dancers, the bright kimonos, the paper lanterns bobbing in the wind, the fireflies . . . How nostalgic. Oh, how nostalgic.

> *[EMIKO appears from the side of the house. Her hair is down; she wears an old straw hat. She dances in front of the MURATAS. They are startled.]*

> *[After the first shock, they watch with frozen smiles. They try to join EMIKO's mood, but something is missing. OKA is grieved. He finally stands as though he's had enough. EMIKO, now close to the door, ducks into the house.]*

HANA: That was pretty. Very nice.

> *[OKA settles down and grunts. MURATA clears his throat, and MASAKO returns from her bath.]*

MURATA: You're done already? *[He's glad to see her.]*

MASAKO: I wasn't very dirty. The water was too hot.

MURATA: Good! Just the way I like it.

HANA: Not dirty?

MURATA *[picking up his towel]*: Come on, Mama . . . scrub my back.

HANA *[laughing with embarrassment]*: Oh, oh . . . well . . . *[She stops the player.]* Masako, now don't forget. Crank the machine and change the needle now and then.

MASAKO: I didn't bring them.

HANA: Oh. Oh . . . all right. I'll be back soon. Don't forget . . . Crank. *[She leaves with her husband.]*

> *[OKA and MASAKO are alone. OKA is awkward and falsely hearty.]*

OKA: So! So you don't like hot baths, eh?

MASAKO: Not too hot.

OKA *[laughing]*: I thought you like it real hot. Hot enough to burn the house down.

> *[MASAKO doesn't laugh.]*

OKA *[continuing]*: That's a little joke.

> *[MASAKO busies herself to conceal her annoyance.]*

OKA *[continuing]*: I hear you're real good in school. Always top of the class.

MASAKO: It's a small class. Only two of us.

OKA: When Kiyoko comes, you'll help her in school, yeah? You'll take care of her . . . a favor for me, eh?

MASAKO: Okay.

OKA: You'll be her friend, eh?

MASAKO: Okay.

OKA: That's good. That's good. You'll like her. She's a nice girl too.

> *[OKA stands, yawns, and stretches.]*

OKA *[continuing]*: I'll go for a little walk now. *[He touches his crotch to indicate his purpose.]*

> *[MASAKO turns her attention to the records and selects one, "And the Soul Shall Dance," and begins to sway with*

the music. The song draws EMIKO from the house. She looks out the window, sees MASAKO is alone, and slips into a dance.]

EMIKO: Do you like that song, Masa-chan?

> *[MASAKO is startled. She remembers her mother's warning. She doesn't know what to do. She nods.]*

EMIKO *[continuing]*: That's one of my favorite songs. I remember in Japan I used to sing it so often. My favorite song. *[She sings along with the record.]* Akai kuchibiru / Kappu yosete / Aoi sake nomya / Kokoro ga ordoru. Do you know what that means, Masa-chan?

MASAKO: I think so. The soul will dance?

EMIKO: Yes, yes, that's right. The soul shall dance. Red lips against a glass, drink the green . . .

MASAKO: Wine?

EMIKO *[nodding]*: Drink the green wine . . .

MASAKO: Green? I thought wine was purple.

EMIKO: Wine is purple, but this is a green liqueur.

> *[EMIKO holds up one of the cups as though it were crystal and looks at the light that would shine through the green liquid.]*

EMIKO *[continuing]*: It's good. It warms your heart.

MASAKO: And the soul dances.

EMIKO: Yes . . .

MASAKO: What does it taste like? The green wine?

EMIKO: Oh, it's like . . . it's like . . .

> *[The second verse starts: Kurai yoru noy ume / Setsu nasa yo / Aoi sake nomya / Yume ga odoru.]*

MASAKO: In the dark night . . .

EMIKO: Dreams are unbearable . . .

MASAKO: Drink the . . .

EMIKO: Drink the green wine . . .

MASAKO: And the dreams will dance.

EMIKO *[softly]*: I'll be going back one day.

170 – And the Soul Shall Dance

MASAKO: Where?

EMIKO: My home. Japan. My real home. I'm going back one day.

MASAKO: By yourself?

EMIKO: Oh, yes. It's a secret. You can keep a secret?

MASAKO: Un-hunh. I have lots of secrets. All my own.

> [*The music stops. EMIKO sees OKA approaching and disap-
> pears into the house. MASAKO attends to the record and
> does not know EMIKO is gone.*]

MASAKO [*continuing*]: Secrets I never tell anyone . . .

OKA: Secrets? What kind of secrets? What did she say?

MASAKO [*startled*]: Oh! Nothing.

OKA: What did you talk about?

MASAKO: Nothing. Mrs. Oka was talking about the song. She was telling me
what it meant . . . about the soul.

OKA [*scoffing*]: Heh! What does she know about soul? [*calming down*] Ehhh . . .
Some people don't have them—souls.

MASAKO [*timidly*]: I thought . . . I thought everyone has a soul. I read in a
book . . .

OKA [*laughing*]: Maybe . . . maybe you're right. I'm not an educated man, you
know. I don't know too much about books. When Kiyoko comes you can talk
to her about it. Kiyoko is very . . .

> [*From inside the house, we hear EMIKO begin to sing loudly
> at the name KIYOKO as though trying to drown it out.
> OKA stops talking, then resumes.*]

OKA [*continuing*]: Kiyoko is very smart. You'll have a good time with her. She'll
learn your language fast. How old did you say you are?

MASAKO: Almost twelve.

> [*By this time OKA and MASAKO are shouting to be heard
> above EMIKO's singing.*]

OKA: Kiyoko is fifteen. Kiyoko . . .

> [*OKA is exasperated. He rushes into the house seething.
> MASAKO hears OKA's muffled rage. "Behave yourself"
> and "Kitchigai" come through. MASAKO slinks to the
> window and looks in. OKA slaps EMIKO around. MASAKO
> reacts to the violence. OKA comes out. MASAKO returns to*

the bench in time. He pulls his fingers through his hair and sits next to MASAKO. *She draws away.]*

OKA: Want me to light a lantern?

MASAKO *[shaken]*: No . . . ye . . . okay.

OKA: We'll get a little light here.

> *[He lights the lantern as the* MURATAS *return from their bath. They are in good spirits.]*

MURATA: Ahhh . . . Nothing like a good hot bath.

HANA: So refreshing.

MURATA: A bath should be taken hot and slow. Don't know how Masako gets through so fast.

HANA: She probably doesn't get in the tub.

MASAKO: I do.

> *[Everyone laughs.]*

MASAKO *[continuing]*: Well, I do.

> *[*EMIKO *comes out. She has a large purple welt on her face. She sits on the separate chair, hands folded, quietly watching the* MURATAS. *They look at her with alarm.* OKA *engages himself with his fan.]*

HANA: Oh! Emiko-san . . . what . . . a . . . a . . . whaa . . . *[She draws a deep breath.]* What a nice bath we had. Such a lovely bath. We do appreciate your hos . . . pitality. Thank you so much.

EMIKO: Lovely evening, isn't it?

HANA: Very lovely. Very. Ah, a little warm, but nice. Did you get a chance to hear the records? *[turning to* MASAKO*]* Did you play the records for Mrs. Oka?

MASAKO: Ye . . . no. The needle was . . .

EMIKO: Yes, she did. We played the records together.

MURATA: Oh, you played the songs together?

EMIKO: Yes . . . yes.

MURATA: That's nice. Masako can understand pretty good, eh?

EMIKO: She understands everything. Everything I say.

MURATA *[withdrawing]*: Oh, yeah? Eh, Mama, we ought to be going. *[He closes the player.]* Hate to bathe and run but . . .

HANA: Yes, yes. Tomorrow is a busy day. Come, Masako.

EMIKO: Please . . . stay a little longer.

MURATA: Eh, well, we got to be going.

HANA: Why, thank you, but . . .

EMIKO: It's still quite early.

OKA *[ready to say good-bye]*: Enjoyed the music. And the sake.

EMIKO: The records are very nice. Makes me remember Japan. I sang those songs . . . those very songs . . . Did you know I used to sing?

HANA *[politely]*: Why, no. No. I didn't know that. You must have a very lovely voice.

EMIKO: Yes.

HANA: No, I didn't know that. That's very nice.

EMIKO: Yes, I sang. My parents were very strict. They didn't like it. They said it was frivolous. Imagine?

HANA: Yes, I can imagine. Things were like that . . . in those days singing was not considered proper for nice . . . I mean, only for women in the profess . . .

MURATA: We better get home, Mama.

HANA: Yes, yes. What a shame you couldn't continue with it.

EMIKO: In the city I did do some classics: the dance, and the koto, and the flower, and of course, the tea. *[She makes the gestures for the disciplines.]* All those. Even some singing. Classics, of course.

HANA *[politely]*: Of course.

EMIKO: All of it is so disciplined . . . so disciplined. I was almost a *natori*.

HANA: How nice!

EMIKO: But everything changed.

HANA: Oh!

EMIKO: I was sent here to America. *[She glares at OKA.]*

HANA: Oh, too bad. I mean, too bad about your *natori*.

MURATA *[loudly to OKA]*: So did you see Nagata-san today?

OKA: Oh, yeah, yeah.

MURATA: What did he say? Is he interested?

OKA: Yeah. Yeah. He's interested.

MURATA: He likes the horse, eh?

OKA: Ah . . . yeah.

MURATA: I knew he'd like him. I'd buy him myself if I had the money.

OKA: Well, I have to take him over tomorrow. He'll decide then.

MURATA: He'll buy. He'll buy. You'd better go straight over to the ticket agent and get that ticket. Before you [ha-ha] spend the money.

OKA: [ha-ha] Yeah.

HANA: It'll be so nice when Kiyoko-san comes to join you. I know you're looking forward to it.

EMIKO [confused]: Oh . . . oh . . .

HANA: Masako is so happy. It'll be good for her too.

EMIKO: I had more freedom in the city. I lived with an aunt and she let me . . . she wasn't so strict.

> [MURATA and MASAKO have their gear together and are ready to leave.]

MURATA: Good luck on the horse tomorrow.

OKA: Yeah.

HANA [bowing]: Many, many thanks.

OKA: Thanks for the sake.

HANA [bowing again]: Good night, Emiko-san. We'll see you again soon. We'll bring the records too.

EMIKO [softly]: Those songs. Those very songs.

MURATA: Let's go, Mama.

> [The MURATAS pull away. Light follows them and grows dark on the OKAS. The MURATAS begin walking home.]

HANA: That was uncomfortable.

MASAKO: What's the matter with . . .

HANA: Shhh!

MURATA: I guess Oka has his problems.

MASAKO: Is she really kitchigai?

HANA: Of course not. She's not crazy. Don't say that word.

MASAKO: I heard Mr. Oka call her that.

HANA: He called her that?

MASAKO: I . . . I think so.

HANA: You heard wrong, Masako. Emiko-san isn't crazy. She just likes her drinks. She had too much to drink tonight.

MASAKO: Oh.

HANA: She can't adjust to this life. She can't get over the good times she had in Japan. Well, it's not easy. But one has to know when to bend . . . like the bamboo. When the winds blow, bamboo bends. You bend or crack. Remember that, Masako.

MURATA [wryly]: Bend, eh? Remember that, Mama.

HANA [softly]: You don't know. It isn't ever easy.

MASAKO: Do you want to go back to Japan, Mama?

HANA: Everyone does.

MASAKO: Do you, Papa?

MURATA: I'll have to make some money first.

MASAKO: I don't. Not me. Not Kiyoko.

HANA: After Kiyoko-san comes, Emiko will have company and things will straighten out. She has nothing to live on but memories. She doesn't have any friends. At least I have my friends at church. At least I have that. She must get awful lonely. . . .

MASAKO: I know that. She tried to make friends with me.

HANA: She did? What did she say?

MASAKO: Well, sort of . . .

HANA: What did she say?

MASAKO: She didn't say anything. I just felt it. Maybe you should be her friend, Mama.

MURATA: Poor woman. We could have stayed longer.

HANA: But you wanted to leave. I tried to be friendly. You saw that. It's not easy to talk to Emiko. She either closes up, you can't pry a word from her, or else she goes on and on. All that . . . that . . . about the koto and tea and the flower . . . I mean, what am I supposed to say? She's so unpredictable. And the drinking . . .

MURATA: All right, all right, Mama.

MASAKO: Did you see her black eye?

HANA [*calming down*]: She probably hurt herself. She wasn't very steady.

MASAKO: Oh, no. Mr. Oka hit her.

HANA: I don't think so.

MASAKO: He hit her. I saw him.

HANA: You saw? Papa, do you hear that? She saw them. That does it. We're not going there again.

MURATA: Aw . . . Oka wouldn't do that. Not in front of a kid.

MASAKO: Well, they didn't do it in front of me. They were in the house.

MURATA: You see?

HANA: That's all right. You just have to fix the bathhouse. Either that or we're going to bathe at home . . . in a bucket, if we have to. We're not going . . . we'll bathe at home.

[*MURATA mutters to himself.*]

HANA: What?

MURATA: I said all right, it's the bucket then. I'll get to it when I can.

[*HANA passes MURATA and walks ahead.*]

[*Fade out*]

ACT I
Scene iii

The same evening

ON RISE: *The exterior of the Oka house. The MURATAS have just left. EMIKO sits on the bench, her back to OKA. OKA, still standing, looks at her contemptuously as she pours herself a drink.*

OKA: Nothing more disgusting than a drunk woman.

[*EMIKO ignores him.*]

OKA [*continuing*]: You made a fool of yourself. You made a fool of *me!*

EMIKO: One can only make a fool of one's self.

OKA: You learn that in the fancy schools, eh?

[*EMIKO examines the pattern of her cup.*]

176 – And the Soul Shall Dance

OKA *[continuing]*: Eh? Ehhh? *[pause]* Answer me!

> *[EMIKO ignores him.]*

OKA *[continuing]*: I'm talking to you. Answer me! *[threatening]* You don't get away with that. You think you're so fine. . . .

> *[EMIKO looks off at the horizon. OKA roughly turns her around.]*

OKA *[continuing]*: When I talk, you listen!

> *[EMIKO turns away again. OKA pulls the cup from her hand.]*

OKA *[continuing]*: Goddammit! What'd you think my friends think of you? What kind of ass they think I am?

> *[He grabs her shoulders.]*

EMIKO: Don't touch me. Don't touch (me) . . .

OKA: Who the hell you think you are? "Don't touch me, don't touch me." Who the hell! High and mighty, eh? Too good for me, eh? Don't put on the act for me. I know who you are.

EMIKO: Tell me who I am, Mister Smart Peasant.

OKA: Shut your fool mouth, goddammit! Sure. I'll tell you. I know all about you. Shizue told me. The whole village knows.

EMIKO: Shizue!

OKA: Yeah, Shizue. Embarrassed the hell out of her, your own sister.

EMIKO: Embarrassed? I have nothing to be ashamed of. I don't know what you're talking about.

OKA *[derisively]*: You don't know what I'm talking about. I know. The whole village knows. They're all laughing at you. At me! Stupid Oka got stuck with a secondhand woman. I didn't say anything because . . .

EMIKO: I'm not secondhand!

OKA: Who you trying to fool? I know. Knew long time ago. Shizue wrote me all about your . . . your affairs in Tokyo. The men you were mess(ing) . . .

EMIKO: Affairs? Men?

OKA: That man you were messing with. I knew all along. I didn't say anything because you . . . I . . .

EMIKO: I'm not ashamed of it.

OKA: You're not ashamed! What the hell! Your father thought he was pulling a fast one on me . . . thought I didn't know nothing . . . thought I was some kind of dumb ass . . . I didn't say nothing because Shizue's dead. Shizue's dead. I was willing to give you a chance.

EMIKO [*laughing*]: A chance? Give me a chance?

OKA: Yeah. A chance! Laugh! Give a *joro* another chance. Sure, I'm stupid . . . dumb.

EMIKO: I'm not a whore. I'm true. He knows I'm true.

OKA: True! [*Hah!*]

EMIKO: You think I'm untrue just because I let . . . let you . . . There's only one man for me.

OKA: Let me [*obscene gesture*]? I can do what I want with you. Your father palmed you off on me – like a dog or cat – animal. Couldn't do nothing with you. Even the rich dumb Yamato wouldn't have you. Your father – greedy father – so proud . . . making big plans for you . . . for himself. [*Humh!*] The whole village laughing at him.

[*EMIKO hangs her head.*]

OKA [*continuing*]: Shizue told me. And she was working like a dog . . . trying to keep your goddam father happy . . . doing my work and yours.

EMIKO: My work?

OKA: Yeah, your work too! She killed herself working. She killed herself. [*He has tender memories of his uncomplaining wife.*] Up in the morning getting the fires started, working the bellows, cleaning the furnace, cooking, and late at night working with the sewing . . . tending the baby. [*He mutters.*] The goddam family killed her. And you . . . you out there in Tokyo with the fancy clothes, doing the [*sneering*] dance, the tea, the flower, the [*obscene gesture*] . . .

EMIKO [*hurting*]: Ahhhhh . . .

OKA: Did you have fun? Did you have fun on your sister's blood?

[*EMIKO doesn't answer.*]

OKA [*continuing*]: Did you? He must have been a son-of-a-bitch. What would make that goddam greedy old man send his prize mare to a plow horse like me? What kind of bum was he that your father would . . .

EMIKO: He's not a bum. He's not a bum.

OKA: Was he Korean? Was he *Etta?* That's the only thing I could figure.

EMIKO: I'm true to him. Only him.

OKA: True? You think he's true to you? You think he waits for you? Remembers you? *Aho!* Think he cares?

EMIKO: He does.

OKA: And waits ten years? *Baka!* Go back to Japan and see. You'll find out. Go back to Japan. *Kaire!*

EMIKO: In time.

OKA: In time. How about now?

EMIKO: I can't now.

OKA: *[Hah!]* Now! Go now! Who needs you? Who needs you? You think a man waits ten years for a woman? You think you're some kind of . . . of diamond . . . treasure . . . he's going to wait his life for you? Go to him. He's probably married with ten kids. Go to him. Get out! Goddam *joro.* Go! Go!

[OKA sweeps EMIKO off the bench.]

EMIKO: Ahhh! I . . . I don't have the money. Give me money to . . .

OKA: If I had money I would give it to you ten years ago. You think I been eating this *kuso* for ten years because I like it?

EMIKO: You're selling the horse. Give me the (money) . . .

OKA *[scoffing]*: That's for Kiyoko. I owe you nothing.

EMIKO: Ten years, you owe me.

OKA: Ten years of what? Misery? You gave me nothing. I give you nothing. You want to go, pack your bag and start walking. Try cross the desert. When you get dry and hungry, think about me.

EMIKO: I'd die out there.

OKA: Die? You think I didn't die here?

EMIKO: I didn't do anything to you.

OKA: No, no, you didn't. All I wanted was a little comfort and you . . . no, you didn't. No. So you die. We all die. Shizue died. If she was here, she wouldn't treat me like this. Ah, I should have brought her with me. She'd be alive now. We'd be poor but happy like . . . like Murata and his wife . . . and the kid.

EMIKO: I wish she were alive too. I'm not to blame for her dying. I didn't know. I was away. I loved her. I didn't want her to die. I . . .

OKA *[softening]*: I know that. I'm not blaming you for that. And it's not my fault what happened to you either.

[OKA is encouraged by EMIKO's silence which he mistakes for a change of attitude.]

OKA *[continuing]*: You understand that, eh? I didn't ask for you. It's not my fault you're here in this desert with . . . with me.

[EMIKO weeps. OKA reaches out.]

OKA *[continuing]*: I know I'm too old for you. It's hard for me too. But this is the way it is. I just ask you be kinder . . . understand it wasn't my fault. Try make it easier for me. For yourself too.

[OKA touches her and she shrinks from his hand.]

EMIKO: Ach!

OKA *[humiliated again]*: Goddam it! I didn't ask for you! *Aho!* If you was smart, you'da done as your father said . . . cut out that *saru shibai* with the *Etta* . . . married the rich Yamato. Then you'd still be in Japan. Not here to make my life so miserable.

[EMIKO is silent.]

OKA *[continuing]*: And you can have your *Etta* . . . or anyone else you want. Take them all on.

[OKA is worn out. It's hopeless.]

OKA *[continuing]*: God, why do we do this all the time? Fighting all the time. There must be a better way to live. There must be another way.

[OKA waits for a response, gives up, and enters the house. EMIKO watches him leave and pours another drink. The storm has passed, the alcohol takes over.]

EMIKO: I must keep the dream alive. The dream is all I live for. I am only in exile now. If I give in, all I've lived before will mean nothing . . . will be for nothing. Nothing. If I let you make me believe this is all there is to my life, the dream would die. I would die.

[She pours another drink and feels warm and good.]

[Fade out]

ACT II
Scene i

Mid-September afternoon

ON RISE: *Muratas' kitchen. The calendar reads September. MASAKO is at the kitchen table with several books. She thumbs through a Japanese magazine. HANA is with her sewing.]*

MASAKO: Do they always wear kimonos in Japan, Mama?

HANA: Most of the time.

MASAKO: I wonder if Kiyoko will be wearing a kimono like this.

HANA [*looking at the magazine*]: They don't dress like that. Not for every day.

MASAKO: I wonder what she's like.

HANA: Probably a lot like you. What do you think she's like?

MASAKO: She's probably taller.

HANA: Mr. Oka isn't tall.

MASAKO: And pretty.

HANA [*laughing*]: Mr. Oka . . . Well, I don't suppose she'll look like her father.

MASAKO: Mrs. Oka is pretty.

HANA: She isn't Kiyoko-san's real mother, remember?

MASAKO: Oh, that's right.

HANA: But they are related. Well, we'll soon see.

MASAKO: I thought she was coming in September. It's already September.

HANA: Papa said Oka-san went to San Pedro a few days ago. He should be back soon with Kiyoko-san.

MASAKO: Didn't Mrs. Oka go too?

HANA [*glancing toward the Oka house*]: I don't think so. I see lights in their house at night.

MASAKO: Will they bring Kiyoko over to see us?

HANA: Of course. First thing, probably. You'll be very nice to her, won't you?

[*MASAKO finds another book.*]

MASAKO: Sure. I'm glad I'm going to have a friend. I hope she likes me.

HANA: She'll like you. Japanese girls are very polite, you know.

MASAKO: We have to be or our mamas get mad at us.

HANA: Then I should be getting mad at you more often.

MASAKO: It's often enough already, Mama. [*She opens the book.*] Look at this, Mama. I'm going to show her this book.

HANA: She won't be able to read at first.

MASAKO: I love this story. Mama, this is about people like us—settlers—it's about the prairie. We live in a prairie, don't we?

HANA: Prairie? Does that mean desert?

MASAKO: I think so.

HANA [*looking at the bleak landscape*]: We live in a prairie.

MASAKO: It's about the hardships and the floods and droughts and how they have nothing but each other.

HANA: We have nothing but each other. But these people . . . they're white people.

MASAKO: Sure, Mama. They come from the east. Just like you and Papa came from Japan.

HANA: We come from the far far east. That's different. White people are different from us.

MASAKO: I know that.

HANA: White people among white people . . . that's different from Japanese among white people. You know what I'm saying?

MASAKO: I know that. How come they don't write books about us . . . about Japanese people?

HANA: Because we're nobodies here.

MASAKO: If I didn't read these, there'd be nothing for me.

HANA: Some of the things you read, you're never going to know.

MASAKO: I can dream though.

HANA [*sighing*]: Sometimes the dreaming makes the living harder. Better to keep your head out of the clouds.

MASAKO: That's not much fun.

HANA: You'll have fun when Kiyoko-san comes. You can study together, you can sew, and sometime you can try some of those fancy American recipes.

MASAKO: Oh, Mama. You have to have chocolate and cream and things like that.

HANA: We'll get them.

> [*We hear the sound of Oka's old car. MASAKO and HANA pause and listen. MASAKO runs to the window.*]

MASAKO: I think it's them!

HANA: Oka-san?

MASAKO: It's them! It's them!

> [*HANA stands and looks out. She removes her apron and puts away her sewing.*]

HANA: Two of them. Emiko-san isn't with them. *[pause]* Let's go outside.

> *[OKA and KIYOKO enter. OKA is wearing his going-out clothes: a sweater, white shirt, dark pants, but no tie. KIYOKO walks behind him.]*
>
> *[KIYOKO is short, broad-chested, and very self-conscious. Her hair is straight and banded into two shucks. She wears a conservative cotton dress, white socks, and two-inch heels.]*
>
> *[OKA is proud. He struts in, his chest puffed out.]*

OKA: Hello, hello! We're here. We made it! *[He pushes KIYOKO forward.]* This my daughter, Kiyoko. *[to KIYOKO]* Murata-san. Remember, I was talking about? My friends . . .

KIYOKO *[bowing deeply]*: Hajime mashite yoroshiku onegai shimasu.

HANA *[also bowing deeply]*: I hope your journey was pleasant.

OKA *[pushing KIYOKO to MASAKO while she still bows]*: This is Masako-chan; I told you about her.

> *[MASAKO is shocked at KIYOKO's appearance. The girl she expected is already a woman. She stands with her mouth agape and withdraws noticeably. HANA rushes in to fill the awkwardness.]*

HANA: Say hello, Masako. My goodness, where are your manners? *[She laughs apologetically.]* In this country they don't make much to-do about manners. *[She stands back to examine KIYOKO.]* My, my, I didn't picture you so grown up. My, my . . . Tell me, how was your trip?

OKA *[proudly]*: We just drove in from Los Angeles this morning. We spent the night in San Pedro, and the next two days we spent in Los Angeles . . . you know, Japanese town.

HANA: How nice!

OKA: Kiyoko was so excited. Twisting her head this way and that–couldn't see enough with her big eyes. *[He imitates her fondly.]* She's from the country, you know . . . just a big country girl. Got all excited about the Chinese dinner–we had a Chinese dinner. She never ate it before.

> *[KIYOKO covers her mouth and giggles.]*

HANA: Chinese dinner!

OKA: Oh, yeah. Duck, *pakkai,* chow mein, seaweed soup . . . the works!

HANA: A feast!

OKA: Oh, yeah. Like a holiday. Two holidays. Two holidays in one.

[HANA pushes MASAKO forward.]

HANA: Two holidays in one! Kiyoko-san, our Masako has been looking forward to meeting you.

KIYOKO *[bowing again]*: Hajime mashite . . .

HANA: She's been planning all sorts of things she'll do with you: sewing, cooking . . .

MASAKO: Oh, Mama . . .

[KIYOKO covers her mouth and giggles.]

HANA: It's true, Kiyoko-san. She's been looking forward to having a best friend.

[KIYOKO giggles and MASAKO pulls away.]

OKA: Kiyoko, you shouldn't be so shy. The Muratas are my good friends, and you should feel free with them. Ask anything, say anything. Right?

HANA: Of course, of course. *[She is annoyed with MASAKO.]* Masako, go in and start the tea.

[MASAKO enters the house.]

HANA *[continuing]*: I'll call Papa. He's in the yard. Papa! Oka-san is here! *[to KIYOKO]* Now tell me, how was your trip? Did you get seasick?

KIYOKO *[bowing and nodding]*: Eh *[affirmative]*. A little.

OKA: Tell her. Tell her how sick you got.

[KIYOKO covers her mouth and giggles.]

HANA: Oh, I know, I know. I was too. That was a long time ago. I'm sure things are improved now. Tell me about Japan. What is it like now? They say it's so changed . . . modern.

OKA: Kiyoko comes from the country . . . backwoods. Nothing changes much there from century to century.

HANA: Ah! That's true. That's why I love Japan. And you wanted to leave. It's unbelievable. To come here!

OKA: She always dreamed about it.

HANA: Well, it's not really that bad.

OKA: No, it's not that bad. Depends on what you make of it.

HANA: That's right. What you make of it. I was just telling Masako today . . .

[MURATA enters. He rubs his hands to remove the soil and comes in grinning. He shakes OKA's hand.]

MURATA: *Oi, oi* . . .

OKA: *Yah* . . . I'm back. This is my daughter.

MURATA: No! She's beautiful!

OKA: Finally made it. Finally got her here.

MURATA *[to KIYOKO]*: Your father hasn't stopped talking about you all summer.

HANA: And Masako too.

KIYOKO *[bowing]*: *Hajime mashite* . . .

MURATA *[with a short bow]*: *Yah*. How'd you like the trip?

OKA: I was just telling your wife . . . had a good time in Los Angeles. Had a couple of great dinners, took in the cinema – Japanese pictures, bought her some American clothes . . .

HANA: Oh, you bought that in Los Angeles.

MURATA: Got a good price for your horse, eh? Lots of money, eh?

OKA: Nagata-kun's a shrewd bargainer. Heh. It don't take much money to make her happy. She's a country girl.

MURATA: That's all right. Country's all right. Country girl's the best.

OKA: Had trouble on the way back.

MURATA: Yeah?

OKA: Fan belt broke.

MURATA: That'll happen with these old cars.

OKA: Lucky I was near a gasoline station. We were in the mountains. Waited in a restaurant while it was getting fixed.

HANA: Oh, that was good.

OKA: Guess they don't see Japanese much. Stare? Terrible! Took them a long time to wait on us. Dumb waitress practically threw the food at us. Kiyoko felt bad.

HANA: Ah! That's too bad . . . too bad. That's why I always pack a lunch when we take trips.

MURATA: They'll spoil the day for you . . . those barbarians!

OKA: Terrible food too. Kiyoko couldn't swallow the dry bread and bologna.

HANA: That's the food they eat!

MURATA: Let's go in . . . have a little wine. Mama, we got wine? This is a celebration.

HANA: I think so. A little.

> *[They enter the house talking. MASAKO has made tea and HANA serves the wine.]*

HANA *[continuing]*: How is your mother? Was she happy to see you?

KIYOKO: Oh, she . . . yes.

HANA: I just know she was surprised to see you so grown up. Of course, you remember her from Japan, don't you?

KIYOKO *[nodding]*: *Eh* (affirmative). I can barely remember. I was very young.

HANA: Of course. But you do, don't you?

KIYOKO: She was gone most of the time . . . at school in Tokyo. She was very pretty, I remember that.

HANA: She's still very pretty.

KIYOKO: Yes. She was always laughing. She was much younger then.

HANA: Oh, now, it hasn't been that long ago.

> *[MASAKO goes outside. The following dialogue continues muted as the light goes dim in the house and focuses on MASAKO. EMIKO enters, is drawn to the Murata window, and listens.]*

OKA: We stayed at an inn on East First Street. *Shizuokaya.* Whole inn filled with Shizuoka people . . . talking the old dialect. Thought I was in Japan again.

MURATA: That right?

OKA: Felt good. Like I was in Japan again.

HANA *[to KIYOKO]*: Did you enjoy Los Angeles?

KIYOKO: Yes.

OKA: That's as close as I'll get to Japan.

MURATA: *Mattakuna!* That's for sure. Not in this life.

> *[Outside MASAKO is aware of EMIKO.]*

MASAKO: Why don't you go in?

EMIKO: Oh. Oh. Why don't you?

MASAKO: They're all grown-ups in there. I'm not grown up.

EMIKO *[softly]*: All grown-ups. Maybe I'm not either. *[Her mood changes.]* Masa-chan, do you have a boyfriend?

186 – And the Soul Shall Dance

MASAKO: I don't like boys. They don't like me.

EMIKO: Oh, that will change. You will change. I was like that too.

MASAKO: Besides, there's none around here . . . Japanese boys. There are some at school, but they don't like girls.

HANA *[calling from the kitchen]*: Masako . . .

[MASAKO doesn't answer.]

EMIKO: Your mother is calling you.

MASAKO *[to her mother]*: *Nani?* (What?)

HANA *[from the kitchen]*: Come inside now.

EMIKO: You'll have a boyfriend one day.

MASAKO: Not me.

EMIKO: You'll fall in love one day. Someone will make the inside of you light up, and you'll know you're in love. Your life will change . . . grow beautiful. It's good, Masa-chan. And this feeling you'll remember the rest of your life . . . will come back to you . . . haunt you . . . keep you alive . . . five, ten years . . . no matter what happens. Keep you alive.

HANA *[from the house]*: Masako . . . Come inside now.

[MASAKO turns aside to answer and EMIKO slips away.]

MASAKO: What, Mama?

[HANA comes out.]

HANA: Come inside. Don't be so unsociable. Kiyoko wants to talk to you.

MASAKO *[watching EMIKO leave]*: She doesn't want to talk to me. You're only saying that.

HANA: What's the matter with you? Don't you want to make friends with her?

MASAKO: She's not my friend. She's your friend.

HANA: Don't be silly. She's only fourteen.

MASAKO: Fifteen. They said fifteen. She's your friend. She's an old lady.

HANA: Don't say that.

MASAKO: I don't like her.

HANA: Shhh! Don't say that.

MASAKO: She doesn't like me either.

HANA: Ma-chan. Remember your promise to Mr. Oka? You're going to take her to school, teach her the language, teach her the ways of Americans.

MASAKO: She can do it herself. You did.

HANA: That's not nice, Ma-chan.

MASAKO: I don't like the way she laughs. *[She imitates KIYOKO holding her hand to her mouth and giggling and bowing.]*

HANA: Oh, how awful! Stop that. That's the way the girls do in Japan. Maybe she doesn't like your ways either. That's only a difference in manners. What you're doing now is considered very bad manners. *[She changes her tone.]* Ma-chan, just wait: when she learns to read and speak, you'll have so much to say to each other. Come on, be a good girl and come inside.

MASAKO: It's just old people in there, Mama. I don't want to go in.

[HANA calls to KIYOKO inside.]

HANA: Kiyoko-san, please come here a minute. Maybe it's better for you to talk to Masako alone.

[KIYOKO dutifully goes outside.]

HANA *[continuing]*: Masako has a lot of things to tell you . . . about what to expect in school and . . . things.

MURATA *[calling from the table]*: Mama, put out something . . . chiles—for Oka-san.

[HANA enters the house. KIYOKO and MASAKO stand awkwardly facing each other, KIYOKO glancing shyly at MASAKO.]

MASAKO: Do you like it here?

KIYOKO *[nodding]*: *Eh* (affirmative).

[There is an uncomfortable pause.]

MASAKO: School will be starting next week.

KIYOKO *[nodding]*: *Eh*.

MASAKO: Do you want to walk to school with me?

KIYOKO *[nodding]*: *Hai*.

[MASAKO rolls her eyes and tries again.]

MASAKO: I leave at 7:30.

KIYOKO: *Eh*.

[There's a long pause. MASAKO gives up and moves offstage.]

MASAKO: I have to do something.

> [*KIYOKO watches her leave and uncertainly moves back to the house. HANA looks up at KIYOKO coming in alone, sighs, and quietly pulls out a chair for her.*]

> [*Fade out*]

ACT II
Scene ii

November night

ON RISE: *Interior of the Murata home. Lamps are lit. The family is at the kitchen table. HANA sews, MASAKO does her homework, MURATA reads the paper. They're dressed in warm robes and are having tea.*

Outside, thunder rolls in the distance and lightning flashes.

HANA: It'll be *ohigan* (autumn festival) soon.

MURATA: Something to look forward to.

HANA: We'll need sweet rice for *omochi* (rice cakes).

MURATA: I'll order it next time I go to town.

HANA [*to MASAKO*]: How is school? Getting a little harder?

MASAKO: Not that much. Sometimes the arithmetic is hard.

HANA: How is Kiyoko-san doing? Is she getting along all right?

MASAKO: She's good in arithmetic. She skipped a grade already.

HANA: Already? That's good news. Only November and she skipped a grade! At this rate she'll be through before you.

MASAKO: Well, she's older.

MURATA: Sure, she's older, Mama.

HANA: Has she made any friends?

MASAKO: No. She follows me around all day. She understands okay, but she doesn't talk. She talks like, you know . . . she says "ranchi" for lunch and "ranchi" for ranch too, and like that. Kids laugh and copy behind her back. It's hard to understand her.

HANA: You understand her, don't you?

MASAKO: I'm used to it.

HANA: You should tell the kids not to laugh. After all, she's trying. Maybe you should help her practice those words . . . show her what she's doing wrong.

MASAKO: I already do. Our teacher told me to do that.

MURATA [looking up from his paper]: You ought to help her all you can.

HANA: And remember, when you started school, you couldn't speak English either.

MASAKO: I help her.

> [MURATA goes to the window. The night is cold. Lightning flashes and the wind whistles.]

MURATA: Looks like a storm coming up. Hope we don't have a freeze.

HANA: If it freezes, we'll have another bad year. Maybe we ought to start the smudge pots.

MURATA [listening]: It's starting to rain. Nothing to do now but pray.

HANA: If praying is the answer, we'd be in Japan now. Rich.

MURATA [wryly]: We're not dead yet. We still have a chance.

> [HANA glares at the small joke.]

MURATA [continuing]: Guess I'll turn in.

HANA: Go to bed, go to bed. I'll sit up and worry.

MURATA: If worrying was the answer, we'd be around the world twice and in Japan. Come on, Mama. Let's go to bed. It's too cold tonight to be mad.

> [There's an urgent knock on the door. The MURATAS react.]

MURATA [continuing]: Dareh da! (Who is it?)

> [MURATA goes to the door and hesitates.]

MURATA [continuing]: Who is it!

KIYOKO [weakly]: It's me . . . help me . . .

> [MURATA opens the door and KIYOKO stumbles in. She wears a kimono with a shawl thrown over. Her legs are bare except for a pair of straw zori. Her hair is wet and stringy, and she trembles uncontrollably.]

Murata: My God! Kiyoko-san! What's the matter?

HANA [overlapping]: Kiyoko-san! What is it?

MURATA: What happened?

KIYOKO: They're fighting, they're fighting!

MURATA: Oh, don't worry. Those things happen. No cause to worry. Mama, make tea for her. Sit down and catch your breath. Don't worry. I'll take you home when you're ready.

HANA: Papa, I'll take care of it.

MURATA: Let me know when you're ready to go home.

HANA: It must be freezing out there. Try to get warm. Try to calm yourself.

MURATA: Kiyoko-san, don't worry. *[He puts his robe around her.]*

> *[HANA waves MASAKO and MURATA off. MURATA leaves. MASAKO goes to her bed in the kitchen.]*

HANA: Papa, I'll take care of it.

KIYOKO *[looking at Murata's retreating form]*: But I came to ask your help. . . .

HANA: You ran down here without a lantern? You could have fallen and hurt yourself.

KIYOKO: I don't care . . . I don't care . . .

HANA: You don't know, Kiyoko-san. It's treacherous out there – snakes, spiders . . .

KIYOKO: I must go back! I . . . I . . . you . . . please come with me. . . .

HANA: First, first we must get you warm. Drink your tea.

KIYOKO: But they'll kill each other. They're fighting like animals. Help me stop them!

> *[HANA warms a pot of soup.]*

HANA *[calmly]*: I cannot interfere in a family quarrel.

KIYOKO: It's not a quarrel. It's a . . . a . . .

HANA: That's all it is. A family squabble. You'll see. Tomorrow . . .

> *[KIYOKO pulls at HANA's arm.]*

KIYOKO: Not just a squabble! Please . . . please . . .

> *[KIYOKO starts toward the door, but HANA stops her.]*

HANA: Now listen. Listen to me, Kiyoko-san. I've known your father and mother a little while now. I suspect it's been like this for years. Every family has some kind of trouble.

KIYOKO: Not like this, not like this.

HANA: Some have it better, some worse. When you get married, you'll understand. Don't worry. Nothing will happen. *[She takes a towel and dries Kiyoko's hair.]* You're chilled to the bone. You'll catch your death.

KIYOKO: I don't care. . . . I want to die.

HANA: Don't be silly. It's not that bad.

KIYOKO: It is! They started drinking early in the afternoon. They make some kind of brew and hide it somewhere in the desert.

HANA: It's illegal to make it. That's why they hide it. That home brew is poison to the body. The mind too.

KIYOKO: It makes them crazy. They drink it all the time and quarrel constantly. I was in the other room studying. I try so hard to keep up with school.

HANA: We were talking about you just this evening. Masako says you're doing so well. You skipped a grade?

KIYOKO: It's hard . . . hard. I'm too old for the class and the children . . .

[She remembers all her problems and starts crying again.]

HANA: It's always hard in a new country.

KIYOKO: They were bickering and quarreling all afternoon. Then something happened. All of a sudden they were on the floor . . . hitting and . . . and . . . He was hitting her in the stomach, the face . . . I tried to stop them, but they were so . . . drunk.

HANA: There, there. It's probably all over now.

KIYOKO: Why does it happen like this? Nothing is right. Everywhere I go. Masa-chan is so lucky. I wish my life was like hers. I can hardly remember my real mother.

HANA: Emiko-san is almost a real mother to you. She's blood kin.

KIYOKO: She hates me. She never speaks to me. She's so cold. I want to love her, but she won't let me. She hates me.

HANA: I don't think so, Kiyoko-san.

KIYOKO: She does! She hates me.

HANA: No. I don't think you have anything to do with it. It's this place. She hates it. This place is so lonely and alien.

KIYOKO: Then why didn't she go back? Why did they stay here?

HANA: You don't know. It's not so simple. Sometimes I think . . .

KIYOKO: Then why don't they make the best of it here? Like you?

HANA: That isn't easy either. Believe me. *[She leaves KIYOKO to stir the soup.]* Sometimes . . . sometimes the longing for home . . . the longing fills me with despair. Will I never return again? Will I never see my mother, my father, my sisters again? But what can one do? There are responsibilities here . . . children . . . *[pause]* And another day passes . . . another month . . . another year. *[She takes the soup to KIYOKO.]* Did you have supper tonight?

KIYOKO *[bowing]*: Ah. When my . . . my aunt gets like this, she doesn't cook. No one eats. I don't get hungry anymore.

HANA: Cook for yourself. It's important to keep your health.

KIYOKO: I left Japan for a better life.

HANA: It isn't easy for you, is it? But you must remember your filial duty.

KIYOKO: It's so hard.

HANA: But you can make the best of it here, Kiyoko-san. And take care of yourself. You owe that to yourself. Eat. Keep well. It'll be better, you'll see. And sometimes it'll seem worse. But you'll survive. We do, you know.

HANA *[continuing]*: It's getting late.

KIYOKO *[apprehensively]*: I don't want to go back.

HANA: You can sleep with Masako tonight. Tomorrow you'll go back. And you'll remember what I told you. *[She puts her arm around KIYOKO.]* Life is never easy, Kiyoko-san. Endure. Endure. Soon you'll be marrying and going away. Things will not always be this way. And you'll look back on this . . . this night and you'll . . .

> *[There is a rap on the door. HANA exchanges glances with KIYOKO and opens the door a crack.]*
>
> *[OKA has come looking for KIYOKO. He wears an overcoat and holds a wet newspaper over his head.]*

OKA: Ah! I'm sorry to bother you so late at night—the fact is . . .

HANA: Oka-san.

OKA *[jovially]*: Good evening, good evening. *[He sees KIYOKO.]* Oh, there you are. Did you have a nice visit?

HANA *[irritated]*: Yes, she's here.

OKA *[still cheerful]*: Thought she might be. Ready to come home now?

HANA: She came in the rain.

OKA *[ignoring HANA's tone]*: That's foolish of you, Kiyoko. You might catch cold.

HANA: She was frightened by your quarreling. She came for help.

OKA [*laughing with embarrassment*]: Oh! Kiyoko, that's nothing to worry about. It's just we had some disagreement.

HANA: That's what I told her, but she was frightened just the same.

OKA: Children are . . .

HANA: Not children, Oka-san. Kiyoko. Kiyoko was terrified. I think that was a terrible thing to do to her.

OKA [*rubbing his head*]: Oh, I . . . I . . .

HANA: If you had seen her a few minutes ago . . . hysterical . . . shaking . . . crying . . . wet and cold to the bone . . . out of her mind with worry.

OKA [*rubbing his head*]: Oh, I don't know what she was so worried about.

HANA: You. You and Emiko fighting like you were going to kill each other.

OKA [*lowering his head in penitence*]: Aaaaaaahhhhhhhh . . .

HANA: I know I shouldn't tell you this, but there's one or two things I have to say: You sent for Kiyoko-san, and now she's here. You said yourself she had a bad time in Japan, and now she's having a worse time. It's not easy for her in a strange country; the least you can do is try to keep from worrying her . . . especially about yourselves. I think it's terrible what you're doing to her . . . terrible!

OKA [*bowing in deep humility*]: I am ashamed.

HANA: I think she deserves better. I think you should think about that.

OKA [*still bowing*]: I thank you for this reminder. It will never happen again. I promise.

HANA: I don't need that promise. Make it to Kiyoko-san.

OKA: Come with Papa now. He did a bad thing. He'll be a good Papa from now. He won't worry his little girl again. All right?

> [*They move toward the door.* KIYOKO *tries to return* MURATA's *robe.*]

KIYOKO: Thank you so much.

OKA: Thank you again.

HANA [*to* KIYOKO]: That's all right. You can bring it back tomorrow. Remember . . . remember what we talked about. [*loudly*] Good night, Oka-san.

> [*They leave.* HANA *goes to* MASAKO, *who pretends to sleep. She covers her.* MURATA *appears from the bedroom.*]

He's heard it all. He and HANA exchange a quick glance and together they retire to their room.]

[Fade out]

ACT II
Scene iii

The next morning

ON RISE: The Murata house and yard. HANA and MURATA have already left the house to examine the rain damage in the fields.

MASAKO prepares to go to school. She puts on a coat and gets her books and lunch bag. Meanwhile, KIYOKO slips quietly into the yard. She wears a coat and carries Murata's robe and sets it on the outside bench.

MASAKO walks out and is surprised to see KIYOKO.

MASAKO: Hi. I thought you'd be . . . sick today.

KIYOKO: Oh. I woke up late.

MASAKO *[scrutinizing KIYOKO's face]*: Your eyes are red.

KIYOKO *[averting her face]*: Oh. I . . . got . . . sand in it. Yes.

MASAKO: Do you want eye drops? We have eye drops in the house.

KIYOKO: Oh, no. That's all right.

MASAKO: That's what's called bloodshot.

KIYOKO: Oh.

MASAKO: My father gets it a lot. When he drinks too much.

KIYOKO: Oh.

[MASAKO notices KIYOKO doesn't carry a lunch.]

MASAKO: Where's your lunch bag?

KIYOKO: I . . . forgot it.

MASAKO: Did you make your lunch today?

KIYOKO: Yes. Yes, I did. But I forgot it.

MASAKO: Do you want to go back and get it?

KIYOKO: No. *[pause]* We will be late.

MASAKO: Do you want to practice your words?

KIYOKO *[thoughtfully]*: Oh . . .

MASAKO: Say, "My."

KIYOKO: My?

MASAKO: Eyes . . .

KIYOKO: Eyes.

MASAKO: Are . . .

KIYOKO: Are.

MASAKO: Red.

KIYOKO: Red.

MASAKO: Your eyes are red.

> *[KIYOKO will not repeat it.]*

MASAKO *[continuing]*: I . . .

> *[KIYOKO doesn't cooperate.]*

MASAKO *[continuing]*: Say, "I."

KIYOKO: I.

MASAKO: Got . . .

KIYOKO: Got.

MASAKO: Sand . . .

> *[KIYOKO balks.]*

MASAKO *[continuing]*: Say, "I."

KIYOKO *[sighing]*: I.

MASAKO: Reft . . .

KIYOKO: Reft.

MASAKO: My . . .

KIYOKO: My.

MASAKO: Runch.

KIYOKO: Run . . . Lunch. *[pause]* Masako-san, you are mean. You are hurting me.

MASAKO: It's a joke! I was just trying to make you laugh!

196 — And the Soul Shall Dance

KIYOKO: I cannot laugh today.

MASAKO: Sure you can. You can laugh. Laugh! Like this! *[She makes a hearty laugh.]*

KIYOKO: I cannot laugh when you make fun of me.

MASAKO: Okay, I'm sorry. We'll practice some other words then, okay?

> *[KIYOKO doesn't answer.]*

MASAKO *[continuing]*: Say, "Okay."

KIYOKO *[reluctantly]*: Okay.

MASAKO: Okay, then . . . um . . . um . . . Say . . . um . . . *[rapidly]* "She sells seashells by the seashore."

> *[KIYOKO turns away indignantly.]*

MASAKO *[continuing]*: Aw, come on, Kiyoko! It's just a joke. Laugh!

KIYOKO *[sarcastically]*: Ha-ha-ha. Now you say, "*Kono kyaku wa yoku kaki ku kyaku da!*"

MASAKO: Sure! I can say it. *Kono kyaku waki ku kyoku kaku* . . .

KIYOKO: That's not right.

MASAKO: *Koki kuki kya* . . .

KIYOKO: No. No-no-no.

MASAKO: Okay, then. You say, "Sea sells she shells . . . shu . . . sh."

> *[They both laugh, KIYOKO with her hands over her mouth. MASAKO takes KIYOKO's hands away.]*

MASAKO: Not like that. Like this! *[She makes a big laugh.]*

KIYOKO: Like this? *[She imitates MASAKO.]*

MASAKO: Yeah, that's right! *[pause]* You're not mad anymore?

KIYOKO: I'm not mad anymore.

MASAKO: Okay. You can share my lunch because we're . . .

KIYOKO: "Flends?"

> *[MASAKO looks at KIYOKO. They giggle and move on.]*
>
> *[HANA and MURATA come in from assessing the storm's damage. They are dressed warmly. HANA is depressed. MURATA tries to be cheerful.]*

MURATA: It's not so bad, Mama.

HANA: Half the ranch is flooded. At least half.

MURATA: No-no. Quarter, maybe. It's sunny today. It'll dry.

HANA: The seedlings will rot.

MURATA: No-no. It'll dry. It's all right. Better than I expected.

HANA: If we have another bad year, no one will lend us money for the next crop.

MURATA: Don't worry. If it doesn't drain by tomorrow, I'll replant the worst places. We still have some seed left. Yeah, I'll replant.

HANA: More work.

MURATA: Don't worry, Mama. It'll be all right.

HANA [quietly]: Papa, where will it end? Will we always be like this – always at the mercy of the weather . . . prices . . . always at the mercy of the Gods?

MURATA [patting HANA's back]: Things will change. Wait and see. We'll be back in Japan by . . . in two years. Guarantee. Maybe sooner.

HANA [dubiously]: Two years . . .

MURATA [finding the robe on the bench]: Ah, look, Mama. Kiyoko-san brought back my robe.

HANA [sighing]: Kiyoko-san . . . poor Kiyoko-san. And Emiko-san . . .

MURATA: Ah, Mama. We're lucky. We're lucky, Mama.

[Fade out]

ACT II
Scene iv

The following spring afternoon

ON RISE: *Exterior of the Oka house. OKA is dressed to go out. He wears a sweater, long-sleeved white shirt, dark pants, no tie. He puts his foot to the bench to wipe off his shoe with the palm of his hand. He straightens his sleeve, removes a bit of lint, and runs his fingers through his hair. He hums softly.*

             KIYOKO comes from the house. Her hair is frizzled in a permanent wave, she wears a gaudy new dress and a pair of new shoes. She carries a movie magazine.

OKA [appreciatively]: Pretty. Pretty.

KIYOKO [*turning for him*]: It's not too *hadeh?* I feel strange in colors.

OKA: Oh, no. Young girls should wear bright colors. Time enough to wear gray when you get old. Old-lady colors.

[*KIYOKO giggles.*]

OKA [*continuing*]: Sure you want to go to the picture show? It's such a nice day . . . shame to waste in a dark hall.

KIYOKO: Where else can we go?

OKA: We can go to Murata-san's.

KIYOKO: All dressed up?

OKA: Or Nagata-san's. I'll show him what I got for my horse.

KIYOKO: I love the pictures.

OKA: We don't have many nice spring days like this. Here the season is short. Summer comes in like a dragon . . . right behind . . . breathing fire . . . like a dragon. You don't know the summers here. They'll scare you.

[*He tousles KIYOKO's hair and pulls a lock of it. It springs back. He shakes his head in wonder.*]

OKA [*continuing*]: Goddam. Curly hair. Never thought curly hair could make you so happy.

KIYOKO [*giggling*]: All the American girls have curly hair.

OKA: Your friend Masako like it?

KIYOKO [*nodding*]: She says her mother will never let her get a permanent wave.

OKA: She said that, eh? Bet she's wanting one.

KIYOKO: I don't know about that.

OKA: Bet she's wanting some of your pretty dresses too.

KIYOKO: Her mother makes all her clothes.

OKA: Buying is just as good. Buying is better. No trouble that way.

KIYOKO: Masako's not interested in clothes. She loves the pictures, but her mother won't let her go. Someday, can we take Masako with us?

OKA: If her mother lets her come. Her mother's got a mind of her own. Stiff back.

KIYOKO: But she's nice.

OKA [*dubiously*]: Oh, yeah. Can't be perfect, I guess. Kiyoko, after the harvest I'll have money, and I'll buy you the prettiest dress in town. I'm going to be lucky this year. I feel it.

KIYOKO: You're already too good to me . . . dresses, shoes, permanent wave . . . movies . . .

OKA: That's nothing. After the harvest, just wait . . .

KIYOKO: . . . magazines. You do enough. I'm happy already.

OKA: You make me happy too, Kiyoko. You make me feel good . . . like a man again. *[That bothers him.]* One day you're going to make a young man happy.

[*KIYOKO giggles.*]

OKA *[continuing]*: Someday we going to move from here.

KIYOKO: But we have good friends here, Papa.

OKA: Next year our lease will be up and we got to move.

KIYOKO: The ranch is not ours?

OKA: No. In America Japanese cannot own land. We lease and move every two to three years. Next year we going go someplace where there's young fellows. There's none good enough for you here. Yeah. You going to make a good wife. Already a good cook. I like your cooking.

KIYOKO *[a little embarrassed]*: Shall we go now?

OKA: Yeah. Put the magazine away.

KIYOKO: I want to take it with me.

OKA: Take it with you?

KIYOKO: Last time, after we came back, I found all my magazines torn in half. Even the new ones.

OKA *[looking toward the house]*: Torn?

KIYOKO: This is the only one I have left.

OKA: All right, all right.

> [*The two prepare to leave when EMIKO lurches through the door. Her hair is unkempt—she looks wild. She holds an empty can in one hand, the lid in the other.*]

EMIKO: Where is it?

> [*OKA tries to make a hasty departure.*]

KIYOKO: Where is what?

> [*OKA pushes KIYOKO ahead of him, still trying to make a getaway.*]

EMIKO: Where is it? Where is it? What did you do with it?

200 — And the Soul Shall Dance

[EMIKO moves toward OKA.]

OKA *[with false unconcern to KIYOKO]*: Why don't you walk on ahead to Murata-san's.

KIYOKO: We're not going to the pictures?

OKA: We'll go. First you walk to Murata-san's. Show them your new dress. I'll meet you there.

> *[KIYOKO enters the house, pushing past EMIKO, emerges with a small package, and exits, looking worriedly back at OKA and EMIKO. OKA sighs and shakes his head.]*

EMIKO *[shaking the can]*: Where is it? What did you do with it?

OKA *[feigning surprise]*: With what?

EMIKO: You know what. You stole it. You stole my money.

OKA: *Your* money?

EMIKO: I've been saving that money.

OKA: Yeah? Well, where'd you get it? Where'd you get it, eh? You stole it from me! Dollar by dollar! You stole it from me! Out of my pocket!

EMIKO: I saved it!

OKA: From *my* pocket!

EMIKO: It's mine! I saved for a long time. Some of it I brought from Japan.

OKA: *Bakayuna!* What'd you bring from Japan? Nothing but some useless kimonos.

> *[OKA tries to leave, but EMIKO hangs on to him.]*

EMIKO: Give back my money! Thief!

> *[OKA swings around and balls his fists but doesn't strike.]*

OKA: Goddam! Get off me!

EMIKO *[now pleading]*: Please give it back . . . please . . . please . . .

> *[EMIKO strokes his legs, but OKA pulls her hands away and pushes her from him.]*

EMIKO *[continuing]*: Oni!

OKA *[seething]*: Oni? What does that make you? *Oni-baba?* Yeah, that's what you are . . . a devil!

EMIKO: It's mine! Give it back!

And the Soul Shall Dance — 201

OKA: The hell! You think you can live off me and steal my money too? How stupid you think I am?

EMIKO [*tearfully*]: But I've paid. I've paid . . .

OKA: With what?

EMIKO: You know I've paid.

OKA [*scoffing*]: You call that paying?

EMIKO: What did you do with it?

OKA: I don't have it.

EMIKO: It's gone? It's gone?

OKA: Yeah! It's gone. I spent it. The hell! Every last cent.

EMIKO: The new clothes . . . the curls . . . restaurants . . . pictures . . . shoes . . . My money. My going-home money.

OKA: You through?

EMIKO: What will I do? What (will) . . .

OKA: I don't care what you do. Walk. Use your feet. Swim to Japan. I don't care. I give you no more than you gave me. Now I don't want anything. I don't care what you do. [*He walks away.*]

> [EMIKO *still holds the empty can. Offstage we hear Oka's car start off. Accustomed to crying alone, she doesn't utter a sound. Her shoulders shake, her dry soundless sobs turn to a silent laugh. She wipes the dust gently from the can as though comforting a friend. Her movements grow sensuous, her hands move to her own body, around her throat, over her breasts, to her hips, caressing, soothing, reminding her of her lover's hands.*]
>
> [*Fade out*]

ACT II
Scene v

Same day, late afternoon

ON RISE: *Exterior of the Murata house. The light is soft.* HANA *sweeps the yard;* MASAKO *hangs a glass wind chime on the wall.*]

HANA [*directing MASAKO*]: There. There. That's a good place.

MASAKO: Here?

HANA [*nodding*]: It must catch the slightest breeze. [*sighing and listening*] It brings back so much. That's the reason I never hung one before. I guess it doesn't matter much anymore.

MASAKO: I thought you liked to think about Japan.

HANA [*laughing softly*]: I didn't want to hear that sound too often . . . get too used to it. Sometimes you hear something too often, after a while you don't hear it anymore. I didn't want that to happen. The same thing happens to feelings too, I guess. After a while, you don't feel anymore. You're too young to understand that yet.

MASAKO: I understand, Mama.

HANA: Wasn't it nice of Kiyoko-san to give you the *furin?*

MASAKO: I love it. I don't know anything about Japan, but it makes me feel something too.

HANA: Maybe someday when you're grown up, gone away, you'll hear it and remember yourself as this little girl . . . remember this old house, the ranch, and . . . your old mama.

MASAKO: That's kind of scary.

> [*EMIKO enters unsteadily. She carries a bundle wrapped in a colorful scarf* (furoshiki). *In the package are two beautiful kimonos.*]

HANA: Emiko-san! What a pleasant surprise! Please sit down. We were just hanging the wind chime. It was so sweet of Kiyoko-san to give it to Masako. She loves it.

> [*EMIKO looks mildly interested. She acts as normal as she can throughout the scene, but at times drops the facade, revealing her desperation.*]

EMIKO: Thank you. [*She sets the bundle on the bench but keeps her hand on it.*]

HANA: Your family was here earlier.

> [*EMIKO smiles vaguely.*]

HANA [*continuing*]: On their way to the pictures, I think. Make tea for us, Ma-chan.

EMIKO: Please don't.

HANA: Kiyoko-san was looking so nice . . . her hair all curly. Of course, in our day, straight black hair was desirable. Of course, times change.

And the Soul Shall Dance – 203

EMIKO: Yes . . .

HANA: But she did look fine. My, my, a colorful new dress, new shoes, a permanent wave – looked like a regular American girl. Did you choose her dress?

EMIKO: No . . . I didn't go.

HANA: You know, I didn't think so. Very pretty though. I liked it very much. Of course, I sew all Masako's clothes. It saves money. It'll be nice for you to make things for Kiyoko-san too. She'd be so pleased. I know she'd be pleased.

> *[While HANA talks, EMIKO plucks nervously at the package. She waits for HANA to stop.]*

HANA *[continuing]*: Emiko-san, is everything all right?

EMIKO *[smiling nervously]*: Yes.

HANA: Masako, please go make tea for us. See if there aren't any more of those crackers left. Or did you finish them? *[to EMIKO]* We can't keep anything in this house. She eats everything as soon as Papa brings it home. You'd never know it, she's so skinny. We never have anything left for company.

MASAKO: We hardly ever have company anyway.

> *[HANA gives MASAKO a strong look before MASAKO leaves. EMIKO is lost in her own thoughts.]*

HANA: Is there something you . . . I can help you with? *[very gently]* Emiko-san?

EMIKO *[suddenly frightened]*: Oh, no. I was thinking . . . Now that . . . now that . . . Masa-chan is growing up . . . older . . .

HANA: Oh, yes.

EMIKO: I was thinking . . .

> *[She stops, puts the package on her lap, and is lost again.]*

HANA: Yes, she *is* growing. Time goes so fast. I think she'll be taller than me soon. *[She laughs weakly but looks puzzled.]*

EMIKO: Yes . . .

> *[EMIKO's depression pervades the atmosphere. HANA is affected by it. The two women sit in silence. A small breeze moves the wind chimes. At the moment, light grows dim on the two lonely figures.]*

> *[MASAKO brings the tray of tea. The light returns to normal.]*

HANA *[gently]*: You're a good girl.

[MASAKO looks first to EMIKO, then to her mother. She sets the tray on the bench and stands near EMIKO. EMIKO seems to notice her for the first time.]

EMIKO: How are you?

[HANA pours the tea.]

HANA: Emiko-san, is there something I can do for you?

EMIKO: There's . . . I was . . . I . . . Masa-chan will be a young lady soon. . . .

HANA: Well, I don't know about "lady."

EMIKO: Maybe she would like a nice . . . nice . . . *[She unwraps the package.]* I have kimonos I wore in Japan for dancing. Maybe she can . . . if you like, I mean. They'll be nice on her. She's so slim.

[EMIKO shakes out a robe. HANA and MASAKO are impressed.]

HANA: Ohhh! Beautiful!

MASAKO: Oh, Mama! Pretty!

[They touch the material.]

MASAKO *[continuing]*: Gold threads, Mama.

HANA: Brocade!

EMIKO: Maybe Masa-chan would like them. I mean for her school programs . . . Japanese school.

HANA: Oh, no! Too good for country. People will be envious of us . . . wonder where we got them.

EMIKO: I mean for festivals. *Obon, Hana Matsuri* . . .

HANA: Oh, but you have Kiyoko-san now. You should give them to her. Has she seen them?

EMIKO: Oh. No.

HANA: She'll love them. You should give them to her – not our Masako.

EMIKO: I thought . . . I mean, I was thinking of . . . if you could give me a little . . . if you could pay . . . manage to give me something for . . .

HANA: But these gowns, Emiko-san – they're worth hundreds.

EMIKO: I know, but I'm not asking for that. Whatever you can give. Only as much as you can give.

MASAKO: Mama?

And the Soul Shall Dance – 205

HANA: Masako, Papa doesn't have that kind of money.

EMIKO: Anything you can give. Anything . . .

MASAKO: Ask Papa.

HANA: There's no use asking. I *know* he can't afford it.

EMIKO *[looking at MASAKO]*: A little at a time . . .

MASAKO: Mama?

HANA *[firmly]*: No, Masako. This is a luxury.

> *[HANA folds the gowns and puts them away. EMIKO is decimated. HANA sees this and tries to find a way to help.]*

HANA *[continuing]*: Emiko-san, I hope you understand.

> *[EMIKO is silent, trying to gather her resources.]*

HANA *[continuing]*: I know you can sell them and get the full price somewhere. Let's see . . . a family with lots of growing daughters . . . someone who did well last year. Nagata-san has no girls. Umeda-san has girls but no money. Well, let's see . . . Maybe not here in this country town. Ah . . . you can take them to the city–Los Angeles–and sell them to a store. Or Terminal Island. Lots of wealthy fishermen there. Yes, that would be the place. Why, it's no problem, Emiko-san. Have your husband take them there. I know you'll get your money. He'll find a buyer. I know he will.

EMIKO: Yes . . . *[She ties the bundle and sits quietly.]*

HANA: Please have your tea. I'm sorry. I really would like to take them for Masako, but it just isn't possible. You understand, don't you?

> *[EMIKO nods.]*

HANA *[continuing]*: Please don't feel so . . . so bad. It's not really a matter of life or death, is it? Emiko-san?

> *[EMIKO nods again. HANA sips her tea.]*

MASAKO: Mama? If you could ask Papa . . .

HANA: Oh, the tea is cold. Masako, could you heat the kettle?

EMIKO: No more. I must be going. *[She picks up her package and rises slowly.]*

HANA *[helplessly]*: So soon? Emiko-san, please stay.

> *[EMIKO starts to go.]*

HANA *[continuing]*: Masako will walk with you. *[She pushes MASAKO forward.]*

EMIKO: It's not far.

HANA: Emiko-san? You'll be all right?

EMIKO: Yes . . . yes . . . yes . . .

HANA [calling after EMIKO]: I'm sorry, Emiko-san.

EMIKO: Yes.

> [MASAKO and HANA watch as EMIKO leaves. The light grows dim as though a cloud passed over. HANA strokes MASAKO's hair.]

HANA: Your hair is so black and straight . . . nice.

> [They stand close. The wind chimes tinkle; light grows dim. Light returns to normal.]

> [MURATA enters. He sees the tableau of mother and child and is puzzled.]

MURATA: What's going on here?

> [The women part.]

HANA: Oh . . . nothing. Nothing.

MASAKO: Mrs. Oka was here. She had two kimo(nos) . . .

HANA [putting her hand on MASAKO's shoulder]: It was nothing.

MURATA: Eh? What'd she want?

HANA: Later, Papa. Right now, I'd better fix supper.

MURATA [looking at the sky]: Strange how that sun comes and goes. Maybe I didn't need to irrigate . . . looks like rain. [He remembers.] Ach! I forgot to shut the water!

MASAKO: I'll do it, Papa.

HANA: Masako, that gate's too heavy for you.

MURATA: She can handle it. Take out the pin and let the gate fall all the way down. All the way. And put the pin back. Don't forget to put the pin back.

HANA: And be careful. Don't fall in the canal.

> [MASAKO leaves.]

MURATA: What's the matter with that girl?

HANA: Nothing. Why?

MURATA: Usually have to beg her to (do) . . .

HANA: She's growing up.

MURATA: Must be that time of the month.

HANA: Oh, Papa, she's too young for that yet.

MURATA *[genially as they enter the house]*: Got to start sometime. Looks like I'll be outnumbered soon. I'm outnumbered already.

> *[HANA glances at him and quietly begins preparations for supper. MURATA removes his shirt and picks up a paper. Light fades slowly.]*

> *[Fade out]*

ACT II
Scene vi

Same evening

ON RISE: *Exterior, desert. There is at least one shrub, a tumbleweed maybe. MASAKO walks slowly. From a distance we hear EMIKO singing the song, "And the Soul Shall Dance." MASAKO looks around, sees the shrub, and crouches by it. EMIKO appears. She wears her beautiful kimono tied loosely at her waist. She carries a branch of sage. Her hair is loose.]*

EMIKO: *Akai kuchibiru / Kappu ni yosete / Aoi sake nomya / Kokoro ga odoru Kurai yoru no yume / Setsu nasa yo.* . . .

> *[EMIKO breaks into a dance, laughs mysteriously, turns round and round acting out a fantasy. MASAKO stirs uncomfortably. EMIKO senses a presence. She stops, drops her branch, empties out her sleeve of imaginary flowers at MASAKO, and exits singing.]*

EMIKO *[continuing]*: *Aoi sake nomya / Yume ga odoru.* . . .

> *[MASAKO watches as EMIKO leaves. She rises slowly and picks up the branch EMIKO has left. She moves forward a step and looks off to the point where EMIKO disappeared.]*

> *[Light slowly fades on MASAKO, and the image of her forlorn form remains etched on the retina.]*

> *[Fade out]*

Recollections

Makapuu Bay

That was the time I went to Hawaii, the first real vacation I'd ever had; one I'd earned myself. I'd had a small windfall, a story I wrote was accepted for television, and also I was asked to do a presentation in Hawaii for an Ethnic-American Writers' Conference, and so my airfare, a per diem, and a small fee was offered. I'd invited Kay to come with me. She'd been my cook, confidante, and nurse since the time of my divorce from her father. In spite of the uneven marriage, I had expected to always be married to Joe; divorce among Japanese Americans is uncommon, and I was not prepared for it.

That was the worst period of my life. I became a walking zombie with no interest at all in the living reality—the eating, sleeping, excreting, the laughing, loving, and crying of life. I finally pulled through without a psychiatrist; I made Kay the receptacle for all my poisonous feelings, and she held them for me (I didn't know this then) until I could put them in their proper places, which I have since done, and I wanted to thank her for her support.

And for a change she agreed to go with me.

I look at these vacation snaps and relive that time; I take a magnifying glass (my eyes are getting so bad) and minutely examine the surface of the pictures in case there's an expression I'd missed, a mood I'd lost—in case I'd forgotten the time of day for each picture. I look for the source of light: shadows are long on this one, changing the green on the ground; a yellow glow catches the tall palm fronds; skies are heavy for the night's rain.

And the pictures of Makapuu—that hot day at the bay—those tiny figures in the background of a family on a picnic, so long gone (the children must be grown now), strangers caught in my camera, strangers sitting in my album. I had nearly forgotten how white the sand was in the afternoon light, or the magnificent and intense blues of the sea. And the hot sun, yes.

Today I sit with my album and peruse the pictures as though my life depended on remembering the sand, the afternoon light, the sea at Makapuu Bay.

I did not mean to think about it today.

It was a wonderful conference with writers, poets, chanters, dancers, and actors. Kay and I had agreed, both of us being of consenting age, not to stay too close to each other. I noticed at the dining hall she was often in the company of one young man whom she did not introduce to me, and when I veered near, I heard the kind of laughter a mother does not often hear from her daughter. And I was happy.

Kay was fifteen when Joe and I split up, and though I didn't relate it to the divorce then, I noticed that she began to stick very close to home, and the few attachments she formed were one-to-one, as though she reasoned that the more people she involved herself with, the more chances there were for abandonment. It wasn't until much later, in fact just before we left for Hawaii, that she confessed the best time of her life was the fifteen years prior to the divorce, and though intellectually she realized her father was happier now with his new wife and family, and I was happier with my many love affairs (actually there were only two, but Kay tends to exaggerate to make a point), we had left her at that place in the past. For years, even after her father had remarried and had his first child, she had prayed that we would return for her at that place so she could resume her life too.

I cried then and said I was returning for her now. I told her that some of the old concepts I'd been taught and also imposed on her, of nucleus—one man, one family—were no longer viable for us, and we must push on, not necessarily together, but forward to explore and discover more workable philosophies for ourselves. I told her I would never withdraw my love and support so that no matter where she stood, she would not be alone, and that she should not be afraid to love; that joy was worth the risk of pain. After all, one does not die from pain unless one chooses to. I am witness to that.

With those things out of the way, we went to Hawaii to have a good time, and I was happy to hear that tinkling laughter from Kay.

Hawaii would not have been my first choice of places to visit. I'd heard how commercialized the islands had become, high-rise hotels dominating the landscape, waters sullied by tourist droppings. I was not prepared for the incredible beauty of the islands, the magnificent colors, the trade winds and tropical rains.

I asked Kay as I have always done, "Are you having fun?"

She answered as she has always done, "Yes."

I asked, "Don't you just love it here?"

She said, "Yes, I do."

My presentation was scheduled for the last day of the conference. I was asked to speak on the literature of the camp experience in World War II. During the war with Japan, all Japanese and Japanese Americans were incarcerated in internment centers in the more remote areas of the U.S. Midwest. These places were loosely called camps. The year before, I'd done a similar paper on camp poetry, so I added some new material and read the piece and quickly went on to the discussion. The first question was so involved, I simply shrugged and said, "I don't know." I've found it's better to pass as uneducated than as stupid. The rest was easy; questions dealt with my own writing, where my characters come from, where the plot originates, do I outline first, etc., like the questions people ask painters: what size brush do you use; do you make small sketches first. I paint too. I said, no, no, my stories start with a character and a situation, then they write themselves, although . . . yes, there is an underlying vein, like an earthquake fault that yields to a certain destiny.

After the talk my throat felt dry, so I went out to find a coffee machine. Several people followed me out, some to congratulate me while I edged my way to the coffee. I was fumbling for coins in my purse when someone slipped the money in for me and asked, "Black, wasn't it, Pinky?"

Pinky! I hadn't heard that name for twenty-five years. After I married Joe, he decided it was too cute, too frivolous a name for his wife and banned it, stamped it out wherever he heard it.

I got the name in camp – Poston, Arizona – where my father and I were sent (my mother had died two years before the war). The dust there was so malevolent I was often afflicted with a condition called pinkeye. They called me "Pinky" and the name stuck even after my environment changed. Until, that is, Joe decided to obliterate the name along with my past.

My heart leaped and connected immediately to camp and Mitch Ochiai.

I'd met him at the camp swimming hole. The "hole" was a deep excavation filled with stagnant Colorado River water set in the center of a firebreak. On one end was a crude diving board, and in the deepest middle was a floating barge. I passed by the swimming hole one evening while Mitch was doing one of his perfect swan dives, and for several evenings thereafter, I watched for his dive and then moved on. He was always alone – a young man of twenty who swam alone and sat on the barge and watched the sun go down; a man who could soar like a bird and suspend himself in the Arizona sky.

I couldn't swim, but I decided to get in the same water with this young man and for a while endured the murky green water, the ripe smell, the slimy mud and algae, to stand neck deep in it until I worked up the courage to ask him (as he moved close to the shallow edge) if he would teach me to swim.

Mitch was an enthusiastic teacher. He manually worked my head and arms to get the technique right, and otherwise tried hard to teach me the rudiments – even going underwater to watch my kick. But I was terribly inept and could not even float without his hand under my belly. Besides, I had other things in mind. Between gurgles ("Pinky, you'll get sick drinking all that bad water") I learned that Mitch had been attending the university in Berkeley at the outbreak of the war and was originally sent to a camp in Utah. He had enlisted in a special military service and was scheduled to train in the fall in Minneapolis. He had come to Poston to spend his remaining time as a civilian with his father. I learned also that Mitch was gentle and unlike other boys I knew; he was not forever trying to impress me with his cleverness or what we now call "machismo," or trying desperately to move with the crowd ("I have no herd instinct"). I was a loner too, and it seemed I had at last found one of my own.

Mitch did not speak of a mother. We were both motherless.

One evening while we were laughing and splashing at the pool edge, I noticed an old man watching us carefully. Mitch introduced him as his father, and they invited me to their barracks. While Mr. Ochiai brewed tea, he sent Mitch to the canteen for cookies, and as he went slowly through the ritual of tea—the boiling of the water, the mixing of herbs, and the steeping, he talked about Mitch—that he was a brilliant scholar and had many stories published in the university magazine, and that finally in his junior year he'd been made the editor of it.

"I'm proud of Michio. He's the first Japanese American in the university's history to become editor of this scholarly journal—the only Japanese," he said. He brought out the paperback and pointed to Mitch's name—a trump card to play against anyone who dared to tamper with his Mitch.

"How old are you, Pinky-san?" he asked.

"Eighteen," I said.

"Ah!" He was delighted. "You are so young. You have much to look forward to, so many boyfriends . . . a pretty girl like you will have many boyfriends."

Then summer was over. Those were the war years, and men and boys were constantly leaving us; and our lives, further complicated by the incarceration and hostilities with the country of our heritage, were always threatened with separations that were conceivably final. Mitch went away to Minneapolis.

He wrote wonderful letters with that writer's eye, that observing eye. He was often very funny. Sometimes he remembered our summer idyll; he was lonely too.

Within a short time I cleared the camp security board, and my father and the government released me to go to Chicago. I got a job in a candy factory and shared an apartment with a religious old lady from Crovatus and waited for Mitch's letters and his weekend passes. Mrs. Creta did not like me to keep company with Mitch in the apartment, so we went to movies and coffee shops and walked up and down the deserted avenues at night. When the weather warmed we walked barefoot along the shores of Lake Michigan.

That's the way it was. We sang songs, we laughed, talked, and often walked hand in hand in silence. In spite of the harried times, the imminence of separation, I felt a quiet joy with him. We did not speak of marriage or of love. I lived simply for these weekends, those letters. I smile now at the things that gave me such intense pleasure: a pressure on the arm, a certain look, a space between words. It was a different time.

The last time I saw Mitch, he kissed me ("I think you are as innocent as I am in these matters"). And shortly after that I was called back to Poston by Joe Noda, who was our block manager at that time. My father was dying.

The train from Chicago took three days; I did not get back to Poston in time. I arrived on the night of the wake. Joe and the mortician arranged the funeral for the next day; they explained the weather was too warm to delay the ceremony. I was now an orphan.

I was in Poston two weeks putting my father's affairs in order when I got a letter forwarded from Chicago in Mrs. Creta's wavering and inaccurate hand. Mitch said he had gone to see me and a strange young woman had answered the door . . . no, she knew no Pinky; no, Mrs. Creta was out of town. He walked down the stairs and for the first time noticed how worn the steps were. He said he smelled cabbage cooking in the hall (Was it suppertime then?). He said he was shipping out to parts unknown in the morning and had come to say good-bye to me.

By this time the dispersal of camp was ordered and I had to decide where to relocate. I didn't have heart enough to return to Chicago. Joe then suggested I go along with his family to Los Angeles. I thought in Los Angeles I might still make contact with Mitch. Maybe he would be detained there.

I stayed in a hostel until I could find an apartment and a job. I ended up hand-painting shower curtains in a factory and spent a bleak year waiting to hear from Mitch. When Joe Noda pressed me for attention, I explained about Mitch, and Joe waited a while and then pressed me again, and finally I put an end to that incredibly lonely year. It's at that point that Joe began to call me by my given name: Sachiko.

Much later I read in the Japanese papers that Mr. Ochiai died in San Francisco (did he wait for Mitch to return to the university?), and I supposed that Mitch, listed as his surviving son, had come back to claim his father. By that time I had little Kay and I'd begun to write and paint, and my life with Joe was secure in its ups and downs. I did not care to see Mitch.

Still, once in a while he would appear in my dreams and the sweet-sad feeling of unfinished business, of being close to something very important awakened me, and I would wonder if I didn't try hard enough to contact him or he me, those many years ago. Or was it something else? The morning's reality— Joe's warm body against me, Kay's need for attention—returned and put these feelings back, back, like songs sung from another room, like stories of another person's pain. I supposed Mitch, like me, had gone on to marry someone and probably had family and certainly would have written several novels. If there was a memory of me at all, it was probably as distant as mine of him.

My marriage almost lasted forever, but not quite long enough or short enough, and in my middle age, I was facing life alone again. No, not alone. Kay was with me this time—a child leading me, picking our way back to sanity, following the bread crumbs back. Then through a fluke, some of the stories I'd written while still married found their way to publication, and one was bought for television and voila! I was doing a minor lecture circuit.

And so in Hawaii, with the word "Pinky," feelings of youth and love and girlish laughter returned to me, and my heart jumped there in front of the coffee machine. I didn't raise my head until it cleared.

He hadn't changed much – a little gray, a little more weight, a tired look around his eyes, but still the boyish smile. With our two coffees in our hands, our embrace was only a body contact, a kiss like a wind against my cheek (the smell of wine – "Has it been so long? I thought of you so often"). He'd read in the papers of the conference and the presentation on camp literature, and he'd wondered if Sachiko Noda could be the Pinky he once knew. And he'd come to see. He lived in Honolulu.

We drove to Waikiki and the shallows of Hanauma, and we stopped at Makapuu Bay. Mitch pointed out Rabbit Island and the cove where he spent much of his free time ("Waves come fast and clean here – the best for body surfing"). We briefly remembered the Poston swimming hole ("Why wouldn't you learn to swim, Pinky?"); we did not speak of the days in Chicago, what took me away, the death of his father or mine. We passed over the years between:

"You've never married?" I asked.

"No, I'm free still."

"You like it this way?"

"Well, it's better for me. I'm free."

"Of course, your writing . . . ,"

"I've freed myself from that too. I have no novel for you, Pinky."

"But why, Mitch?"

"Because . . . ," he laughed dryly. "Here you are, still literally seething with innocence, even after all these years, and I must be the one to tell you things are not what they seem; that sometimes the illusion and the enlightenment are found at the same place, are one and the same. So does it matter whether one takes the entire trip around to arrive at the same place?"

"Is this the truth or is it your theory?"

"Each finds his own truth."

"And you've wandered over the face of the earth?"

"In a manner of speaking, yes."

"To the Himalayas – the Gurus of Inja?" I tried to make light.

"The Diamond Head of Oahu."

"The monasteries of Japan, at least . . ."

"At least."

"And you've chosen this green and blue and gold island with the swaying palms. . . ."

"Well, I'm stationed here, Pinky."

"You're still with the military."

"Yes." A smile died in his eyes.

We returned to Makapuu the next day. Mitch swam while I waited on the rocks, tasting the salt wind, snapping pictures, writing in my journal, trying to find the exact words for the color of the sea, trying to nail down an elusive feeling of living a recurring dream. But this was Makapuu – another time, another era, not a fragment of the past dislodged from its time frame. This was now, and Mitch was one of those little dots in the changing blue, moving with the surf, almost coming ashore, drawing out to sea again. I wrote in my journal: "This moment *is*. No more, no less." I stood on the black rocks and snapped a family of picnickers under the palms, freezing an instant of their laughter.

We went one more time to Makapuu ("I'll wave my arm and you'll know which dot is me") and later stopped at a cafe terrace facing the sea. We were alone, the sun was setting, and a quiet sense of endlessness prevailed. I was thinking that we were the intruders here, that the sun would continue to set like this on this island forever while we died in agony or joy or ennui and cafe terraces crumbled and cities decayed, and so why shouldn't a small persistent dream also perish here in Makapuu with the last of the day's sun? Mitch touched my hand.

"You look so sad," he said.

"I'm releasing a dream."

"The past is not retrievable," he said.

Kay and I finished the vacation with a tour of the outer islands. We tramped through miles of volcanic ash, cane and pineapple fields and factories thereof, lush valleys, stuffy museums, and scores of souvenir shops. In Lahaina I found a paperweight – a fragile heart-shaped shell, a heart cockle – encased in a bubble of plastic. A man I know said he'd been twenty years in medicine but had never seen the cockles of one's heart, and I meant to carry it two thousand miles across the emerald sea to him ("You've been looking in the wrong places"). I bought strings of coral, T-shirts, black sand in tiny bottles, and I bought ti-leaf booze and macadamia-nut chocolates.

That was a long time ago – seven, eight years? When I look at these Hawaii snaps, I can almost smell that salt spray; the sun is forever suspended at late afternoon, a moment standing still, and sometimes along with a certain sadness, a joy returns. It's good. Then I remember Mitch again, the conference, and I remember Kay's laughter.

Kay was never the same after Hawaii. She dropped out of college, enrolled in a training program with an airline, and became a stewardess and now sleeps in many of the major cities of the world. She stops by now and then with expensive gifts which I've put in the room that used to be hers: a samovar, Persian stone rubbings, Indian baskets, ivory and jade carvings, a piece of Roman relic. I keep the Roman relic in a dish with the broken coral we collected in Maui.

The heart-cockle paperweight is in the room too. I didn't give it to my friend; I couldn't part with it. It has all the beautiful colors of the shores of

Hawaii, and depending on how I hold it, it is greener or bluer, and sometimes the light catches on the shell and it shines all gold and white and blue and green. And I recall once more the sand and sun and surf at Makapuu. Yet if I hold it directly at eye level, it is clearly only a plastic bubble, and one can see that the colors are just at the base of the paperweight. I suspect that there is a way to look at things so the truth clearly separates itself from the illusion.

A Veteran of
Foreign Wars

I t wasn't until several years after Bill and I moved to the neighborhood that
I saw him. In fact it was quite a bit later . . . after my marriage failed, after
the terrible depressions, after I'd pulled myself together somewhat and
began to look cautiously out of my window, began to water my front yard
again, to notice the warm sun on my skin, to touch the camellias that somehow
survived my neglect and year after year bloomed pure and perfect – like the part
of me that refuses to lie down and die and continues to peer out from a dung
heap, expecting a more sufferable world.

I was already walking as far as three houses to the north and four south
when I noticed him, a one-legged man in a wheelchair. We were cool to each
other as though by association; we could call attention to our condition – a
blot on the Nisei horizon – the two that did not make it past the war and,
through the subsequent years, did not become wiser, more self-assured, pros-
perous, smug and secure middle-class middle-aged Japanese Americans. The
model minority.

After I started a routine of walking around the block every morning (my
doctor said I was getting sallow), I passed the small frame house where he
seemed to live, and if he was out sunning, I sent a short nod toward him,
affecting a kind of busy how'd-you-do, and he sometimes waved a scarred arm
at me. When I dared look an instant longer, I could see that he was once a
handsome young man. He looks a bit bloated now; soft fat plumps his hands,
his fingers, and stomach. The right leg is gone at the groin. I suppose the
absence of a leg does not permit him to work off the fat.

There are some days in my life that come and go, come and go, and suddenly I see that another winter has passed and the camellias are blooming once more and children scream and laugh on the streets again. When I try to reclaim the time that moved along without me, the illusion of yellow leaves scattering in the wind, and rain falling on my wool cape and sending out animal smells to my nose, and soggy dog droppings on the sidewalk appear like a montage on a TV melodrama. And like the trick they do on TV with matter slowly swirling and finally forming a definite image, my memory coagulates to two gray forms, a man and a woman, sitting on a curb. On a misty morning I pass them.

I see them again on another morning. They sit on the curb near the park. The woman is middle-aged. Her face is red from the cold, and her gray hair is wet and stringy. She wears an oversized man's sport coat and clutches her waist, trying to keep her warmth from leaking out of the cavernous coat. The man is young. His boyish skin is clear, and a lock of curly brown hair falls forward like a young Frank Sinatra. He holds the woman with one arm in an indefinable attitude – not sensual, not like a son – an attitude of mutual comfort and need – without possession. The woman accepts this as natural.

She looks at me as I pass, and she smiles, seeking my eyes (which I avert) and says, "Nice," in a tone that sane people use. I'm not sure what it is that's nice, but I'm afraid to ask because maybe it is I who lost the first part of the conversation. I've lost things before, and she seems to know what she's talking about. They get up as one, as though it were preplanned, or maybe there is a hidden signal in my look. I see the back of her legs; she does not wear stockings, and her heels have turned blue. They move briskly on and (again as though on signal) part to go to the restrooms in the park. I see her blue heels disappear behind the ladies' door, and walking on, I cry.

The little girl next door tells me his name is Jimmy – the man in the wheelchair. She says Jimmy asked about me and my divorce, and she starts to look very silly like she already knows what's supposed to be funny. "I think he likes you," she says. She's eleven, which means I've been here eleven years. She was an infant when we moved in. She tosses her long taffy hair and the sun shimmers on it. I don't know whether I cry because of the sun on the hair – so golden, so temporal – or because the time from infancy and innocence to knowing too much is too fleeting, or whether I cry for the man in the wheelchair who reaches to me (oh, but I am maimed too and I cannot accommodate you).

I cried a lot during the autumn the leaves fell twice. I know that's not logical; I'm aware of that, but if I were to try putting the succession of days in proper sequence, I may stay too long in one place.

Now, of course, I could no longer face the man in the wheelchair. I avoid him – checking from my window each time before stepping out of the house. He wants to talk to everyone on the street. He strokes the cold, unyielding aluminum arm of his chair like a friend; his left leg curls inward so the outer foot skims the sidewalk as he moves along. He does not lace his shoe, and like the gray woman in the park, he wears no socks.

He talked to everyone but me. He pretended not to want my company and I—if I happened on him inadvertently—would shuffle off in another direction.

But spring came back again and the days grew long, the evenings longer, and he was on the sidewalks all day (growing brown to the roots of his silver hair) and long into the cool gray evenings, talking with people, cocking his head upward to them, and stroking their dogs.

On Thursday evenings a fish man comes in a green van to sell fish and Japanese products: tofu, *kamaboko,* jars of *tsukemono,* and other things. Often Jimmy spends a long time with the man, but he buys only a small package of something. Peeking from my window, lifting the curtain ever so slightly, I always watch to see if Jimmy is there, and when I find he's left, I rush out and do my buying.

This time I was too early. By the time I paid for my tofu (my doctor said tofu is a good source of protein, and it's also easy to swallow), Jimmy came scooting down the block. I was still on the top step of the van, and he looked surprised to see me. His mouth dropped. My face grew warm and I said, "Excuse me," and more than see, I could feel him turn his chair to try to say hello before I passed him. A foot looks defenseless in a shoe without lace, without socks, and without its mate. I know how much loneliness a body can endure before it mortifies itself (but I am disabled and I cannot carry your wounds too). I rushed to get behind my door.

The day it was announced on TV that a drought condition existed and lawns should be watered in early morning or late afternoon, I was aware enough of civic duty to perform my obligations. I was almost through watering. The sun was not yet out. Through the half-light I saw Jimmy rush toward me. For a moment I felt the old panic. My doctor said there's nothing to fear in a man in a wheelchair. I held my ground.

Because of the running water I couldn't hear him, so I had to watch his face to understand what he was saying—watch his lips move to decipher the sounds. He pointed to my open garage door.

"You leave your garage open."

"Oh." I think I smiled.

"It makes my skin crawl when I see your garage door open."

"Oh." There are deep lines in his brown neck. Thirty-five years ago he was a callow youth with a firm neck. He would be in camp, maybe Gila, maybe Poston. His hair is black—a glossy pompadour in front. Sweet-faced Nisei girls whisper and giggle when he passes. A navy peacoat with the collar turned up, tight jeans, and heavy boots . . .

"You know there's an arsonist loose in the neighborhood. Burning cars is his thing."

Both legs slim and strong. "Is that so?"

"You should keep your car locked and the door closed." He looked toward my garage.

"Oh. All right."

"You know, sometimes I can't sleep. . . ." He rubbed his scarred left arm. The lower half was wrapped in an ACE bandage.

"Really?"

"Two o'clock, three, four o'clock in the morning . . . when I can't sleep . . ." He indicated his arm again.

"Oh, I see . . ." He would endure incredible pain.

"I scoot around here in my . . ." He tapped the arm of his trusty Silver.

"In the dark?" He would be fearless.

"I see some character walking around, and I see your garage open. I kinda wait around till he leaves."

"Oh, thank you."

There were too many cute girls in camp. He would not have noticed me then. Boys, good-looking boys rarely paid attention to me. My mother said good-looking boys will leave you. She was right. She said they don't make good husbands. They don't make a good living, she said.

"It makes my skin crawl." His eyes turned inward, remembering his scarred skin.

"Oh, thank you."

He stroked the arm of his chair. "Lots of times I can't sleep, you know." He tucked in the flap of the ACE bandage. "This arm is practically reconstructed."

"Is that so?"

"Well, I've lived with it over thirty years."

Thirty years ago, a whole young man. "An accident?"

"The war."

"Oh!" Young and strong and torn in a second; torn and thrown away.

"In Luzon . . ."

"Oh!" Fighting against our own. He pulled a gun against a face that looked like a brother. A man that could be his brother tore off his leg.

"I was the only one—there were four of us Nisei in the battalion—I was the only one that got wounded. The only one."

"Too bad . . ." Why just you? Why just me?

"Most Nisei were in the military intelligence."

"Oh, Fort Snelling."

"That's right. The battle of Luzon changed the tide of the war. That's where I was wounded. We were called 'MacArthur's Pets.' Hey, you all right? You look kind of pale."

"How long have you lived here?"

"Fifteen years this August."

"I don't remember you from that far back."

"Oh, now wait: I *saw* you move in: you, your husband, and . . . didn't you have a son? He moved out, right?"

"You didn't get a prosthesis?"

"I'm used to it now. Twenty-five years since they cut it off. They tried to save it. They tried for five years. In and out of hospitals for five years. Then they cut it off."

"How terrible it must be to lose a piece of yourself." I almost did.

"It was the second most awful thing. . . . ," he said.

That was in the spring. It's autumn again now, and somehow the days since have spun by in a more orderly fashion. The doctor told me it would happen this way. Slowly, slowly, I would regain my memory and life would be good again, he said. It is. After rock bottom, everything thereafter is up.

I still see Jimmy gliding up and down the street. We always exchange pleasantries now. He doesn't seem to need to talk so much anymore, or then again, that may have been my distorted view. I don't know. I explained how patchy my memory of the last few years is. His smile was benign. I suppose a man who loses his leg and considers it the second most awful thing to happen to him has seen pain that rends without tearing.

I've not yet assimilated all the leftover images of that period. They bob into my conscious like globules of dreams, rising and dipping, seemingly independent of each other. But I know there is an invisible thread that runs through, stringing together my lost years, Jimmy and his unspoken first most awful thing that happened to him, and the gray winter lovers who sit on the curb near the park.

I cannot forget them. The condition the world has created has forged them together, and they have condensed life to its final essence: a coat to keep warm in, and food to keep alive with, so they could do the only thing that is important to their lives. Love.

By luck they found each other.

Old Times, Old Stories

mong Japanese, bathing is a ritual often performed with family members and friends. One of my earliest memories is that of taking baths with a bunch of boisterous children. These were the Nakayama kids: Kei, Ben, Fumi, and Saburo, and my sister and brother. I was about three, and their splashing, dunking, and raw energy frightened me.

My father had come to America in his youth and had spent some years in rural California. He worked in a white-man's dairy for a time and sent the money he could spare to his family in Japan. This gave them the impression that he was a man of considerable means. He was a quiet man and did not himself tell me; I gleaned it from my mother and from what he would reveal in his more garrulous moments.

He was past thirty when he went back to Japan to marry my mother. It was an arranged marriage. My mother was from a merchant family, tea packers, but by the time she was of age, the business had gone bankrupt through the mismanagement of one of her sisters' husbands, and her marriage prospects had narrowed down to a farmer from America. Still, on the eve of her departure, full of confidence, she told her favorite sister that she would return to Japan, a rich woman.

On the first day of their arrival, my mother was detained in prison, probably in quarantine. It was New Year's Day, 1920. She never forgot that.

My father took his bride to a desert farm in Imperial Valley near the Mexican border. He had leased fifteen acres in Westmorland and had built a house not far from the Nakayama family. They had come to America earlier and already had two sons, Kei and Ben. The Nakayamas were my mother's first friends.

My mother and Mrs. Nakayama grew very close. They had children together: my sister and Fumi (a girl) were born in the same year; my brother and Saburo (a boy), a year later, and I came along alone, two years later.

The house we were born in burned to the ground when I was three, and the five of us went to live with the Nakayamas for a short while. The baths are the only memory I have of that period.

At that time Japanese, by law, were not allowed to own land in America. At best, land leases were for three years, usually two, so the Japanese farmers and their families were always on the move, like desert nomads. We loaded the houses on trucks and relocated sometimes five, ten miles away, sometimes to another township.

After we moved, we saw very little of the Nakayamas. My affection and knowledge of them come solely from the stories my mother told. Mrs. Nakayama's name was Sono; my mother was named Hama, which means seaside. The children took to calling each other's mothers by their first names: Sono-chan (a diminutive) and Hama-chan. My father rarely used my mother's name, and when he did, he seemed to be calling more for a weapon than a wife. But I know he loved her, because when he could afford it, he bought her pretty presents. For us he bought candy.

My memory of the Nakayama kids, too, was kept alive by my mother's stories. Often they were hilarious tales of innocents in America, of mischief and mayhem that Kei and Ben created, but sometimes the unspoken yearning for Sono-chan and a time gone would make me want to cry.

Nakayama-san took sick and was moved to a sanitarium three hundred miles away. A kindly white man named Morann sometimes drove Sono-chan and her youngest two to the hospital. I suppose our family did not own a car. The children would wait outside, and Morann would lift them to the window so they could see their father. This is the last memory they have of him – the long car rides, the hot-dog lunches, and Morann's face come together with their father's raised hand beyond a glass window.

In 1929 when Nakayama-san died, Sono-chan took the insurance money and her children and returned to Japan. My mother was inconsolable. The two women vowed to meet again – I think they surmised that when my father's fortunes changed, he would take her back to Japan. This was never to happen; the two women did not meet again.

Yamada-san was a man from the same era, a friend from my father's bachelor days. His face appears before me now – calm and handsome. He was not a transient laborer as so many single Japanese men were; he leased his own farm and lived alone in limited elegance. He had a phonograph, Japanese records, some Carusos, and he sometimes wore a gray felt hat and a white scarf which he tucked in the collar of his overcoat on cold days. My father did not own a suit or an overcoat, and he couldn't have cared less. He wore a visored cap for all occasions. On Yamada-san's bureau, he kept a pale green vase with a single wax rose. Later, when I showed such longing for it, he gave it to me.

I'm sure we stayed with him for a while, because I remember the morning meals: toast, butter, jam, grapefruit halves, and coffee. Different from the breakfasts my mother prepared for us: hot rice and miso soup.

We left Yamada-san when my father got a job in a produce company as foreman on a lettuce ranch. We moved into a green frame house in district number five. It was a company house—a white-man's house. There were two bedrooms, a porch, a long kitchen, a parlor–dining room with a couch, a heavy oak table, and bentwood chairs. On the kitchen wall there was a telephone which kept ringing. My father, who didn't speak English well, would pick up the earpiece and listen without saying anything. My mother wouldn't speak the language at all, and we were too short to reach the phone. Every time it rang, one of us would fetch my father, and he'd pick up the receiver and listen. After a few days of this, my father got mad and tore the box off the wall.

My mother said I was so eager to start school that she sent me there before I turned five. She said she was tired of fighting me. I knew school was serious business by the way my sister and brother solemnly marched off in the morning and returned in the afternoon with books and drawings. Sometimes they brought home a lollipop for me which was sold at school. They never spoke of the humiliation they endured from not knowing the language. I found that out for myself. Nor did my brother tell of the teasing he took from the big white boys. I saw this for myself too.

But we were happy in the green house. I remember Christmas trees that reached the ceiling. Even though we were Buddhists, we observed the holiday and there were presents for us. My mother acquired a set of American dishes and a pink-and-white jacquard bedspread. She bought nice dresses—I remember one of rose-colored silk with a short pleated skirt. She had a string of garnet beads to go with it and high-heeled shoes and a matching hat with a white silk rose. My father bought a car with Eisenglass windows. It was what Americans enjoyed in the roaring twenties.

From time to time Yamada-san dropped by. He brought gifts and suffered my excessive gratitude and demonstrations of affection. My mother used to pull me off of him, scolding me for my lack of restraint. My father had not started drinking yet. This was the longest we lived in any one place.

Then my father lost his job. It was a bad time for the whole nation. We left the green house, taking with us the dishes, the bedspread, the bentwood chairs, and the oak table (I remember these as remnants of better times), and we changed schools in the middle of the semester.

In those days, even in that backcountry town, Mexican, Indian, and Black children were segregated in separate schools. The bus dropped them off first. The Japanese kids were allowed to attend white schools (I learned later that the Japanese government protested our segregation), but the effect of prejudice had already taken its toll, and we were regarded as socially backward and cliquish. My sister and brother survived the change, but I flunked third grade. My mother said it was no shame—I was too young for the class anyway; it was good I was kept back. We moved yet again to another school district, so I was spared some of the embarrassment, but the trauma remained with me for a long time.

In the valley, houses were built as simple one-room structures to facilitate moving. I have a memory of two bachelors who farmed together and doubled up one summer so we could live in one of their houses.

There were many single Japanese men then. My father had lucked out and married my mother before the Asian Exclusion Act, but after 1924, it was against the law to bring in brides, and other laws prohibited out-of-race marriages. Many men remained single all their lives.

One of the bachelors owned a rumble-seat coupe and sometimes would take my mother and us for rides. My mother was a beautiful woman, and my sister and brother were well behaved in company, and I suppose it was nice to cart around a borrowed family and to treat them like he would have treated his own. I have no recollection of where my father was at these times. When the other man came with us, I had to sit on his lap. I remember his warm hands folded heavily on my lap. They wouldn't let me sit in the rumble seat with my sister and brother while the car was moving.

I didn't like these men. To be sure, they were genial, clean, and dressed well enough, but with the exception of Yamada-san, I thought farmers should be unaffected and a bit unappealing—like my father. One of them, the one who owned the car, was an illegal alien, had come over the Mexican border, and every time we passed the immigration inspection station (which was whenever we left the valley), he would sweat and tremble noticeably. The other bachelor had an ingratiating smile I didn't quite trust or understand. My father was not by nature a cheerful man. My mother said he sometimes had the expression of someone who had stepped in dung. He seldom smiled, and I never saw him tremble or cry, though I'm sure there were times he wanted to.

Later my father bought two old houses (no doubt from a family who gave up the ghost), set them together, bought a galvanized tin trough to join them at the roofs, and put up the connecting walls with my brother's help. He was about twelve. So we had a two-room house with a short hallway between where my mother could store things. And we had plenty of noise when it rained on the tin trough.

Yamada-san still came by then, though not on rainy days. "Too noisy," he said. That was when we needed him most—those dreary days when it rained without end and my mother's voice turned dead. The men who came in winter were unemployed laborers, and they would sit by the hour drinking with my father. It was a difficult time for him, and no one made it easier.

My mother hated my father's drinking, but he said he would not stop until it was time to wear the stone hat, meaning a tombstone. In her women's magazines, my mother read up on sneaky ways to cure alcoholism, such as putting sake in his morning soup and increasing the dosage until he unconsciously began to despise the taste. It didn't work.

We lived in the house with the tin trough for two or three years—until we lost it. I don't know why. Maybe the former owners repossessed it; maybe my father lost it on a bet. The possibilities were numerous and scary, and my mother was not above a little hair-raising. That's when we moved into an abandoned house at the crossing of two alkaline roads.

Small glass windows and carved porch supports easily identified the house as built by white men. The shattered glass and empty rooms testified to a past of failure and desertion. Although we lived there only a month (waiting for a deal to come through), this is the house that haunts me in recurring dreams. The shape changes—sometimes an apartment, sometimes a mansion—but always there are the vacant rooms, always the familiar sense of loss and the search for a vague and nameless something.

We waited for the school bus under the shade of an old cottonwood tree. My sister had a habit of swinging her arms and clapping her hands, once in front, once in back, over and over, no doubt reviewing her Latin verbs. She was in high school. My brother recited poetry for his English class—Longfellow, Wordsworth, Tennyson. I knew from the way he rolled his words, from the way he moved his hands, it wasn't just the lesson or the poetry that held him. When I looked at him, his gestures narrowed. It wasn't good to appear to like it; it would be unseemly to let a dream like this show through. He would appear to want too much, to dream too broadly, too foolishly. It was the thirties, and a Japanese American boy's chances of getting off the farm were slim. Our mother's repeated assurance that we were cut from racially superior cloth didn't change the facts: young men from college returned to their hometowns to work in fruit stands, and women lucky enough to go came back to wait to marry.

About this time Kei and Ben Nakayama returned to America. They separated—Kei going inland to Colorado and Ben coming back to the valley. Barren as it was, no doubt happier memories brought him back to us. But now eighteen, an adult, he had to make his own way. And now he was also a "kibei," an American-born educated in Japan and returned to America—a man with one foot in Japan and the other here—neither fish nor foul—rejected by Japanese and Japanese American alike.

Ben was ensconced in a bitter plot of land (through the "generosity" of a family friend), to work, sleep, and eat alone. Once in a while he came by to share our meal and give us news of Sono and the family. But he was not talkative; he did not speak of his disappointments nor of his wants. It was hard to picture him as the kid in my mother's stories who was so mischievous, so naughty.

In the summer of 1940, Imperial Valley suffered a severe earthquake. It only damaged the property of people who owned buildings and store merchandise. The rest of us were only shaken up. Our houses were built to withstand considerable shifting, so they were undamaged. But the earthquake did jolt a large part of the Japanese community, both farmers and townspeople, and there was a small exodus to Oceanside. The living wasn't better there, but it was cooler and the change brought back the old pioneer spirit and the feeling that we were all in it together. Most went back to rural living; our family moved to the city, where my mother started a boarding house for itinerant laborers.

Ben Nakayama also left the valley. He moved inland from Oceanside to a place called Vista, and he worked on a truck farm hauling produce to the market. I think it was during this period that my sister fell in love with him. I say this because it's hard to picture Ben making the first move even though my sister had grown to be a beautiful woman. Or maybe there are certain signals a man of this type puts out. I don't know.

Ben was drafted in the army just before the attack on Pearl Harbor. We have a picture of him at the bus station preparing to report to his post. My sister is there along with my mother and another girl who also had her eye on him. My father is not there. My brother and I are also present. Kei, in Colorado, successfully evaded the draft with a punctured eardrum.

In early 1942 we were to experience another exodus—the evacuation of all Japanese and Japanese Americans living on the West Coast during the war with Japan. First, all the men of consequence (my father was not one of them), men who were active in Japanese societies and who might have found a way to save us from the humiliation of being incarcerated, were picked up by the FBI and put in detention centers. Yamada-san was among them. He had not come to Oceanside with us, so we had lost touch with him, but this is what I was told. Then the rest of us, alien and citizen, women and children, old and infirm alike were sent to ten concentration camps in the most desolate places in the country. This move changed all our lives and continues to be felt in succeeding generations.

Ben, already in the U.S. Army, refused to bear arms against Japan—against his brother Saburo who was eligible for Japan's Imperial Army. But Saburo was sickly and died during the war of the same disease that killed his father. Ben was put in a labor battalion to spend World War II digging ditches and building roads in southern swamps. My sister applied for a release from camp and went to Arkansas to marry him. My brother was transferred to Tule Lake—a camp for dissidents and troublemakers, and I left my father and mother and relocated to Chicago (we were not permitted to return to the West Coast at this time). My father died in October of 1946, his health failing steadily after the bombing of Hiroshima. I am told that Yamada-san, while incarcerated, was shot in the back by a sentry. He had walked too close to the barbed-wire fence and either did not hear or did not choose to obey the order to halt. They say he died without regaining consciousness.

After the war, most Japanese returned to California—the state that cast us out—straggling in like stepchildren asking to be loved, asking for another chance. Ben was discharged from the army, my brother was released from Tule Lake, I left Chicago, and all of us, my father in ashes, returned to California too. Kei died of cirrhosis of the liver, alone in Colorado, alienated from his wife and children. A few years after that, our mother died from a heart attack.

In 1983, Ben Nakayama and my sister, my brother and his wife and I went to Japan to visit our families in Shizuoka. My mother's favorite sister was still alive then, eighty-eight, the last of that large family of girls. She sang songs for us, songs she and my mother sang together as children. She would not take us to the tea plantation where they lived so long ago. It was not there anymore . . . everything had changed, she said. I wanted to see the well where my mother said they chilled melons on summer evenings, but she said that was gone too. She told us of the hard times she had feeding her children during the war with her husband dead.

Sono Nakayama at eighty-six was bent over with osteoporosis. When we first arrived, her mind was clear, but toward the end of our visit, she grew confused and forgot that Kei was dead, forgot who I was, and she asked me to take care of Kei because he was all alone in America. She didn't remember Ben either. Before we left, I went to her room to say good-bye. She was on the tatami, her back toward the door, and she appeared to be sleeping under the futon. I whispered very softly, "Sayonara, Sono-chan," like my mother might say, thinking I would probably never see her again. Without turning, Sono said, "Good-bye," in remarkably clear English.

Fumi, sixty-four, forgot most of her English. She did not forget the taste of her favorite foods—wieners, tortillas, and cheese. She remembered the stand of eucalyptus on the spine of the hill where we had the Japanese picnics, the dust from the footraces turning gold in the sunset. She remembered, too, the high heels her mother wore on the day they left America, and she remembered how my mother had cried. She and Saburo had often talked about the valley, about their father, his face beyond the smudged glass and his raised hand, Mr. Morann, and the hot dogs. They had yearned to return to America for a long time, but gradually the language was forgotten and the memories faded too. Saburo died at twenty-one and very nearly broke Sono's heart, Fumi said. Sono also had wanted to go back to America, but of course, that was not possible, Fumi said. My mother had always wanted to return to Japan, but that too was not possible.

A year after our visit to Japan, my mother's favorite sister died, and Sono followed a few months later. So Mr. Nakayama, my father, mother, Yamada-san, Kei, Saburo, my mother's favorite sister, and now Sono are gone. If there is an afterlife, maybe they are all together in some desert paradise where they live again in what was (in looking back) the happiest time of their lives. Maybe I will be there too one day, along with my brother reciting poetry, my sister swinging her arms and clapping her hands, once in front, once in back, over and over and over.

So What; Who Cares?

"C lose your mouth when you chew," she says.

I close my mouth. Hunh!

She reaches across the table to wipe my chin. I rear back and grab her arm.

"There's gravy on your chin, Ma!" she says loudly.

"Shhh . . ." I hiss. She thinks because I don't talk, I can't hear. In spite of myself, a tear sneaks down my face.

"What are you crying about now?" She is exasperated. "Those are the very things you taught me: 'Close your mouth, please, and thank you,' all that. Remember?"

She dabs my cheek with the same napkin (I smell the food on it) and spoons mashed potato into a puddle of gravy. I shake my head. "Just one more bite," she coos, making up for the other, harsh words. I open my mouth.

I can feed myself. Most of the time I insist on it, but I'm slow and she often glances at her watch, sometimes taking the fork from me, like now, and I must swallow half-masticated food to accommodate her—especially on holidays when she comes with my dinner and rushes back to serve her family. I'd rather go to her house to eat—I can still walk, I can take a bus—but she never invites me. I depress her husband. His mother died a few years ago in a convalescent home, and why should he do for me what he never did for his mother? Oh, he gave her money and things; she had the woolliest lap robe in the ward, they say, the grandest slippers, but who cares about that? I know. Not much gets past me.

And it doesn't matter to me either, but it's the children I miss–the girls. I like to hear their silly chatter, the giggling. Soon their words will grow too clever, their eyes will change, their thoughts will turn to designer labels. They live in a storybook world now, where princesses don't die, only sleep–no wrinkled faces, no gnarled fingers, no stroke to remind them of reality. No pyorrhea.

She takes me to her dentist, but my teeth are going anyway. That's why she brings me dinner every night. I can cook; I can putter around, but she's afraid I'll die of malnutrition with the rice gruel I keep cooking. It's easy. It goes down fast. But what's my hurry?

"How's the food? Good?" she asks sweetly.

I nod. Juicy dark meat–she always remembers I prefer dark–finely sliced and crushed with a fork–tender garden peas, also crushed, a wedge of cranberry jelly, a mound of mashed potato with a crater of gravy, dark and smooth, like I taught her, a tablespoon of dressing–not my favorite–she knows me well. "A devoted daughter," one of her friends said. They think I'm deaf.

She didn't bring dessert. Maybe she didn't want to cut into the meringue (her meringues are famous). Her husband may have told her to let the kids have the first pieces. Like Joe always said: "Let the baby have the first piece."

I'd almost forgotten him, he died so long ago. What would he think of me now–so old and gap-toothed. He wouldn't like me. "Straighten up," he'd say. "Put on some lipstick; wear something pretty; go to a hairdresser." He liked pretty. Everything had to be pretty and smell nice. He wouldn't have liked growing old.

He died in the Vosges Mountains, Joe, in beautiful France. He saw some awful things there: torn bodies, ruined villages, broken families–not pretty or nice smelling.

He loved the baby. He said, "If I don't come back, promise you won't let her forget me."

"You won't die," I said.

"If I do, will you marry again?"

"No," I said. "If I marry again, she'll forget you. And I would too."

I have anyway. And she has. And I've grown old enough to be your mother, Joe, plus you should see her now.

I didn't get a chance to love you, you know. I was five years out of high school and sitting up there on the farm sorting tomatoes every spring. When you asked, it seemed like a good idea to marry. Then the baby came and the war and the awful relocation camps–the price of being a Japanese in America. Then you left with the volunteers, returned once on a furlough, and never came back.

There were lots of handsome guys in camp, and lots of cute girls. A widow with a baby didn't have a chance. The smart people got out as soon as possible and pursued careers. They became nurses, engineers, secretaries, some even doctors. Me, I stayed the whole four years. It was easier that way, with my father and little sister helping with the baby. My mother died the first year we were there. With a lot of pain–she had ulcers.

I was old then already, a mother of a baby, a gold-star wife and nothing more. I was never young.

Except that once.

He came in while my father and sister were at a camp movie or someplace–I don't remember. He waited until he saw them leave. He lived in another block, a stranger. Well, not really. I'd seen him once or twice at the canteen. He had smiled at me. He was older, a Kibei, born in America, educated in Japan. He spoke mostly Japanese. He knocked and opened the door at the same time. I didn't know what to do–what to say. The baby cried and he picked her up. "*Yoshi-yoshi,*" he crooned. Then he put her in my arms and left.

I lied. I had seen him often. I've told myself so many variations of the story, I can't separate fact from fiction anymore. At the camp talent shows he sang romantic Japanese songs of longing and loneliness. He was not good looking, not very tall, but his arms were strong and his eyes–they looked through you, past your fluttering heart, and all the way down to you-know-where. And when he finally came to see me, I didn't know what to do. Then the baby cried and he sang to her and he left. The only time a man came near me the whole four years. I've clung to this memory through four decades, embellishing it, stripping it to its bone, and putting on the flesh again.

He's probably dead now anyway. Everyone is dead: my mother, father, my little sister. I loved her so much. She died before she could fall in love and marry. I had looked forward to it like a mother might; I could share her excitement, I could be happy too. But she died. It was harder to take than Joe's death. I don't know why. I lived with her longer, maybe; I loved her more, maybe. It nearly broke my heart. It broke Pop's, because he didn't live long after that. Everyone was gone then. Joe's parents had returned to Japan with the repatriates (they didn't want Joe to volunteer), and it was just the baby and me. Sometimes in my dreams it all comes back with a suffocating longing. Then I wake up and see it's just another day.

She efficiently slides the leftovers into one large dish and sets it in the refrigerator. "I put it here, Mom," she says. "Tomorrow you'll set it in the microwave. One minute–no more. Okay? And you'll have a nice turkey dinner again."

That means she won't be coming tomorrow. A four-day holiday. Maybe they're going on a trip. That's okay; that's good. I'm glad she's doing for her girls what I couldn't do for her.

She was a latchkey kid. By the time we were released from camp, she was in school. I had to go to work. I tied the key on colored ribbons to match her dress. Maybe it's one of those traumas that haunt you later in life, but at the time, she didn't seem to mind. She grew up fast, learning to start dinner, learning to mend and sew her own clothes.

She was proud of her competence. She joined every school activity. She got a part-time job – maybe to keep from coming home to an empty apartment. It seems so sad to me now, I want to grab her and say, "I couldn't help it, Baby, forgive me." But she wouldn't like that. She hates tears. She won't let herself cry, and she won't forgive anyone who does.

She went to college and got a good job as a legal secretary. That's where she met Fred – a lawyer. She made me take a night course in typing and insisted I apply for civil service. She made me quit my sewing job so I stopped embarrassing her with the lint in my hair and threads on my clothes. It got so you couldn't tell who was the mother and who was the child. Even before the stroke. But I was lucky. I got disability and a pension of sorts.

What's she doing now? Running water? But I took a bath yesterday. Oh. She's not coming tomorrow, that's why. She doesn't like me to bathe when she's not here. She's afraid I'll have a stroke and drown, and she'll come by the next day or the day after that and find me in the cold water, face down, my hair floating, the soap all soft and gummy.

I want her to say it: "I'm not coming tomorrow," so I shake my head.

"You have to take your bath today; I'm not coming by tomorrow," she says. She gets a fresh towel and my change of underwear and hands it to me.

Homely underwear. They don't hardly make these anymore. They look like they come from a Salvation Army bin or some cleric's dusty drawer. She thinks I like these no-nonsense kind and goes to considerable lengths to find them.

I never had pretty underwear. Joe was appalled when he first saw them. "I thought girls wore pretty things," he said. Not on a farm, they don't. He later bought some lacy rayon things for me. It took a lot of courage to go into the lingerie department, but he did it. It takes a lot of courage to go to war to be shot at or to shoot someone. He did that too, and someone shot him.

They sent him home a few years after the war ended, when we were already used to not having him around. We buried him in a short Buddhist ceremony in the little cemetery on Normandy Avenue.

When she was little she used to say, "Mama, tell me about him," and I would tell her she was Daddy's little honey and that he called her lots of sweet names (he could not call me), and I told her of some incidents that grew worn and changed with each telling. She would laugh with delight. "More! More!" she'd scream.

We used to take flowers regularly. She would romp around the mounds and pick other people's flowers and bring them to his headstone. "This is for you,

Daddy," she'd say happily. All the people who loved her were buried there or in some other graveyard. She hadn't known any of them, and so she didn't really miss them.

As she grew older, she stopped wanting to go to the cemetery, and after a while, when I told those old stories she started saying, "I don't remember that." We went less and less, and toward the end, we even quit the Memorial Day thing.

We have forgotten you, Joe. That's the way it is when there is no one around to remember. When I am gone, we will all be forgotten. There'll be no one left to remember how young we were, how handsome, and those . . . well, they're stupid stories anyway. No one laughed at them.

The water's too cool for my taste. The bottom of the tub stays cold and I can't warm up. I like my bath hot – the way we always had it, even when we had to draw water from a well and heat it with the desert sage and chaparral. She forgot Mr. Bubbles; the bubbles prevent a ring from forming around the tub. Not that I'm ever that dirty. How dirty can you get moving from bed to TV to table to bath?

"I forgot the bubbles," she screams from the kitchen. She is washing the dishes. She comes to the bathroom door. "Did you hear me?" she asks. I rap on the wall. "Put the bubbles in," she says. I rap again. What's the use of wasting my voice on idle words? The things I want to say, she won't hear. "I don't remember," she'll say, or, "Not that story again," and she'll look at her husband.

I run the hot water.

"Not too hot," she calls. "I don't want you to faint in there."

They say drowning is a pleasant way to go. They say that at the end there is such a feeling of euphoria. Maybe it's like going back to the uterus. They say all dying is that way. There's this wonderful light and feeling of joy, and you see the forms of all those you love who have preceded you. I will see my mother and father and my little sister – I love her still – and Joe. I'd be older than all of them. What fun is that? And him.

I should have done it the night he came over. The baby cried and he held her and began to sing. He drew me close (what a leaping in my heart), and we put her to bed. He said, "Let's go to bed too."

"I can't," I said.

"Why?" he asked.

"I don't know."

"Don't you want me to?" He ended the sentence with a preposition.

"No," I lied.

"Well, then, we won't." He put his hands up. "Good-bye," he said and left.

No, he didn't. He stayed and kissed me and we made love and it was the most wonderful . . . "Wonderful, wonderful," is that the only word I know? He said good-bye and left.

I came out of the bathroom and she says, "Did you hear me?"

What did she say? "Wonderful, wonderful . . ." No, *I* said that. I shrug.

She holds vitamin pills in front of me. "You didn't take them yesterday, did you? I want you to take them while I watch." She gives me a glass of water. I hesitate. "Please?" she asks. She wants me to live longer.

I swallow them down.

"I don't know why I have to keep reminding you," she says. "I swear, you're worse than the girls. At least, the girls . . ."

I should have done it. I should have let him do it.

"At least the girls . . ."

Or did I? Did we do it?

". . . will answer me. At least they do that. I'm not saying . . ."

Did I forget? Could I have forgotten such a thing?

"They don't always mind, but at least they answer me. Here I don't know if you hear me or not."

Naw, I wouldn't have forgotten. Would it have changed my life? I should have. I should have.

"Between you and the girls and Fred pulling me apart . . . I don't know what I did to deserve it."

Naw. But it's something to remember. At least. "At least it's something to . . ." I blurt it aloud. It comes out aloud.

"What?" She's stunned. "What did you say?"

I clamp my mouth. Close the gate.

" 'At least,' you said. 'At least.' "

"So what?" I say.

She shakes me. "You can talk!" she screams.

"So what?" I say. She heaves great humps of dry tears. "What's the use of talking? There's nothing to say anymore." Aloud. Well, that's not exactly true, but that's the way it came out. The truth is, there's nothing anyone wants to hear anymore.

"Mom," she says. She is breathless and almost embraces me but instead veers to the closet. Can't lose your head at a time like this, you know. She riffles through my clothes and brings out a skirt and shirt. She pushes them toward me. "Get dressed," she says, "the girls will want to see you."

She wipes her eyes with the sleeve of my shirt.

Ōtōkō

This is the summer solstice, the longest day of the year. My brother Kiyo drops by with three small boxes of berries his in-laws in West Covina gave him. He also brings a record he found at a Japanese record store, a recent issue of old Japanese songs—songs we used to hear as children. Our mother sang them.

"Listen to this," he says. "Remember?"

Watashya ukiyo no watari dori (I'm a bird of passage in a floating world). . . .

I can hear my mother's voice; I see her dancing. She's younger than I am today.

"Remember that old abandoned house in Westmorland?" Kiyo asks.

That was a few years after my father lost his job with the American Fruit Growers, a job that included housing with the salary. It was nice then—good food, store-bought clothes, and singing and laughing. After the job was terminated, we learned what the depression was all about. They called it *fukeiki*.

My father took our family of four (Sachi was not yet born), borrowed an old house from a friend, leased thirty acres, and went into farming independently. It was a struggle—too much rain, too little rain, frost. And that was the worst of those years. At that point.

The friend reclaimed the house he'd loaned us, and we had to find a place to stay until my father decided what to do. He chose to remain in farming, and he moved us into this deserted house that stood by the dirt road we took to town.

We'd passed it often. Kiyo and I used to throw stones at the windows, called it the haunted house, *obakeyashiki*. We boarded the windows with cardboard and moved in as squatters.

My brother spent that summer working at a packing shed making boxes, hammering nails into wooden slats all day, his small fingers growing raw with tiny splinters. He was eleven or twelve. He gave all his pay to our father; he tells me now he's glad of that, because it turned out that was all he'd ever do for him. His eyes swell with moisture.

Otoko wa iji, onna wa nasake (man is will, mercy is woman). . . . The moisture dries before it falls.

Kiyo says he once drove with our father to Niland, a township in the low desert, to a friend who'd made it good with tomatoes that year. He says now that he believes our father went to borrow money that day. "They were rich. Radio, refrigerator, everything." Kiyo flicks his cigarette. "I guess they turned him down, because Dad didn't say anything all the way home. Twenty miles. I remember that." He takes a deep breath.

"Maybe he didn't ask them," I say, unwilling to picture my father, cap in hand, rubbing the back of his neck—my children are hungry; we have no place to live.

"Yeah, he was proud. Well, he made it without their help," Kiyo says. "I wonder what he was thinking on that ride back." He takes another breath. "I guess he felt bad."

"He." We talk about him as we would a stranger. And he *is* a stranger. I can't speak of his feelings with any accuracy. I suppose his life was a string of enduring humiliations like this one, rotating his failures and hanging in there—drawing strength from beneath the surface of his silent self, from his hope of one day returning to Japan. I heard it in the songs he sang when he had too much wine.

The images come tumbling out. I was a headstrong, impetuous, and demanding child—the second of three issues: my brother Kiyo, myself, and thirteen years below me, a sweet cross-eyed sister, Sachiko. I was the only one of the bunch who was familiar with the knuckles of my father's hand. "*Onna no kuse,*" he said. That's an admonition to know my place as a woman.

There was no doubt I was his offspring: the long face, angular frame, the epicanthic fold. My mother was a beautiful woman, and mercifully the others inherited her looks and my father's suppressed temperament. I was given the other combination: his looks and her tenacious nature.

The spring of the great Imperial Valley earthquake was the culmination of my father's farming career—his biggest failure. One hundred and forty acres of lettuce nobody wanted.

I was fifteen. I was tired of hand-me-downs and recycled clothes and contrived to go to Los Angeles to earn a few dollars to buy a coat of my own and some finery that might help me with the fellows. At that time the only jobs available to Japanese were in markets, garages, and for women, domestic work.

In South Pasadena, I found a job as a "schoolgirl," a euphemism for inexperienced servant. I worked three months at twenty-five dollars a month plus room and board, washing, ironing, polishing furniture, vacuuming, and caring for two small girls. Not a lot of money even for those days. Of the seventy-five dollars I'd earned, I spent twenty-five, mostly for movies and restaurants on my days off. I bought a coral necklace and a pair of blue Gallen Kamp shoes with open toes.

At the end of my stint, I was ready to come home and return to school. In the meantime my family had gone to Oceanside to pick berries for the summer. I'd missed them while I was away serving and living with white people, a life-style I was unfamiliar with, and I needed to return to the warmth of my family, to the language and patterns of my people.

In Oceanside I was appalled to find my father, mother, Kiyo, and two-year-old Sachi living in a makeshift tent, using water from a communal faucet, washing, shaving, brushing teeth where everyone could see. There were other families from Imperial Valley who had come to work too. I had just left a home where bathrooms were mirrored and little girls got up from their naps and changed dresses. In the three months I'd been away, my little sister's front teeth had rotted.

Kiyo would not take the situation seriously: a few months in Oceanside, cool weather, a beach nearby, a few bucks, a kind of vacation. He laughed. My mother's lips curled in a reluctant grin.

I gave my remaining fifty dollars to her. "We'll buy a sweater for Father," she said, "and we'll give money to Kiyo to go to Los Angeles. There is no future for him here."

Kiyo left for L.A. He wrote later that he'd found a day job in a fruit stand and went to vocational school, nights.

And we didn't stay in the tent. A kindly bachelor who farmed a piece of land with a frame house on it offered us a room. "It's not right for a young girl to sleep on the ground," he said.

My mother said, "Michiko, remember this kindness."

"It's only for a short while," I said. "We have to get back to our home. School will start in two weeks."

"We have nothing to return to," my mother said.

The following week my mother was offered a job in town as a cook in a boarding house that accommodated Japanese migratory laborers.

The man who came to see my mother was short and wiry. He wore boots laced to his calves. He said she would cook for thirty, forty men during the peak of the season, and off-season there would be only a few, say, four or five, who chose not to move on. "There're always some of them," Mr. Tano said. "They get tired of moving, and if they don't have money enough to pay, well, I have to carry them. What can you do? They're Japanese too, eh? I'll give you a room for your family. Your husband can work out of the boarding house like the rest of them. We serve as an employment agency, and when farmers need help, they come to the hotel. I'll see that your husband always has work," Mr. Tano said.

My father went to bed that day. He had a stomach condition that had plagued him off and on for years. He took a chalky white liquid for it.

My mother asked him, "What should I do? Should I take the job?" My father's face was ashy. His lips were dry and cracked. On this hot day he pulled the blanket around his neck and turned away from us.

"What should I do?" my mother asked again.

"Do what you want," he said without turning.

We moved to the city and lived in a room with a double bed and two cots and just enough space to move cautiously around them. With the money Mr. Tano gave her, my mother bought the supplies: rice, shoyu, miso, heart, liver, tripe – nether cuts. My father rode to work in a truck with the rest of the men and swallowed prodigious quantities of chalky medicine. My mother bought me a herringbone jacket with shoulder pads that made me look like a grown woman, and I started my junior year at Oceanside Carlsbad Union High School. When the kids at school asked me where I lived, I said, "Out that way," and waved vaguely westward, too ashamed to say I lived in a hotel of transient men, afraid the down-cheeked youngsters would shrink from me, their mouths drawn down.

Nokoru yume wo nanto shyo? (What should I do with the dreams that remain?) . . . Kiyo flips the record.

Most of the men in the boarding house were men over fifty. There were a few in their thirties: Kibei – men who were born in America, sent back to Japan for an education. Still seeking something they'd not found in Japan, they had returned, to join a legion of men who moved with harvests not their own. In this land of plenty, they bought beautiful clothes which they kept in cleaners' bags, and went to movies together, wrote long letters to Japan, and visited neighboring farmers (who had daughters). Sometimes in the evening they would play wistful Japanese melodies on harmonicas or wooden flutes. Songs of longing.

The older men were scruffy and bowed from years of scraping along on their knees picking strawberries (for tables not their own), and from bending over low grapevines. Their pants were caked with mud. They shook them out at night over the balcony. Conversations were colored with sexual references, and they laughed lewdly at the jokes. They spent their leisure playing *hana* (cards) or drinking sake which my mother kept warm for them at ten cents a cup.

Once a man staggered off to the courtyard and passed out on the dirt, the ocean breeze cooling him, the sun warming him like the fruit he's spent his youth harvesting. In the late afternoon he woke and walked away brushing himself off, without shame, as though it were his natural right as a man. Fruit of the land.

Within months the hotel was condemned by the Oceanside Department of Health and Sanitation. Not enough bathrooms; too many men in one room.

The men scattered and Mr. Tano left. We stayed in the shack in the back where Mr. Tano had lived and waited for something to turn up. Again squatters.

The landlord came to check on his property and found us there. He saw my little sister with the rotten teeth and the lazy eye and me, haughty and cold. My sister sang *"Cielito Lindo"* for him—a song she'd learned from the Mexican family next door. The landlord asked me to tell my mother that he was willing to remodel to meet health standards if she would run the hotel. He said he was through dealing with Tano.

My mother pointed a forefinger to the sky and said to me, "You see? Someone is watching."

My father wasn't home that day—just my mother; and Sachi, smiling and showing her nubs of teeth, confident the world was safe and loving; and me, unrelenting.

We stayed in the shack during the repairing and later moved into a room until the shack was redone. My father worked when he could, grim but uncomplaining.

By the time the hotel was habitable, it was winter, and though a few men returned, most of the rooms were empty. I asked my mother if I could have one for myself; I would give it up during the busy season, I promised. She said no. I begged and pleaded and sulked, slammed doors and cupboards, and banged dishes until she screamed, "All right! You can have the room!" She said I was a graceless child—determined and self-centered. She said if I didn't change my ways I would come to great unhappiness. "You'll find out!" she said.

Kiete kureruna, itsumade mo (Don't fade, remain forever) . . .

It was the first time I had a room to myself, excluding the one in South Pasadena. It was on the second floor overlooking the courtyard. I dragged in a table and our two best chairs—in case I had company. I sewed dimity curtains for the window and pushed my cot against it so I could see the stars at night. I bought a vase in a secondhand store for a nickel.

The old men thought I was an upstart. Some devised ways of getting back at me: one used to wait until my mother left the room and then would sensuously rub his leg against mine and laugh at my indignation. One passed me on my way to the bathroom and cackled, "Three. Count them and see. Three holes, count them." Sexuality was man's birthright, and nothing, no circumstance, rags or riches, no employer or landlord or upstart kid would deny them that. From cradle to grave, theirs. *Otoko* was the word that said it all: man, virility, courage, endurance.

Tsuki ga noboreba rantan keshite (As the moon rises, lanterns flicker out) . . .

My father went to work less and less. He found little jobs to do at home: sweeping the sidewalk, emptying ashtrays, turning the *tsukemono* (pickles). In the evenings he joined the gambling and drinking; during the day he administered to his anxieties and griefs, silently, orally, with chalk. My mother sucked in her breath and said to me, "He drinks sake and takes medicine. Sake by night and medicine by day. What good does it do? Sake and medicine . . ."

I went to sleep to the sound of the cursing and laughing and reviling of the men gambling down the hall. My father was always there, taking the house cut and plowing it back onto the table (my mother said) – grimly smiling, squandering the money that meant so much to her, fighting his last battleline: his manhood, his courage, his endurance.

Noda-san was among the group that drifted in from Fresno, leaving the grape harvest early that year. He was about thirty, boyish and quiet. He didn't join the card games nor did he drink much. Sometimes, if I was behind the counter, he'd ask me for a cup of sake, counting the change from his pocket slowly, flashing a shy smile with his white teeth.

One late night I was awakened by a gentle knock.

"Who is it?" I asked.

"*Boku yo. Noda. Chotto akete. Hanashi ga aruno.*" It's me, Noda. Let me in. I must talk to you.

I opened the door and he quickly slipped in. We faced each other in the dark.

"What do you want?" I asked.

"You," he said.

"Well, you can't have me," I said and switched on the light and made for the door. He turned off the light and barred the door with his arm.

"You ought not be here," I said, but his smile was so sad, so much in need, it was hard for me to hurt him. "You can't come in here like this," I said.

"But you let me in." He touched my face with his fingers.

"You asked to come in." I pushed his hand away. "You ought to get out of here. You ought not be here."

"But you let me in."

This went on for a while until he got impatient and reached for me. He tried to kiss me. He stroked my struggling body. He maneuvered me to the cot, squirming and sliding in his arms.

We could hear the gamblers down the hall. "Let me go or I'll scream," I whispered.

"You won't do that." Stroking.

"You can walk out of here. I won't tell anyone. Just let me go." I may have heard that line in the movies.

His hands worked to calm me, to arouse me. "Shhhh . . ."

"One more chance," I warned. Still he didn't stop.

I screamed. I yelled, "Father!" He released me instantly. We heard footsteps thudding down the hall. He jumped away from me, and we stood there facing each other – in the dark – just the way he came in. The door opened. My father and two other men peered into the room.

"Oh," one of them said. No other word was spoken. The two men left, my father waited for Noda-san and followed him out, closing the door quietly behind him.

In the morning my father put a hook and eye on my door. And Noda-san smiled his boyish smile whenever he passed me at the counter.

Shina no yoru, Shina no yoru yo (China nights, nights of China) . . .

My brother says, "This was popular before the war. Remember Oceanside?"

The international tension between Japan and America brought my brother from his fruit stand back to Oceanside to work as a truck driver for a farmer in Vista. "Work days and study nights and still driving a truck," my brother said.

Minato no akari, murasaki no yo ni (The lights of the harbor, against the purple sky) . . .

"I wonder what happened to all those men at the boarding house," I say.

"Why, they went to concentration camps like the rest of us," Kiyo says.

Camp was the place they sent us all, and it mattered not whether one was rich or poor, alien or citizen, loyal or disloyal, we had the face of the enemy, and they herded us all into these camps. And one family, after all those years of struggle, lost the boarding house that was their boat to Japan.

"No, Kiyo, I mean now. What are the men doing now?" I say.

"Why, they were old. They died, of course. Heh, like our father and mother." He lights a cigarette. "They never did get to Japan, did they?"

They never did.

Our father died in camp, after the war ended, just before camp closed. The government had been slowly dispersing the inmates over the past year, and I was in Chicago and Kiyo in Tule Lake, expecting deportation. His citizenship was revoked when he answered "no" to the questionnaire that asked him to go into combat for the country that gave him the opportunity to wash fruit, study nights, and still drive trucks. They took away every inch-by-inch gain in one swift stroke, incarcerated without due process, and gave my brother the choice to bear arms against the country of his ancestry or be deported.

My father had said to him, "*Kimi wa otoko da,*" you are a man, and had let his only son go. I went to Chicago to work in a candy factory.

And so, only my mother and little Sachi, who was eight, were with my father when he died.

Hiroshima had ended the war. My mother said my father grew despondent after the bombing. By this time, the government had set a November deadline for closing the camp. She said she'd asked my father, "Where shall we go? What shall we do?" and he'd not answered. She said he began to vomit black beads of blood and at the end of October died without making that decision. She said, "I joined the last group of people going out. What could I do?" My mother and Sachi left their home of four years with my father's ashes. They had been there longer than they were in Oceanside.

The war ended and Kiyo, still in camp at Tule Lake, was not deported. But my father died believing the nucleus of his small family was shattered.

Yume mo nuremasho; shiwo kaze, yo kaze (Dreams may dampen; salt winds, night winds) . . .

Kiyo says, "These songs really get to me." He thumps his chest. "It's like going back to the past – to Japan. You ever want to go back, Michi?" he asks.

"Go back? Kiyo, we've never been there."

"Yeah, I guess we think of ourselves as them."

"Kiyo? What if there's no such place? What if it only existed in their minds? And we believed them?"

"There is no such place. It's Fantasy Island, Michi," he says.

The record spins silently before Kiyo turns it off. He tucks it in its jacket. "I better get going," he looks at his watch. "Teru's probably wondering what happened to me." He looks out my window. "Hey, I thought you planted agapanthus last year."

"I did. They didn't bloom," I say.

"Did you water them? They're supposed to be the hardiest plant around." He tucks the record under his arm. "Well, maybe next year, hunh?" He laughs.

And on the longest day of the year, he leaves me and hurries home.

Afterword

The Relocation of Identity

A s a child who experienced the Imperial Valley earthquake, Wakako Yamauchi grew up with a consciousness of temblors, of the subtle and dramatic shifts that cause identity to be realigned, reconstructed, relocated. "The spring of the great Imperial Valley earthquake was the culmination of my father's farming career—his biggest failure. One hundred and forty acres of lettuce nobody wanted." ("Ōtōkō ," 238). During teenage years, Yamauchi endured a very different kind of earthquake when she and 120,000 other Japanese Americans were dumped into World War II internment camps. Throughout her versatile, acute, graceful collection, *Songs My Mother Taught Me*, relocation is the prevailing metaphor; Yamauchi's characters survive and ponder enormous shifts in their gender, class, racial, national, cultural, and regional identities.

Relocate here has a number of connotations: To transform. To switch. To pull the rug out from under. To evacuate. To incarcerate. To intern. To humiliate. To liberate. To rename. To metamorphose. To move while staying the same.

Songs My Mother Taught Me is a book about place. Geography is explored in Asian and American and Asian American settings; in rural and urban venues. Inside and outside, Yamauchi is attentive to domestic decor, desert habitat, urban distraction. Social place—the "knowing of one's place"—is observed with close watch on citizenship, economic class, and racial politics. She carefully tracks wavering gender relations between wives and husbands, girls and boys, single women and single men. *Songs My Mother Taught Me* is also very much a book of family narratives, considering birth order, generational affiliation, and duty to extended family members.

I am grateful for these wise, elegant stories, memoirs, and plays. Selfishly, I wish these pieces had been collected long ago, when I was a younger writer, because they offer nourishment and momentum. Yamauchi's passion for truth – at the expense of sentimentality and dogma – gives me permission, no, requires me, to tell the truth in my own work. Her people bring me to tears as I read and re-read their journeys. I can still see Emiko unwrapping her precious kimonos, wagering her tangible link with the past on a desperate hope for the future. I can picture Chizuko cooking dinner after a long day in the fields while her daughter Aki plays the violin. I recall Benji sniffing the bleached handkerchief that evokes his lost mother. I hear the divorced, lonely, nameless narrator of "A Veteran of Foreign Wars" chatting with her disabled neighbor. I read this work with different lenses – as a writer learning technique, as a woman gaining heart, as the daughter of an immigrant, working-class home finding dignity in Yamauchi's immigrant, working-class characters; as a Euro-American, discovering this history of my country untaught in my California public schools.

Thanks to Garrett Hongo and The Feminist Press, I can now add *Songs My Mother Taught Me* to what I have read about these same generations of Japanese Americans in books by Hisaye Yamamoto, Mine Okubo, John Okada, Jeanne Wakatsuki Houston, Toshio Mori, Mitsuye Yamada, and others. Throughout *Songs,* I recall the poem that opens Yamada's *Camp Notes,* "What your mother tells you now / in time / you will come to know." Of course I also acknowledge my gratitude to Yamauchi, herself, for her fine work, for her courage in relocating from visual art to literary art, for her nerve in continuing to write for many years despite the odds and obstacles. These plays, stories, and memoirs are tales of substance, blessedly distinct from the solipsistic products processed and packaged as literature for the current U.S. market. As a writer, a teacher, a reader, I celebrate *Songs My Mother Taught Me,* this powerful antidote to the loud, yawning, present-tense "I" that has infected fashionable American writing and numbed our ability to remember and envision. Yamauchi provokes us to think more intricately, to empathize more broadly, to imagine more deeply. Here are prose and drama that raise moral, philosophical, and political dilemmas for readers, which permit us to look internally and externally at the same time.

Although Yamauchi doesn't write extensively about the camps in *Songs,* her post-camp characters are conscious of the shifts in their attitudes toward the United States, themselves, their relatives, friends, neighbors, strangers. For those characters of the Issei generation, life has already been a series of migrations – from Japan to the United States; within the United States looking for work; from the American places they finally "settle" to the internment camps; from the camps back to the remains of their lives, collecting shards of the past: home, land, relationships, self-respect.

Yamauchi shows us that in a certain perverse way the relocation-internment, for all its horrors and hurtful divisiveness, insured a kind of cohesion between generations. For those families who were interned together (absent the sons who were drafted), the internment camps forced relatives into very close quarters. On another level, the internment experience limited that often irrevocable rift that occurs between immigrant parents and their children in North America, a rift created as the assimilation of the younger generation severs them from family traditions and old-country ideals. So often U.S.-born children, in claiming autonomous selves, separate from what they perceive as their immigrant parents' romanticism or orthodoxy. They are unable to empathize with the older generations' profound sensation of *trespassing*. But these relocated Nisei and Sansei – U.S.-born citizens – were forced also to immigrate, to endure a hardship different from, yet analogous to, the trans-Pacific journey. These Americans were ostracized aliens in their own land, as foreign and suspicious as the older generation. Thus the double helix of international and intranational immigration forced a painful understanding between parents and children, children and parents.

The breadth of Yamauchi's compassion can be gauged by her repertoire of narrators and points of view: female, male, adult, child, Issei, Nisei, Kibei. She writes from within Japanese-American culture, naming and identifying with many aspects of that world. She dramatically chronicles assaults on her people – laws to prohibit Japanese Americans from owning land, from becoming citizens, indeed, eventually, from immigrating, as well as job and school discrimination, internment, extradition, racist brutality. However, she is not uncritical of traditions and individual behaviors within her community. Candidly she portrays the ravages of alcoholism, gambling, battery. For me the book is resonantly literary in how she renders both the particular and the universal in her characters.

Perhaps the most striking aspect of this prose and drama is the dignified, humane voice in which the audience is addressed. Readers (or viewers) are treated with respect, rather than the more chic indifference or even contempt. There is no attempt to manipulate the audience or persuade us. Yamauchi's characters have a plain-spoken eloquence. They are struggling to understand their own situations, to convey emotion, to articulate ideas. The authorial voice is at once wise, tender, tough, vulnerable, and always searching.

Faultlines of Gender

Just as life is geographically mobile for these people, so is it shifting in the territory of gender. The Issei find that sexual relationships have changed here in the looser U.S. environment, away from the support of extended family and the influence of customary social strictures. Attitudes about male and female relationships change – as mores always do – with the passage of time. The fluidity of the war and postwar years exposes families to different cultures and further disrupts traditional gender expectations.

Yamauchi is boldly, thrillingly frank about a spectrum of sexual feelings. The passion between young lovers in "Shirley Temple, Hotcha-cha," "Makapuu Bay," and "Maybe." The confusing, taboo attractions between girls and older men in "That Was All," "In Heaven and Earth," and *The Music Lessons*. The arousal of middle-aged women in "The Coward" and "A Veteran of Foreign Wars." And the vivid erotic memories of an old woman in "So What; Who Cares?"

Sexual attraction—like other fantasies and desires in this promised land—is often abruptly thwarted by the historical moment: "That's the way it was. We sang songs, we laughed, talked, and often walked hand in hand in silence. In spite of the harried times, the imminence of separation, I felt a quiet joy with him. We did not speak of marriage or of love. I lived simply for these weekends, those letters. I smile now at the things that gave me such intense pleasure: a pressure on the arm, a certain look, a space between words. . . . And shortly after that I was called back to Poston by Joe Noda, who was our block manager at that time. My father was dying." ("Makapuu Bay," 214)

A number of Yamauchi's characters are burdened by moral prohibitions, as the narrator in "The Coward" explains: "My mother taught me a lot of things that were pertinent to then and me, a Japanese American country girl in an insecure economy, facing a bleak future. And however unrewarding the virtues she herself practiced, or inequitable the gods that judged her, she still pressed on me a sort of Japanese-Buddhist Victorianism. She spoke a lot about greed and need and hungers of the flesh, and all manner of nonessential material things as the devil's instruments. She taught me not to dream extravagantly, but with both feet on the ground and of attainable goals. She told me to be frugal with love and passion, and she passed on an unspoken distrust of men." (137)

Sexual fulfillment sometimes symbolizes artistic self-expression, and characters are prone to censorship on both fronts. Indeed, the strongest erotic tension in these stories and plays often ends in disappointment or embarrassment. In "That Was All," the family friend comes to dinner, ". . . examining each morsel on his *hashi* before bringing it to his lips and chewing slowly—movements as sensual and private as making love. Once when he caught me watching him, he laughed and slipped some food into my mouth in a gesture so intimate I flushed warm and my father coughed suddenly." (48)

Yamauchi also meditates on the contradictions between the real and ideal in her portraits of motherhood, battery, and divorce. Like the protagonist in Buchi Emecheta's *The Joys of Motherhood*, in Yamauchi's title story, Hatsue Kato is overwhelmed with maternal responsibilities. She does not want to bear the latest child. Already too many burdens drain her of hope. "The baby grew steadily in my mother's belly, distending and misshaping her body. The black hair she wore in a smooth coil at her neck grew crisp and faded. Broken strands hung from her temples like dry summer grass, and brown splotches appeared on her skin." (36) At the end of the story, when the child drowns, we sense there is as much relief as guilt and grief in Hatsue's exhausted heart.

One of the boldest stories is "The Handkerchief," in which Yamauchi explores the forbidden subject of a mother leaving her children with their father and beginning a new life on her own. Although told from the point of view of the smallest son, the story—and this is typical of Yamauchi's loving range—displays an evenhanded sympathy for everyone in the family: the withholding, isolated father; the rigid, scared sister; the two bewildered boys as well as the frustrated mother.

Usually Yamauchi's men leave the women. Divorce is a profound, wounding relocation shared by these female characters who, in midlife, find themselves abandoned by husbands they married in a different world, a distant era. For someone like Mieko, in "Shirley Temple, Hotcha-cha," divorce is another blow after a life of hardship through the war and disruptive postwar years. "Awake, there were other confrontations: What was the reason for surviving the war, to come to this? What is the purpose of heartbreak? And if it all dies with me, what indeed was the use of it? Am I only a segment of a larger drama? Is there still another act?" (120)

The betrayal of divorce causes loneliness, poverty, a shattering of hope. "That was the worst period of my life. I became a walking zombie with no interest at all in the living reality—the eating, sleeping, excreting, the laughing, loving, and crying of life." ("Makapuu Bay," 211)

Sometimes, as in "Charted Lives" and "A Veteran of Foreign Wars," this loss brings the women close together with unpredictable men. And usually there is some reprieve, reawakening, acceptance, as in the stunning last paragraph of "Shirley Temple, Hotcha-cha": "My Shirley doll sits on my dresser now. I bought her a new wig and made a fancy nylon dress for her. She smiles at me. Her lips are cracked, she's a bit sallow, the luster is gone from her blue eyes. She's not what she used to be. But she's been around a long time now." (121)

Class Negotiations

Yamauchi is equally adept at navigating the twists and turns of the covert U.S. class system. Most of her characters come from poor, immigrant families; some wind up in the city as clerical or factory workers. Others—given the rigid restrictions against Japanese Americans owning land—become migrant or tenant farmers in the stark, inhospitable Imperial Valley of southern California.

This arid, dusty, sweltering country is haunted by scorpions and mined with bad dreams. "By May, after the broiling sun had reduced the plants to dry twigs, the plowing began." ("Songs My Mother Taught Me," 32) It is a land to escape, as we see in "And the Soul Shall Dance," "In Heaven and Earth," and *The Music Lessons*. Yet there are tender moments of physical renewal, which perhaps exaggerate the characters' spiritual sense of possibility. "Spring comes early in the valley; in February the skies are clear though the air is still cold. By March, winds are vigorous and warm and wildflowers dot the desert floor, cockleburs are green and not yet tenacious, the sand is crusty underfoot, everywhere there is the smell of things growing, and the first tomatoes are showing green and bald." ("And the Soul Shall Dance," 23)

Farmers here are barely scratching a living from the unforgiving soil. Constantly, they confront the irony that not only does life in the United States fall short of youthful aspirations, it is often worse than the life they left in Japan. Hana says to Oka, "I know I shouldn't tell you this, but there's one or two things I have to say: You sent for Kiyoko-san, and now she's here. You said yourself she had a bad time in Japan, and now she's having a worse time. It's not easy for her in a strange country; the least you can do is try to keep from worrying her . . . especially about yourselves. I think it's terrible what you're doing to her . . . terrible!" (*And the Soul Shall Dance*, 194)

Dreams are central to these people–whether as refuge from their daily lives or as the source of their ongoing grief. In both plays, mothers warn their daughters against dreaming happier lives.

HANA: Some of the things you read, you're never going to know.

MASAKO: I can dream though.

HANA [*sighing*]: Sometimes the dreaming makes the living harder. Better to keep your head out of the clouds. (*And the Soul Shall Dance*, 182)

And in *The Music Lessons,* Chizuko tries to persuade Aki against running off with Kaoru:

AKI: I'm not going to live like you. I'm not going to live all tied up in knots like you: afraid of what people say, afraid of spending money, afraid of laughing, afraid (of) . . .

CHIZUKO: Do you understand my problems? Do you think just once about *my* prob(lems) . . .

AKI: Afraid you're going to love someone. Afraid (you) . . .

CHIZUKO: I have lots to worry about. I got to see you have enough to eat, give you an education, see you're dressed right . . . decent, so people won't say, "Those kids don't have a father." See you're not left with debts, like what happened to me. See you don't make a mess (of your life). . . . (86)

This rural existence is spare, arduous, lonely, monotonous. Disappointing. Not until they arrive, having exhausted life savings, splintered their families, and compromised their dignity, do many immigrants learn they will not be able to buy land, become citizens, marry outside their race, or sponsor spouses from home. The people who do find partners and become parents are refreshed by the possibility of their children's futures just as the children are stranded in the desert of their parents' expectations.

Likewise, people who work in city offices, hotels, and factories constantly face harsh economic realities and racial prejudice. "When the kids at school asked me where I lived, I said, 'Out that way,' and waved vaguely westward, too ashamed to say I lived in a hotel of transient men, afraid the down-cheeked youngsters would shrink from me, their mouths drawn down." ("Ōtōkō ," 240) Often these characters have no financial security or job satisfaction, share crowded housing, drive borrowed cars or take the bus, and, if they do eventually claim middle-class lives, know they are visitors precariously awaiting the next transfer, termination, eviction, relocation.

In each urban tale, a sardonic sense of humor is a crucial survival strategy. "Stephen Turner, the man who interviewed me, looked over my application and said, 'Oh, you paint. My wife paints. She's Japanese too.' But I was ready to accept any advantage. Years ago during World War II, being Japanese was a total nil, and I figured I'd paid my dues." ("Charted Lives," 128)

A similar case of racial insensitivity is used to advantage by the narrator in "Maybe." "Although I was the last hired, I was sent to the end of the belt largely because of Chuck White. White people (no pun intended) do not observe the difference between native Japanese and Japanese Americans. As I said, I was born in the southern California desert, but people are often amazed that I can speak English, and I guess Chuck White associates me with Japanese industry (Sony, Toyota, et cetera), and just for walking in and asking for a job, I went to the back of the line which in this case is the top of the bottom." (147)

"Maybe" is one of the classics of American working-class fiction in its powerful evocation of labor, the relationships among workers, the tensions between boss and worker, the aspirations of progress, the inevitable threat of layoff. Gaps between employee and employer are apparent from the outset with Chuck White's misapprehension of Florence's identity. Soon Florence notices the boss's wife suspiciously watching her. "Most of the time, she's busy on the phone or is rushing off somewhere in her silver Mercedes. Probably to the bank. She wears Gloria Vanderbilt jeans and carries a Gucci bag and smells of expensive perfume. When Chuck White is out of town, she moves me from one floor to the other for unimportant reasons. Just to let me know how superfluous I am." (148)

The other workers are mainly Spanish-speaking undocumented immigrants from Mexico and Central America, a couple of decades younger than Florence. She gets along well with them, bound together by their common low wage, their shared disgust at the filthy factory lavatories, their common experiences of white racism. She tries and fails to find someone to marry and "legitimize" her new friend Reynaldo. Eventually the discrimination, hardship, hypocrisy, and stoicism become too much for Florence, and in one of the most moving passages of the book, Florence thinks:

> I'm afraid I shall leave Zodiac soon. In the deceptive simplicity of the lives here, there is a quality I am unable to face. It's the underbelly of a smile. I know it well.

I remember our life in the Arizona camp—the first day our family entered that empty barracks room (our home for the next four years), my father squatted on the dusty floor, his head deep in his shoulders, and my mother unwrapped a roll of salami and sliced it for us. I wanted so much to cry, but my mother gripped my arm and gave me the meat. I turned to my father; he looked up and smiled. Two years later, the day I was to leave them and relocate to Chicago, my mother stood by the army truck that was to take us to the train in Parker. She had not wanted me to leave because my father was in the hospital with stomach ulcers. She did not touch me. The corners of her mouth wavered once, then turned up in a smile. And in the same tradition, I smiled when my husband told me he was marrying a young woman from Japan. "That's good," I said.

It did not seem so brave or so sad then. Maybe living it is easier than remembering or watching someone else living it. (151)

Some of Yamauchi's farmers wind up in Oceanside, San Pedro, Los Angeles, and all of those who survive the 1930s wind up in the camps, which extended suffering beyond the urban and rural hardship. Camps where people died of broken hearts or gunshots in the back. From which they were extradited to Japan or drafted to Europe in the 442nd Battalion, which lost more men than any U.S. battalion in World War II.

"Camp was the place they sent us all, and it mattered not whether one was rich or poor, alien or citizen, loyal or disloyal, we had the face of the enemy, and they herded us all into these camps. And one family, after all those years of struggle, lost the boarding house that was their boat to Japan." ("Ōtōkō ," 243)

Parameters of Home

Yamauchi provides no map, no predictable route for her characters. Scenes shift back and forth: Japan, the United States, memory, time present, premonition, Japan, the United States. Japan is both the country to escape and the romantic memory for which one saves frugally to recapture. In "Shirley Temple, Hotcha-cha," U.S.-born Mieko is sent to the old country to study because the racist U.S. educational system won't do justice to such a promising child. Her parents' old country becomes her new country and then, as war nears and ensues, it becomes the besieged country. When Mieko finally returns "home," married to another Kibei, she has missed the opportunities of both countries.

In "Old Times, Old Stories," friends and relatives are split apart by the Pacific voyage. When the narrator visits her childhood friend, she finds that, "Fumi, sixty-four, forgot most of her English. She did not forget the taste of her favorite foods—wieners, tortillas, and cheese. She remembered the stand of eucalyptus on the spine of the hill where we had the Japanese picnics, the dust from the footraces turning gold in the sunset. She remembered, too, the high heels her mother wore on the day they left America, and she remembered how my mother had cried." (230)

The old country is the abandoned lover who maintains beauty after one's spouse has faded and widened. The unfaithful paramour who may someday reform and offer succor. The romantic ideal who, after a while, exists only in the refigured imagination. Images of various Japans float in and out of Yamauchi's work, fermented into spectral melodies in "The Boatmen on Toneh River," "In Heaven and Earth," "And the Soul Shall Dance," and *The Music Lessons*. In "Ōtōkō ," Kiyo says:

> "These songs really get to me." He thumps his chest. "It's like going back to the past–to Japan. You ever want to go back, Michi?" he asks.
>
> "Go back? Kiyo, we've never been there."
>
> "Yeah, I guess we think of ourselves as them."
>
> "Kiyo? What if there's no such place? What if it only existed in their minds? And we believed them?" (243)

Japan and the United States are different countries. Issei and Nisei are different generations. And yet, all is enmeshed. As Chizuko says to Aki, "Your life is my life. We're one." And as Kimi muses in "The Boatmen on Toneh River":

> What do you want to tell me? That you are me and I am you, and today is the same as yesterday, and tomorrow will be the same as today? I thought I could change the pattern of my life; I thought I could deny your existence, deny our lonely past together, but alas, I had preserved it carefully, and when all the frills and furbelows are stripped away, you are here, the backbone of my life, the bleached hull of my shipwreck. And here between yesterday and today, I sing the same lonely song as you. I should not have denied you; I should not have woven my life within the framework of our past. (44)

Yamauchi's boundaries are permeable. Children are their parents; deserts become fertile valleys; camps become communities; memoirs become stories; stories become plays; inside the stories there are more stories; inside one culture exists a separate one; inside the heart live other people. Never one for static identity, Yamauchi dexterously plays with form–by moving among genres–exposing some of the material twice, first in story, then in drama–by taking a character from one piece to another. Under her wry, perceptive eye, characters find life to be a series of small and large, conscious and unconscious migrations. Identity here is a process, not a fixed claim. The task, Yamauchi seems to be saying, is *not* to reinvent yourself, but to discover yourself. This is both harder and easier when the scenery is moving. As much as her characters adjust their psyches and realign their goals, they maintain some essential core—a kind of grace—which they carry with them and which carries them through to the next, unpredictable place.

Valerie Miner

Publications Chronology

"And the Soul Shall Dance" *(story)*

Growing Up Asian American: An Anthology edited by Maria Hong (New York: William Morrow, 1993)

Women of the Century: Thirty Modern Short Stories edited by Regina Barreca (New York: St. Martin's, 1993)

Literary Cavalcade 46, no. 1 (September 1993)

American Dragon: Twenty-Five Asian American Voices edited by Lawrence Yep (New York: HarperCollins, 1993)

Six Short Stories by Japanese American Writers edited by Iwao Yamamoto, Mie Hihara, and Shigeru Kobayashi (Tsurumi Shoten, 1991)

Home to Stay: Asian American Fiction by Women edited by Sylvia Watanabe and Carol Bruchac (Greenfield, N.Y.: Greenfield Review, 1990)

Literature and Society edited by Pamela J. Annas and Robert C. Rosen (New York: Prentice Hall, 1989)

Solo: Women on Woman Alone edited by Linda Hamalian and Leo Hamalian (New York: Dell, 1977)

Aiiieeeee! An Anthology of Asian American Writers edited by Jeffrey Paul Chang, Frank Chin, Lawson Fusao Inada, and Shawn Wong (Washington, D.C.: Howard University, 1974)

Los Angeles Rafu Shimpo Holiday Supplement, December 1966

And the Soul Shall Dance (play)

Staging Diversity: Plays and Practice in American Theater edited by John R. Wolcott and Michael L. Quinn (Dubuque, Iowa: Kendall/Hunt, 1992)

The Big Aiiieeeee! An Anthology of Chinese and Japanese American Literature edited by Jeffrey Paul Chan, Frank Chin, Lawson Fusao Inada, and Shawn Wong (New York: Meridian/Penguin, 1991)

Between Worlds: Contemporary Asian American Plays edited by Misha Berson (New York: Theater Communications Group, 1990)

New Worlds of Literature edited by Jerome Beaty and J. Paul Hunter (New York: W. W. Norton, 1989)

West Coast Plays 11/12 (California Theatre Council, Winter/Spring 1982)

Burn Mantel Theatre Yearbook of 1976–77 edited by Otis Guernsy (Dodd Mead, 1976)

"The Boatmen on Toneh River"

Structure and Meaning: An Introduction to Literature edited by Anthony Duke, J. Earl Franson, James W. Parins, and Russell E. Murphy (Boston: Houghton Mifflin, 1983)

The Third Woman: Minority Women Writers of the United States edited by Dexter Fisher (Boston: Houghton Mifflin, 1980)

Counterpoint: Perspectives on Asian America edited by Emma Gee (Los Angeles: UCLA Asian American Studies Center, 1977)

Amerasia Journal 2, no. 2 (Fall 1974)

"The Coward"

Los Angeles Rafu Shimpo Holiday Supplement, December 1977

"The Handkerchief"

Amerasia Journal 4, no. 1 (1977)

Los Angeles Rafu Shimpo Holiday Supplement, December 1961

"In Heaven and Earth"

Ayumi: A Japanese American Anthology (Japanese American Anthology Committee, 1980)

The Greenfield Reader 6, nos. 1 and 2 (Spring 1977)

Los Angeles Rafu Shimpo Holiday Supplement, December 1968

"Makapuu Bay"

Making Waves: An Anthology of Writings by and about Asian American Women edited by Asian Women United of California (Boston: Beacon, 1989)

Bamboo Ridge: The Hawaii Writers' Quarterly 3 (June and August 1979)

Los Angeles Rafu Shimpo Holiday Supplement, December 1978

"Maybe"

Home to Stay: Asian American Fiction by Women edited by Sylvia Watanabe and
Carol Bruchac (Greenfield, N.Y.: Greenfield Review, 1990)
Los Angeles Rafu Shimpo Holiday Supplement, December 1984

"Ōtōkō"

Southwest Review 2 and 3 (Spring/Summer 1992)
Los Angeles Rafu Shimpo Holiday Supplement, December 1980

"The Sensei"

Yardbird Reader 3 (Fall 1977)
Southwest: A Contemporary Anthology edited by Jane and Carl Kopp (Norman,
Okla.: Red Earth Press, 1977)

"Shirley Temple, Hotcha-cha"

Los Angeles Rafu Shimpo Holiday Supplement, December 1979

"Songs My Mother Taught Me"

Amerasia Journal 3, no. 2 (1976)

"That Was All"

Charlie Chan Is Dead: An Anthology of Asian American Fiction edited by Jessica
Hagedorn (New York: Viking/Penguin, 1993)
Los Angeles Rafu Shimpo Holiday Supplement, December 1983
Amerasia Journal 7, no. 1 (Spring 1980)

"A Veteran of Foreign Wars"

Los Angeles Rafu Shimpo Holiday Supplement, December 1981

The Feminist Press at The City University of New York offers alternatives in education and in literature. Founded in 1970, this nonprofit, tax-exempt educational and publishing organization works to eliminate stereotypes in books and schools and to provide literature with a broad vision of human potential. The publishing program includes reprints of important works by women, feminist biographies of women, multicultural anthologies, a cross-cultural memoir series, and nonsexist children's books. Curricular materials, bibliographies, directories, and a quarterly journal provide information and support for students and teachers of women's studies. Through publication and projects, The Feminist Press contributes to the rediscovery of the history of women and the emergence of a more humane society.

NEW AND FORTHCOMING BOOKS

The Answer/La Respuesta: The Restored Text and Selected Poems, by Sor Juana Inés de la Cruz. Commentary and Translation by Electa Arenal and Amanda Powell. $12.95 paper, $35.00 cloth.

Australia for Women, edited by Susan Hawthorne and Renate Klein. $17.95 paper.

The Castle of Pictures: A Grandmother's Tales, by George Sand. Translated by Holly Erskine Hirko. $9.95 paper, $23.95 cloth.

Folly, a novel by Maureen Brady. Afterword by Bonnie Zimmerman. $12.95 paper, $35.00 cloth.

Women Composers: The Lost Tradition Found, second edition. By Diane Peacock Jezic. Second Edition Prepared by Elizabeth Wood. $14.95 paper, $35.00 cloth.

Women of Color and the Multicultural Curriculum: Transforming the College Classroom, edited by Liza Fiol-Matta and Mariam Chamberlain. $18.95 paper, $35.00 cloth.

Prices subject to change. *Individuals:* Send check or money order (in U.S. dollars drawn on a U.S. bank) to The Feminist Press at The City University of New York, 311 East 94th Street, New York, NY 10128. Please include $3.00 postage and handling for the first book, $.75 for each additional. For VISA/MasterCard orders call (212) 360-5790. *Bookstores, libraries, wholesalers:* Feminist Press titles are distributed to the trade by Consortium Book Sales and Distribution, (800) 283-3572.